BLACK
SCIENCE

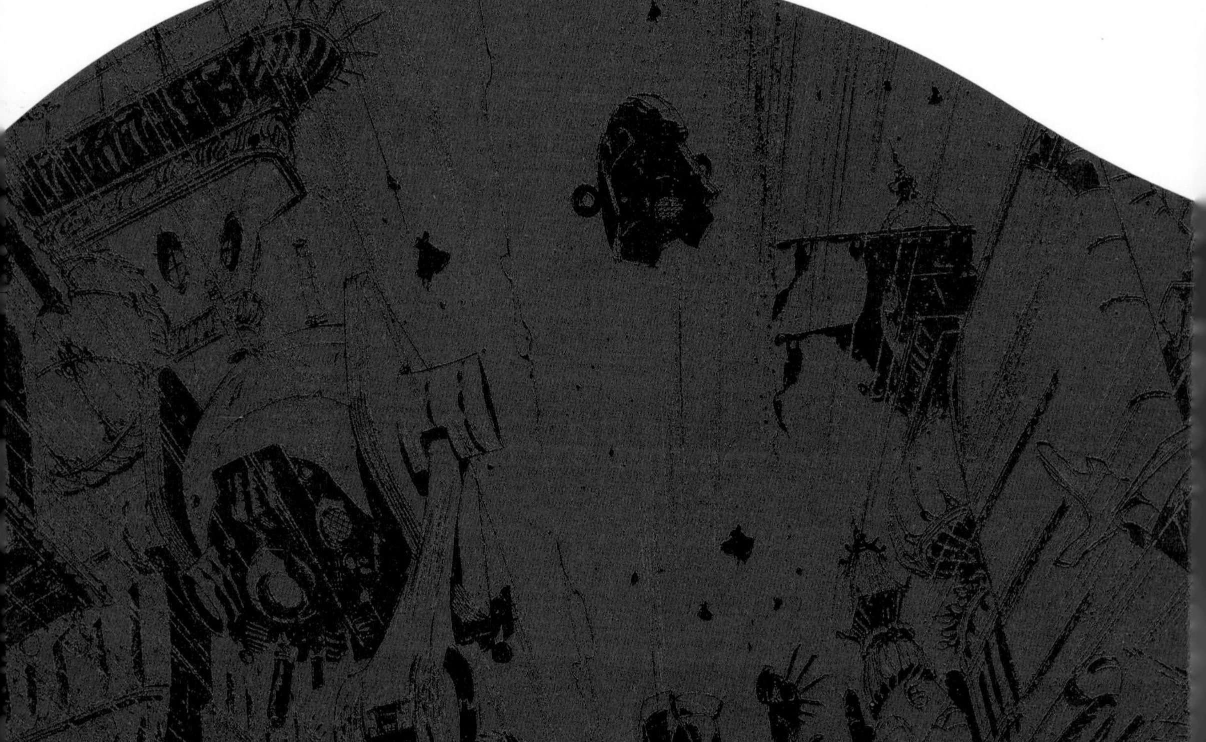

IMAGE COMICS, INC.
Robert Kirkman – Chief Operating Officer
Erik Larsen – Chief Financial Officer
Todd McFarlane – President
Marc Silvestri – Chief Executive Officer
Jim Valentino – Vice-President

Eric Stephenson – Publisher
Corey Murphy – Director of Sales
Jeremy Sullivan – Director of Digital Sales
Kat Salazar – Director of PR & Marketing
Emily Miller – Director of Operations
Branwyn Bigglestone – Senior Accounts Manager
Sarah Mello – Accounts Manager
Drew Gill – Art Director
Jonathan Chan – Production Manager
Meredith Wallace – Print Manager
Randy Okamura – Marketing Production Designer
David Brothers – Branding Manager
Ally Power – Content Manager
Addison Duke – Production Artist
Vincent Kukua – Production Artist
Sasha Head – Production Artist
Tricia Ramos – Production Artist
Emilio Bautista – Sales Assistant
Chloe Ramos-Peterson – Administrative Assistant
IMAGECOMICS.COM

COLLECTION DESIGN: JEFF POWELL

BLACK SCIENCE VOLUME 3: VANISHING PATTERN. First Printing. August 2015. Published by Image Comics, Inc. Office of publication: 2001 Center Street, 6th Floor, Berkeley, CA 94704. Copyright © 2015 Rick Remender & Matteo Scalera. All rights reserved. Originally published in single magazine form as BLACK SCIENCE #12-16. BLACK SCIENCE™ (including all prominent characters featured herein), its logo and all character likenesses are trademarks of Rick Remender & Matteo Scalera, unless otherwise noted. Image Comics® and its logos are registered trademarks of Image Comics, Inc. No part of this publication may be reproduced or transmitted, in any form or by any means (except for short excerpts for review purposes) without the express written permission of Image Comics, Inc. All names, characters, events and locales in this publication are entirely fictional. Any resemblance to actual persons (living or dead), events or places, without satiric intent, is coincidental. PRINTED IN THE U.S.A. For information regarding the CPSIA on this printed material call: 203-595-3636 and provide reference #RICH–630149. For international rights inquiries, contact: foreignlicensing@imagecomics.com.
ISBN 978-1-63215-395-1

RICK REMENDER
WRITER

MATTEO SCALERA
ARTIST

MORENO DINISIO
COLORS

RUS WOOTON
LETTERING + LOGO DESIGN

SEBASTIAN GIRNER
EDITOR

BLACK SCIENCE CREATED BY
RICK REMENDER & MATTEO SCALERA

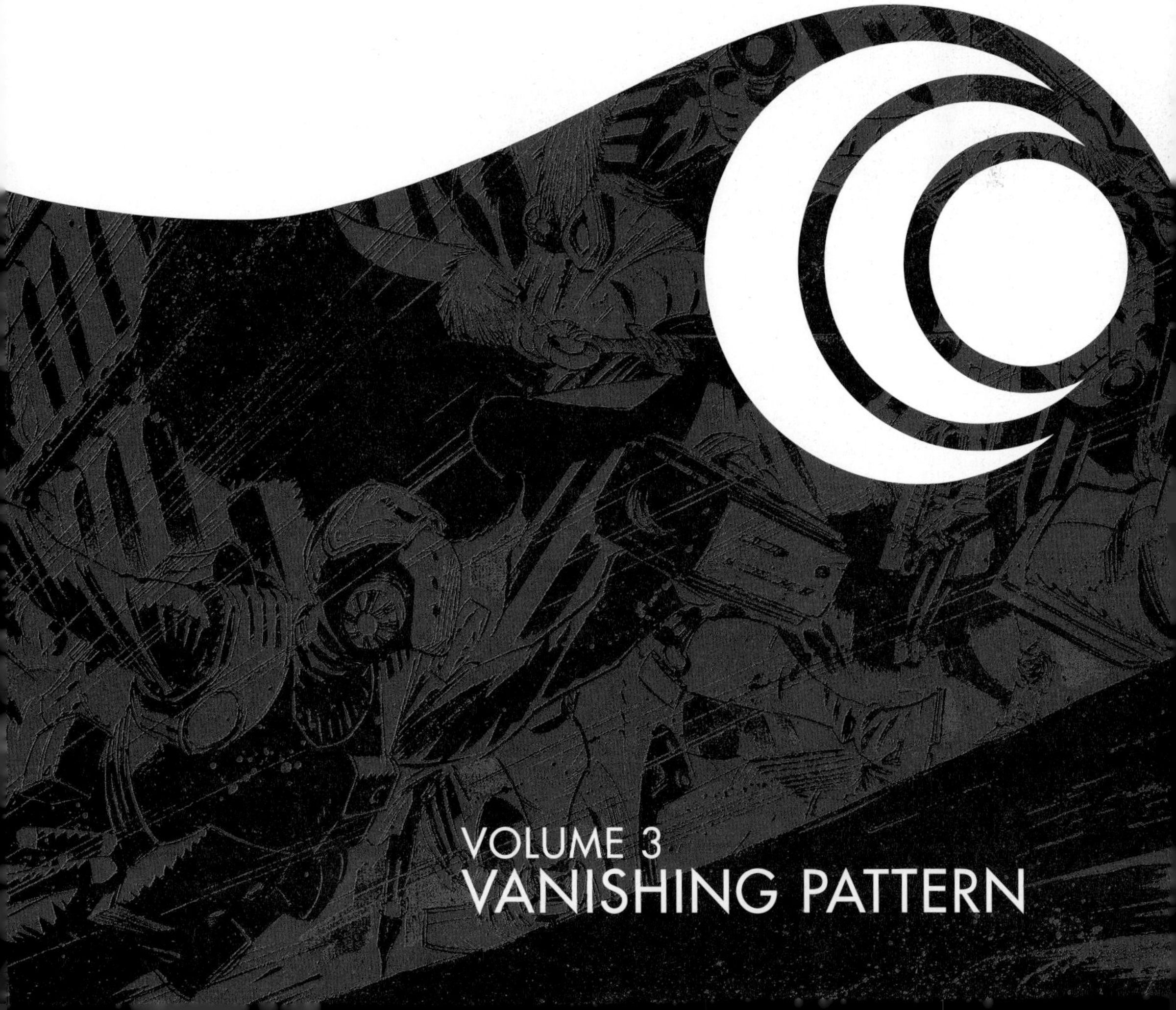

# VOLUME 3
# VANISHING PATTERN

# 12

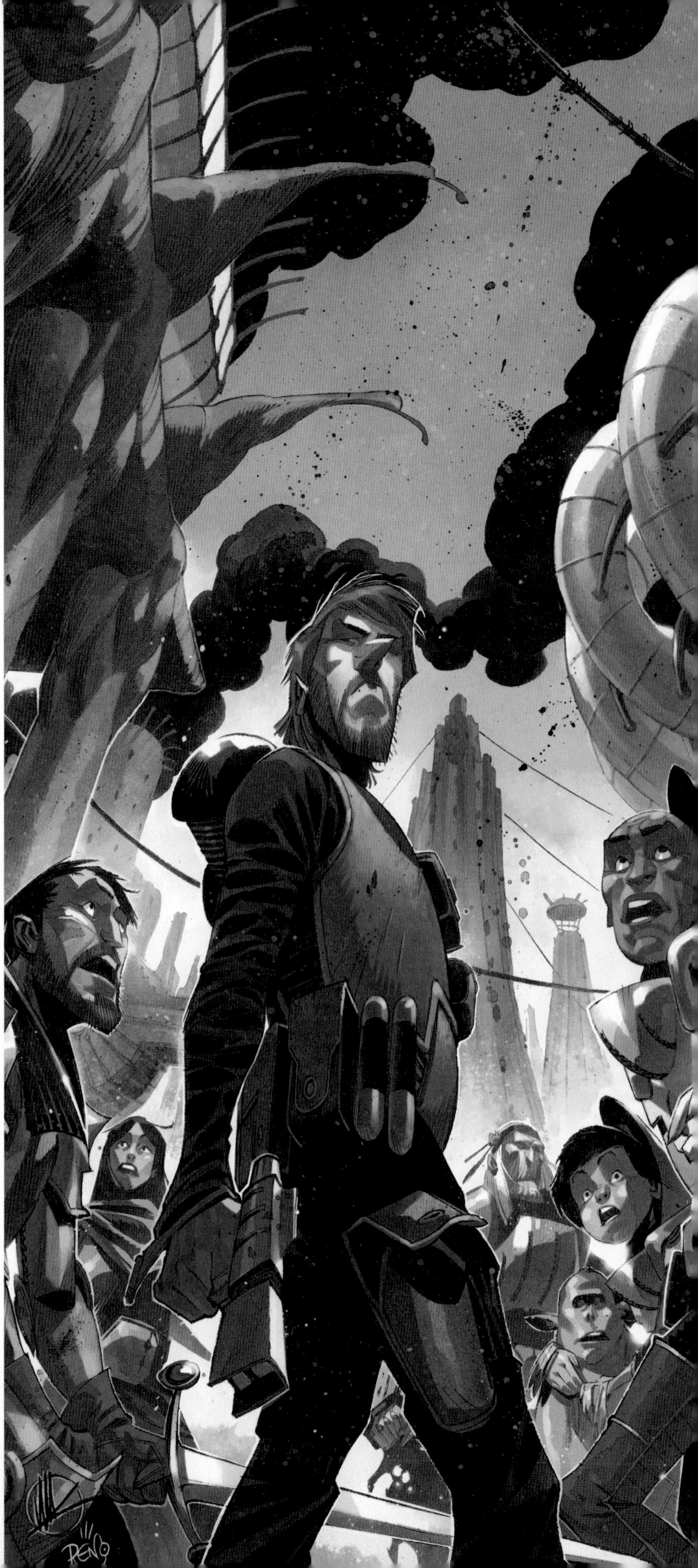

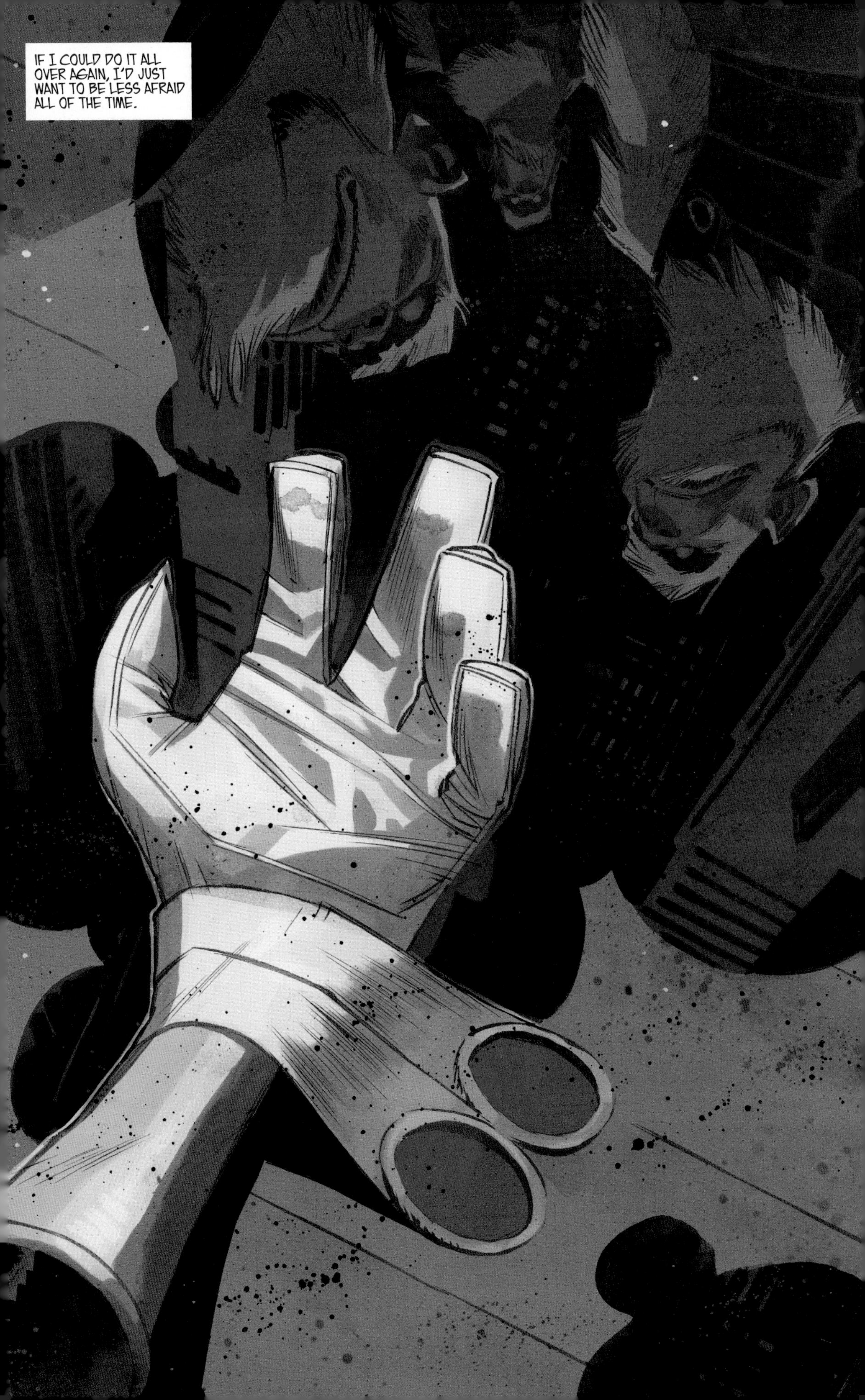
IF I COULD DO IT ALL OVER AGAIN, I'D JUST WANT TO BE LESS AFRAID ALL OF THE TIME.

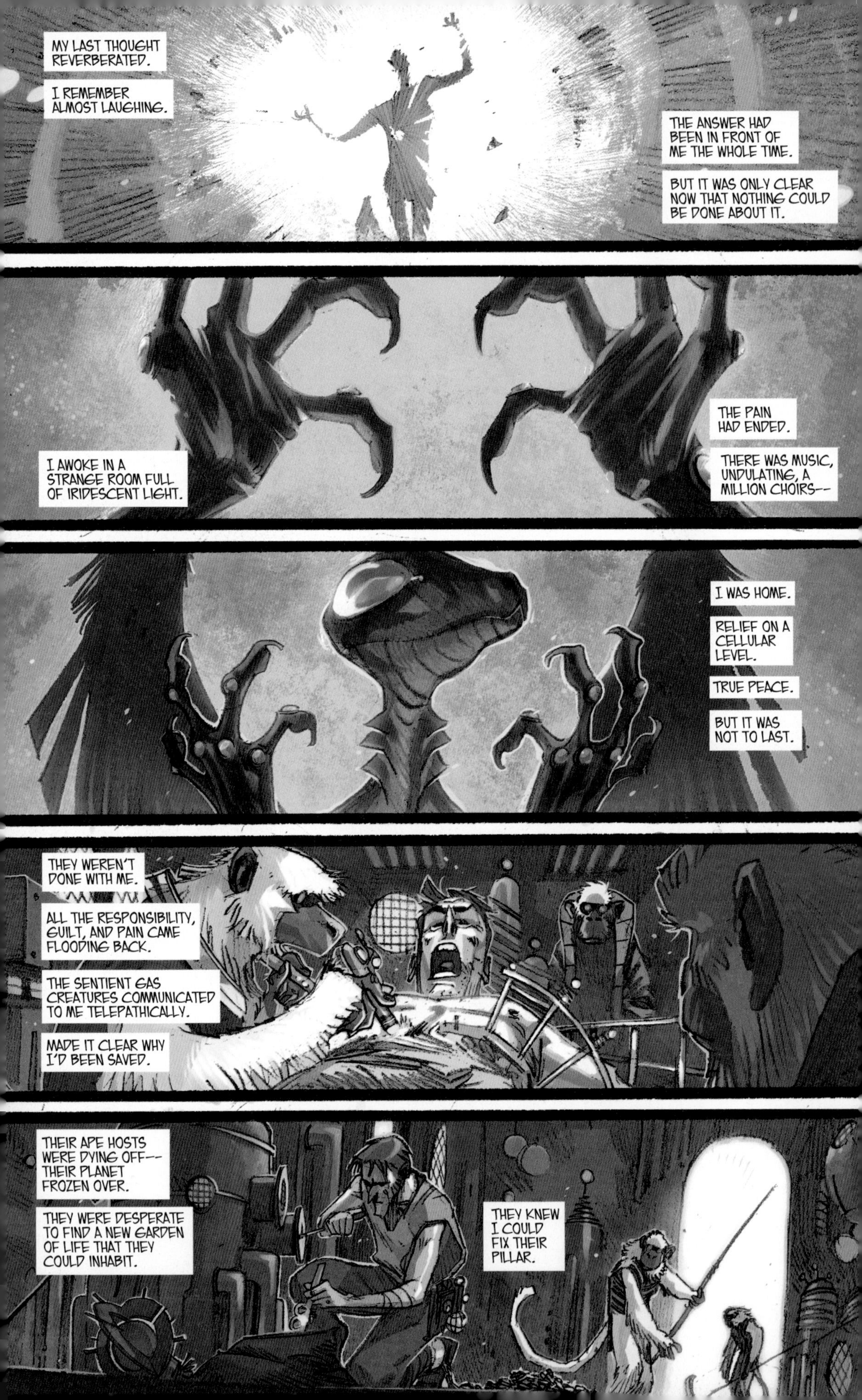

MY LAST THOUGHT REVERBERATED.
I REMEMBER ALMOST LAUGHING.
THE ANSWER HAD BEEN IN FRONT OF ME THE WHOLE TIME.
BUT IT WAS ONLY CLEAR NOW THAT NOTHING COULD BE DONE ABOUT IT.
I AWOKE IN A STRANGE ROOM FULL OF IRIDESCENT LIGHT.
THE PAIN HAD ENDED.
THERE WAS MUSIC, UNDULATING, A MILLION CHOIRS--
I WAS HOME.
RELIEF ON A CELLULAR LEVEL.
TRUE PEACE.
BUT IT WAS NOT TO LAST.
THEY WEREN'T DONE WITH ME.
ALL THE RESPONSIBILITY, GUILT, AND PAIN CAME FLOODING BACK.
THE SENTIENT GAS CREATURES COMMUNICATED TO ME TELEPATHICALLY.
MADE IT CLEAR WHY I'D BEEN SAVED.
THEIR APE HOSTS WERE DYING OFF-- THEIR PLANET FROZEN OVER.
THEY WERE DESPERATE TO FIND A NEW GARDEN OF LIFE THAT THEY COULD INHABIT.
THEY KNEW I COULD FIX THEIR PILLAR.

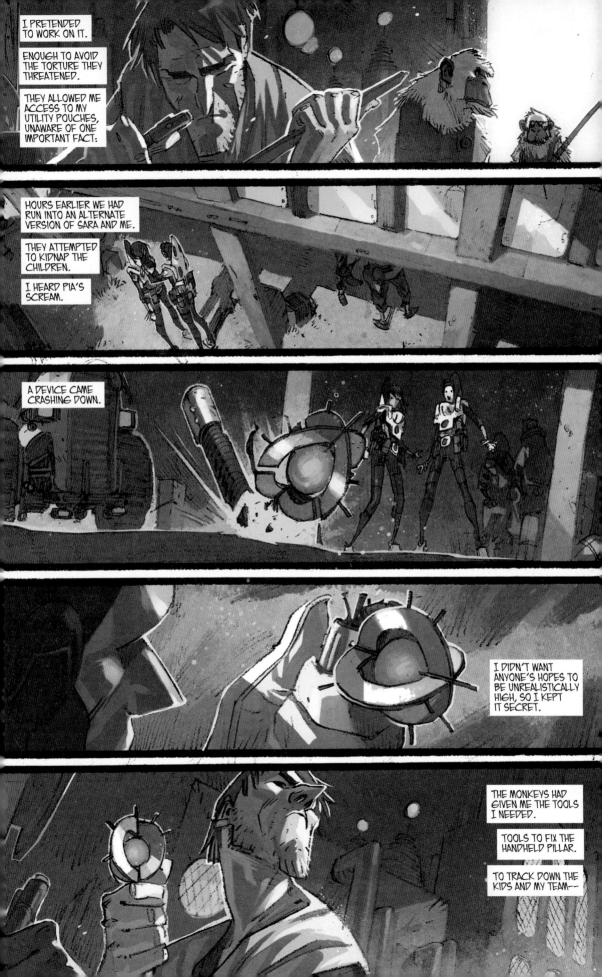

I PRETENDED TO WORK ON IT.

ENOUGH TO AVOID THE TORTURE THEY THREATENED.

THEY ALLOWED ME ACCESS TO MY UTILITY POUCHES, UNAWARE OF ONE IMPORTANT FACT:

HOURS EARLIER WE HAD RUN INTO AN ALTERNATE VERSION OF SARA AND ME.

THEY ATTEMPTED TO KIDNAP THE CHILDREN.

I HEARD PIA'S SCREAM.

A DEVICE CAME CRASHING DOWN.

I DIDN'T WANT ANYONE'S HOPES TO BE UNREALISTICALLY HIGH, SO I KEPT IT SECRET.

THE MONKEYS HAD GIVEN ME THE TOOLS I NEEDED.

TOOLS TO FIX THE HANDHELD PILLAR.

TO TRACK DOWN THE KIDS AND MY TEAM--

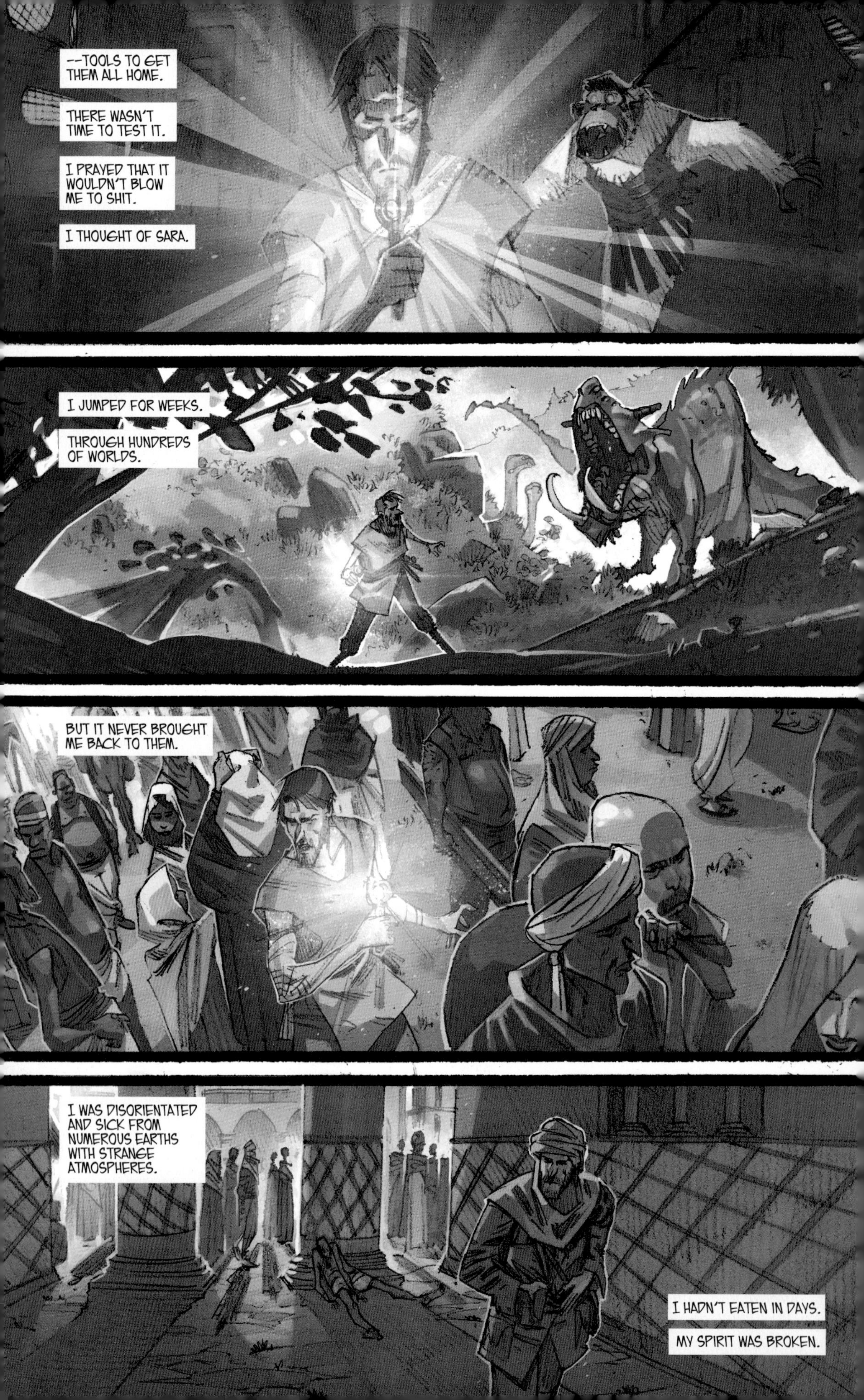
--TOOLS TO GET THEM ALL HOME.
THERE WASN'T TIME TO TEST IT.
I PRAYED THAT IT WOULDN'T BLOW ME TO SHIT.
I THOUGHT OF SARA.
I JUMPED FOR WEEKS.
THROUGH HUNDREDS OF WORLDS.
BUT IT NEVER BROUGHT ME BACK TO THEM.
I WAS DISORIENTATED AND SICK FROM NUMEROUS EARTHS WITH STRANGE ATMOSPHERES.
I HADN'T EATEN IN DAYS.
MY SPIRIT WAS BROKEN.

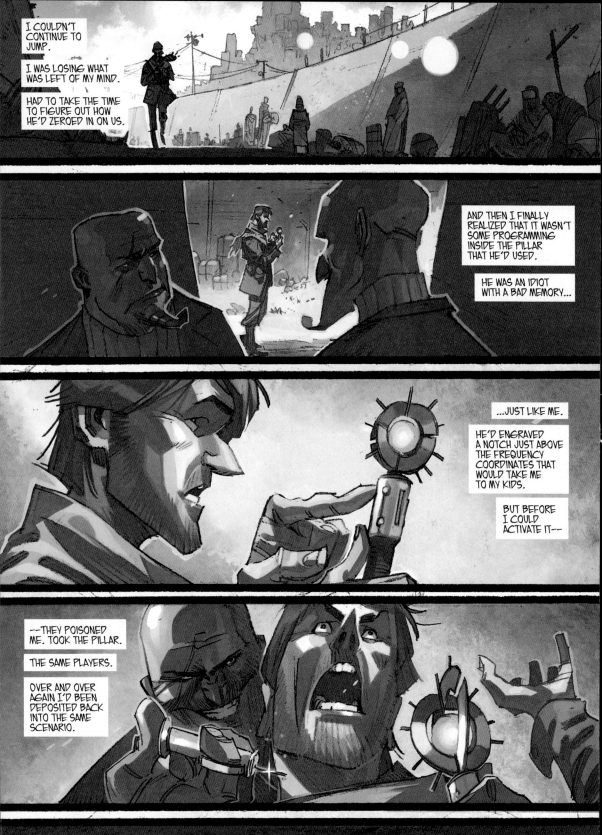

I COULDN'T CONTINUE TO JUMP.

I WAS LOSING WHAT WAS LEFT OF MY MIND.

HAD TO TAKE THE TIME TO FIGURE OUT HOW HE'D ZEROED IN ON US.

AND THEN I FINALLY REALIZED THAT IT WASN'T SOME PROGRAMMING INSIDE THE PILLAR THAT HE'D USED.

HE WAS AN IDIOT WITH A BAD MEMORY...

...JUST LIKE ME.

HE'D ENGRAVED A NOTCH JUST ABOVE THE FREQUENCY COORDINATES THAT WOULD TAKE ME TO MY KIDS.

BUT BEFORE I COULD ACTIVATE IT--

--THEY POISONED ME. TOOK THE PILLAR.

THE SAME PLAYERS.

OVER AND OVER AGAIN I'D BEEN DEPOSITED BACK INTO THE SAME SCENARIO.

MR. BLOCK SOUGHT CONTROL.

KADIR SOUGHT SARA.

GRANT AND SARA ONLY WANTED TO FIND THEIR VERY LIKELY DEAD CHILDREN.

THE SAME PATTERNS PLAYING OUT, REPEATING THROUGH THE ONION.

BUT I DIDN'T STOP FIGHTING. I GOT THE PILLAR--

--AND JUMPED.

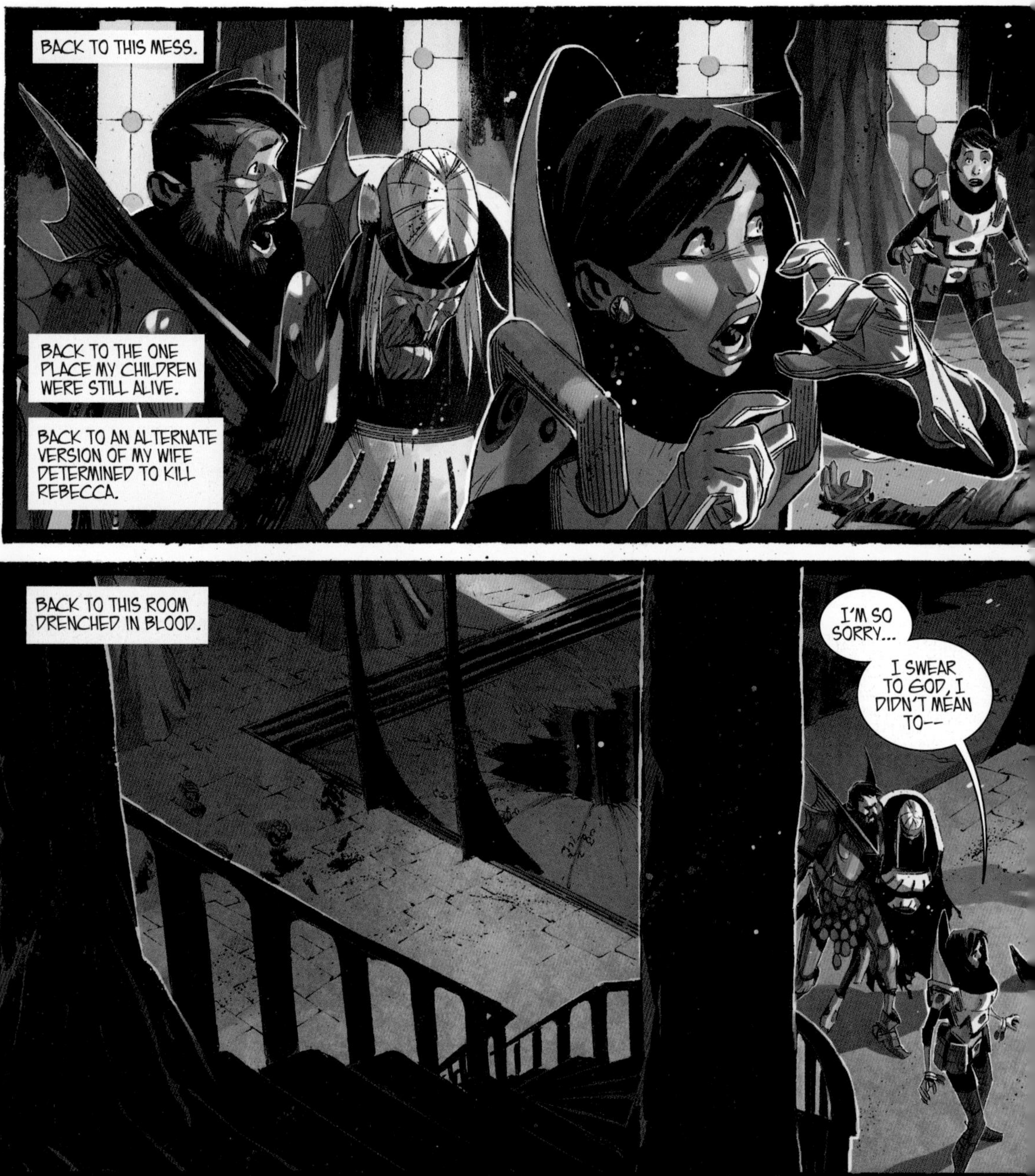
BACK TO THIS MESS.
BACK TO THE ONE PLACE MY CHILDREN WERE STILL ALIVE.
BACK TO AN ALTERNATE VERSION OF MY WIFE DETERMINED TO KILL REBECCA.
BACK TO THIS ROOM DRENCHED IN BLOOD.
I'M SO SORRY...
I SWEAR TO GOD, I DIDN'T MEAN TO--

# BLACK

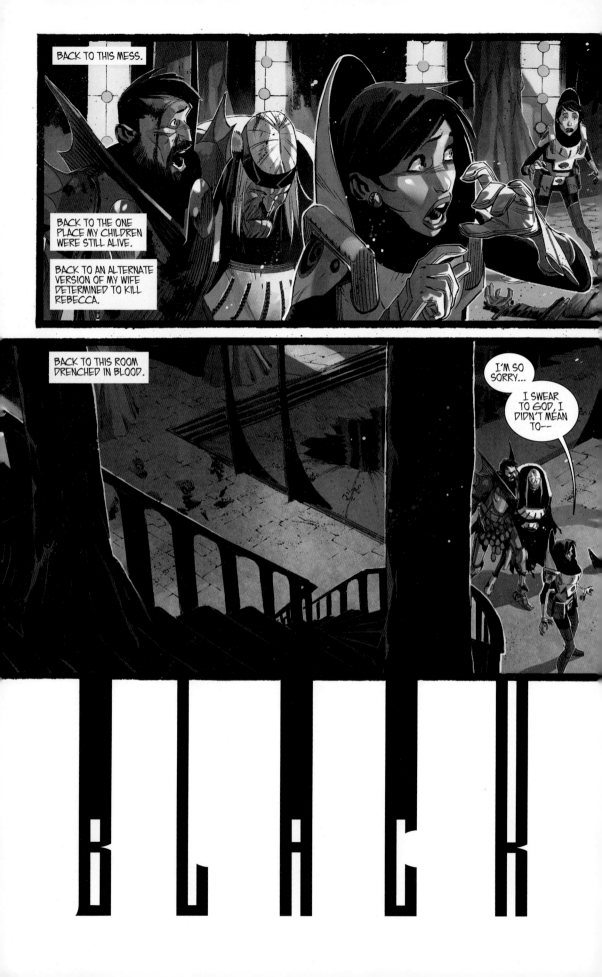

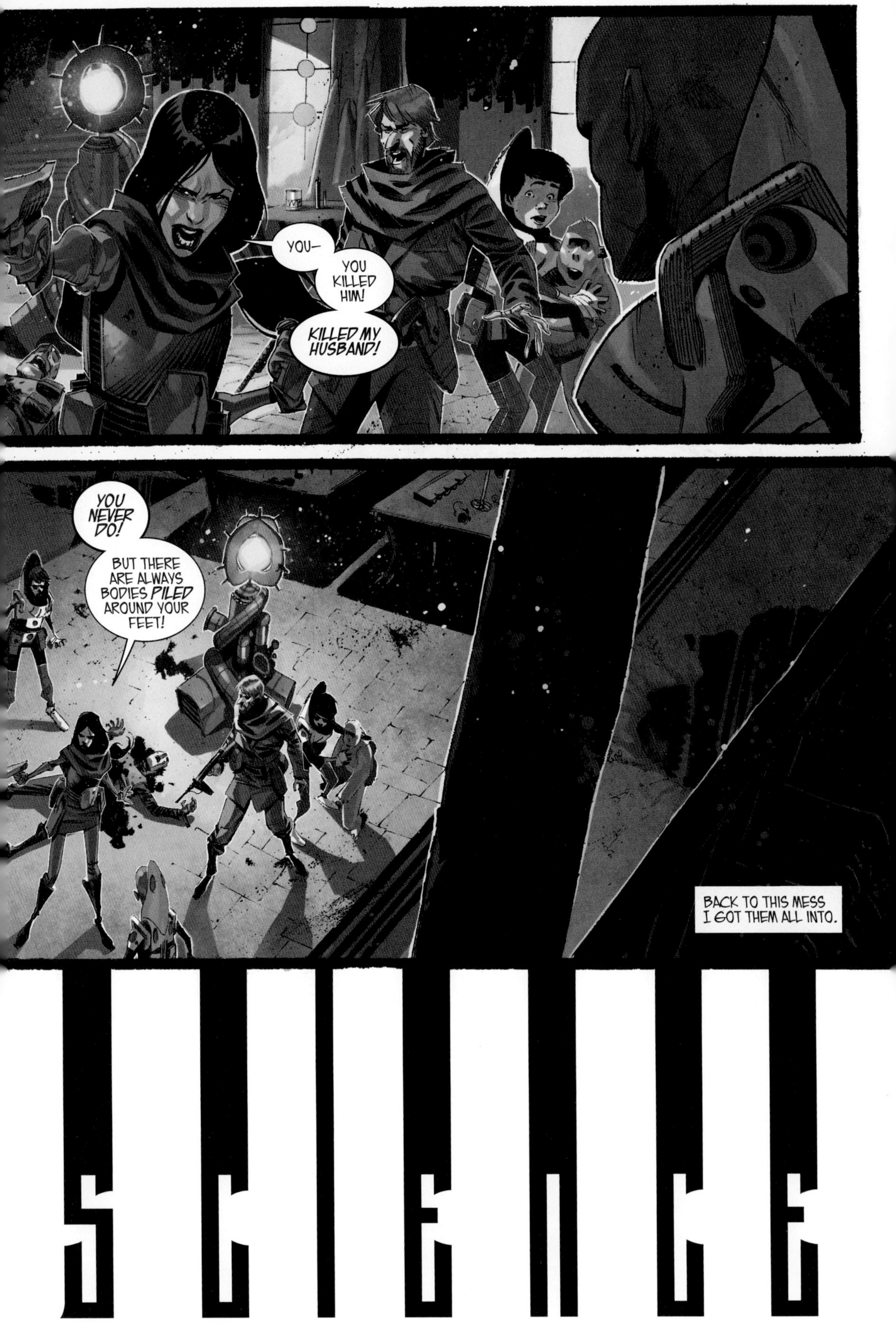
YOU—
YOU KILLED HIM!
KILLED MY HUSBAND!
YOU NEVER DO!
BUT THERE ARE ALWAYS BODIES PILED AROUND YOUR FEET!
BACK TO THIS MESS I GOT THEM ALL INTO.

# SCIENCE

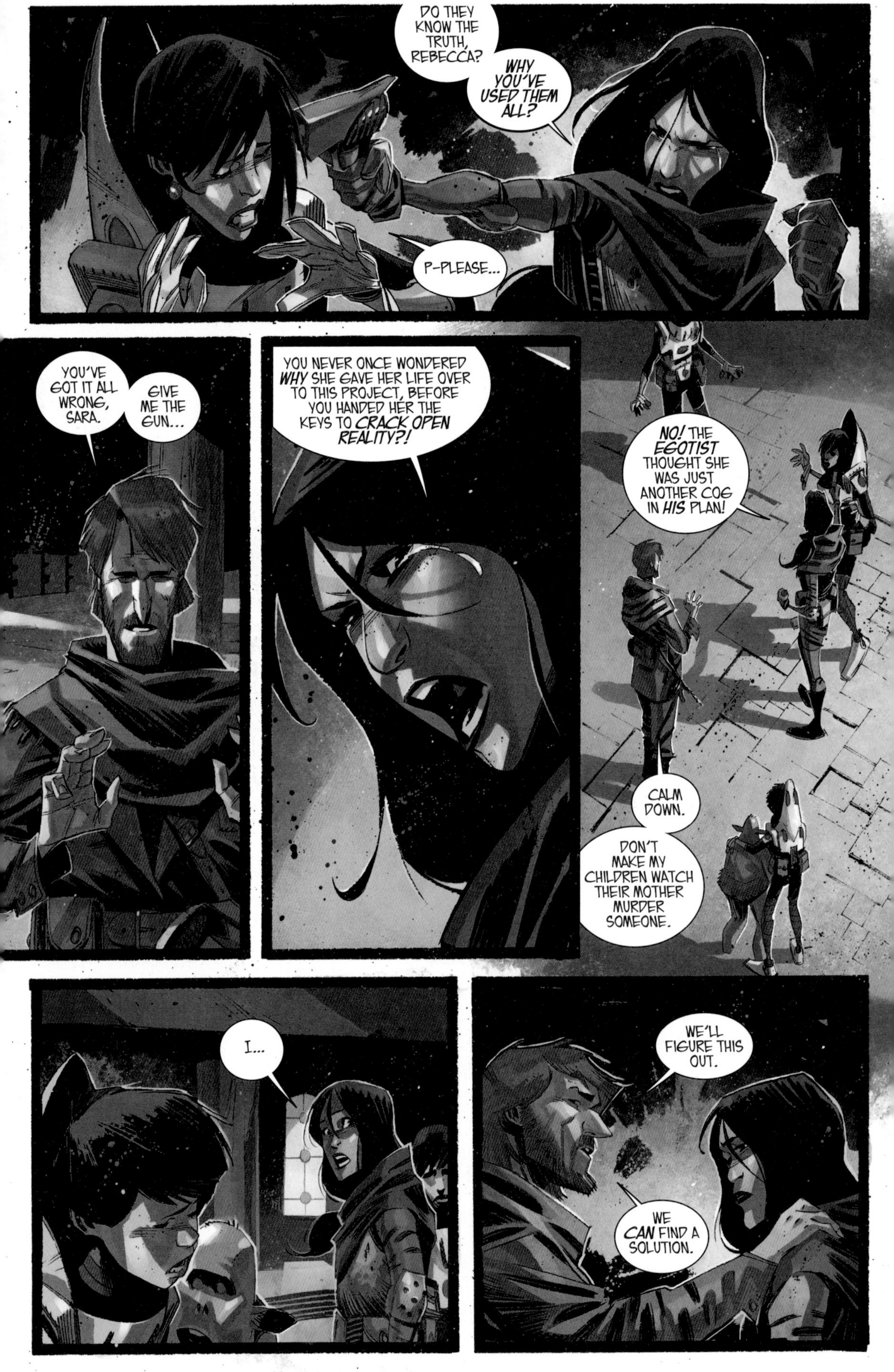
DO THEY KNOW THE TRUTH, REBECCA?
WHY YOU'VE USED THEM ALL?
P-PLEASE...
YOU'VE GOT IT ALL WRONG, SARA.
GIVE ME THE GUN...
YOU NEVER ONCE WONDERED WHY SHE GAVE HER LIFE OVER TO THIS PROJECT, BEFORE YOU HANDED HER THE KEYS TO CRACK OPEN REALITY?!
NO! THE EGOTIST THOUGHT SHE WAS JUST ANOTHER COG IN HIS PLAN!
CALM DOWN.
DON'T MAKE MY CHILDREN WATCH THEIR MOTHER MURDER SOMEONE.
I...
WE'LL FIGURE THIS OUT.
WE CAN FIND A SOLUTION.

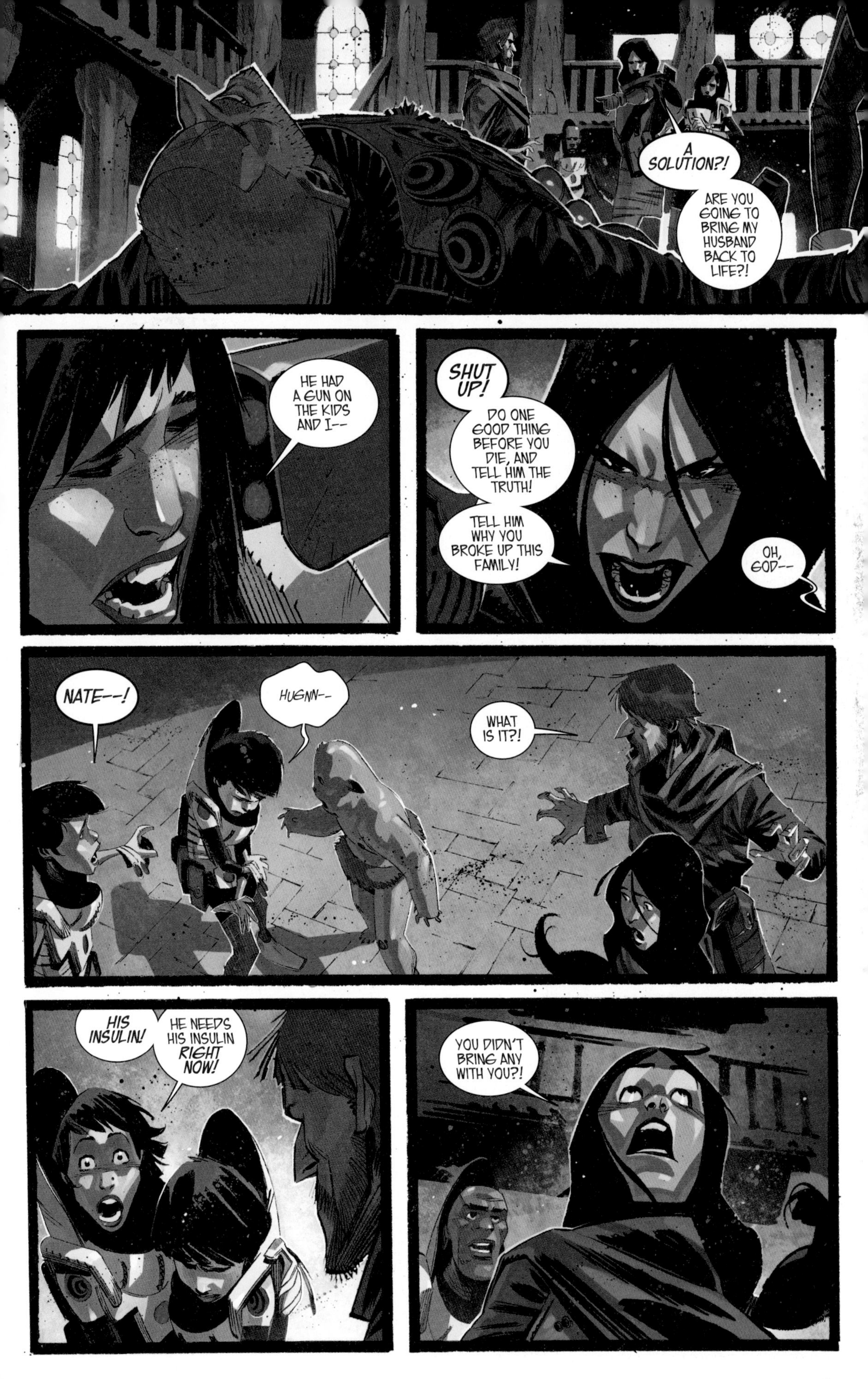
A SOLUTION?!
ARE YOU GOING TO BRING MY HUSBAND BACK TO LIFE?!
HE HAD A GUN ON THE KIDS AND I--
SHUT UP!
DO ONE GOOD THING BEFORE YOU DIE, AND TELL HIM THE TRUTH!
TELL HIM WHY YOU BROKE UP THIS FAMILY!
OH, GOD--
NATE--!
HUGNN--
WHAT IS IT?!
HIS INSULIN!
HE NEEDS HIS INSULIN RIGHT NOW!
YOU DIDN'T BRING ANY WITH YOU?!

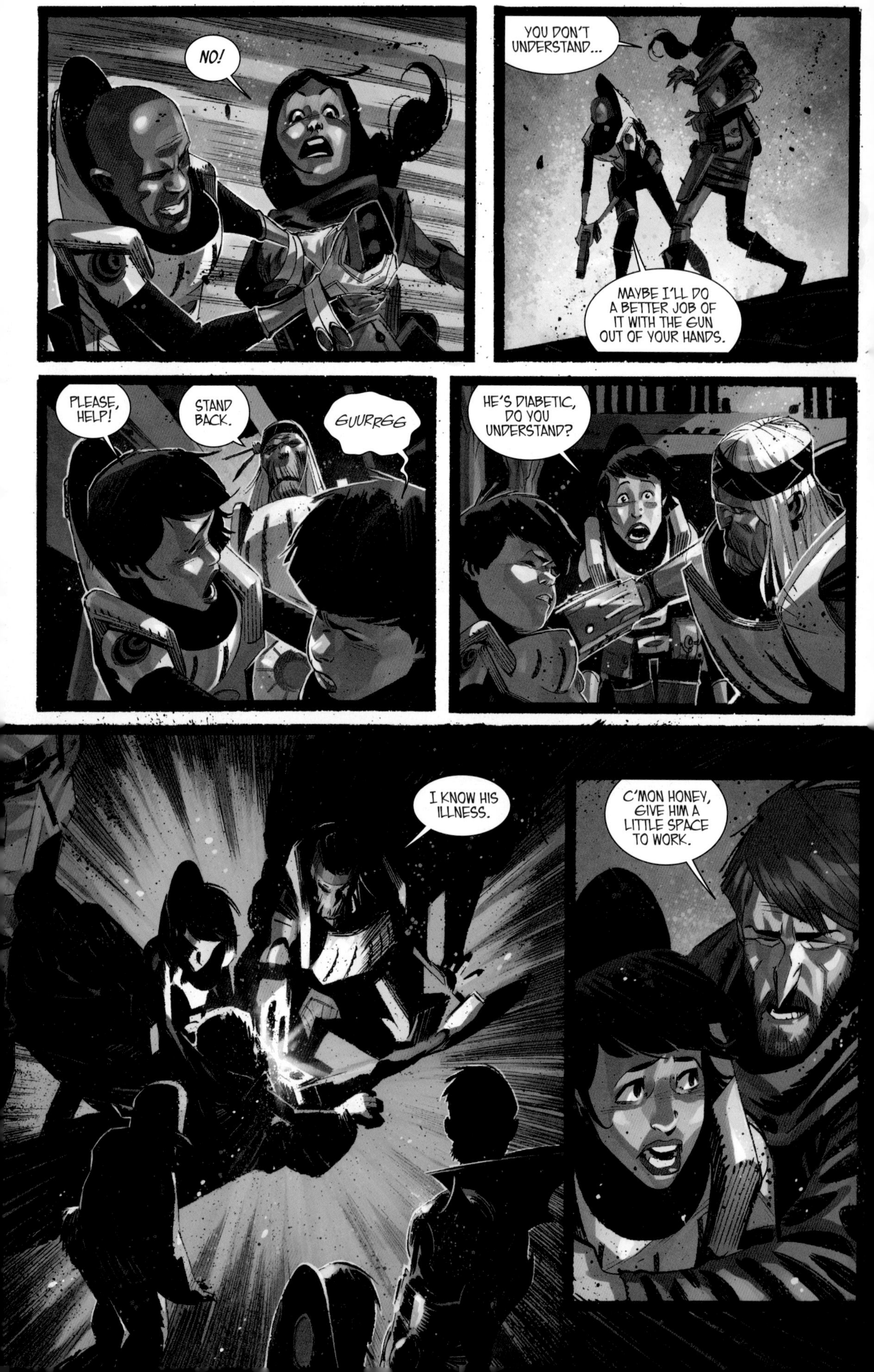
NO!
YOU DON'T UNDERSTAND...
MAYBE I'LL DO A BETTER JOB OF IT WITH THE GUN OUT OF YOUR HANDS.
PLEASE, HELP!
STAND BACK.
GUURRGG
HE'S DIABETIC, DO YOU UNDERSTAND?
I KNOW HIS ILLNESS.
C'MON HONEY, GIVE HIM A LITTLE SPACE TO WORK.

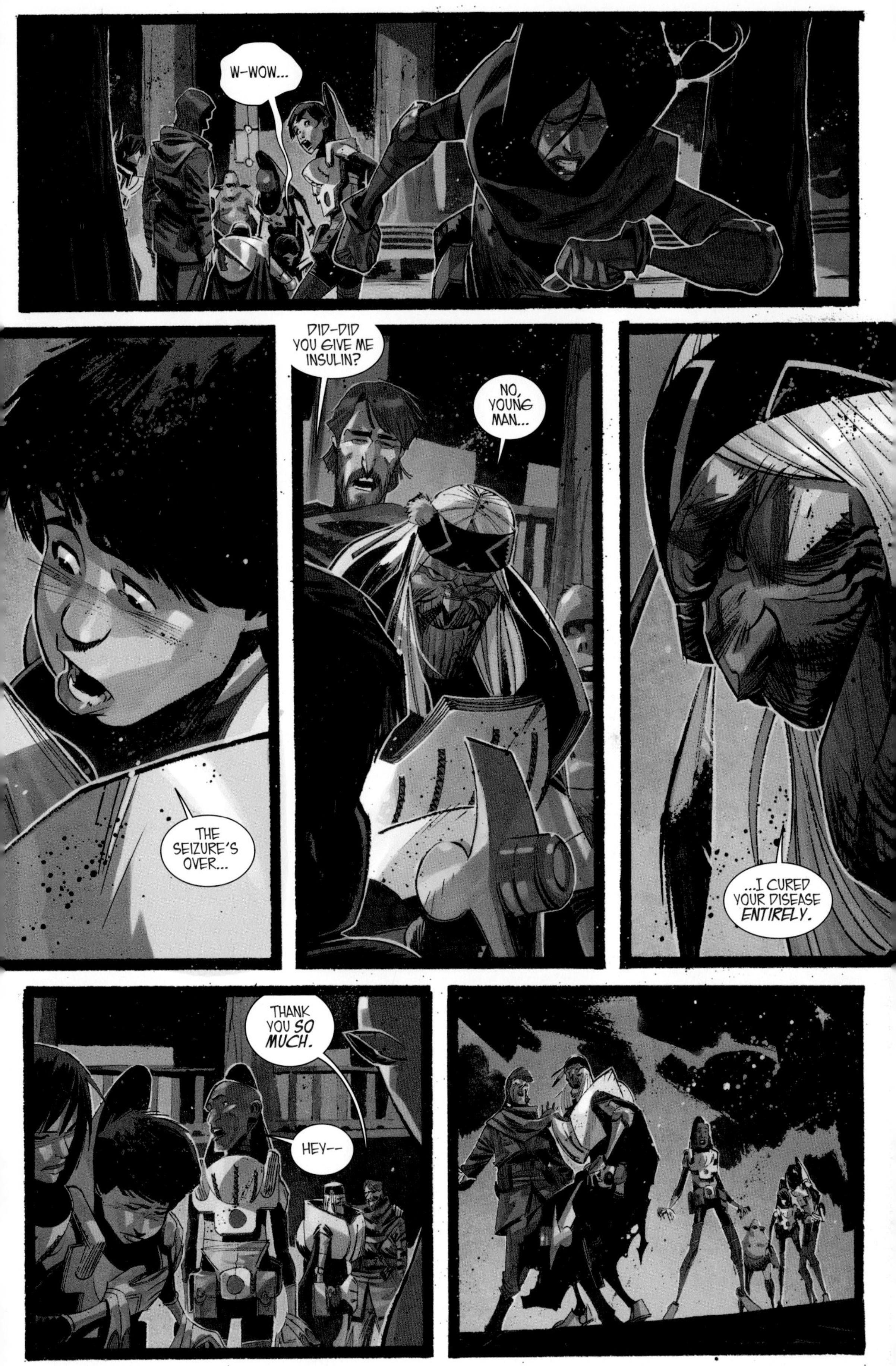
W-WOW...
DID-DID YOU GIVE ME INSULIN?
THE SEIZURE'S OVER...
NO, YOUNG MAN...
...I CURED YOUR DISEASE ENTIRELY.
THANK YOU SO MUCH.
HEY--

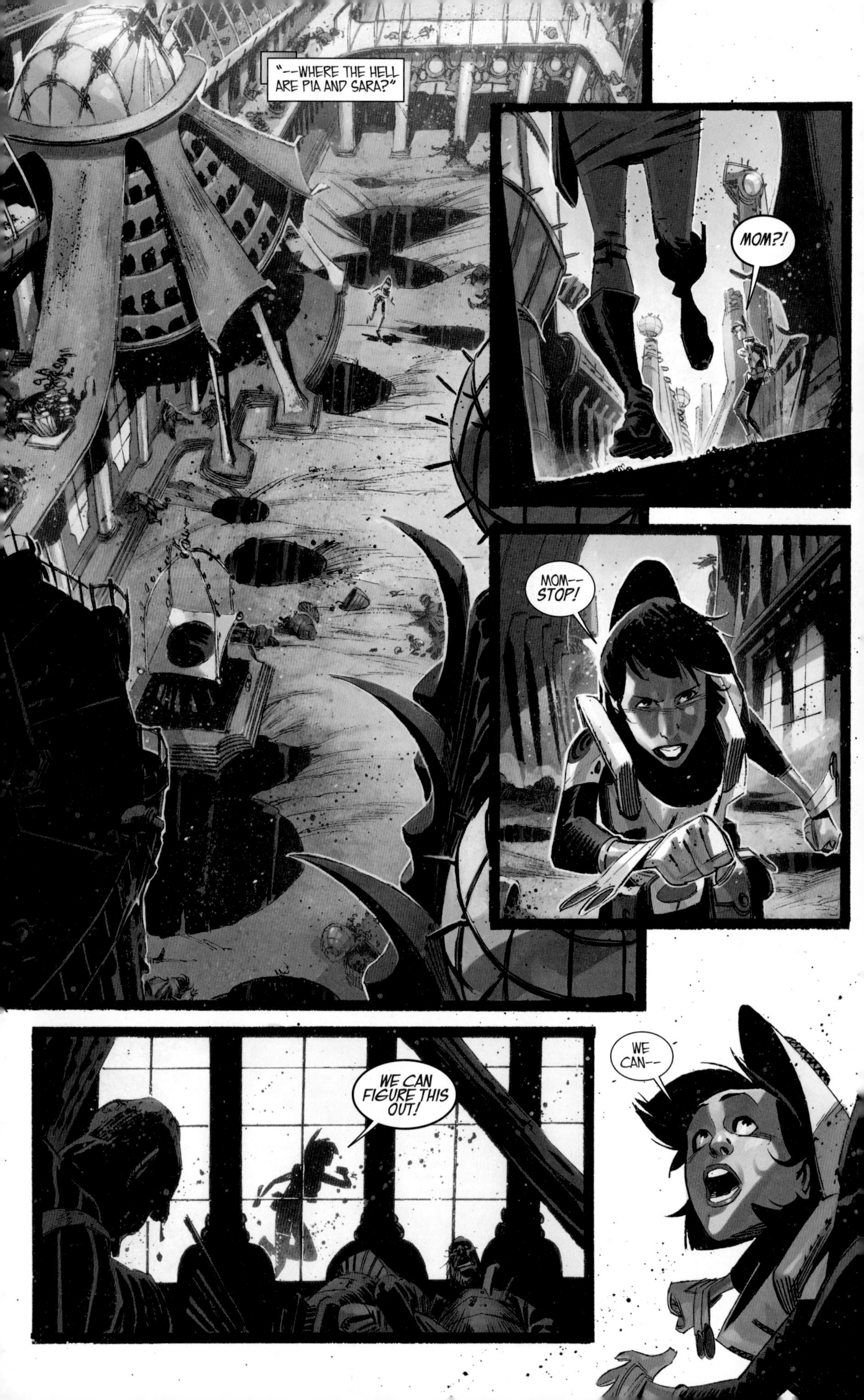
"--WHERE THE HELL ARE PIA AND SARA?"
MOM?!
MOM-- STOP!
WE CAN FIGURE THIS OUT!
WE CAN--

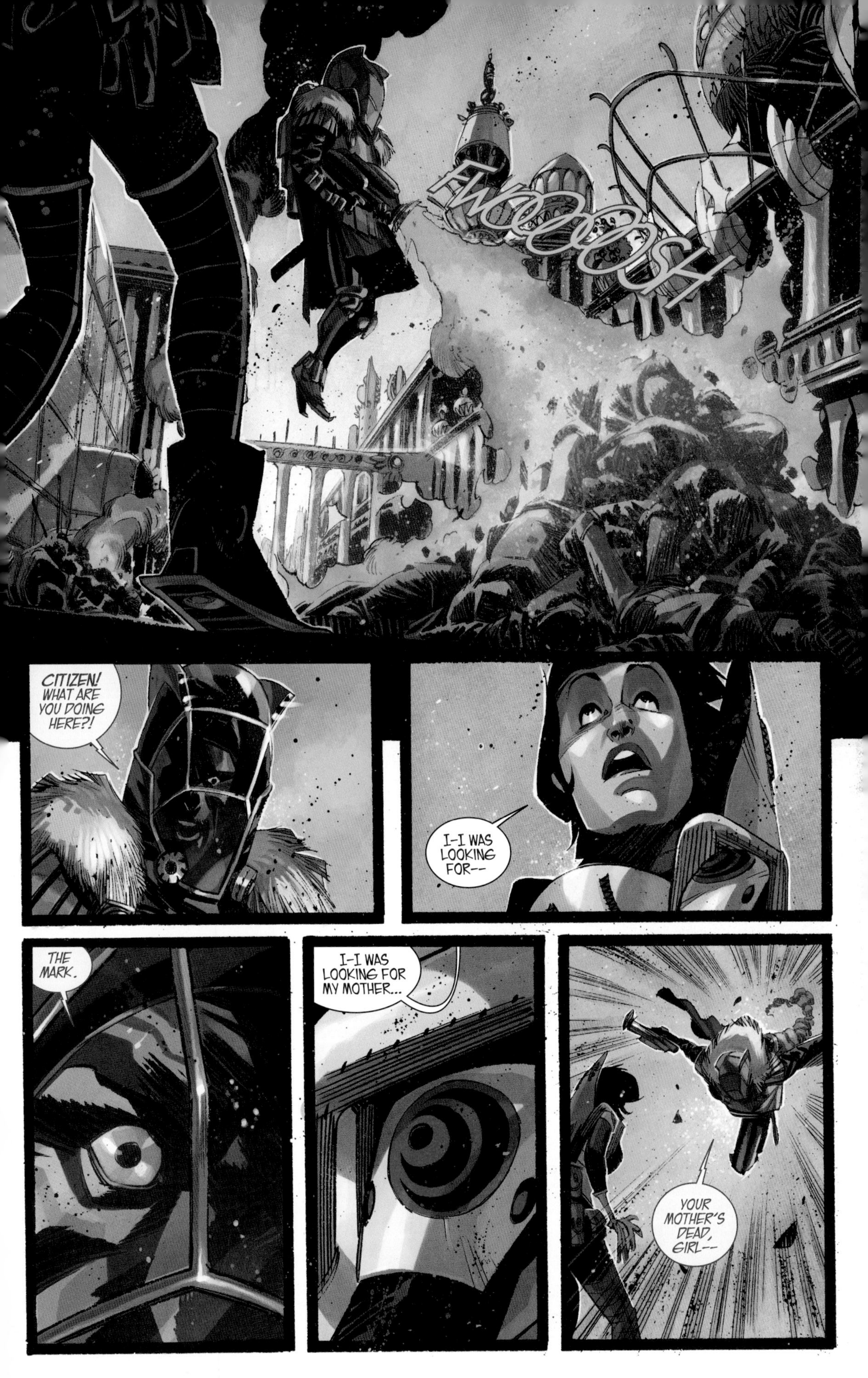
FWOOOOSH
CITIZEN! WHAT ARE YOU DOING HERE?!
I-I WAS LOOKING FOR--
THE MARK.
I-I WAS LOOKING FOR MY MOTHER...
YOUR MOTHER'S DEAD, GIRL--

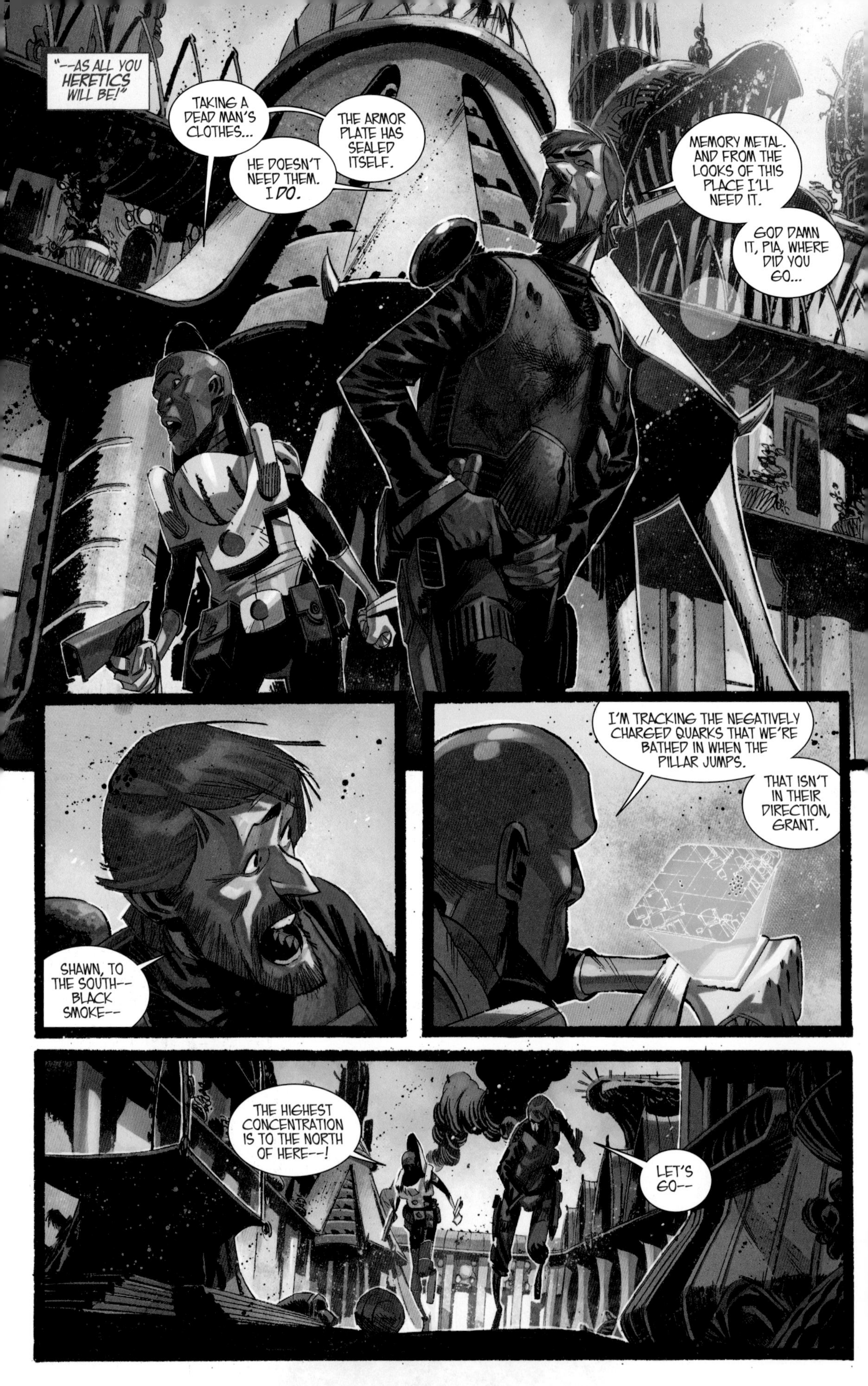
"--AS ALL YOU HERETICS WILL BE!"
TAKING A DEAD MAN'S CLOTHES...
THE ARMOR PLATE HAS SEALED ITSELF.
HE DOESN'T NEED THEM. I DO.
MEMORY METAL. AND FROM THE LOOKS OF THIS PLACE I'LL NEED IT.
GOD DAMN IT, PIA, WHERE DID YOU GO...
SHAWN, TO THE SOUTH-- BLACK SMOKE--
I'M TRACKING THE NEGATIVELY CHARGED QUARKS THAT WE'RE BATHED IN WHEN THE PILLAR JUMPS.
THAT ISN'T IN THEIR DIRECTION, GRANT.
THE HIGHEST CONCENTRATION IS TO THE NORTH OF HERE--!
LET'S GO--

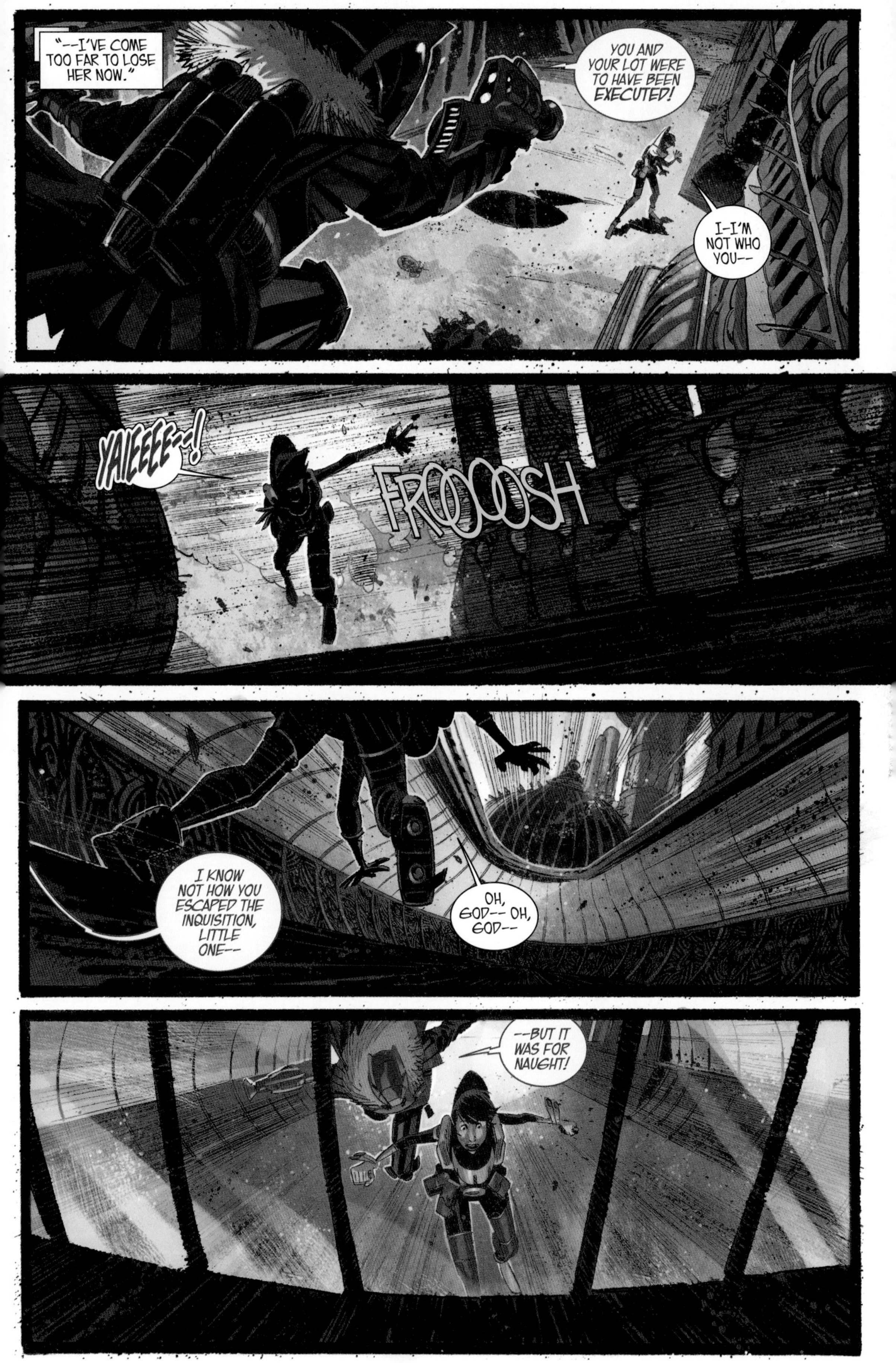
"--I'VE COME TOO FAR TO LOSE HER NOW."
YOU AND YOUR LOT WERE TO HAVE BEEN EXECUTED!
I-I'M NOT WHO YOU--
YAIEEEE--!
FROOOSH
I KNOW NOT HOW YOU ESCAPED THE INQUISITION, LITTLE ONE--
OH, GOD-- OH, GOD--
--BUT IT WAS FOR NAUGHT!

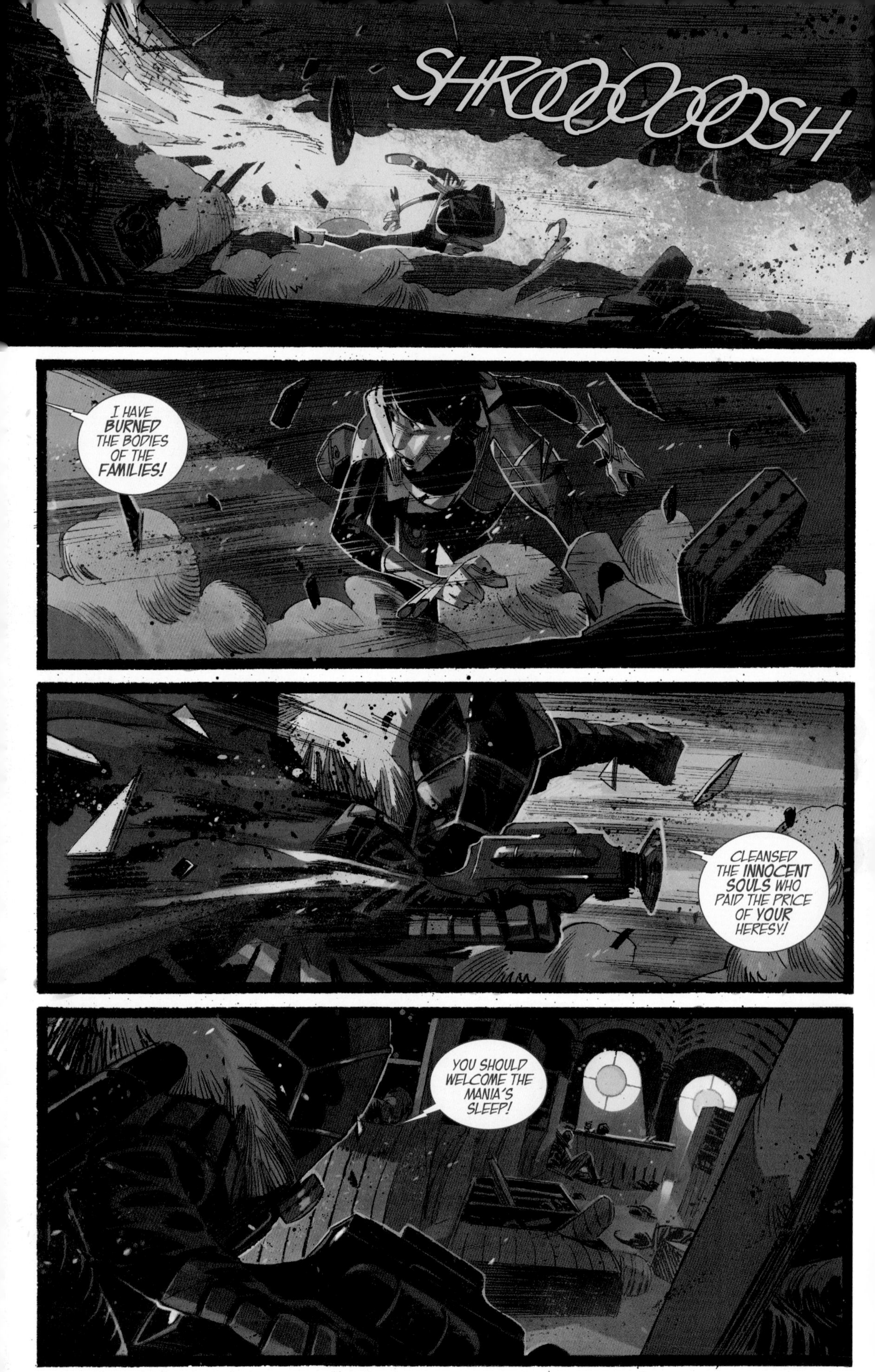
SHROOOOOOSH
I HAVE BURNED THE BODIES OF THE FAMILIES!
CLEANSED THE INNOCENT SOULS WHO PAID THE PRICE OF YOUR HERESY!
YOU SHOULD WELCOME THE MANIA'S SLEEP!

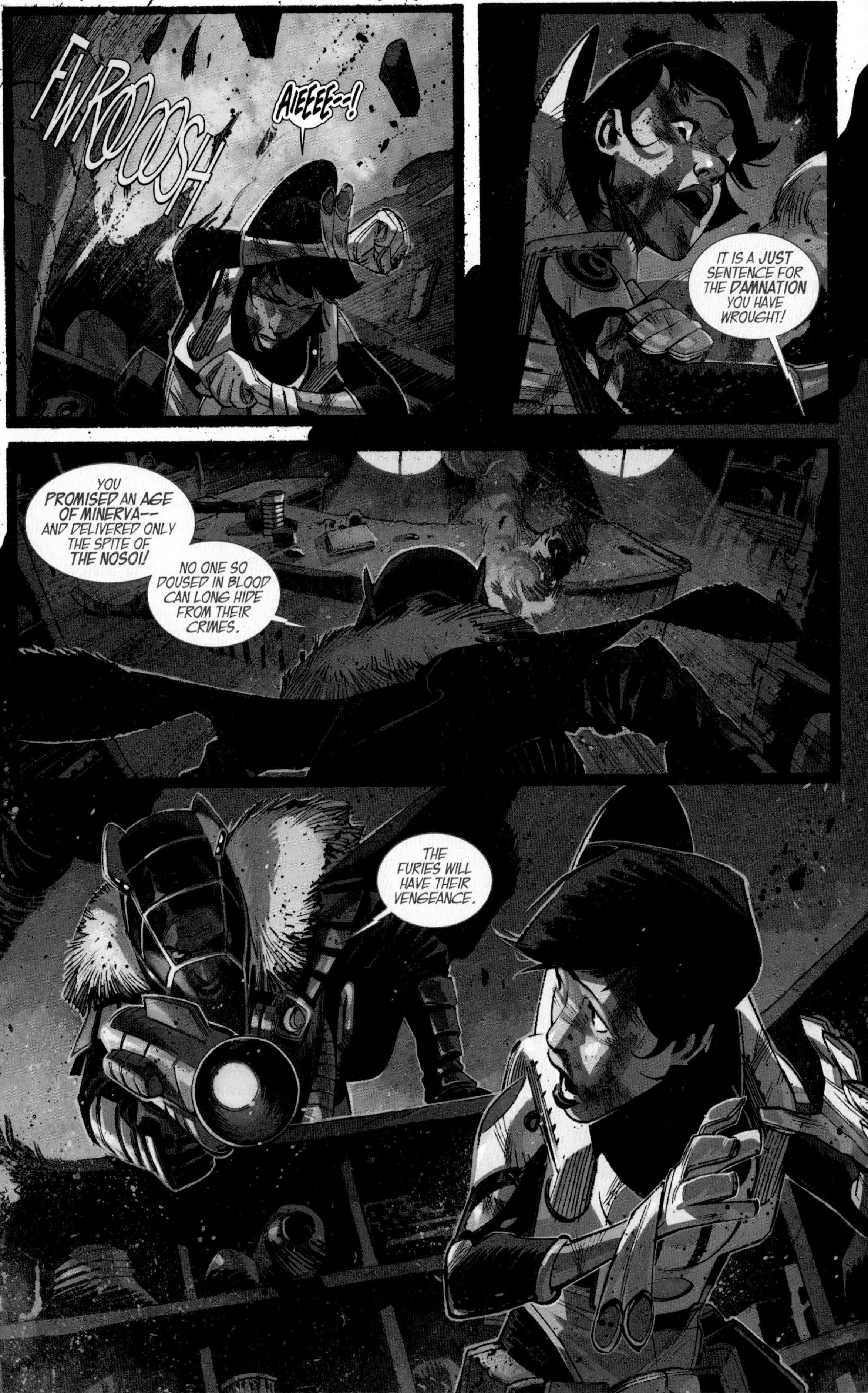
FWROOOOSH
AIEEEE--!
IT IS A JUST SENTENCE FOR THE DAMNATION YOU HAVE WROUGHT!
YOU PROMISED AN AGE OF MINERVA-- AND DELIVERED ONLY THE SPITE OF THE NOSOI!
NO ONE SO DOUSED IN BLOOD CAN LONG HIDE FROM THEIR CRIMES.
THE FURIES WILL HAVE THEIR VENGEANCE.

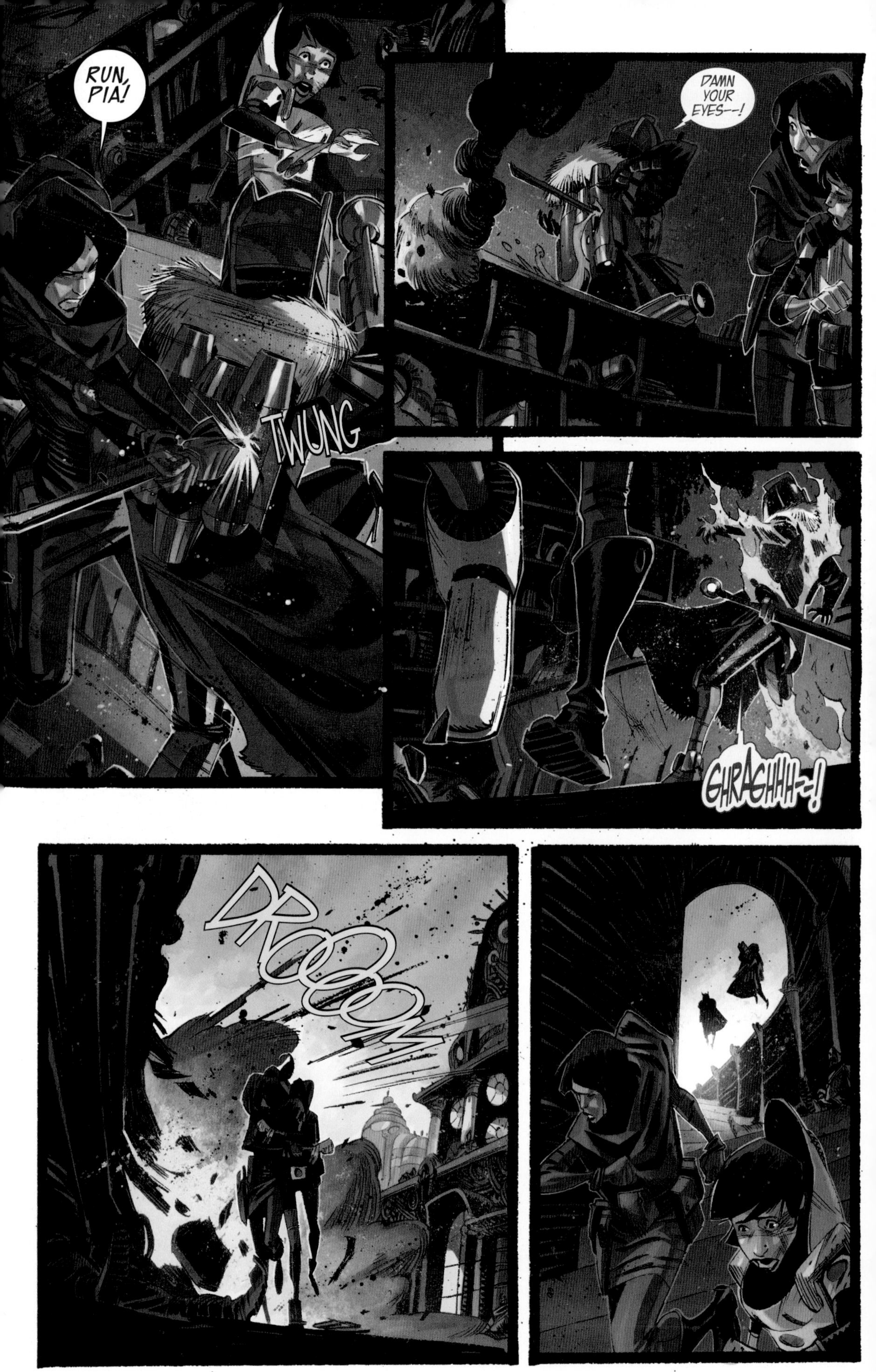
RUN, PIA!
TWUNG
DAMN YOUR EYES--!
GHRAGHHH--!
DROOOOM!

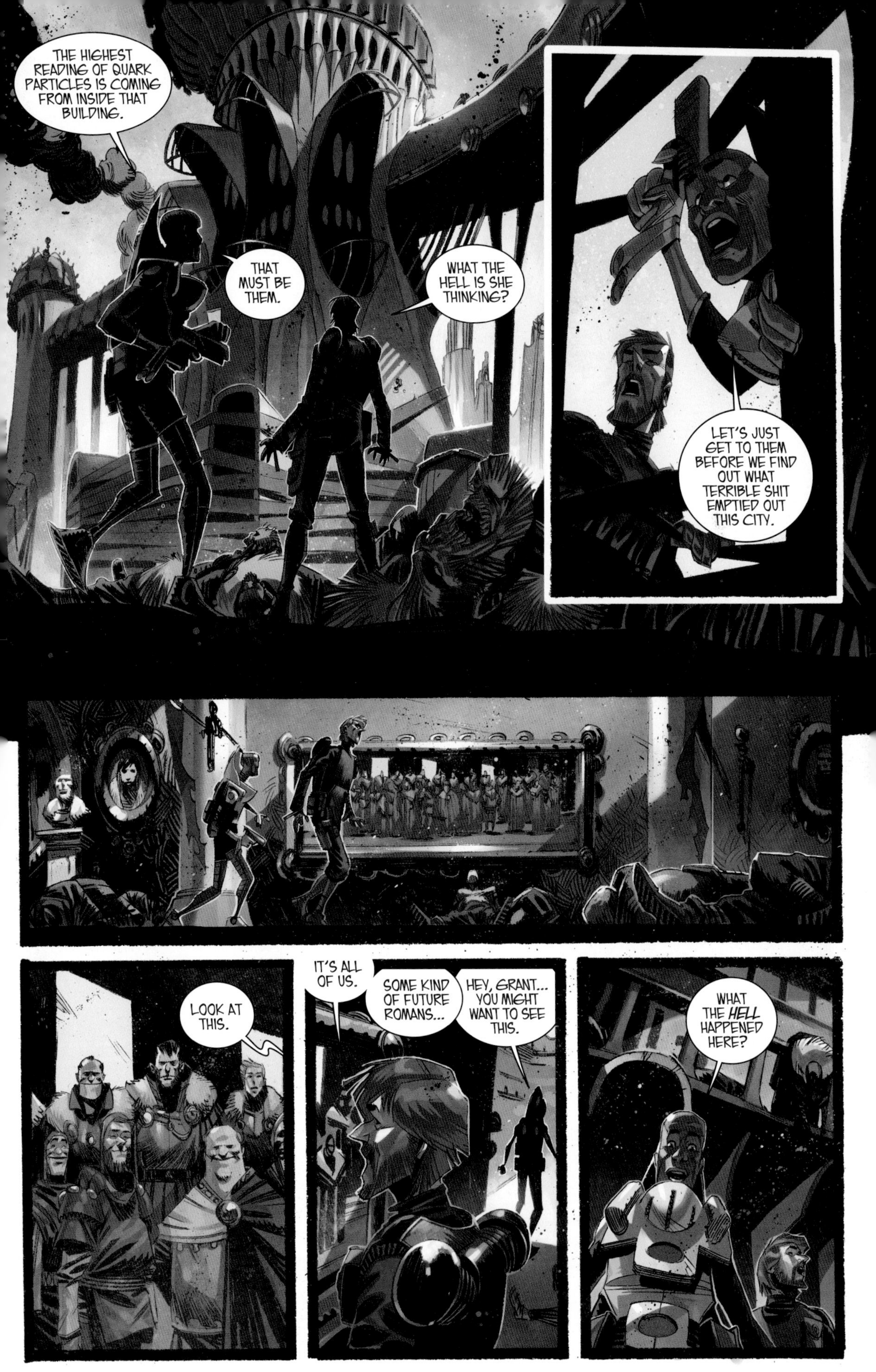
THE HIGHEST READING OF QUARK PARTICLES IS COMING FROM INSIDE THAT BUILDING.
THAT MUST BE THEM.
WHAT THE HELL IS SHE THINKING?
LET'S JUST GET TO THEM BEFORE WE FIND OUT WHAT TERRIBLE SHIT EMPTIED OUT THIS CITY.
LOOK AT THIS.
IT'S ALL OF US.
SOME KIND OF FUTURE ROMANS...
HEY, GRANT... YOU MIGHT WANT TO SEE THIS.
WHAT THE *HELL* HAPPENED HERE?

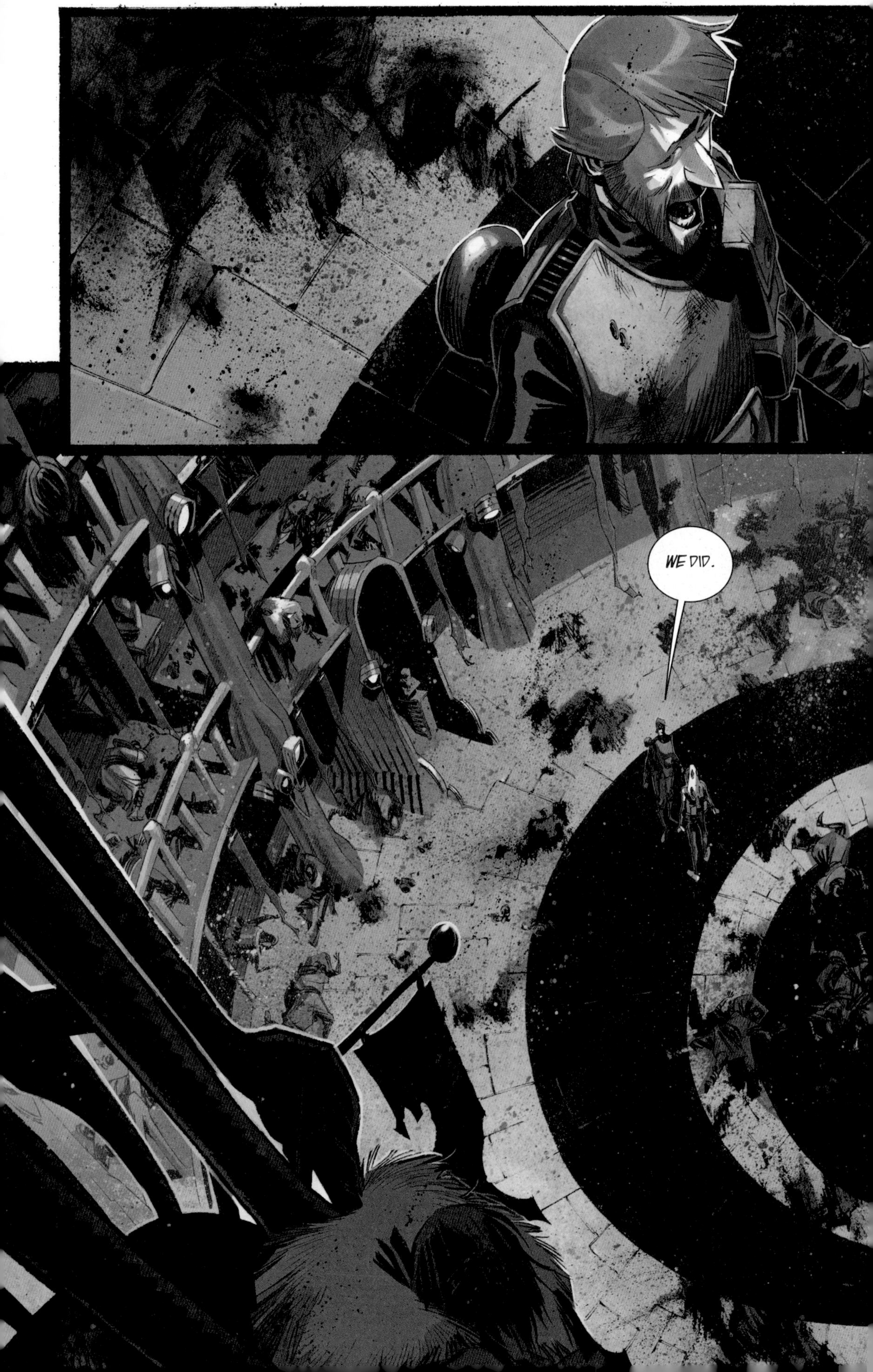
WE DID.

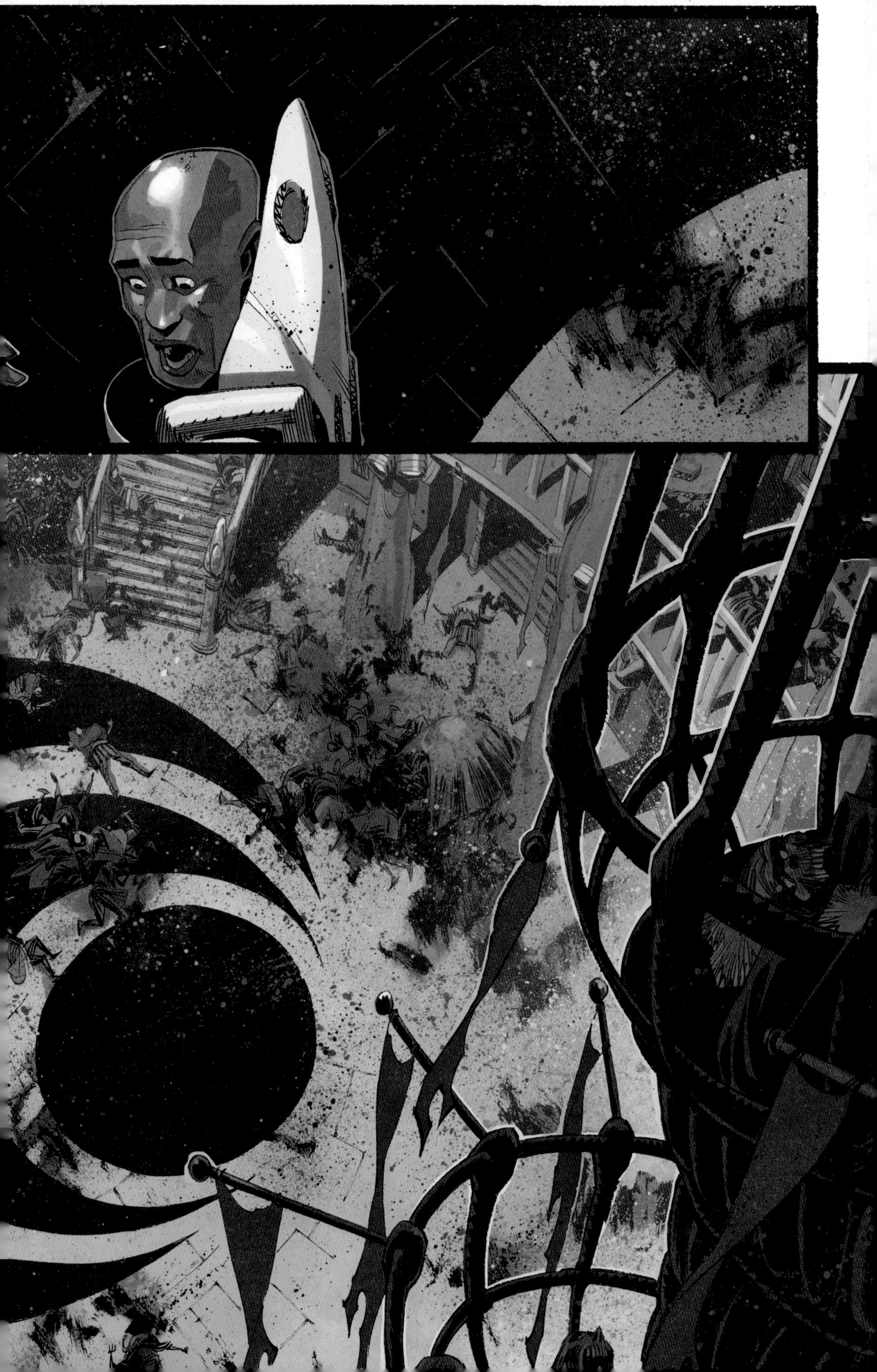

# 13

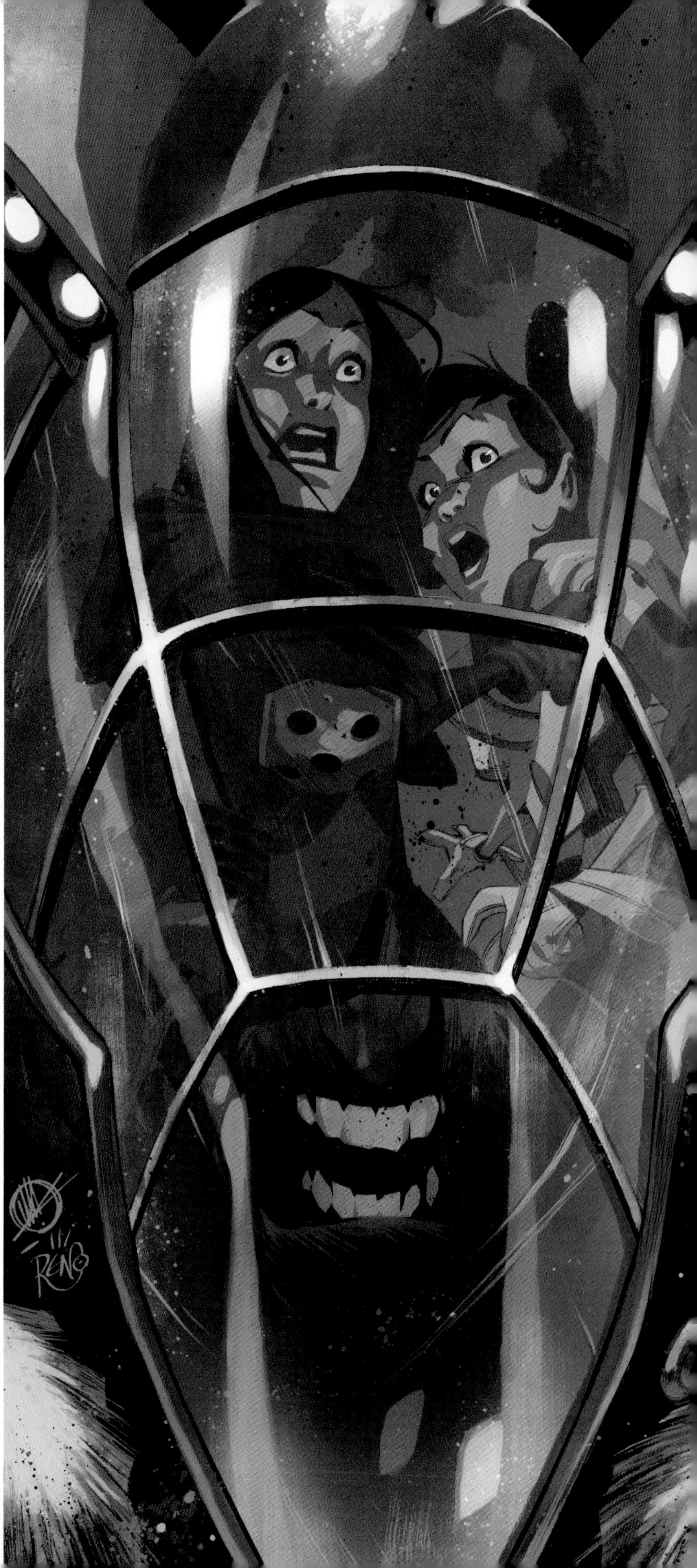
RENO

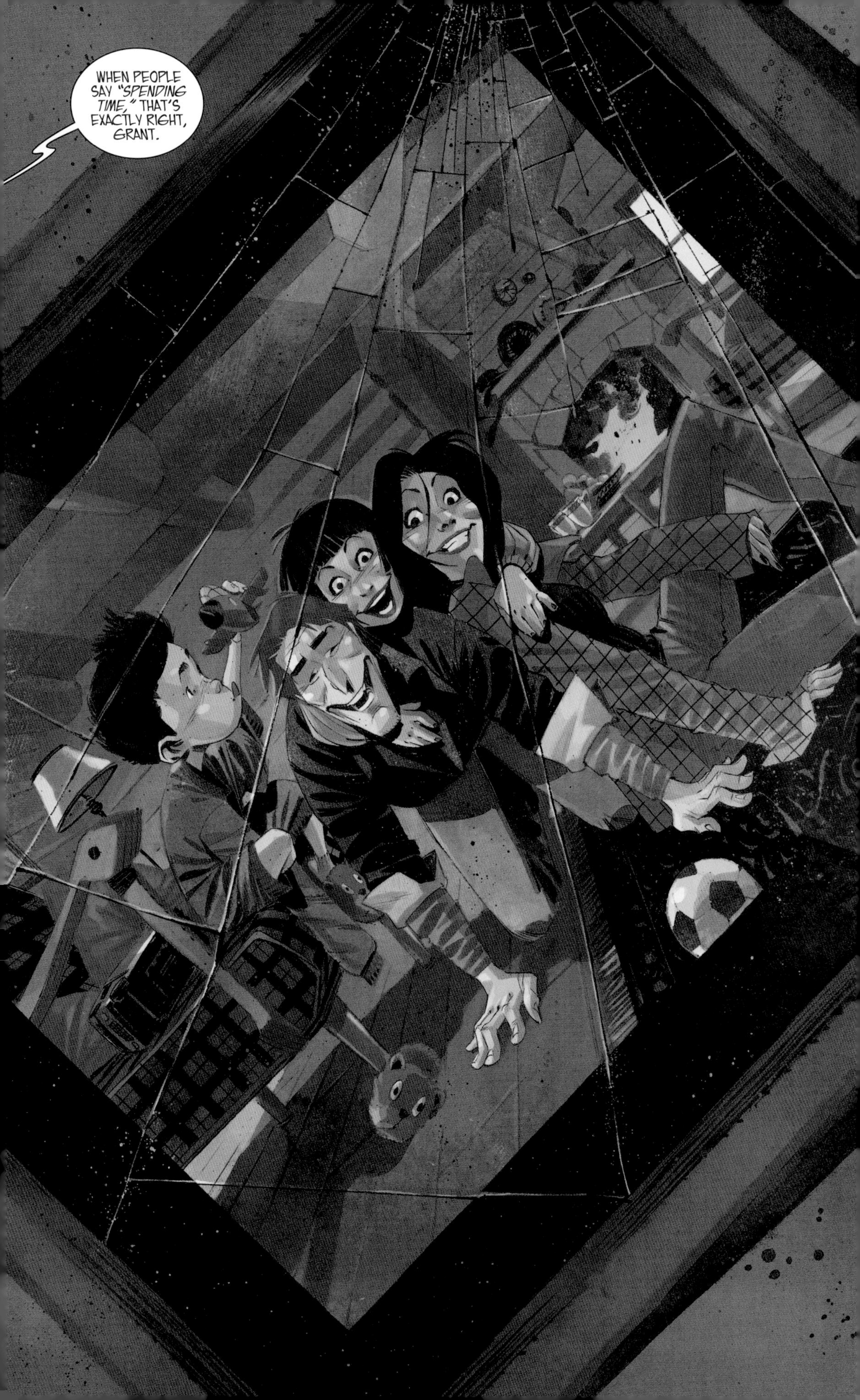
WHEN PEOPLE SAY "SPENDING TIME," THAT'S EXACTLY RIGHT, GRANT.

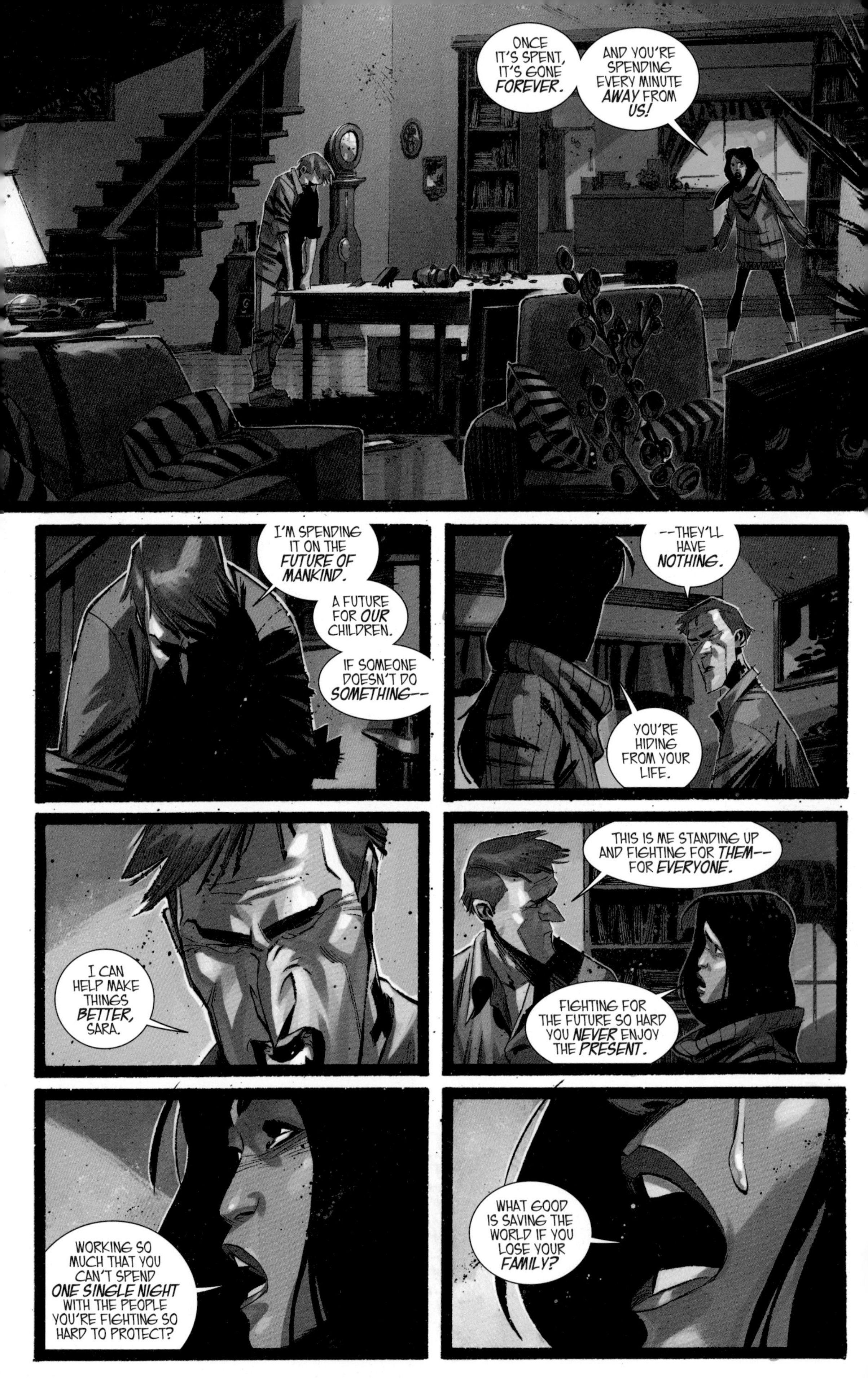
ONCE IT'S SPENT, IT'S GONE FOREVER.
AND YOU'RE SPENDING EVERY MINUTE AWAY FROM US!
I'M SPENDING IT ON THE FUTURE OF MANKIND.
A FUTURE FOR OUR CHILDREN.
IF SOMEONE DOESN'T DO SOMETHING--
--THEY'LL HAVE NOTHING.
YOU'RE HIDING FROM YOUR LIFE.
I CAN HELP MAKE THINGS BETTER, SARA.
THIS IS ME STANDING UP AND FIGHTING FOR THEM--FOR EVERYONE.
FIGHTING FOR THE FUTURE SO HARD YOU NEVER ENJOY THE PRESENT.
WORKING SO MUCH THAT YOU CAN'T SPEND ONE SINGLE NIGHT WITH THE PEOPLE YOU'RE FIGHTING SO HARD TO PROTECT?
WHAT GOOD IS SAVING THE WORLD IF YOU LOSE YOUR FAMILY?

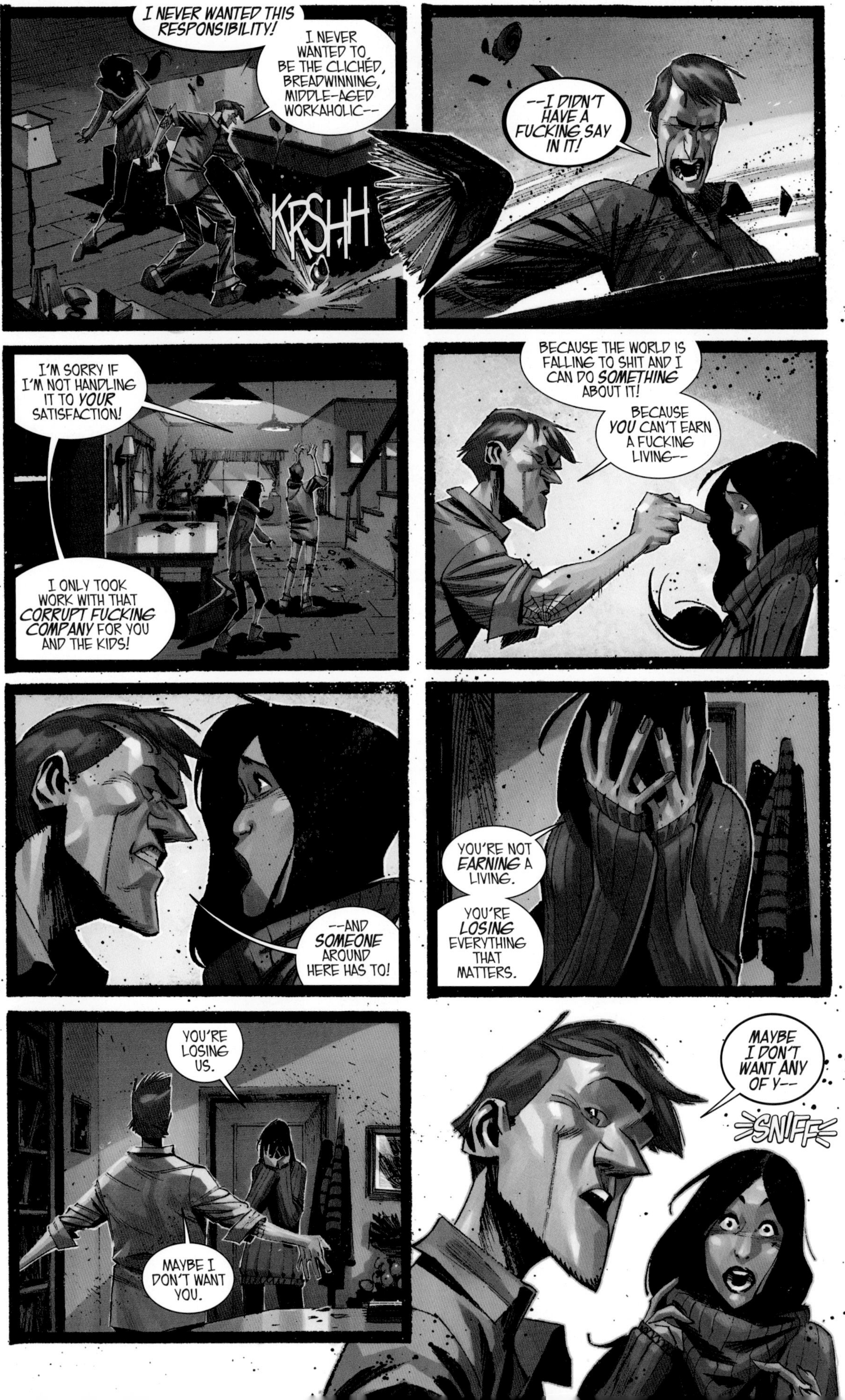
I NEVER WANTED THIS RESPONSIBILITY!
I NEVER WANTED TO BE THE CLICHÉD, BREADWINNING, MIDDLE-AGED WORKAHOLIC--
KRSHH
--I DIDN'T HAVE A FUCKING SAY IN IT!
I'M SORRY IF I'M NOT HANDLING IT TO YOUR SATISFACTION!
I ONLY TOOK WORK WITH THAT CORRUPT FUCKING COMPANY FOR YOU AND THE KIDS!
BECAUSE THE WORLD IS FALLING TO SHIT AND I CAN DO SOMETHING ABOUT IT!
BECAUSE YOU CAN'T EARN A FUCKING LIVING--
--AND SOMEONE AROUND HERE HAS TO!
YOU'RE NOT EARNING A LIVING.
YOU'RE LOSING EVERYTHING THAT MATTERS.
YOU'RE LOSING US.
MAYBE I DON'T WANT YOU.
MAYBE I DON'T WANT ANY OF Y--
SNIFF

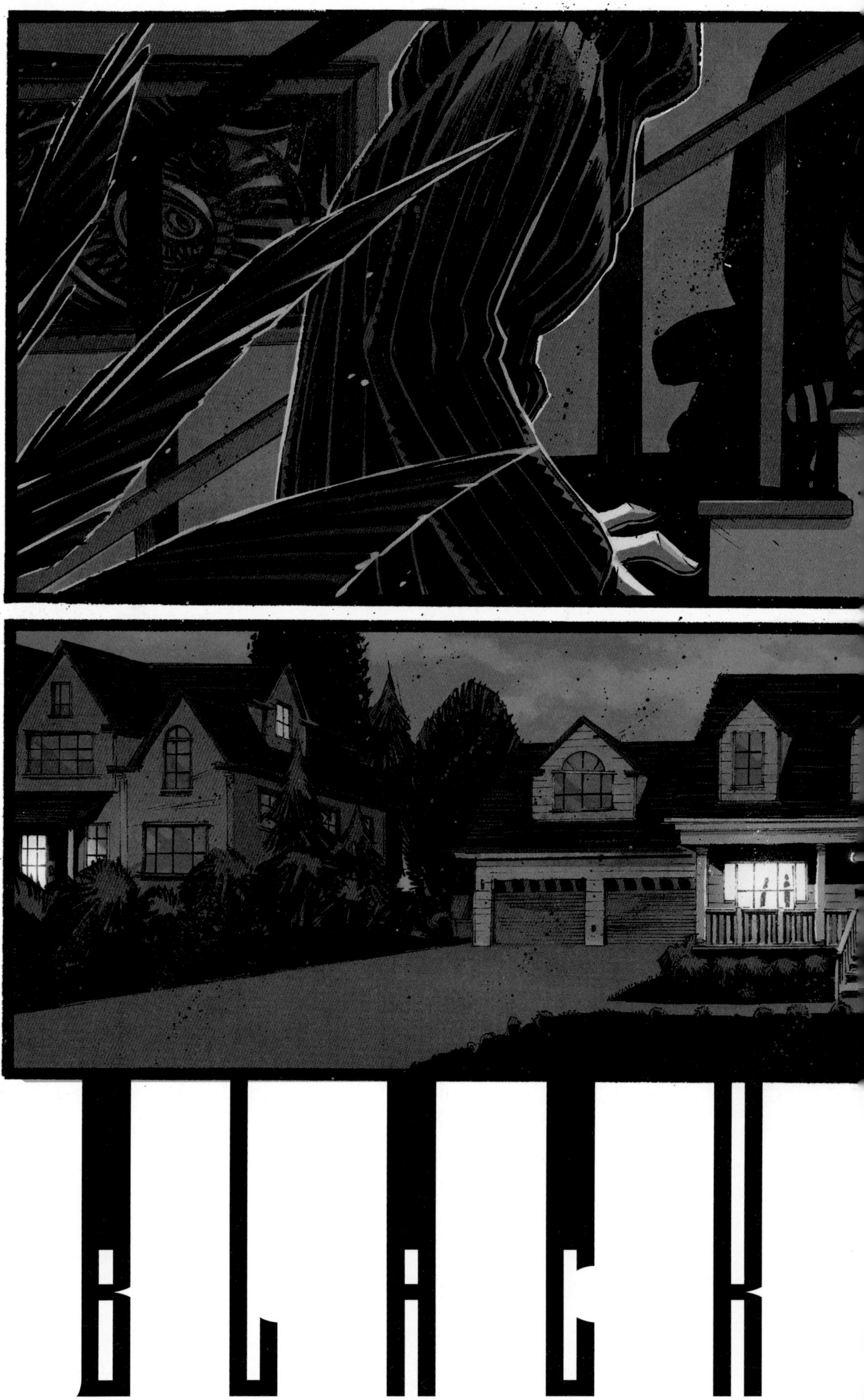

# BLACK

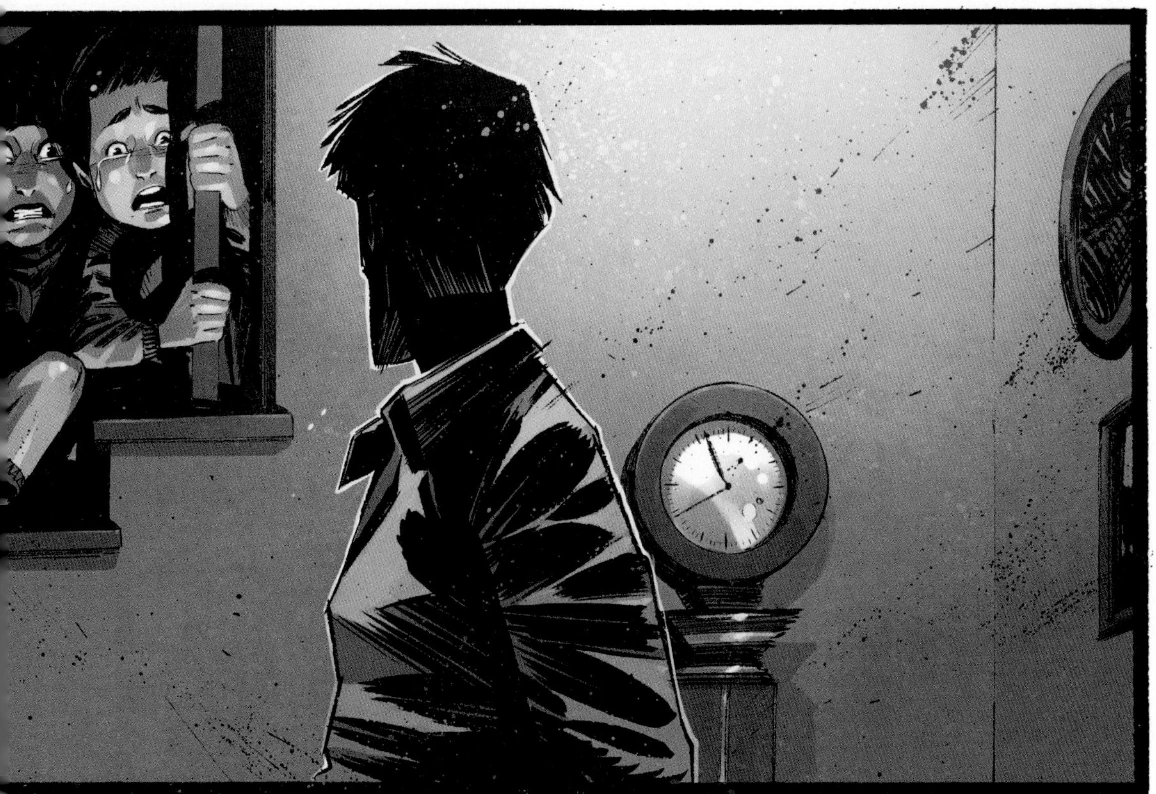

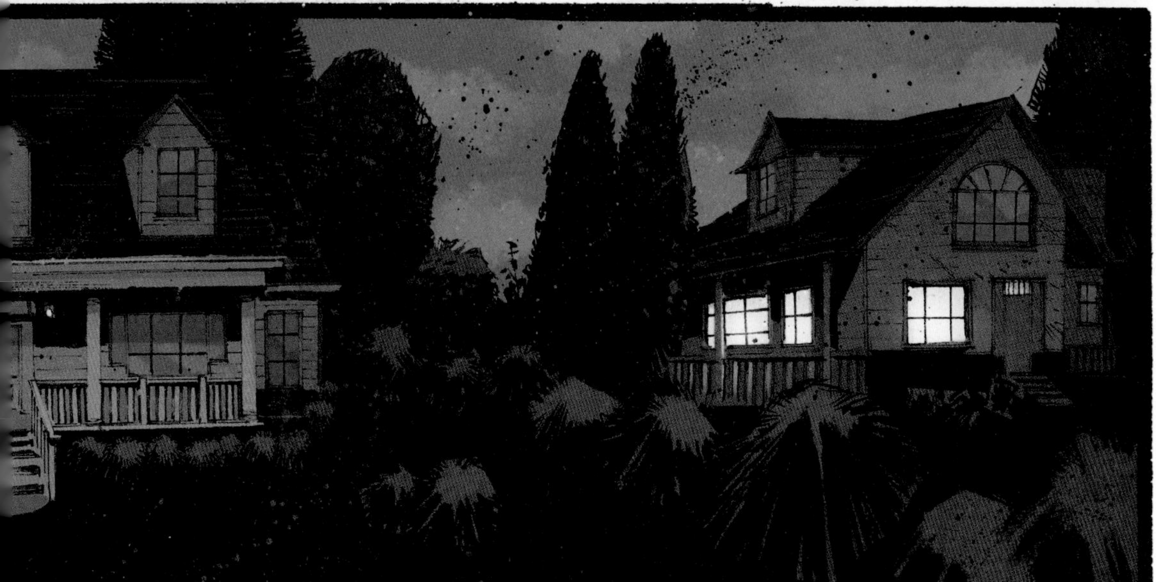

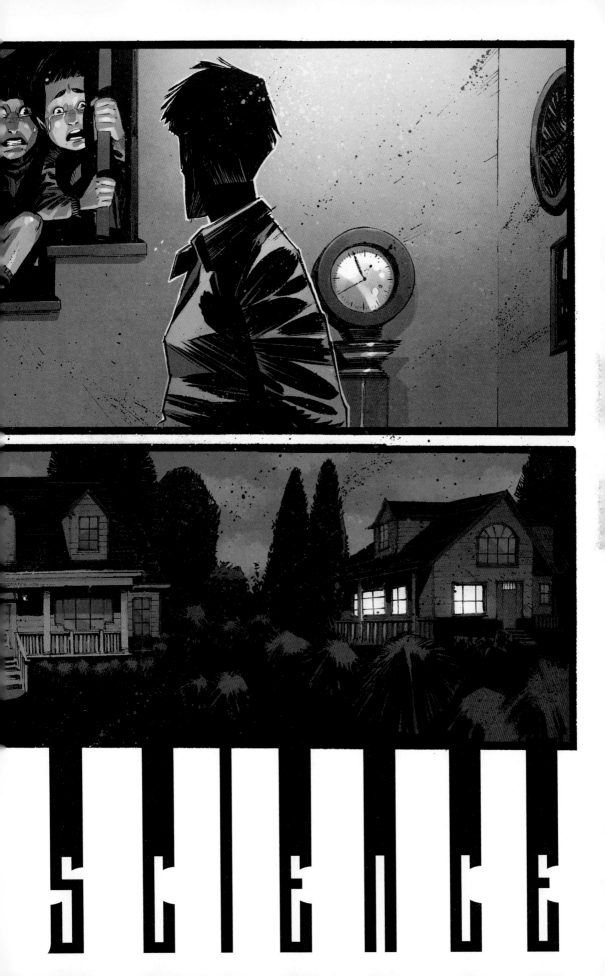

# SCIENCE

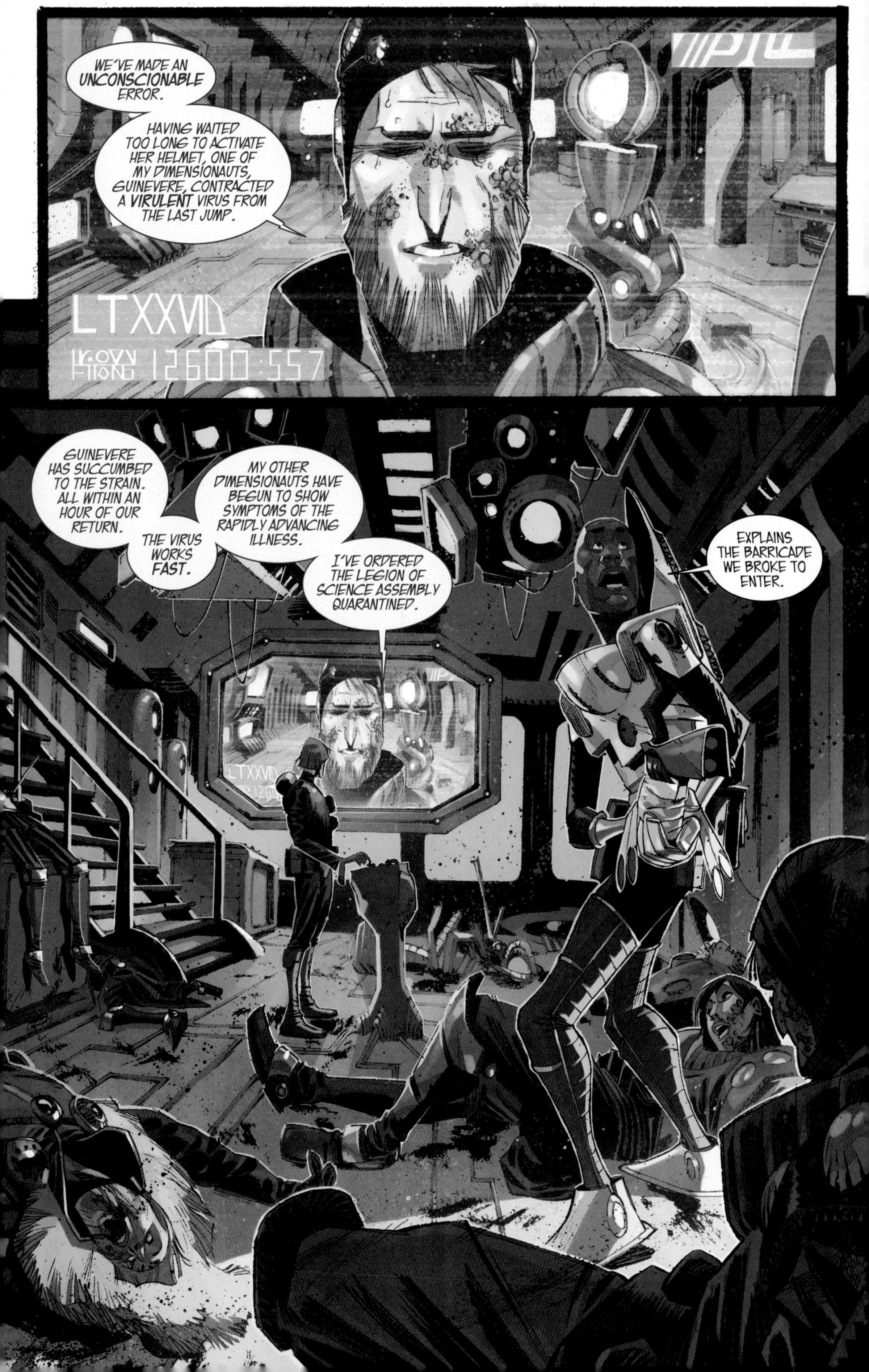
WE'VE MADE AN **UNCONSCIONABLE** ERROR.
HAVING WAITED TOO LONG TO ACTIVATE HER HELMET, ONE OF MY DIMENSIONAUTS, GUINEVERE, CONTRACTED A **VIRULENT** VIRUS FROM THE LAST JUMP.
LTXXVID
12600:557
GUINEVERE HAS SUCCUMBED TO THE STRAIN. ALL WITHIN AN HOUR OF OUR RETURN.
THE VIRUS WORKS **FAST**.
MY OTHER DIMENSIONAUTS HAVE BEGUN TO SHOW SYMPTOMS OF THE RAPIDLY ADVANCING ILLNESS.
I'VE ORDERED THE LEGION OF SCIENCE ASSEMBLY QUARANTINED.
EXPLAINS THE BARRICADE WE BROKE TO ENTER.

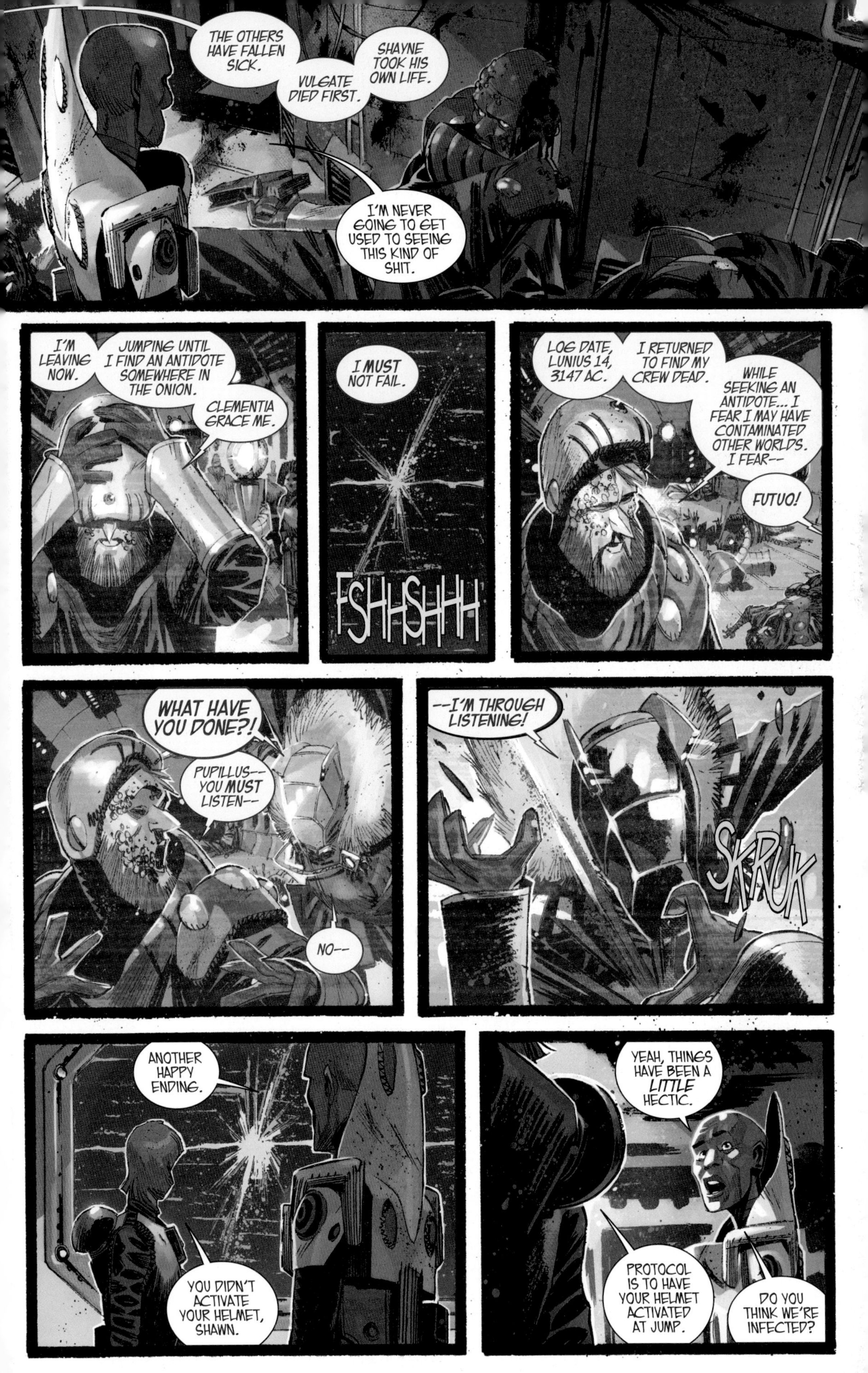
THE OTHERS HAVE FALLEN SICK.
VULGATE DIED FIRST.
SHAYNE TOOK HIS OWN LIFE.
I'M NEVER GOING TO GET USED TO SEEING THIS KIND OF SHIT.
I'M LEAVING NOW.
JUMPING UNTIL I FIND AN ANTIDOTE SOMEWHERE IN THE ONION.
CLEMENTIA GRACE ME.
I MUST NOT FAIL.
FSHHSHHH
LOG DATE, LUNIUS 14, 3147 AC.
I RETURNED TO FIND MY CREW DEAD.
WHILE SEEKING AN ANTIDOTE... I FEAR I MAY HAVE CONTAMINATED OTHER WORLDS. I FEAR--
FUTUO!
WHAT HAVE YOU DONE?!
PUPILLUS-- YOU MUST LISTEN--
NO--
--I'M THROUGH LISTENING!
SKRUK
ANOTHER HAPPY ENDING.
YOU DIDN'T ACTIVATE YOUR HELMET, SHAWN.
YEAH, THINGS HAVE BEEN A LITTLE HECTIC.
PROTOCOL IS TO HAVE YOUR HELMET ACTIVATED AT JUMP.
DO YOU THINK WE'RE INFECTED?

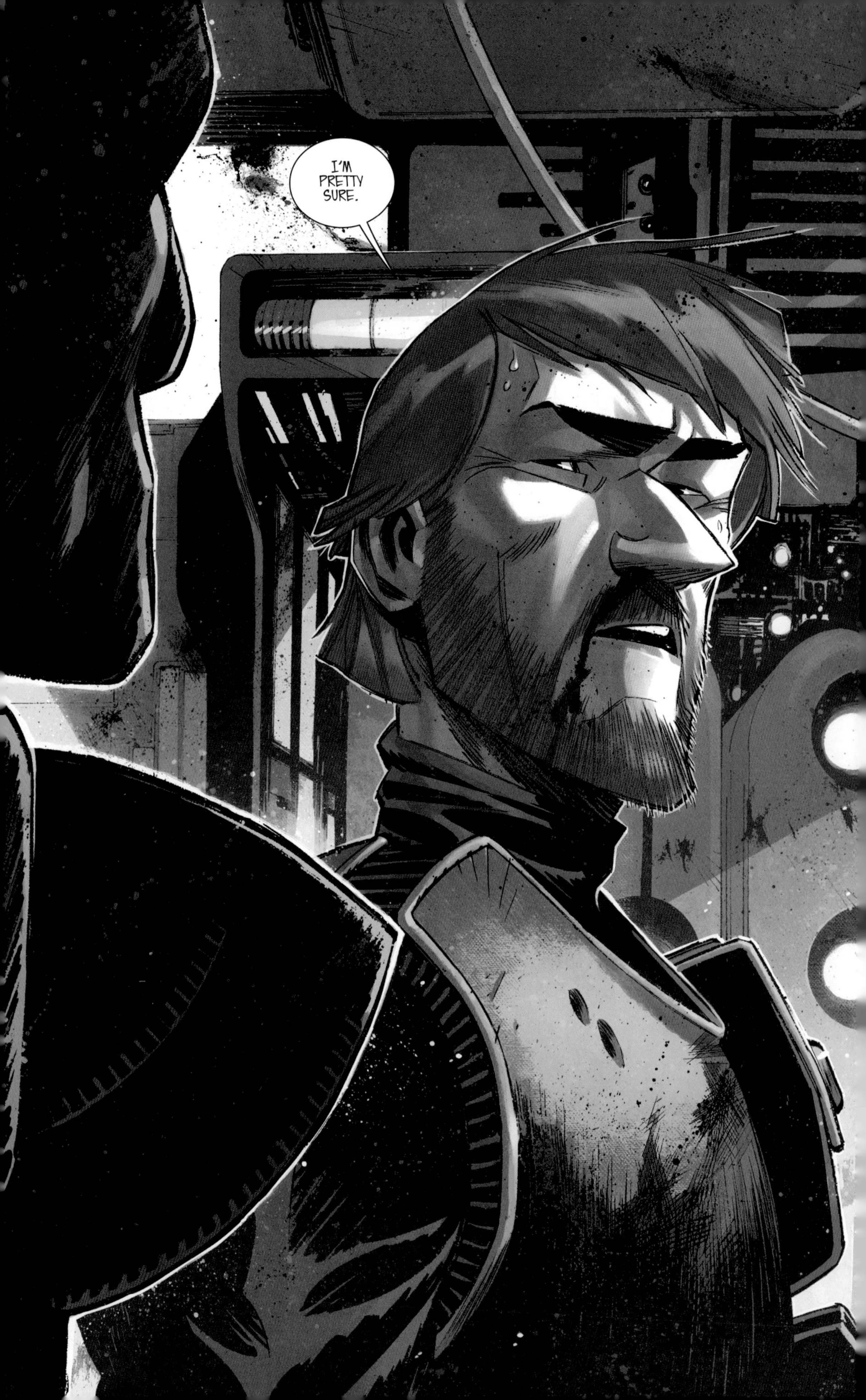
I'M PRETTY SURE.

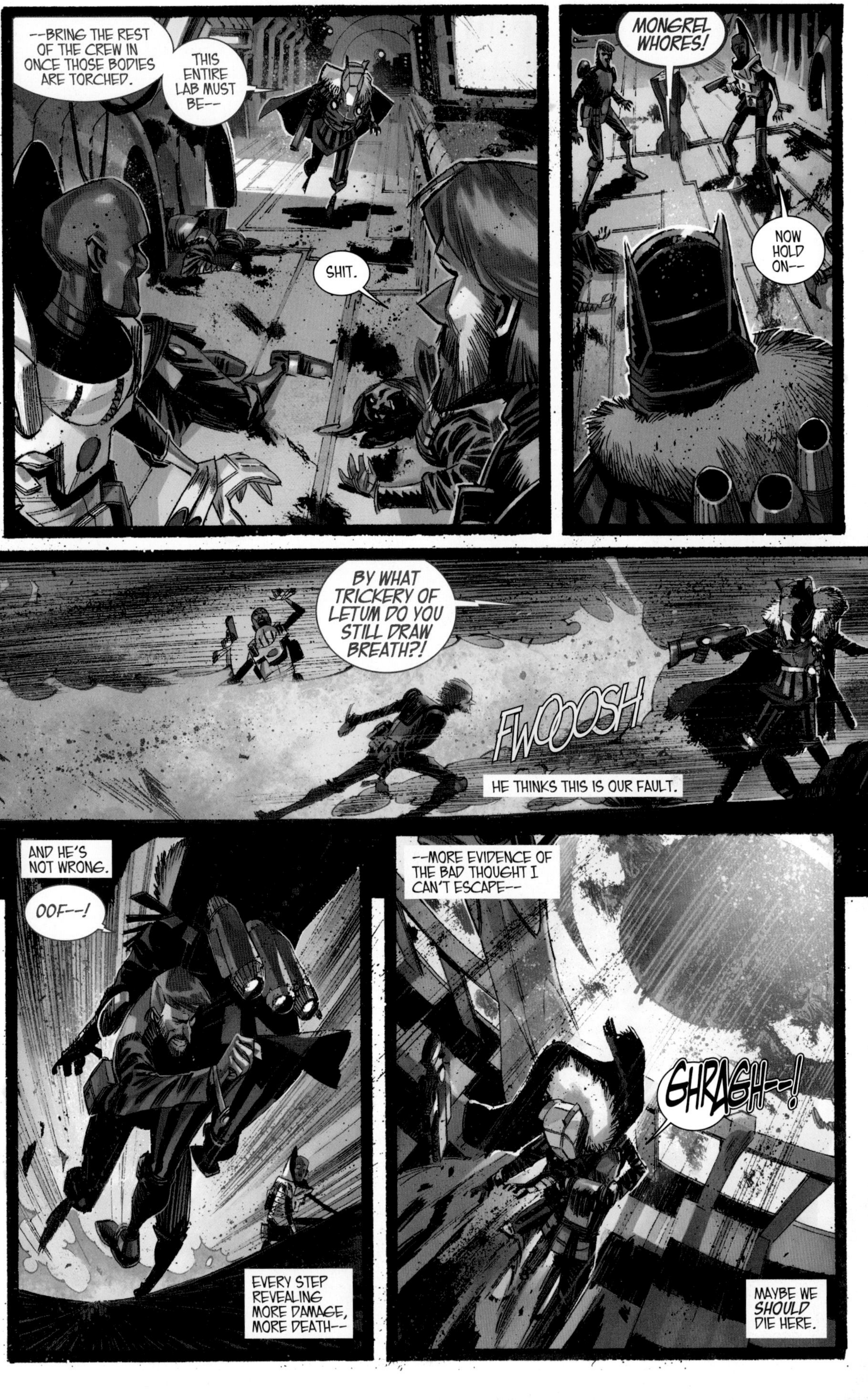
--BRING THE REST OF THE CREW IN ONCE THOSE BODIES ARE TORCHED.
THIS ENTIRE LAB MUST BE--
SHIT.
MONGREL WHORES!
NOW HOLD ON--
BY WHAT TRICKERY OF LETUM DO YOU STILL DRAW BREATH?!
FWOOOSH
HE THINKS THIS IS OUR FAULT.
AND HE'S NOT WRONG.
OOF--!
EVERY STEP REVEALING MORE DAMAGE, MORE DEATH--
--MORE EVIDENCE OF THE BAD THOUGHT I CAN'T ESCAPE--
GHRAGH--!
MAYBE WE SHOULD DIE HERE.

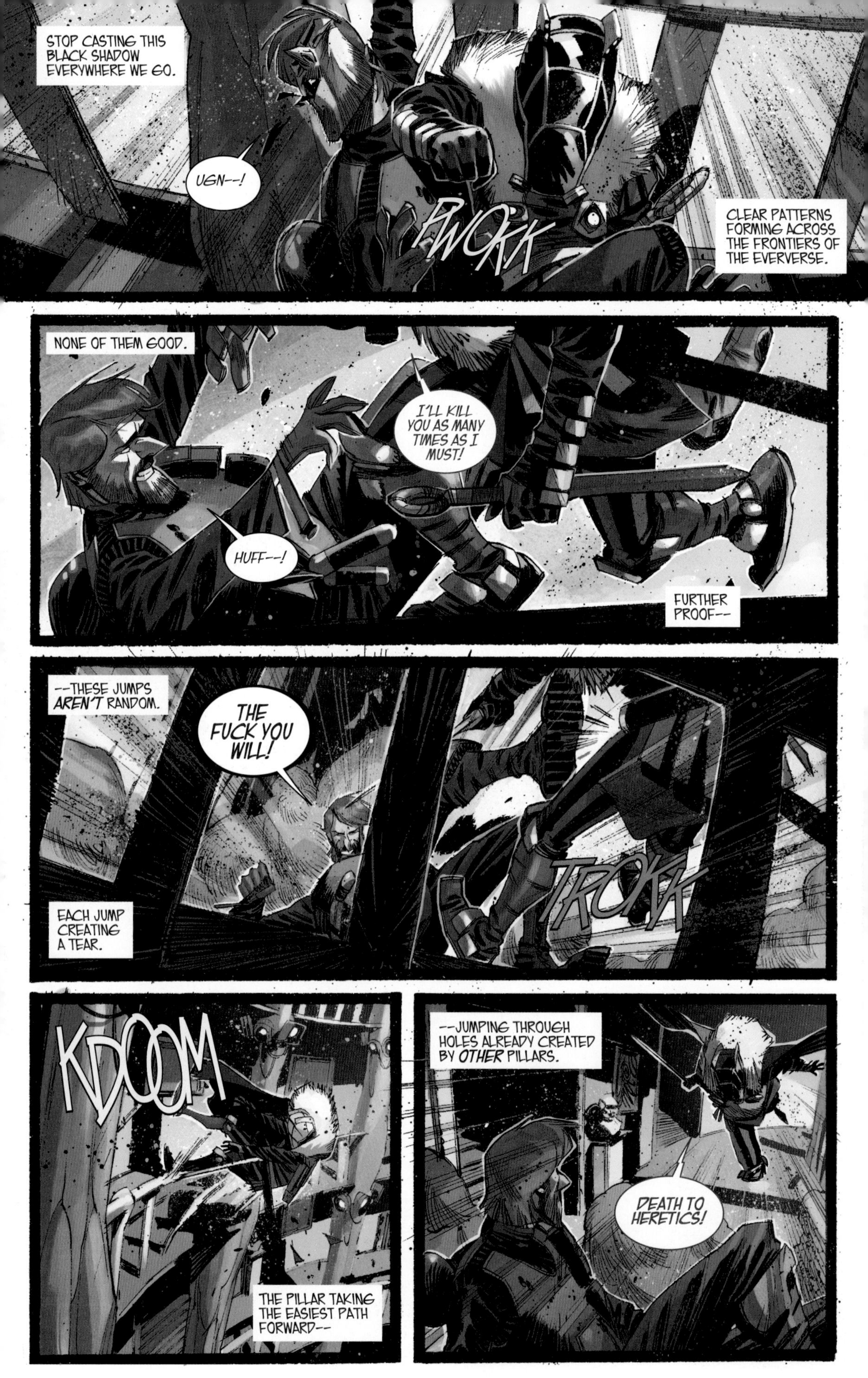
STOP CASTING THIS BLACK SHADOW EVERYWHERE WE GO.
UGN--!
PWOKK
CLEAR PATTERNS FORMING ACROSS THE FRONTIERS OF THE EVERVERSE.
NONE OF THEM GOOD.
I'LL KILL YOU AS MANY TIMES AS I MUST!
HUFF--!
FURTHER PROOF--
--THESE JUMPS AREN'T RANDOM.
THE FUCK YOU WILL!
TROKK
EACH JUMP CREATING A TEAR.
KDOOM
THE PILLAR TAKING THE EASIEST PATH FORWARD--
--JUMPING THROUGH HOLES ALREADY CREATED BY OTHER PILLARS.
DEATH TO HERETICS!

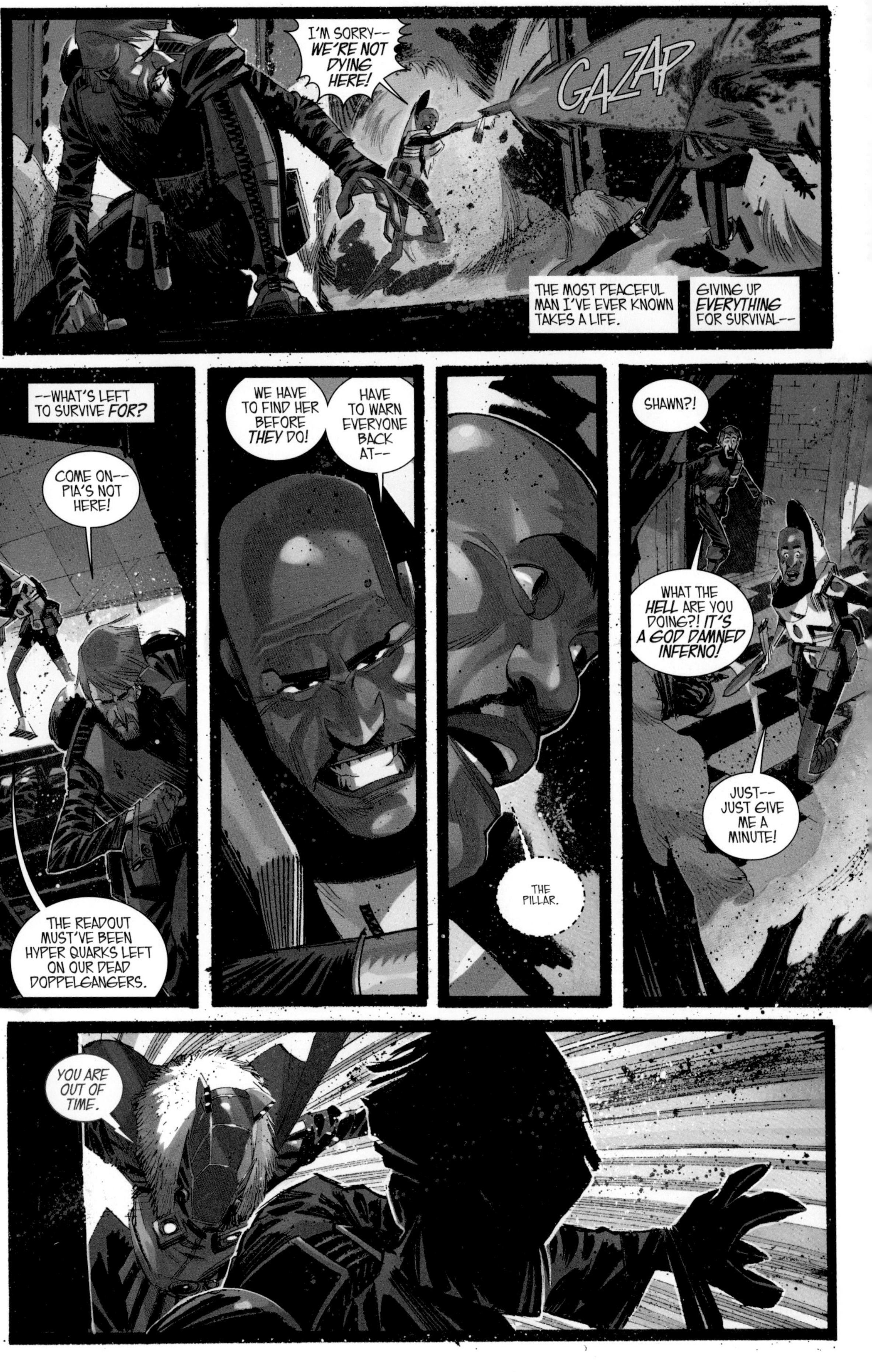

I'M SORRY-- WE'RE NOT DYING HERE!
GAZAP
THE MOST PEACEFUL MAN I'VE EVER KNOWN TAKES A LIFE.
GIVING UP EVERYTHING FOR SURVIVAL--
--WHAT'S LEFT TO SURVIVE FOR?
COME ON-- PIA'S NOT HERE!
THE READOUT MUST'VE BEEN HYPER QUARKS LEFT ON OUR DEAD DOPPELGANGERS.
WE HAVE TO FIND HER BEFORE THEY DO!
HAVE TO WARN EVERYONE BACK AT--
THE PILLAR.
SHAWN?!
WHAT THE HELL ARE YOU DOING?! IT'S A GOD DAMNED INFERNO!
JUST-- JUST GIVE ME A MINUTE!
YOU ARE OUT OF TIME.

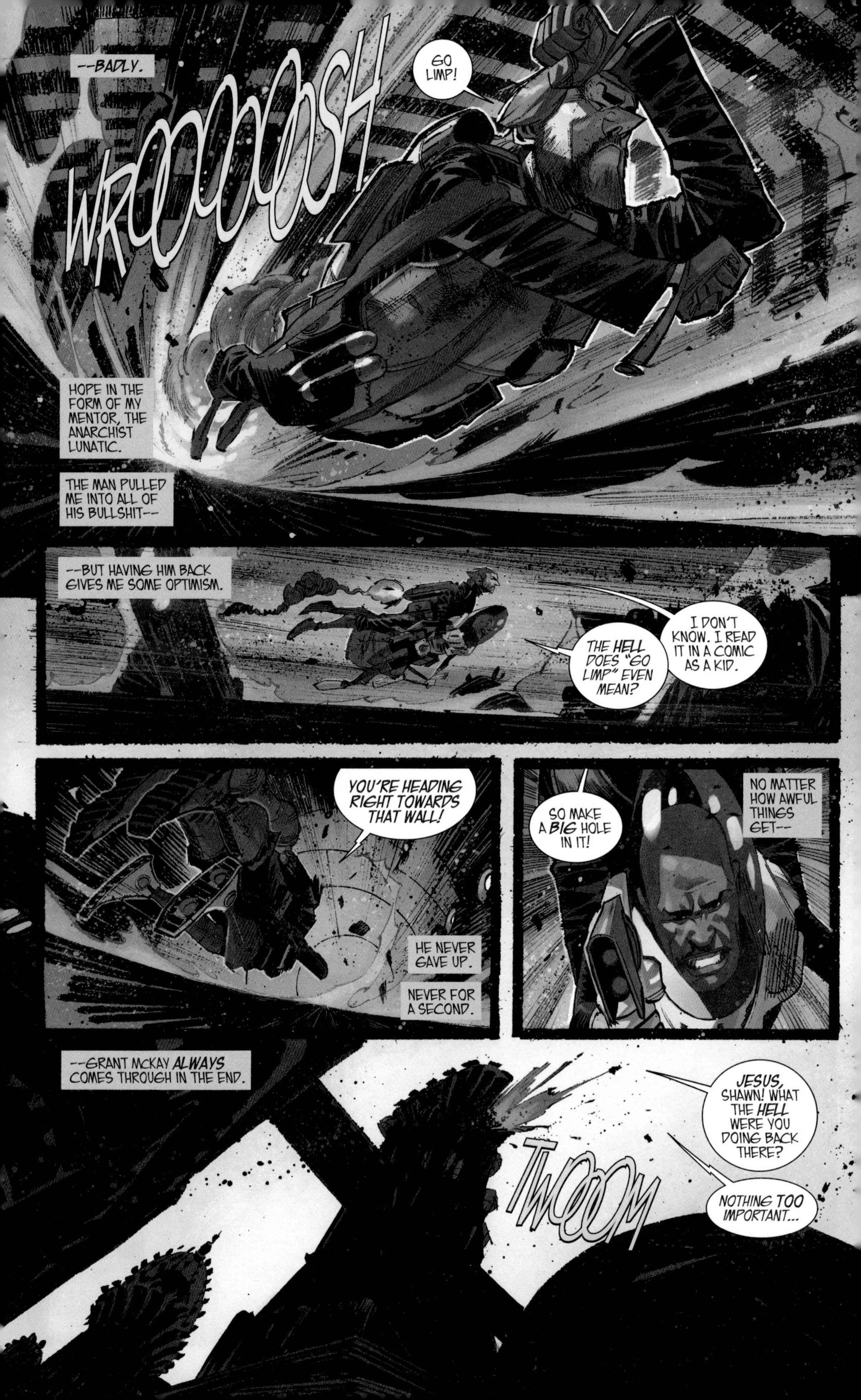
--BADLY.
WROOOOOOSH
GO LIMP!
HOPE IN THE FORM OF MY MENTOR, THE ANARCHIST LUNATIC.
THE MAN PULLED ME INTO ALL OF HIS BULLSHIT--
--BUT HAVING HIM BACK GIVES ME SOME OPTIMISM.
THE HELL DOES "GO LIMP" EVEN MEAN?
I DON'T KNOW. I READ IT IN A COMIC AS A KID.
YOU'RE HEADING RIGHT TOWARDS THAT WALL!
HE NEVER GAVE UP.
NEVER FOR A SECOND.
SO MAKE A BIG HOLE IN IT!
NO MATTER HOW AWFUL THINGS GET--
--GRANT McKAY ALWAYS COMES THROUGH IN THE END.
TWOOOM
JESUS, SHAWN! WHAT THE HELL WERE YOU DOING BACK THERE?
NOTHING TOO IMPORTANT...

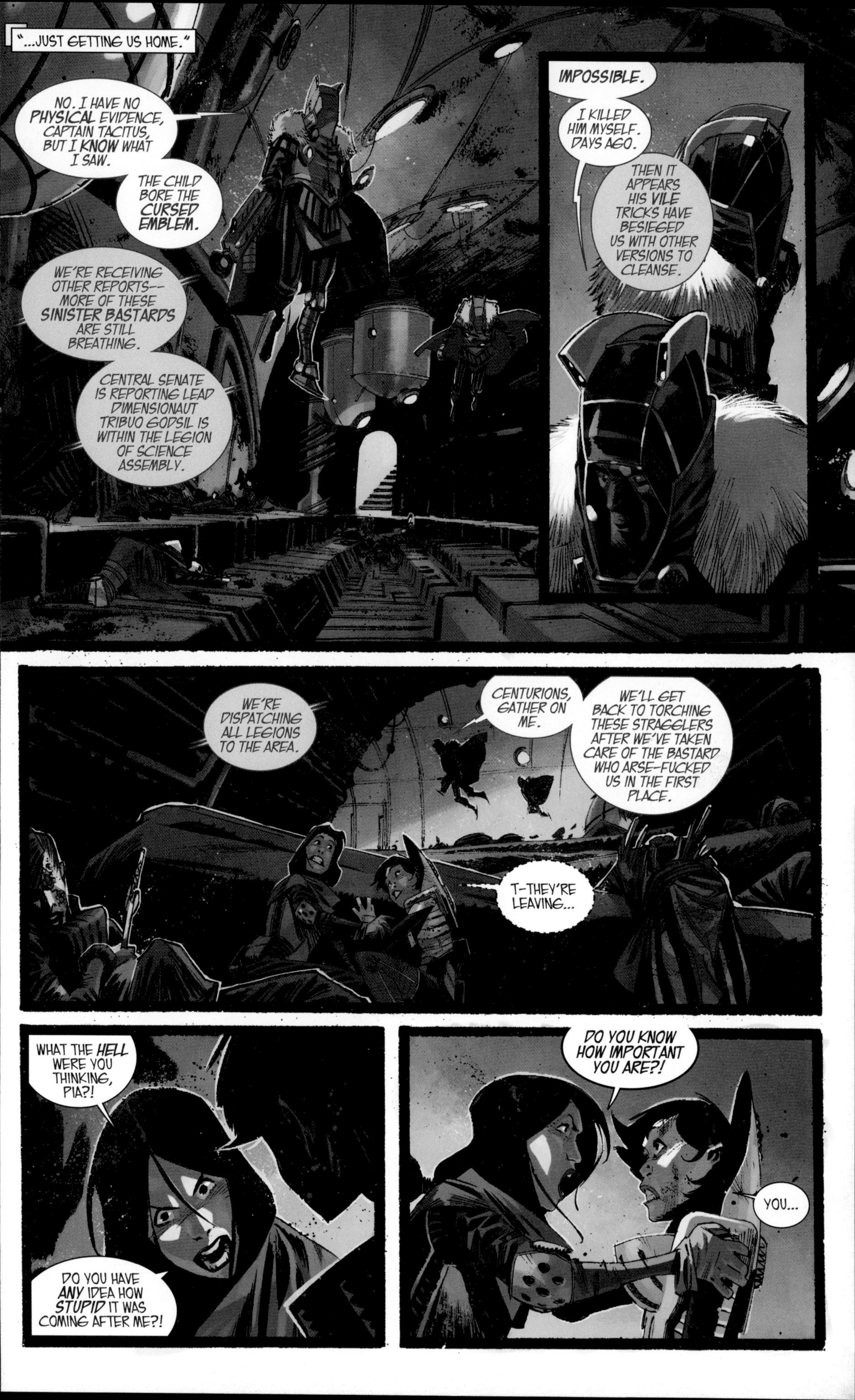
"...JUST GETTING US HOME."
NO. I HAVE NO PHYSICAL EVIDENCE, CAPTAIN TACITUS, BUT I KNOW WHAT I SAW.
THE CHILD BORE THE CURSED EMBLEM.
WE'RE RECEIVING OTHER REPORTS-- MORE OF THESE SINISTER BASTARDS ARE STILL BREATHING.
CENTRAL SENATE IS REPORTING LEAD DIMENSIONAUT TRIBUO GODSIL IS WITHIN THE LEGION OF SCIENCE ASSEMBLY.
IMPOSSIBLE.
I KILLED HIM MYSELF. DAYS AGO.
THEN IT APPEARS HIS VILE TRICKS HAVE BESIEGED US WITH OTHER VERSIONS TO CLEANSE.
WE'RE DISPATCHING ALL LEGIONS TO THE AREA.
CENTURIONS, GATHER ON ME.
WE'LL GET BACK TO TORCHING THESE STRAGGLERS AFTER WE'VE TAKEN CARE OF THE BASTARD WHO ARSE-FUCKED US IN THE FIRST PLACE.
T-THEY'RE LEAVING...
WHAT THE HELL WERE YOU THINKING, PIA?!
DO YOU HAVE ANY IDEA HOW STUPID IT WAS COMING AFTER ME?!
DO YOU KNOW HOW IMPORTANT YOU ARE?!
YOU...

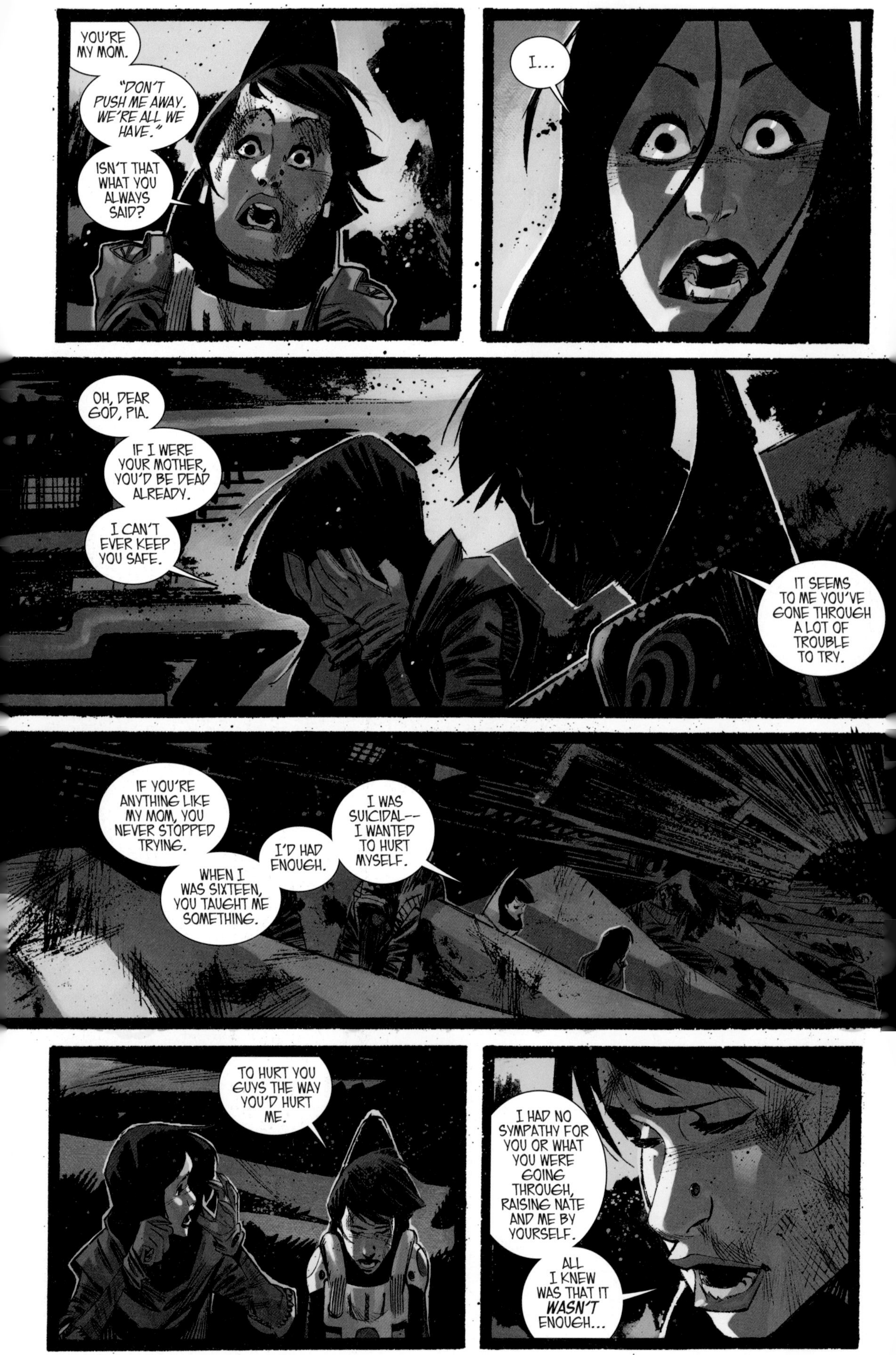
YOU'RE MY MOM.
"DON'T PUSH ME AWAY. WE'RE ALL WE HAVE."
ISN'T THAT WHAT YOU ALWAYS SAID?
I...
OH, DEAR GOD, PIA.
IF I WERE YOUR MOTHER, YOU'D BE DEAD ALREADY.
I CAN'T EVER KEEP YOU SAFE.
IT SEEMS TO ME YOU'VE GONE THROUGH A LOT OF TROUBLE TO TRY.
IF YOU'RE ANYTHING LIKE MY MOM, YOU NEVER STOPPED TRYING.
WHEN I WAS SIXTEEN, YOU TAUGHT ME SOMETHING.
I'D HAD ENOUGH.
I WAS SUICIDAL-- I WANTED TO HURT MYSELF.
TO HURT YOU GUYS THE WAY YOU'D HURT ME.
I HAD NO SYMPATHY FOR YOU OR WHAT YOU WERE GOING THROUGH, RAISING NATE AND ME BY YOURSELF.
ALL I KNEW WAS THAT IT *WASN'T* ENOUGH...

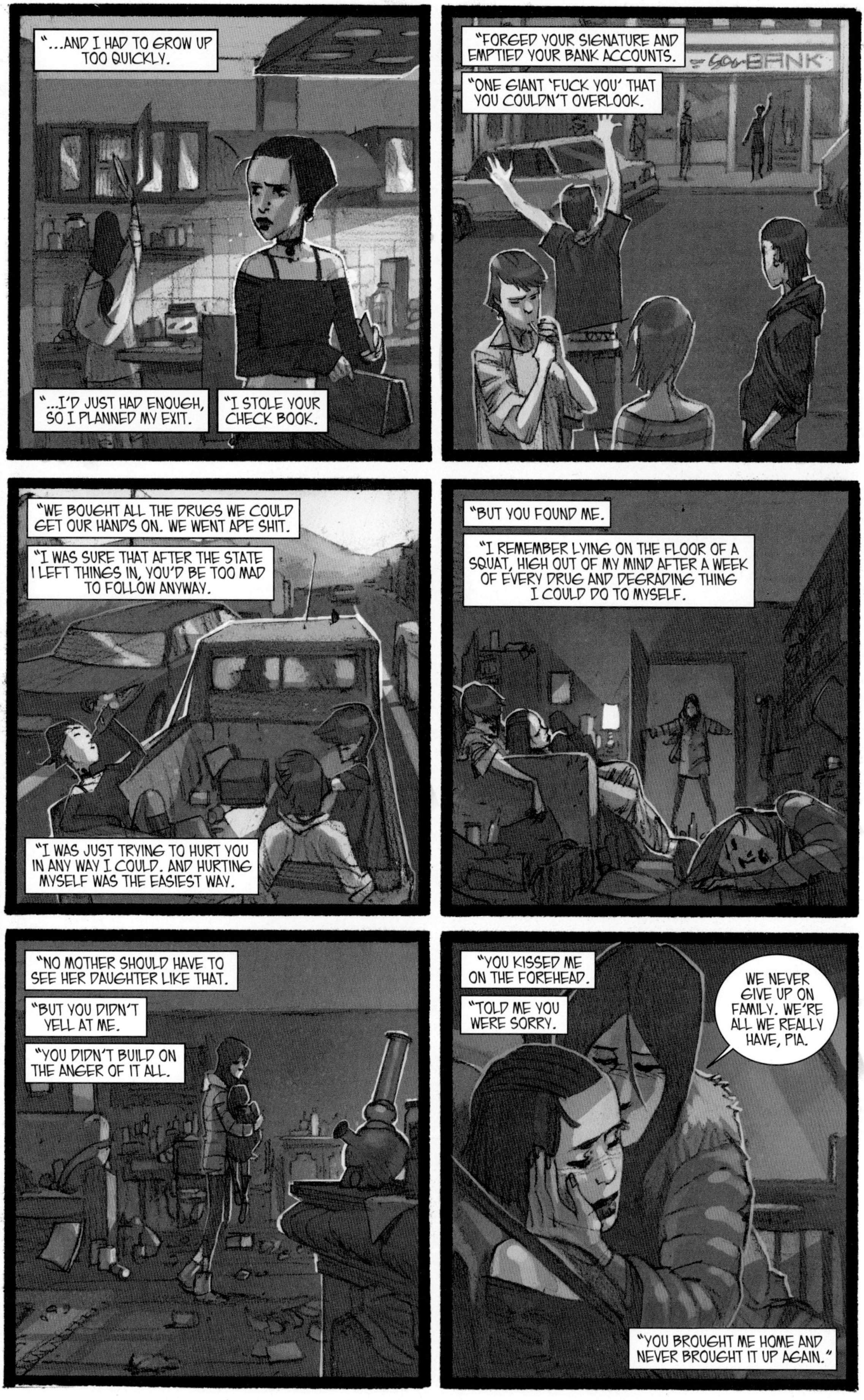
"...AND I HAD TO GROW UP TOO QUICKLY.
"...I'D JUST HAD ENOUGH, SO I PLANNED MY EXIT.
"I STOLE YOUR CHECK BOOK.
"FORGED YOUR SIGNATURE AND EMPTIED YOUR BANK ACCOUNTS.
BANK
"ONE GIANT 'FUCK YOU' THAT YOU COULDN'T OVERLOOK.
"WE BOUGHT ALL THE DRUGS WE COULD GET OUR HANDS ON. WE WENT APE SHIT.
"I WAS SURE THAT AFTER THE STATE I LEFT THINGS IN, YOU'D BE TOO MAD TO FOLLOW ANYWAY.
"I WAS JUST TRYING TO HURT YOU IN ANY WAY I COULD. AND HURTING MYSELF WAS THE EASIEST WAY.
"BUT YOU FOUND ME.
"I REMEMBER LYING ON THE FLOOR OF A SQUAT, HIGH OUT OF MY MIND AFTER A WEEK OF EVERY DRUG AND DEGRADING THING I COULD DO TO MYSELF.
"NO MOTHER SHOULD HAVE TO SEE HER DAUGHTER LIKE THAT.
"BUT YOU DIDN'T YELL AT ME.
"YOU DIDN'T BUILD ON THE ANGER OF IT ALL.
"YOU KISSED ME ON THE FOREHEAD.
"TOLD ME YOU WERE SORRY.
WE NEVER GIVE UP ON FAMILY. WE'RE ALL WE REALLY HAVE, PIA.
"YOU BROUGHT ME HOME AND NEVER BROUGHT IT UP AGAIN."

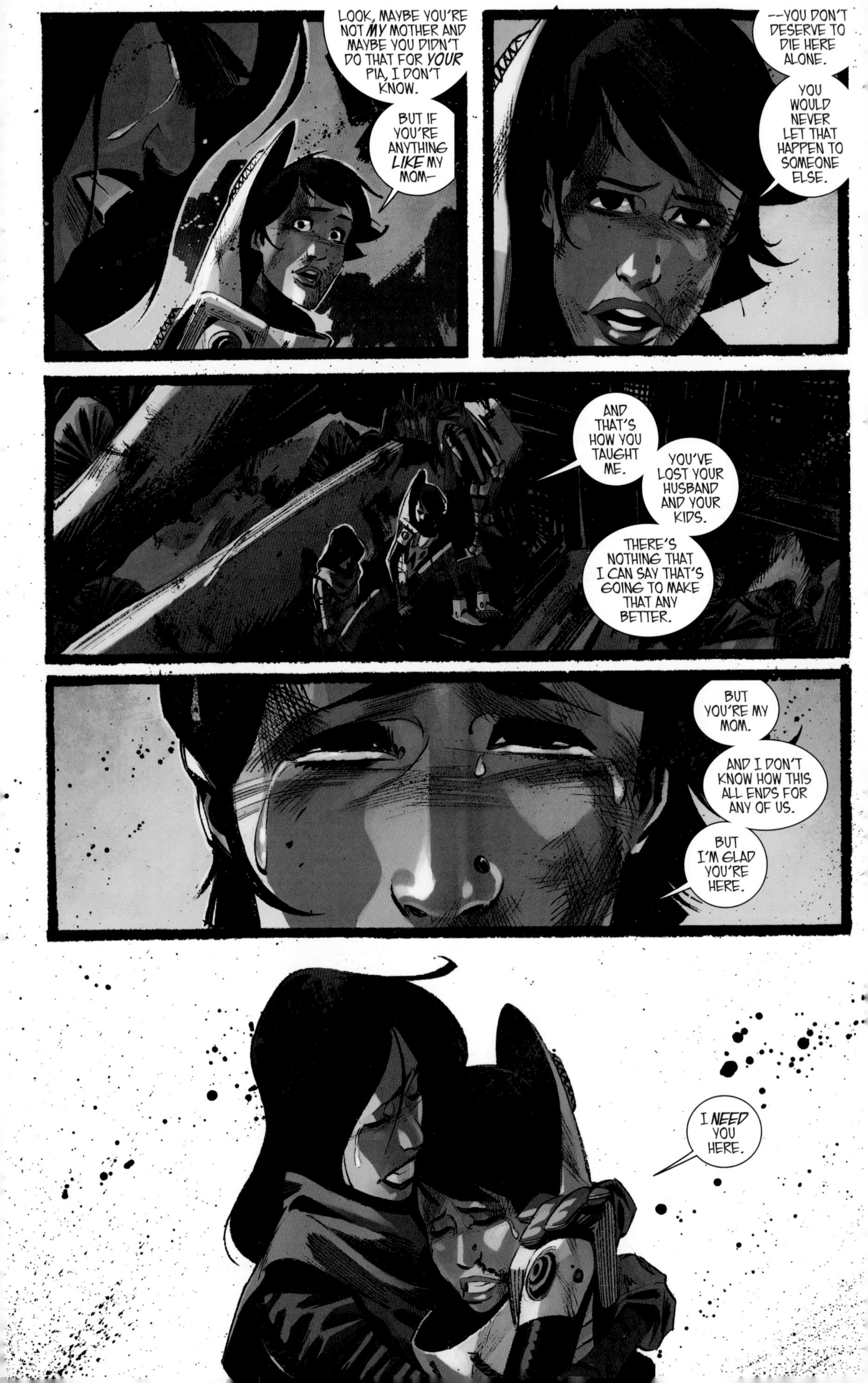
LOOK, MAYBE YOU'RE NOT MY MOTHER AND MAYBE YOU DIDN'T DO THAT FOR YOUR PIA, I DON'T KNOW.
BUT IF YOU'RE ANYTHING LIKE MY MOM–
--YOU DON'T DESERVE TO DIE HERE ALONE.
YOU WOULD NEVER LET THAT HAPPEN TO SOMEONE ELSE.
AND THAT'S HOW YOU TAUGHT ME.
YOU'VE LOST YOUR HUSBAND AND YOUR KIDS.
THERE'S NOTHING THAT I CAN SAY THAT'S GOING TO MAKE THAT ANY BETTER.
BUT YOU'RE MY MOM.
AND I DON'T KNOW HOW THIS ALL ENDS FOR ANY OF US.
BUT I'M GLAD YOU'RE HERE.
I NEED YOU HERE.

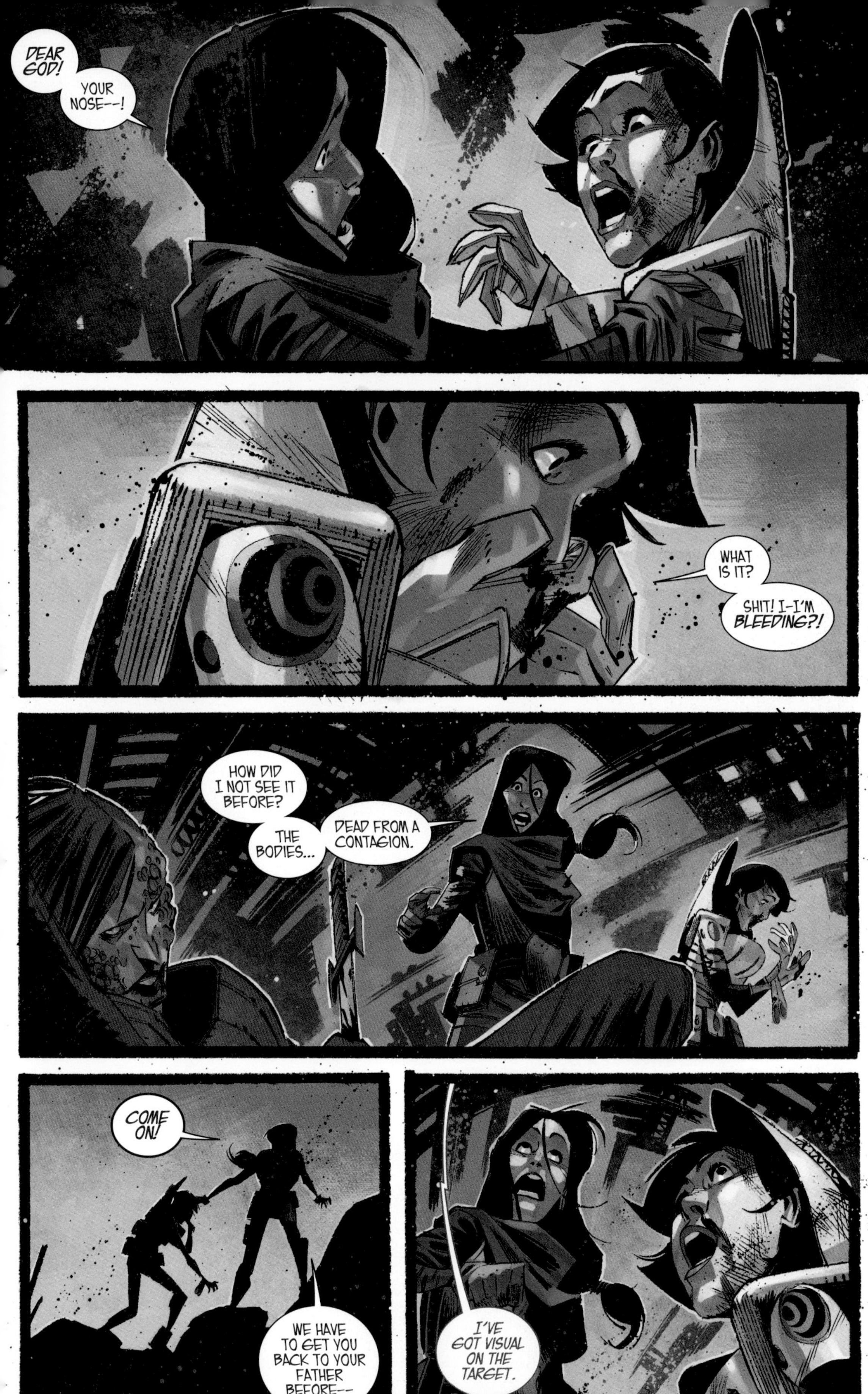
DEAR GOD!
YOUR NOSE--!
WHAT IS IT?
SHIT! I-I'M BLEEDING?!
HOW DID I NOT SEE IT BEFORE?
THE BODIES...
DEAD FROM A CONTAGION.
COME ON!
WE HAVE TO GET YOU BACK TO YOUR FATHER BEFORE--
I'VE GOT VISUAL ON THE TARGET.

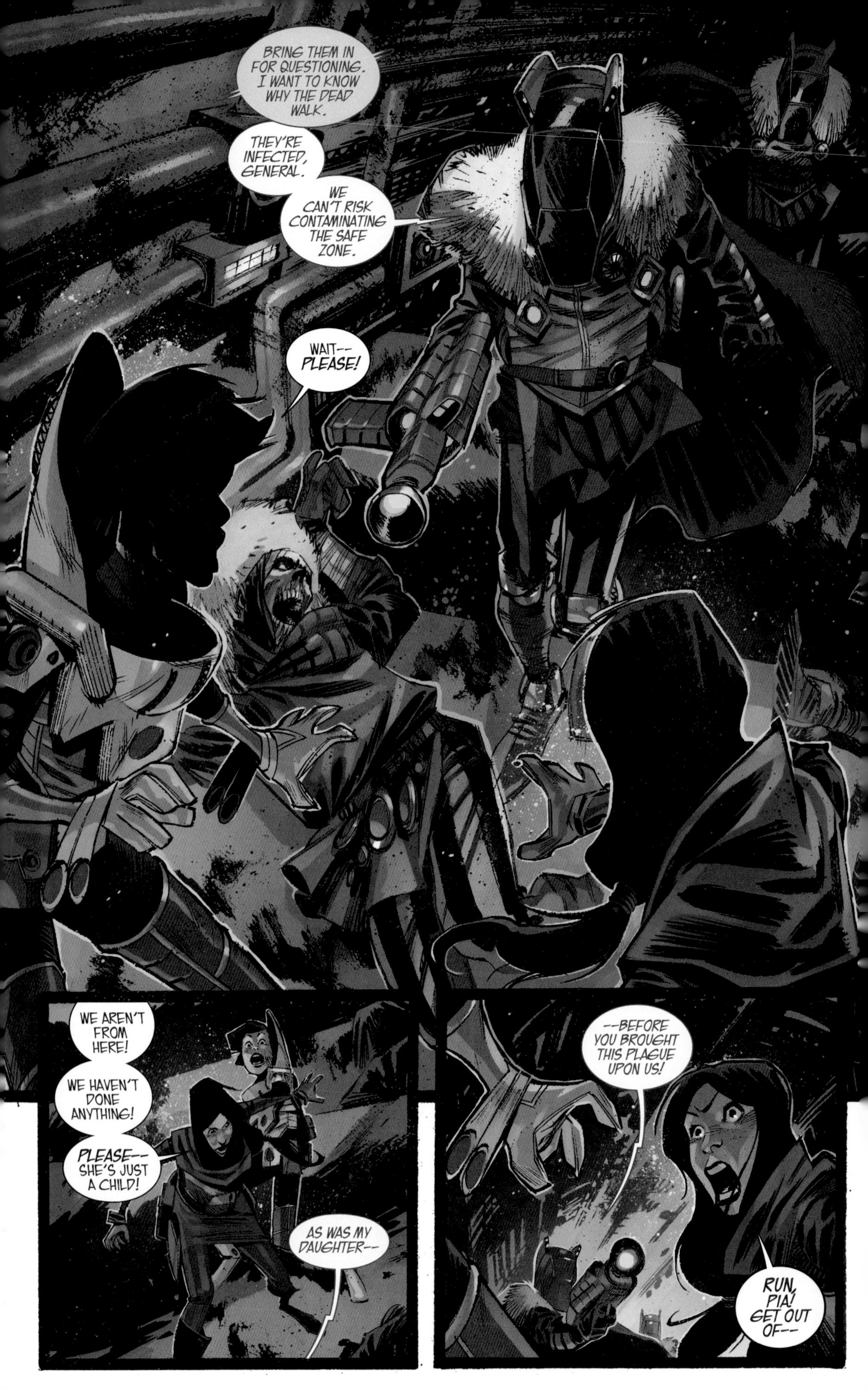
BRING THEM IN FOR QUESTIONING. I WANT TO KNOW WHY THE DEAD WALK.
THEY'RE INFECTED, GENERAL.
WE CAN'T RISK CONTAMINATING THE SAFE ZONE.
WAIT-- PLEASE!
WE AREN'T FROM HERE!
WE HAVEN'T DONE ANYTHING!
PLEASE-- SHE'S JUST A CHILD!
AS WAS MY DAUGHTER--
--BEFORE YOU BROUGHT THIS PLAGUE UPON US!
RUN, PIA! GET OUT OF--

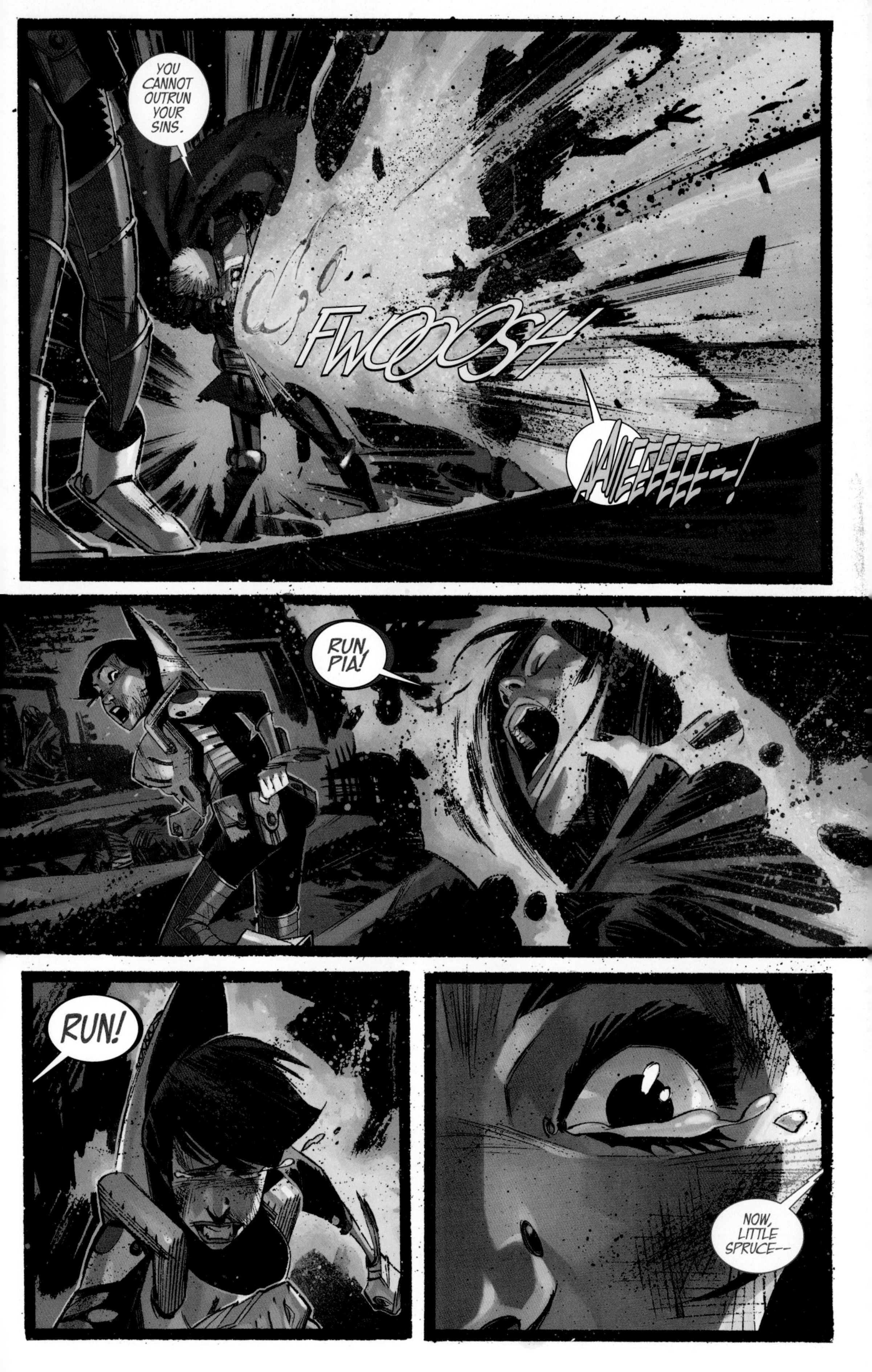
YOU CANNOT OUTRUN YOUR SINS.
FWOOOSH
AAIIEEEEEEE--!
RUN, PIA!
RUN!
NOW, LITTLE SPRUCE--

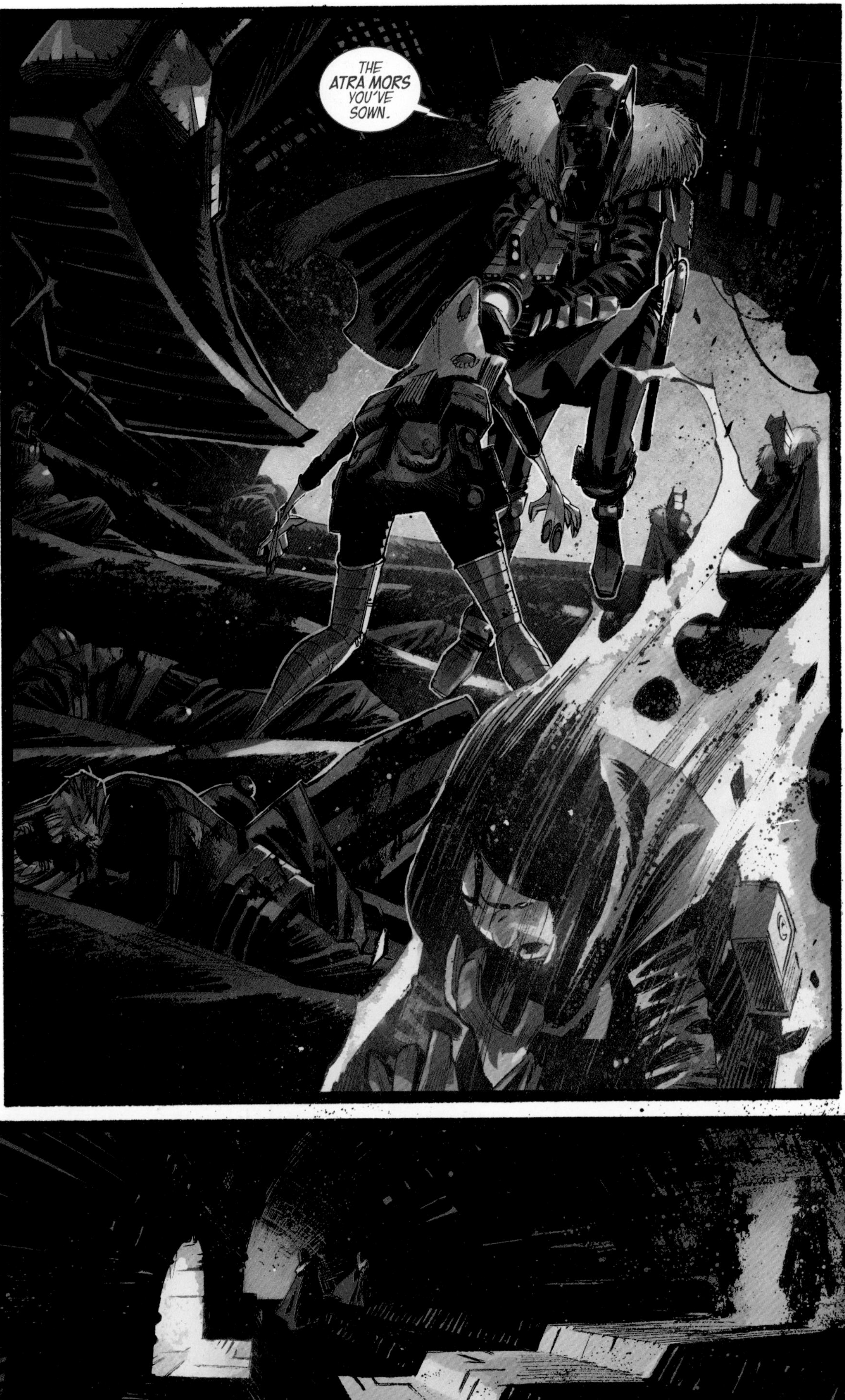
THE ATRA MORS YOU'VE SOWN.

# 14

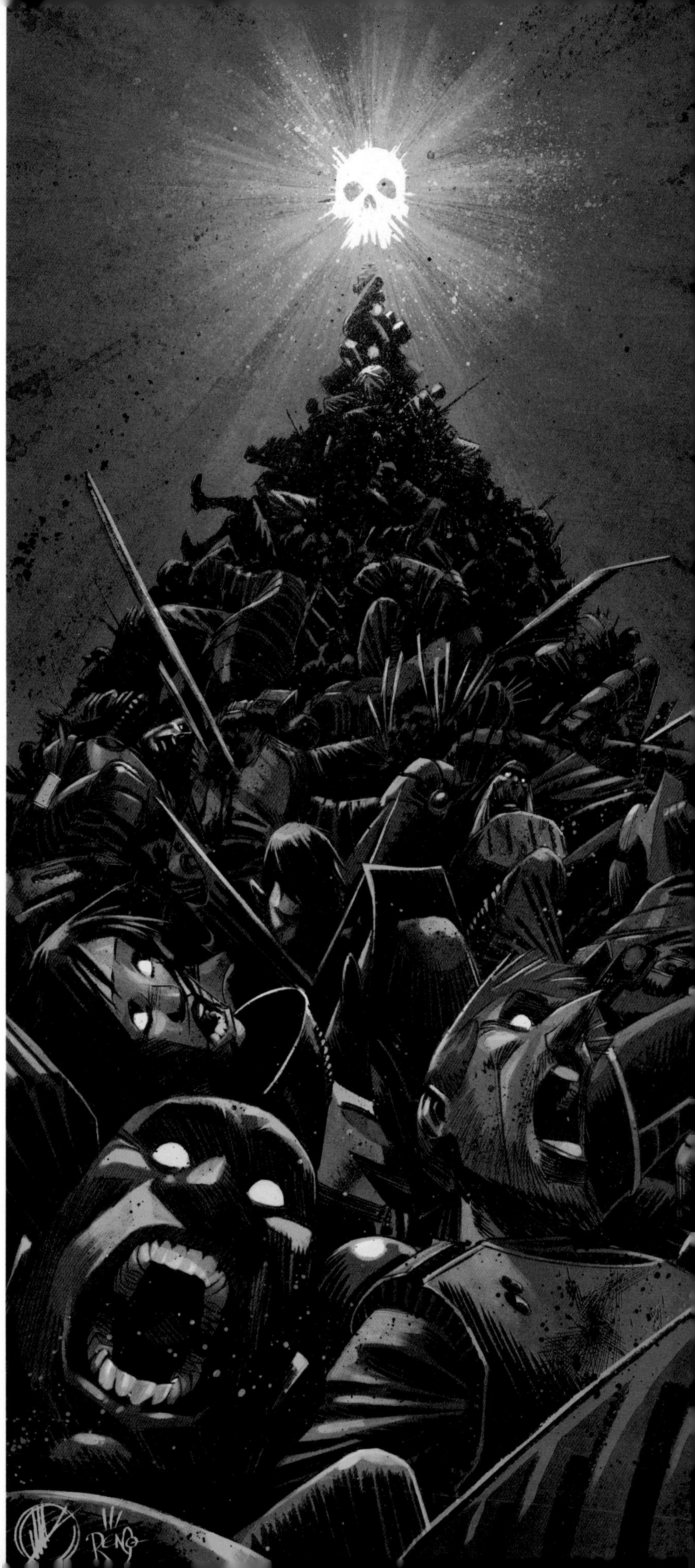

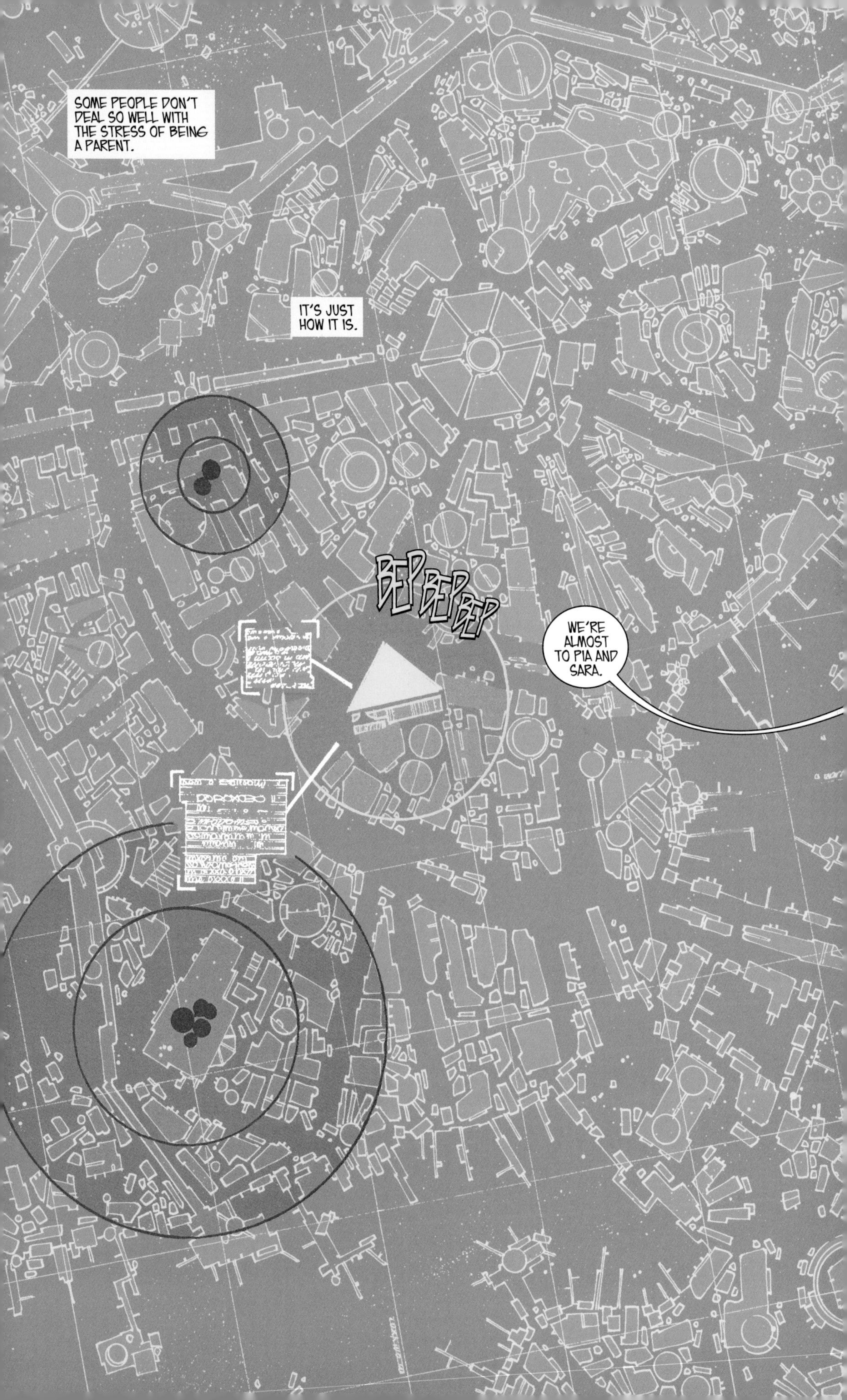
SOME PEOPLE DON'T DEAL SO WELL WITH THE STRESS OF BEING A PARENT.
IT'S JUST HOW IT IS.
BEP BEP BEP
WE'RE ALMOST TO PIA AND SARA.

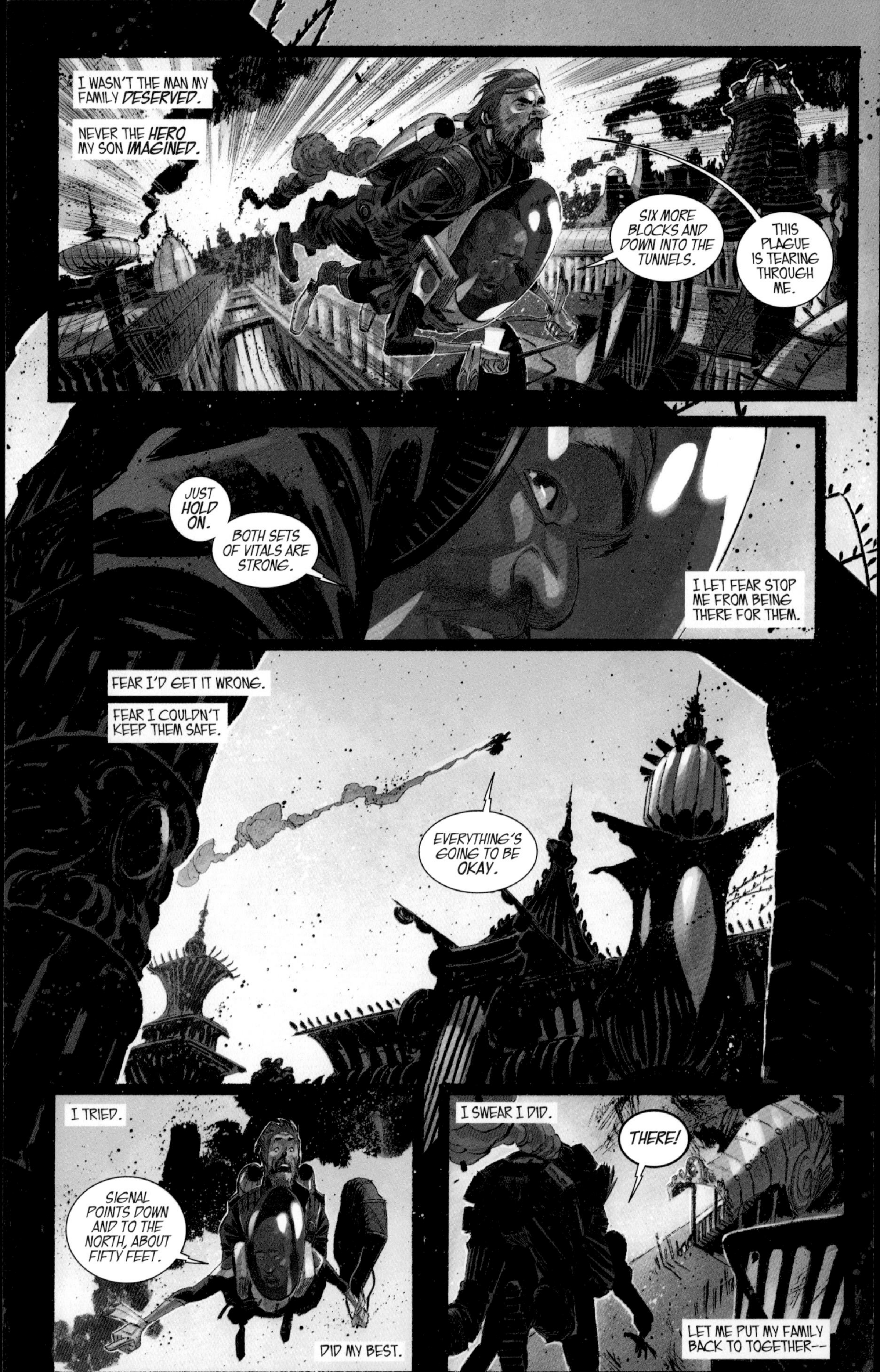
I WASN'T THE MAN MY FAMILY DESERVED.
NEVER THE HERO MY SON IMAGINED.
SIX MORE BLOCKS AND DOWN INTO THE TUNNELS.
THIS PLAGUE IS TEARING THROUGH ME.
JUST HOLD ON.
BOTH SETS OF VITALS ARE STRONG.
I LET FEAR STOP ME FROM BEING THERE FOR THEM.
FEAR I'D GET IT WRONG.
FEAR I COULDN'T KEEP THEM SAFE.
EVERYTHING'S GOING TO BE OKAY.
I TRIED.
SIGNAL POINTS DOWN AND TO THE NORTH, ABOUT FIFTY FEET.
DID MY BEST.
I SWEAR I DID.
THERE!
LET ME PUT MY FAMILY BACK TO TOGETHER--

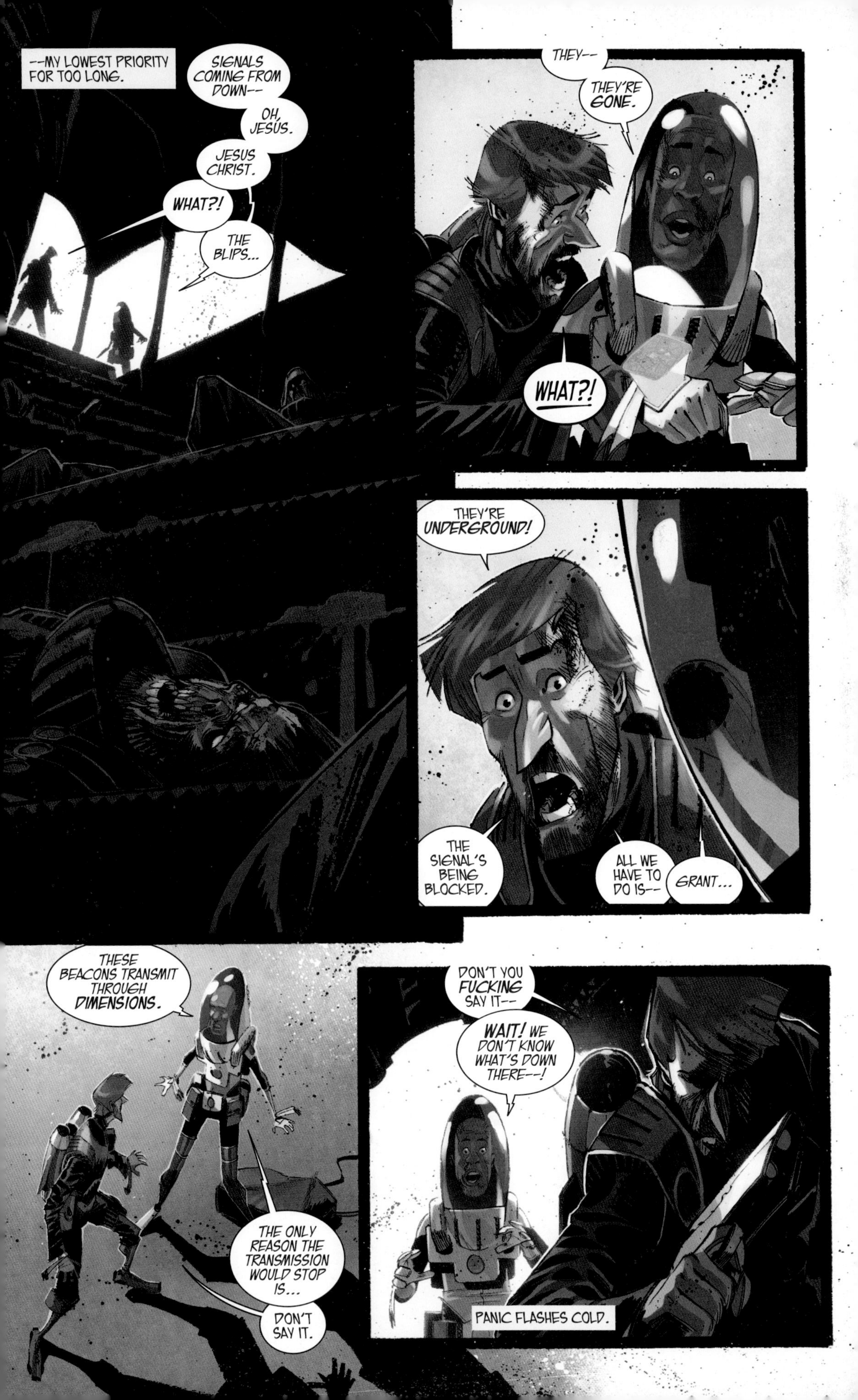
--MY LOWEST PRIORITY FOR TOO LONG.
SIGNALS COMING FROM DOWN--
OH, JESUS.
JESUS CHRIST.
WHAT?!
THE BLIPS...
THEY--
THEY'RE GONE.
WHAT?!
THEY'RE UNDERGROUND!
THE SIGNAL'S BEING BLOCKED.
ALL WE HAVE TO DO IS--
GRANT...
THESE BEACONS TRANSMIT THROUGH DIMENSIONS.
THE ONLY REASON THE TRANSMISSION WOULD STOP IS...
DON'T SAY IT.
DON'T YOU FUCKING SAY IT--
WAIT! WE DON'T KNOW WHAT'S DOWN THERE--!
PANIC FLASHES COLD.

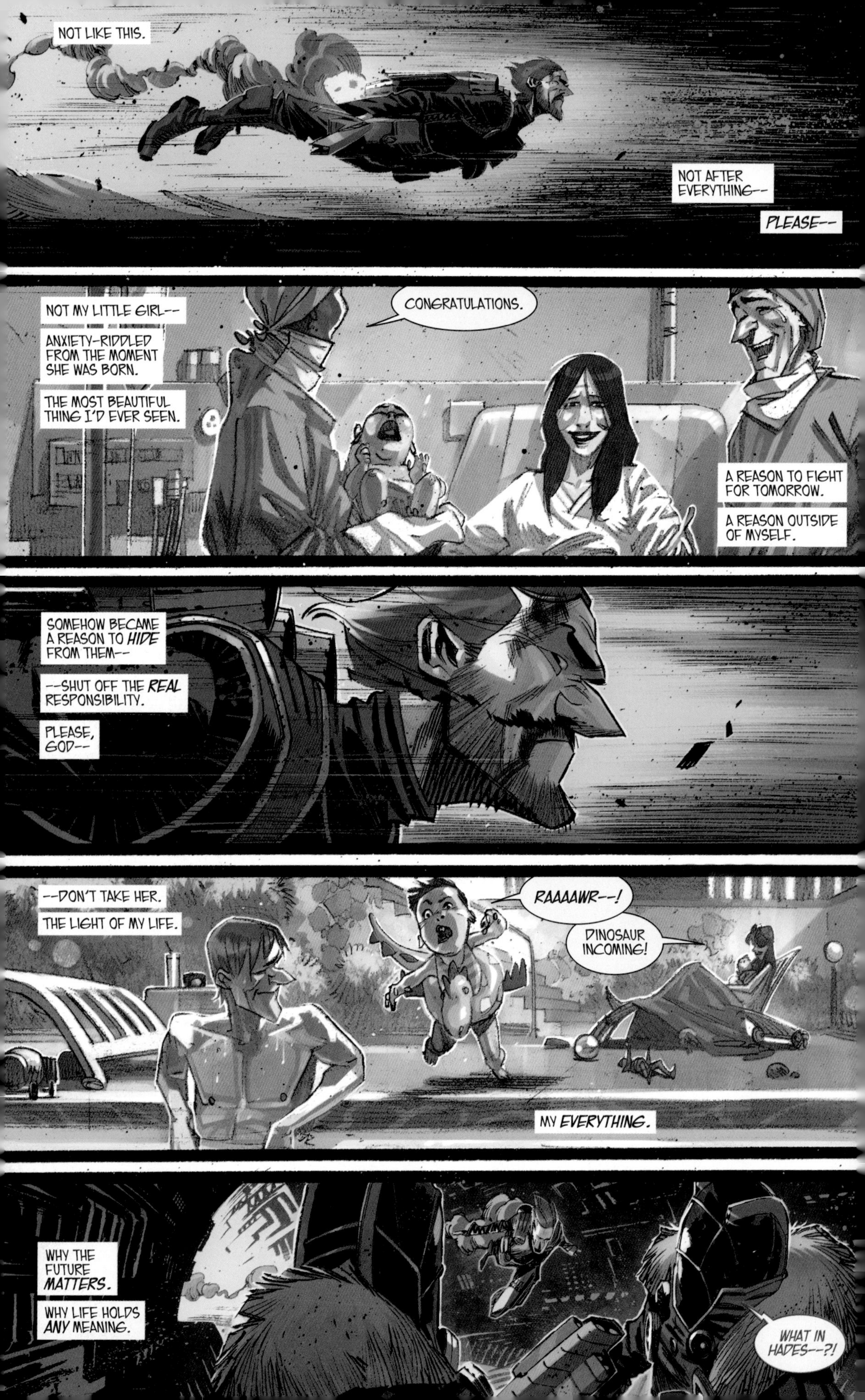
NOT LIKE THIS.
NOT AFTER EVERYTHING--
PLEASE--
NOT MY LITTLE GIRL--
CONGRATULATIONS.
ANXIETY-RIDDLED FROM THE MOMENT SHE WAS BORN.
THE MOST BEAUTIFUL THING I'D EVER SEEN.
A REASON TO FIGHT FOR TOMORROW.
A REASON OUTSIDE OF MYSELF.
SOMEHOW BECAME A REASON TO HIDE FROM THEM--
--SHUT OFF THE REAL RESPONSIBILITY.
PLEASE, GOD--
--DON'T TAKE HER.
THE LIGHT OF MY LIFE.
RAAAAWR--!
DINOSAUR INCOMING!
MY EVERYTHING.
WHY THE FUTURE MATTERS.
WHY LIFE HOLDS ANY MEANING.
WHAT IN HADES--?!

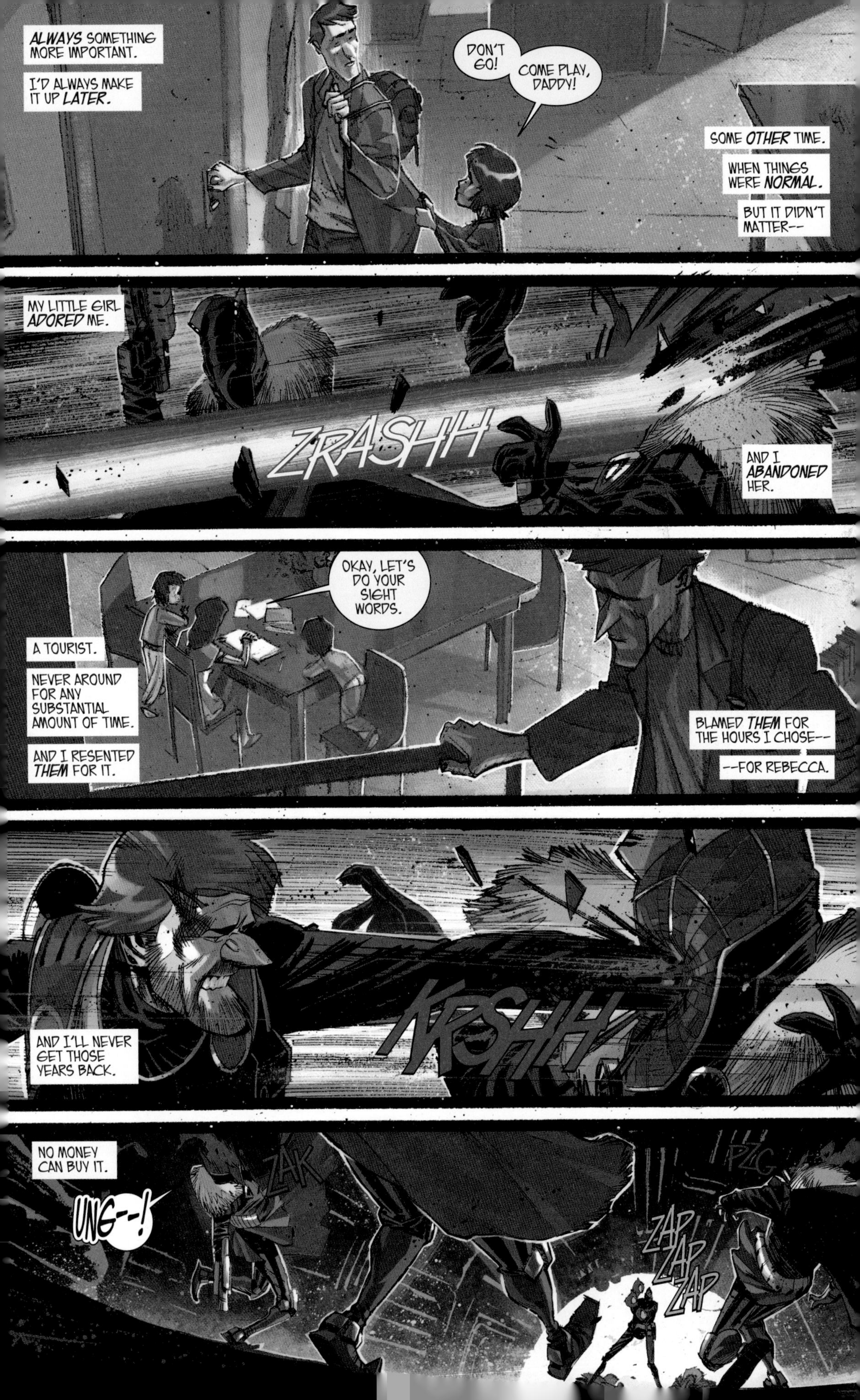
ALWAYS SOMETHING MORE IMPORTANT.
I'D ALWAYS MAKE IT UP LATER.
DON'T GO!
COME PLAY, DADDY!
SOME OTHER TIME.
WHEN THINGS WERE NORMAL.
BUT IT DIDN'T MATTER--
MY LITTLE GIRL ADORED ME.
ZRASHH
AND I ABANDONED HER.
OKAY, LET'S DO YOUR SIGHT WORDS.
A TOURIST.
NEVER AROUND FOR ANY SUBSTANTIAL AMOUNT OF TIME.
AND I RESENTED THEM FOR IT.
BLAMED THEM FOR THE HOURS I CHOSE--
--FOR REBECCA.
KRSHH
AND I'LL NEVER GET THOSE YEARS BACK.
NO MONEY CAN BUY IT.
ZAK
UNG--!
PZZG
ZAP ZAP ZAP

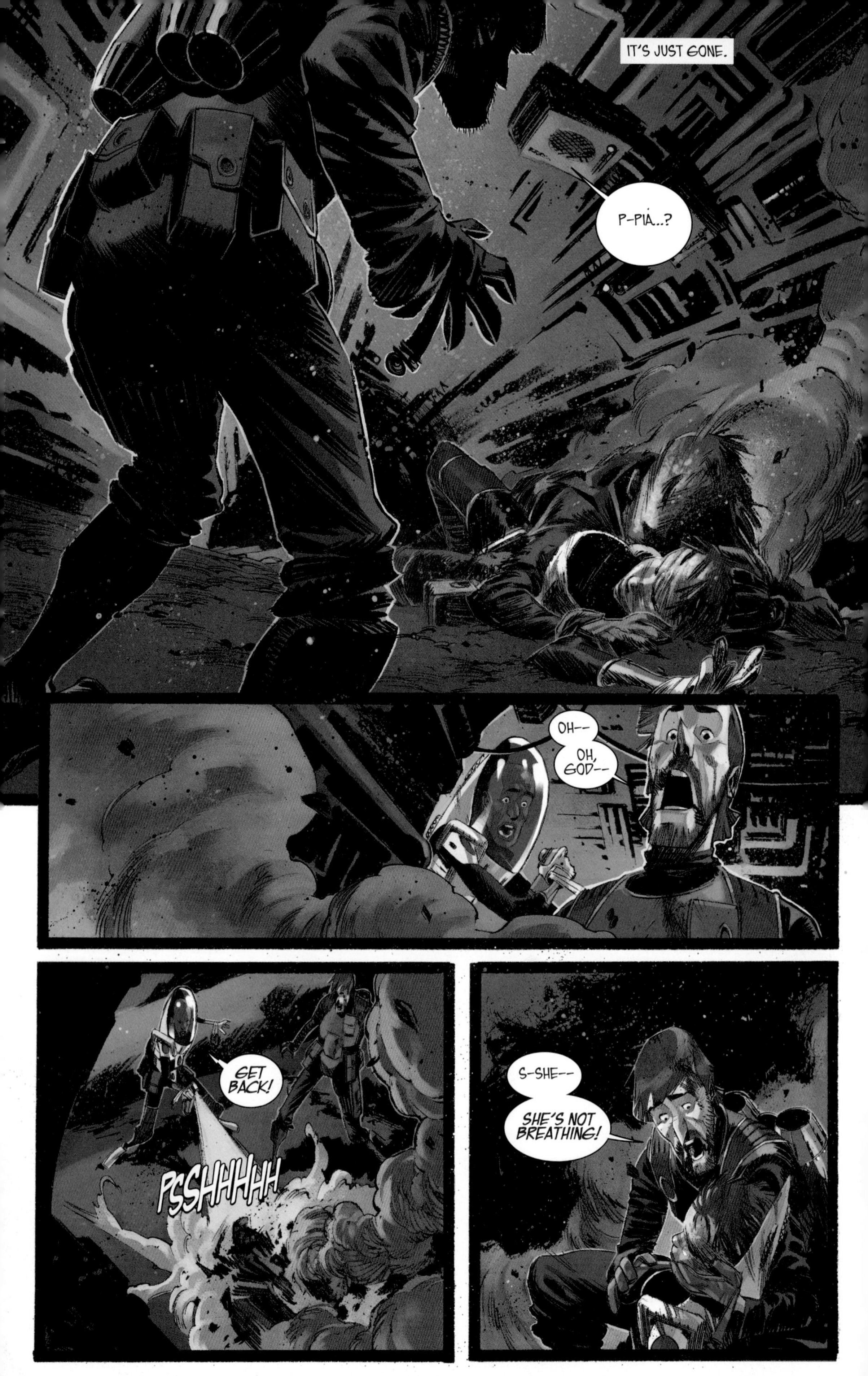
IT'S JUST GONE.
P-PIA...?
OH--
OH, GOD--
GET BACK!
PSSHHHHH
S-SHE--
SHE'S NOT BREATHING!

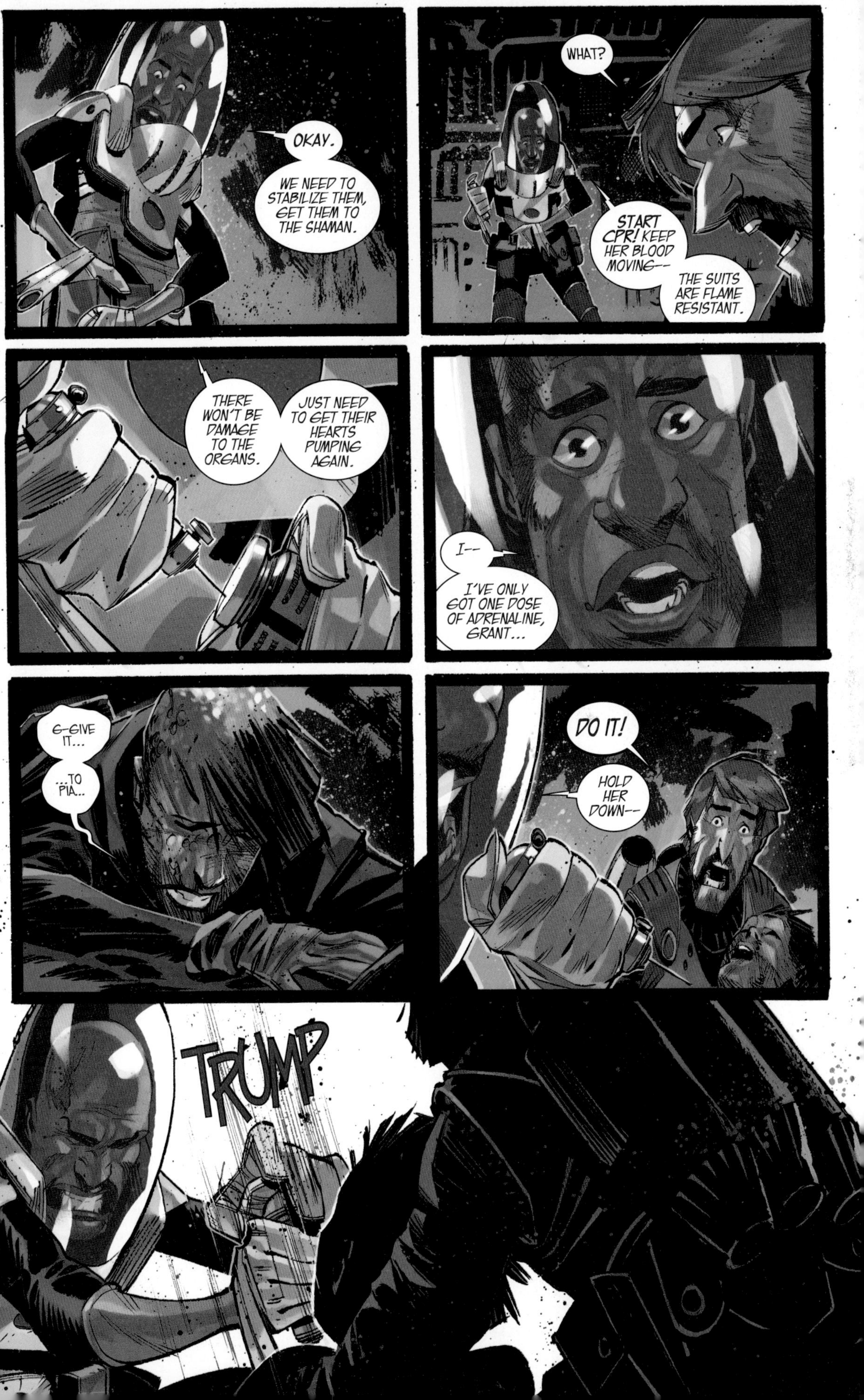
OKAY.
WE NEED TO STABILIZE THEM, GET THEM TO THE SHAMAN.
WHAT?
START CPR! KEEP HER BLOOD MOVING--
THE SUITS ARE FLAME RESISTANT.
THERE WON'T BE DAMAGE TO THE ORGANS.
JUST NEED TO GET THEIR HEARTS PUMPING AGAIN.
I--
I'VE ONLY GOT ONE DOSE OF ADRENALINE, GRANT...
G-GIVE IT...
...TO PIA...
DO IT!
HOLD HER DOWN--
TRUMP

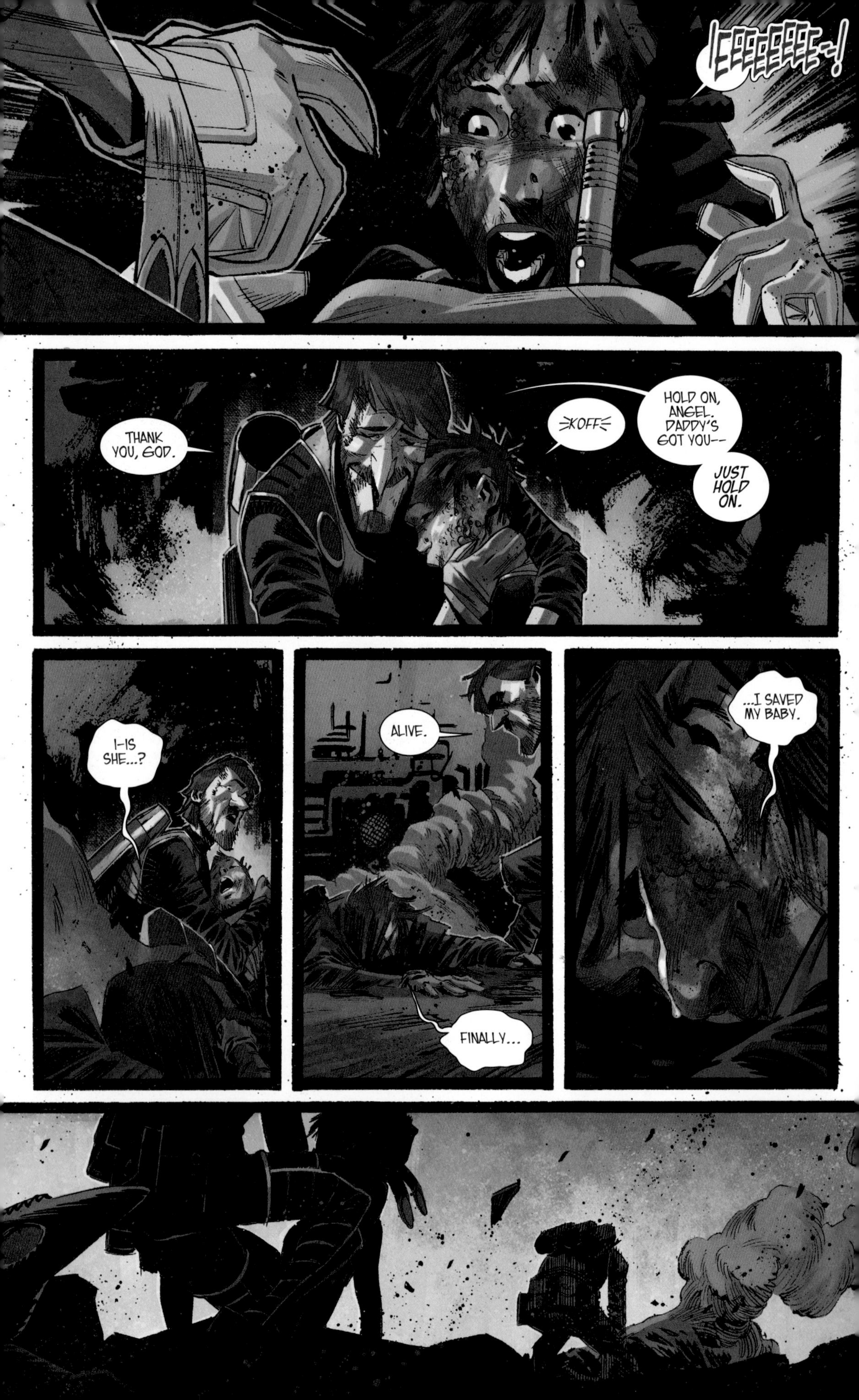
EEEEEEEEEE--!
THANK YOU, GOD.
KOFF
HOLD ON, ANGEL. DADDY'S GOT YOU--
JUST HOLD ON.
I-IS SHE...?
ALIVE.
FINALLY...
...I SAVED MY BABY.

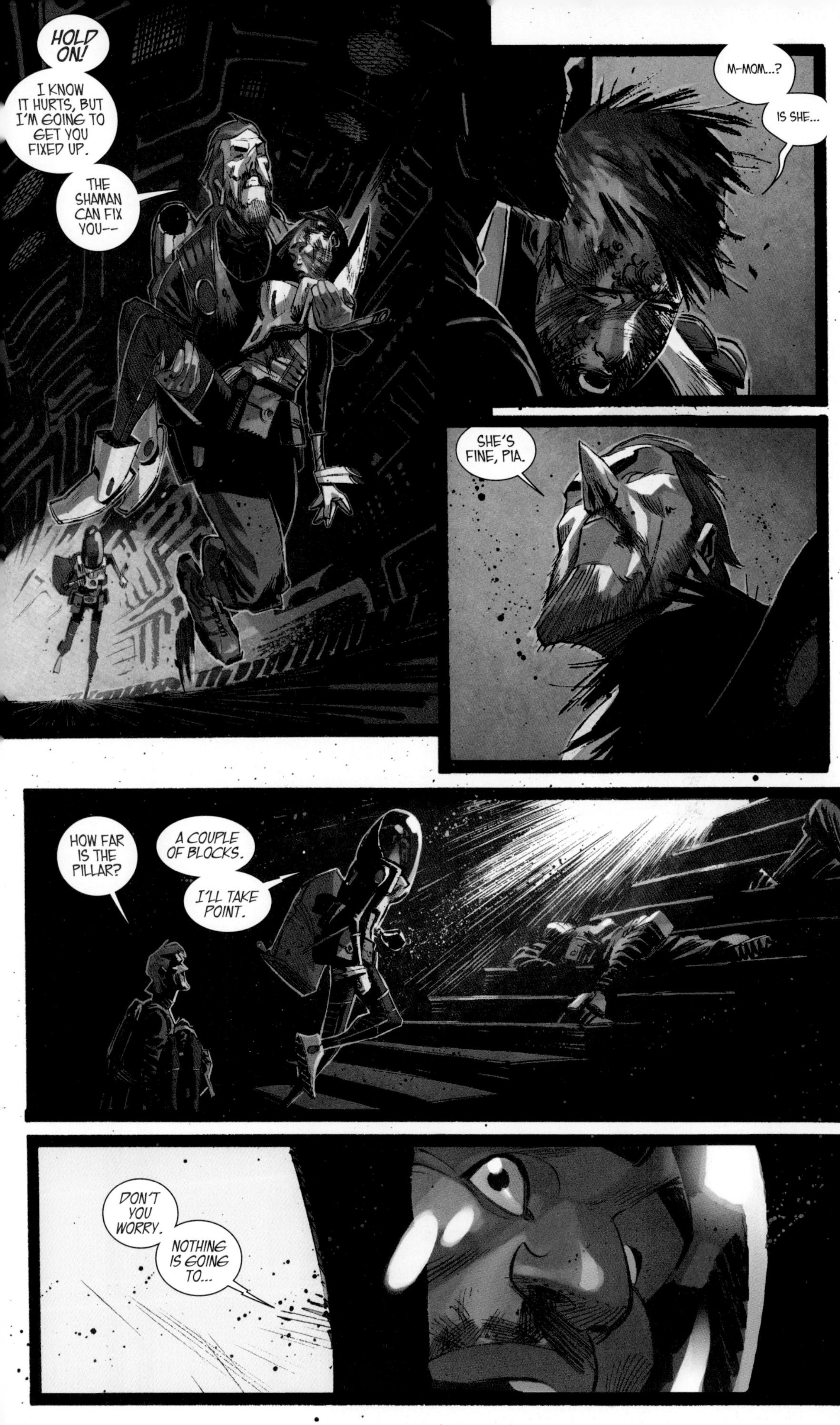
HOLD ON!
I KNOW IT HURTS, BUT I'M GOING TO GET YOU FIXED UP.
THE SHAMAN CAN FIX YOU--
M-MOM...?
IS SHE...
SHE'S FINE, PIA.
HOW FAR IS THE PILLAR?
A COUPLE OF BLOCKS.
I'LL TAKE POINT.
DON'T YOU WORRY.
NOTHING IS GOING TO...

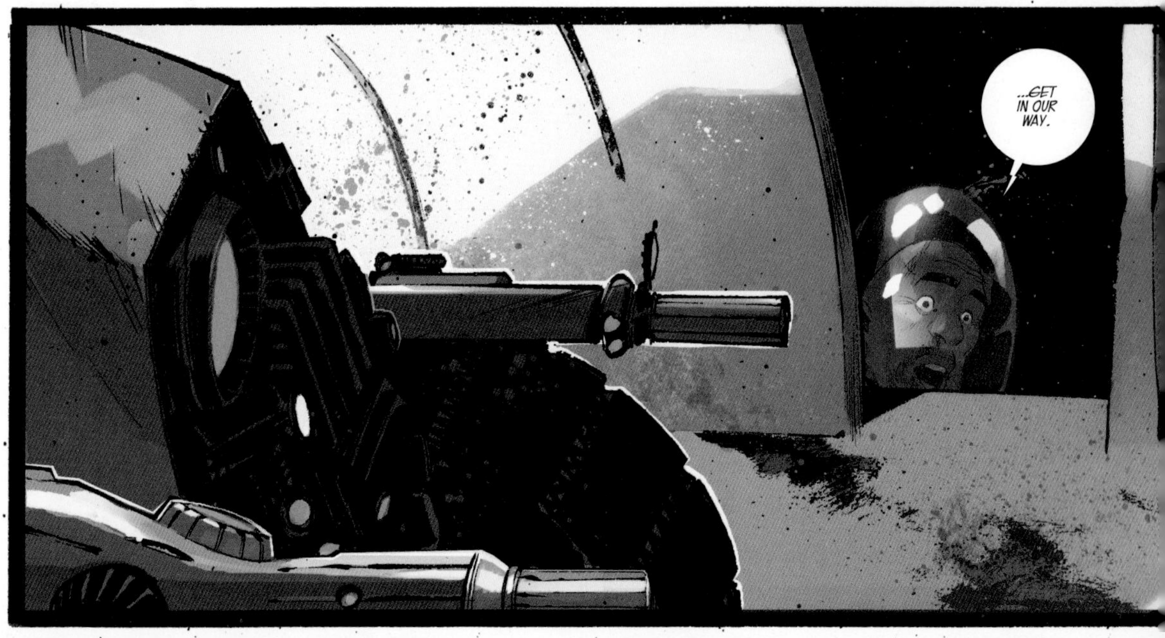
...GET IN OUR WAY.

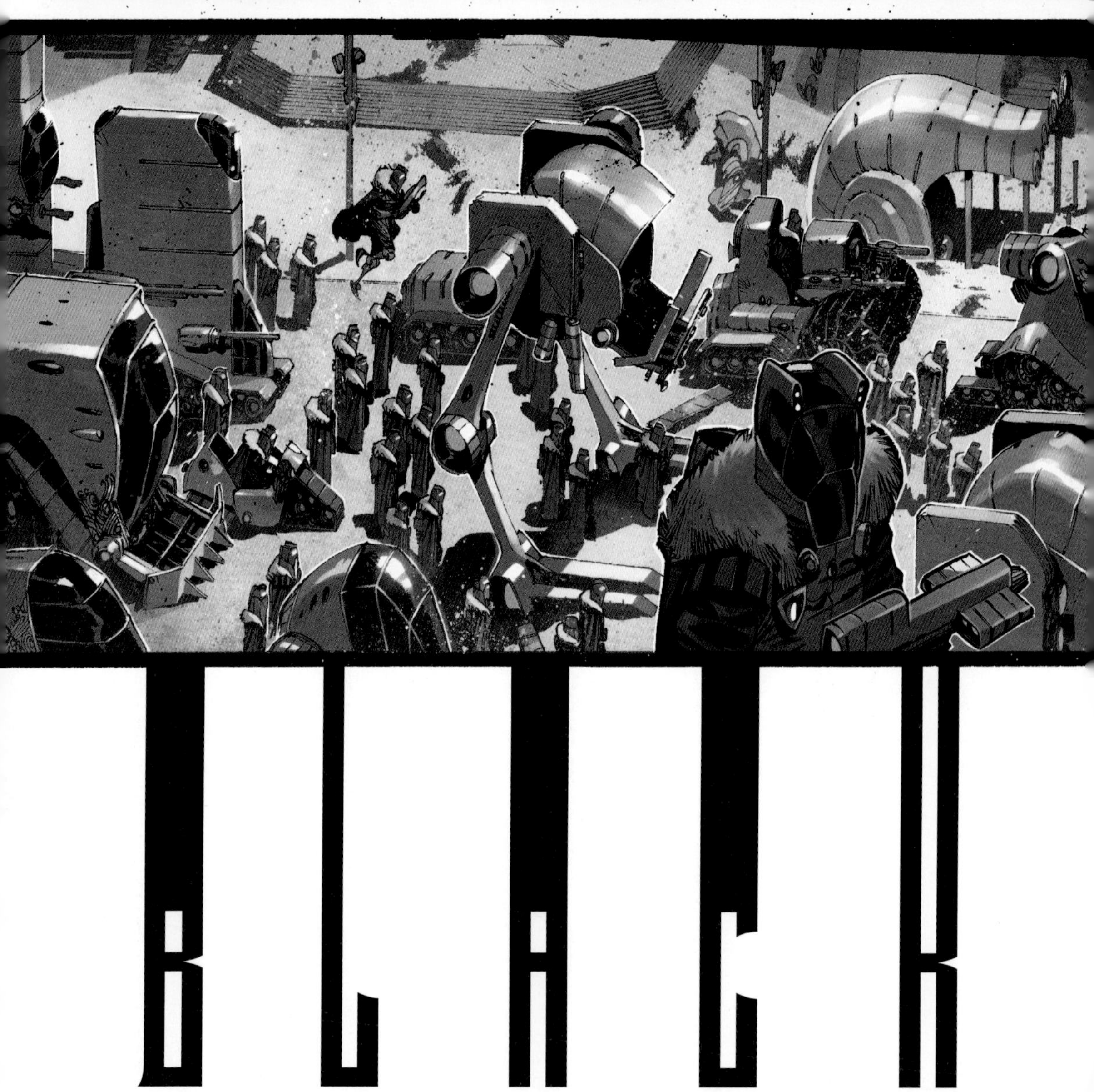

# BLACK

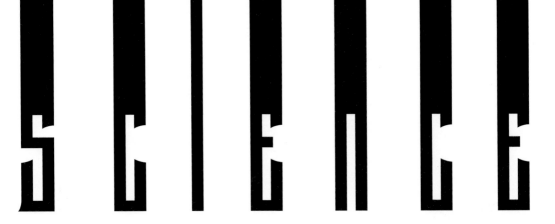

SCIENCE

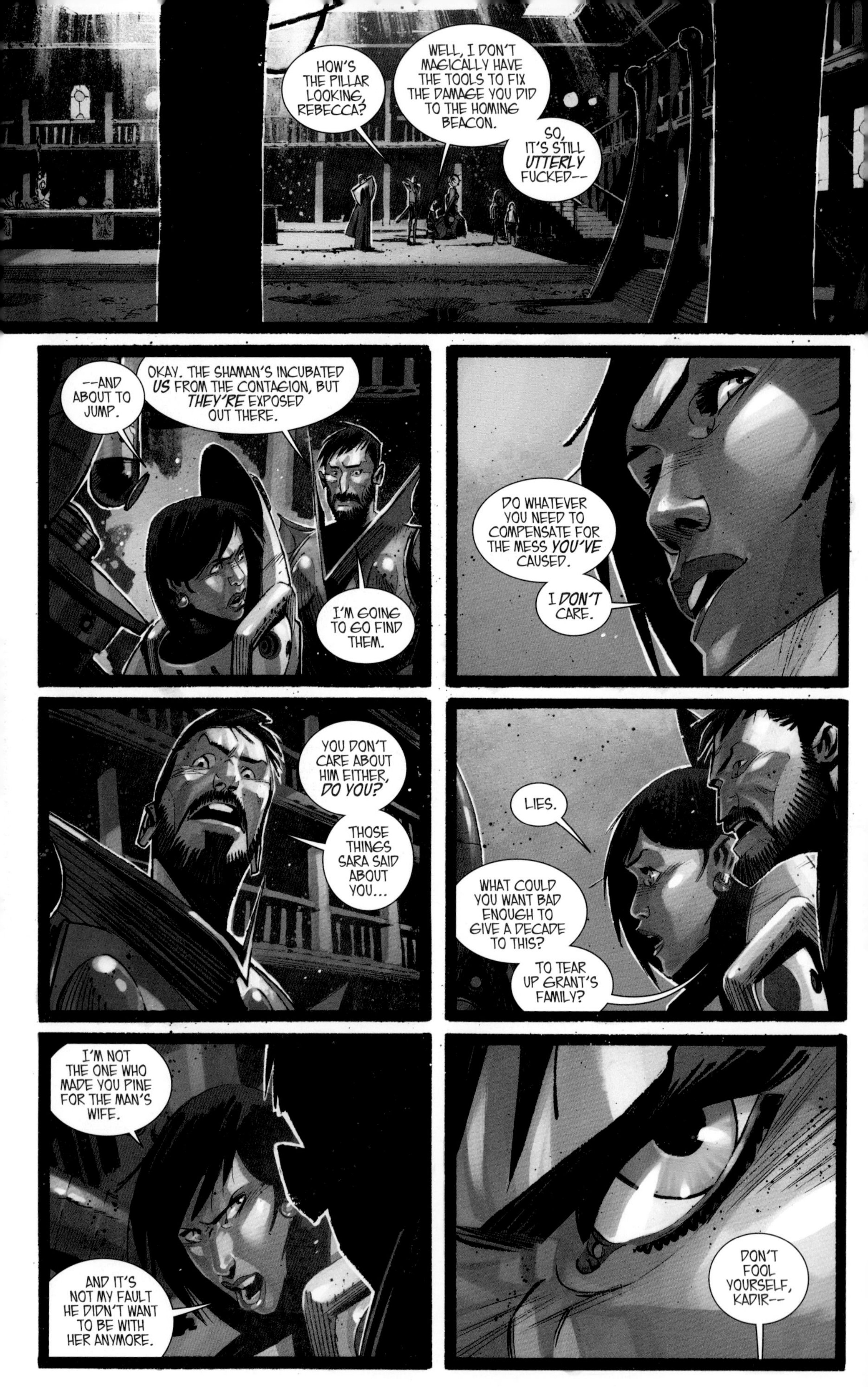
HOW'S THE PILLAR LOOKING, REBECCA?
WELL, I DON'T MAGICALLY HAVE THE TOOLS TO FIX THE DAMAGE YOU DID TO THE HOMING BEACON.
SO, IT'S STILL *UTTERLY* FUCKED--
--AND ABOUT TO JUMP.
OKAY. THE SHAMAN'S INCUBATED *US* FROM THE CONTAGION, BUT *THEY'RE* EXPOSED OUT THERE.
I'M GOING TO GO FIND THEM.
DO WHATEVER YOU NEED TO COMPENSATE FOR THE MESS *YOU'VE* CAUSED.
I *DON'T* CARE.
YOU DON'T CARE ABOUT HIM EITHER, *DO YOU?*
THOSE THINGS SARA SAID ABOUT YOU...
LIES.
WHAT COULD YOU WANT BAD ENOUGH TO GIVE A DECADE TO THIS?
TO TEAR UP GRANT'S FAMILY?
I'M NOT THE ONE WHO MADE YOU PINE FOR THE MAN'S WIFE.
AND IT'S NOT MY FAULT HE DIDN'T WANT TO BE WITH HER ANYMORE.
DON'T FOOL YOURSELF, KADIR--

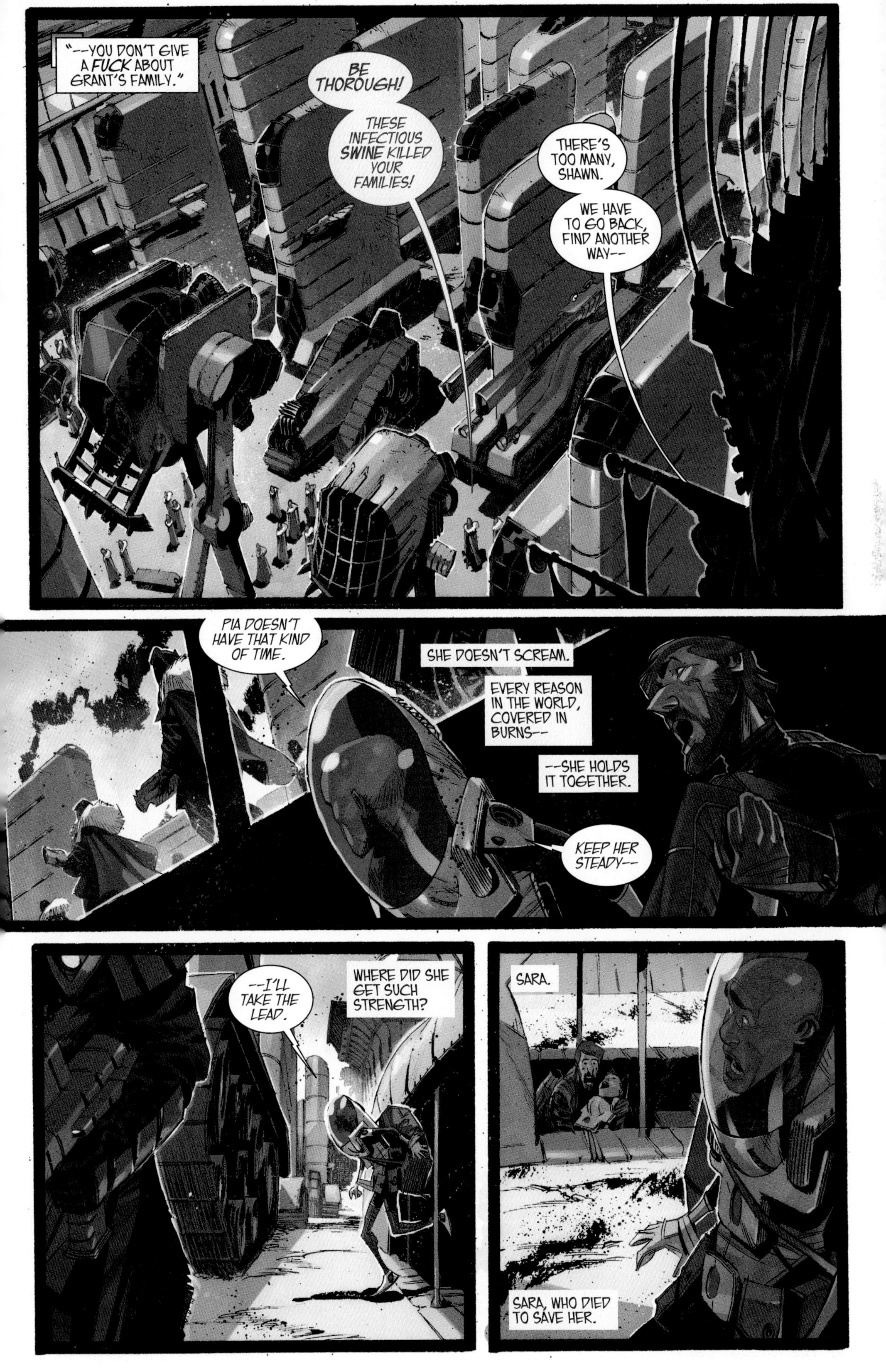

"--YOU DON'T GIVE A FUCK ABOUT GRANT'S FAMILY."
BE THOROUGH!
THESE INFECTIOUS SWINE KILLED YOUR FAMILIES!
THERE'S TOO MANY, SHAWN.
WE HAVE TO GO BACK, FIND ANOTHER WAY--
PIA DOESN'T HAVE THAT KIND OF TIME.
SHE DOESN'T SCREAM.
EVERY REASON IN THE WORLD, COVERED IN BURNS--
--SHE HOLDS IT TOGETHER.
KEEP HER STEADY--
--I'LL TAKE THE LEAD.
WHERE DID SHE GET SUCH STRENGTH?
SARA.
SARA, WHO DIED TO SAVE HER.

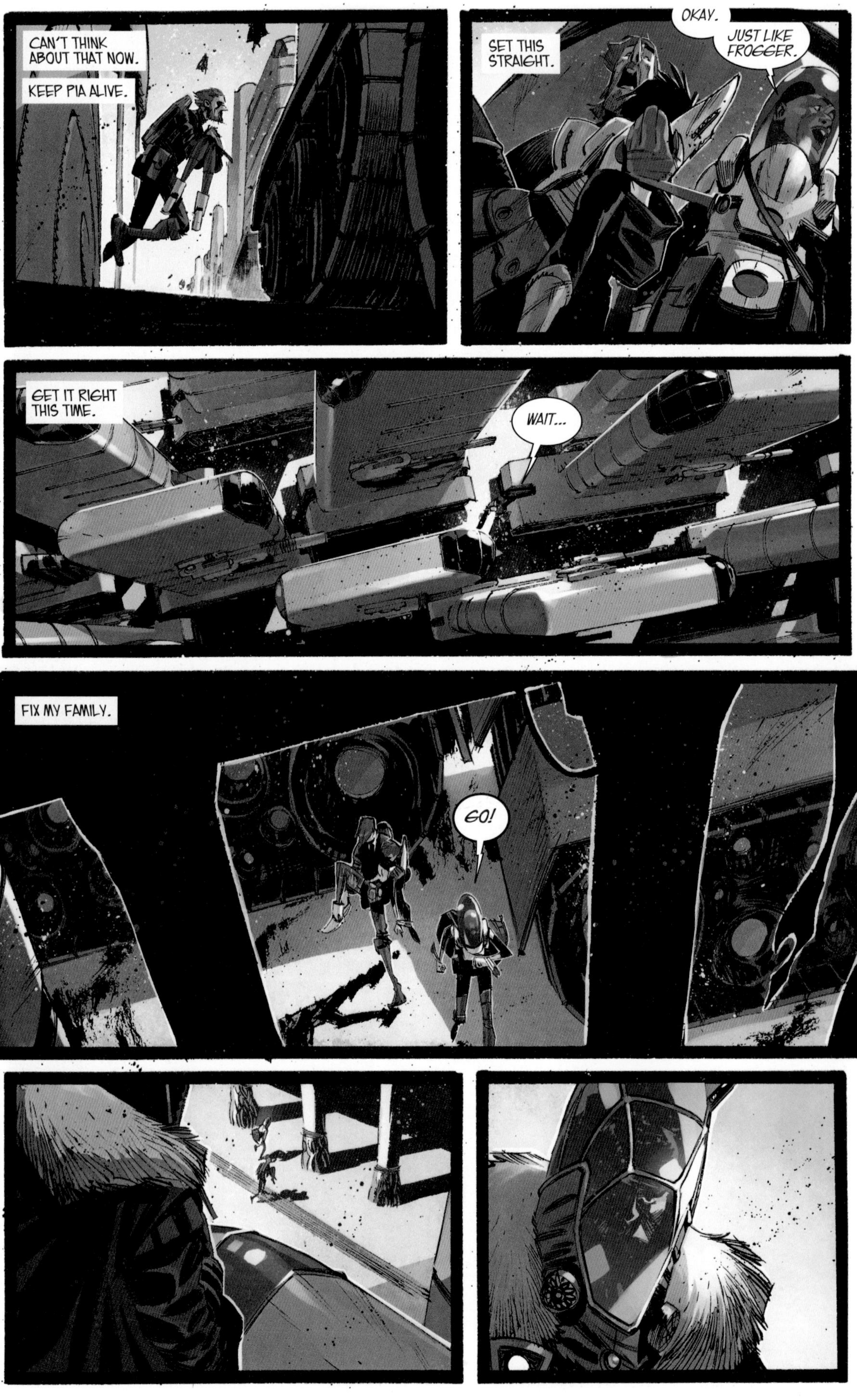
CAN'T THINK ABOUT THAT NOW.
KEEP PIA ALIVE.
SET THIS STRAIGHT.
OKAY.
JUST LIKE FROGGER.
GET IT RIGHT THIS TIME.
WAIT...
FIX MY FAMILY.
GO!

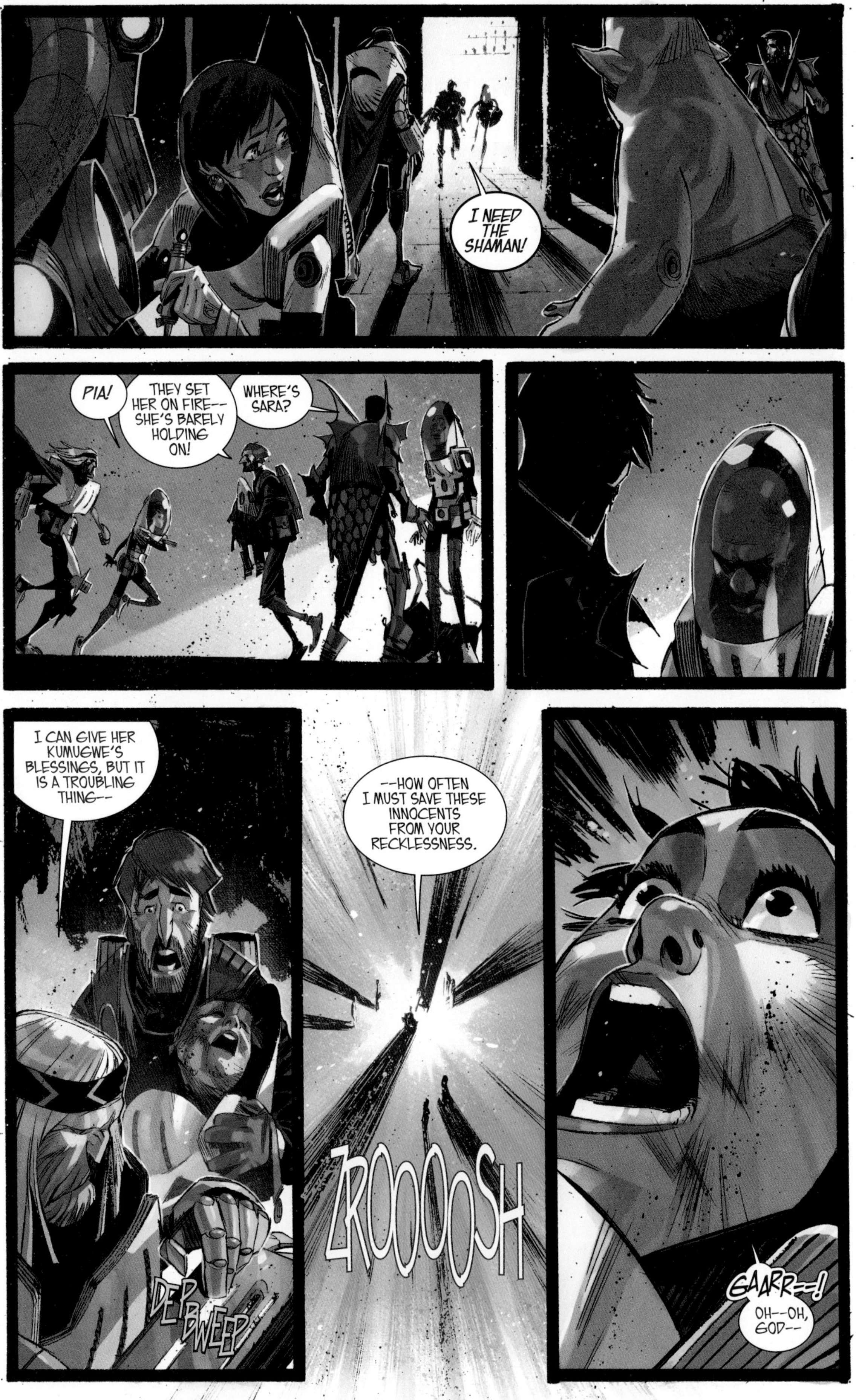
I NEED THE SHAMAN!
PIA!
THEY SET HER ON FIRE-- SHE'S BARELY HOLDING ON!
WHERE'S SARA?
I CAN GIVE HER KUMUGWE'S BLESSINGS, BUT IT IS A TROUBLING THING--
--HOW OFTEN I MUST SAVE THESE INNOCENTS FROM YOUR RECKLESSNESS.
ZROOOOSH
DEP BWEEP
GAARR--!
OH--OH, GOD--

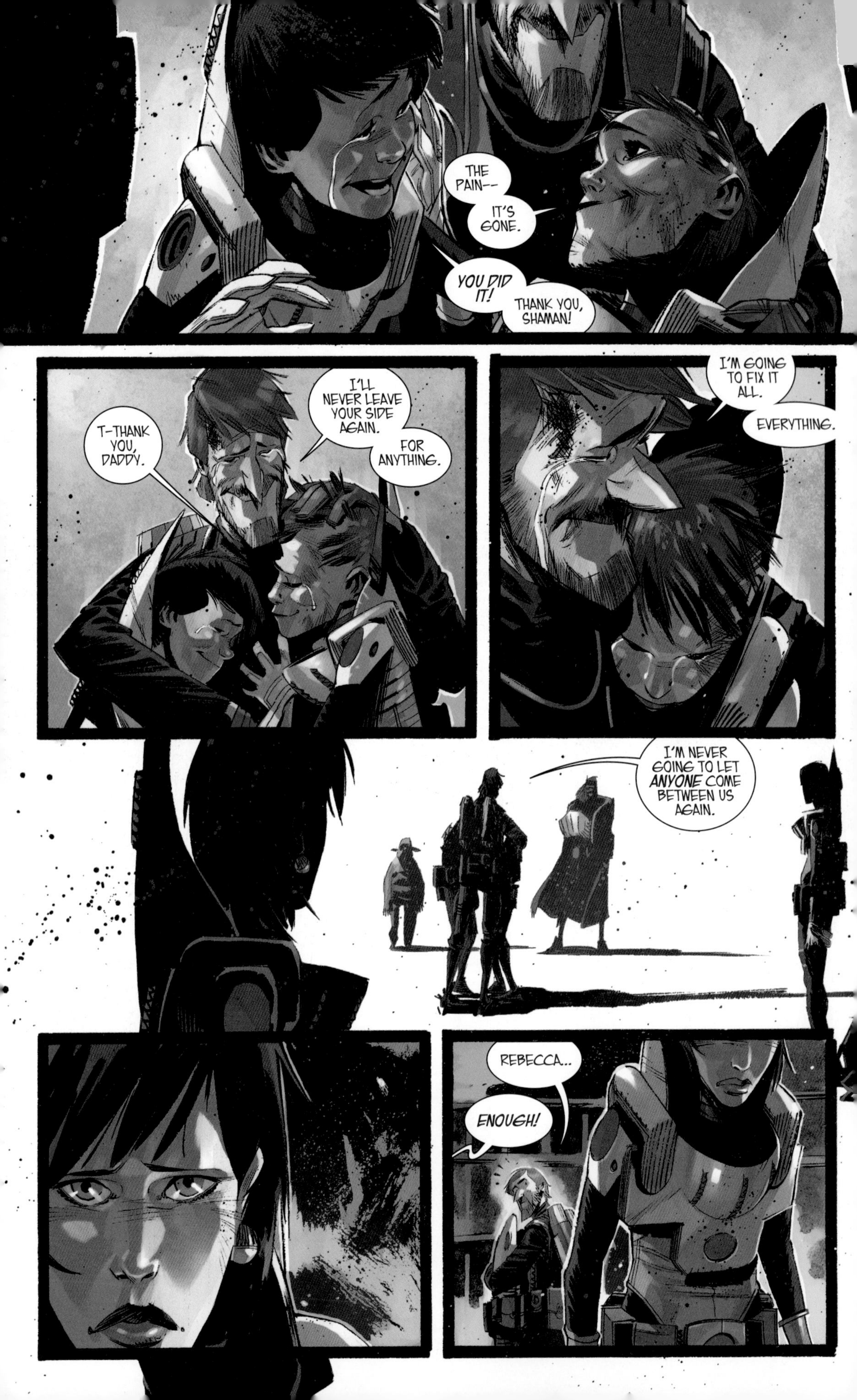
THE PAIN--
IT'S GONE.
YOU DID IT!
THANK YOU, SHAMAN!
T-THANK YOU, DADDY.
I'LL NEVER LEAVE YOUR SIDE AGAIN.
FOR ANYTHING.
I'M GOING TO FIX IT ALL.
EVERYTHING.
I'M NEVER GOING TO LET ANYONE COME BETWEEN US AGAIN.
REBECCA...
ENOUGH!

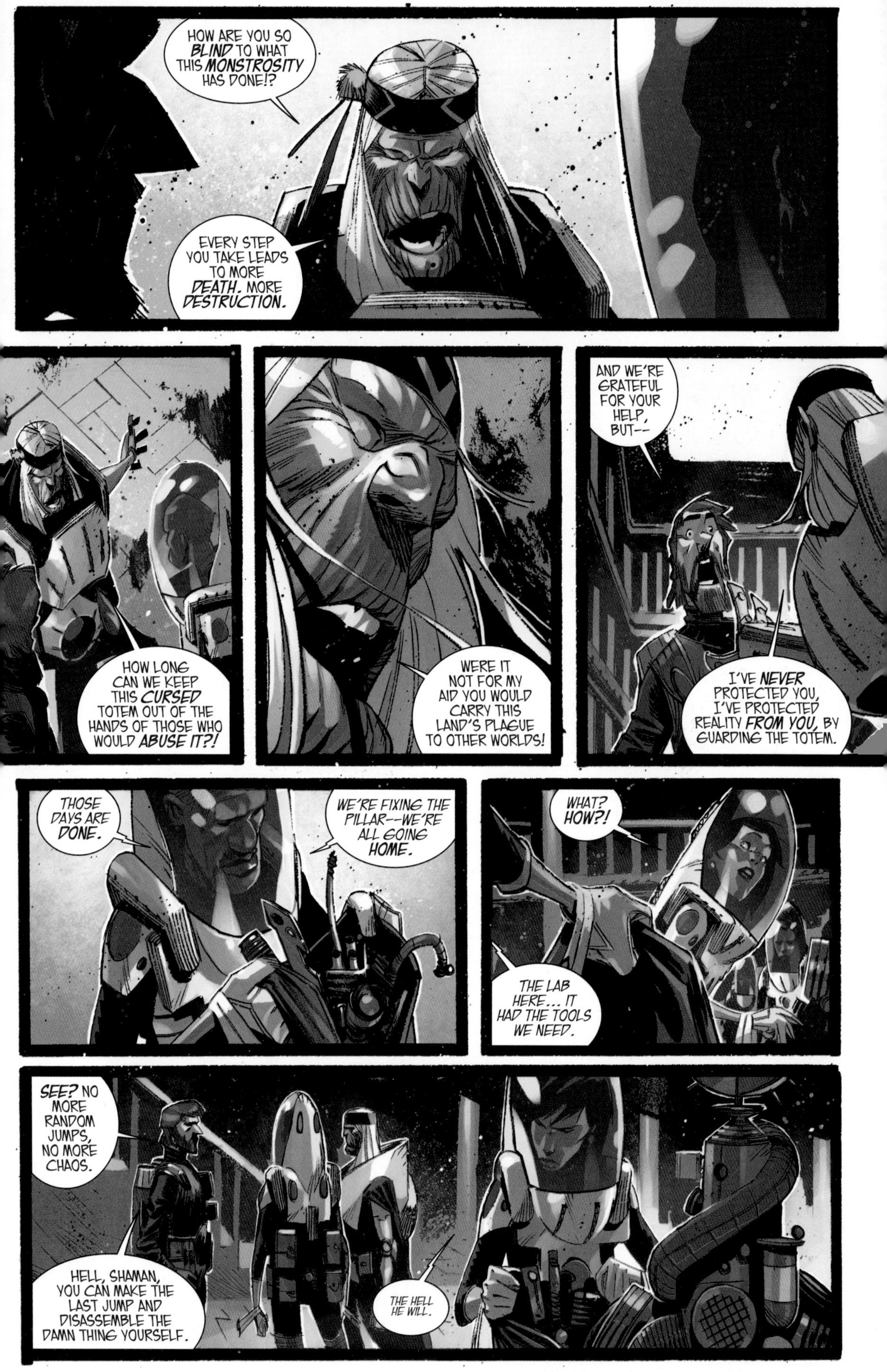
HOW ARE YOU SO BLIND TO WHAT THIS MONSTROSITY HAS DONE!?
EVERY STEP YOU TAKE LEADS TO MORE DEATH. MORE DESTRUCTION.
HOW LONG CAN WE KEEP THIS CURSED TOTEM OUT OF THE HANDS OF THOSE WHO WOULD ABUSE IT?!
WERE IT NOT FOR MY AID YOU WOULD CARRY THIS LAND'S PLAGUE TO OTHER WORLDS!
AND WE'RE GRATEFUL FOR YOUR HELP, BUT--
I'VE NEVER PROTECTED YOU, I'VE PROTECTED REALITY FROM YOU, BY GUARDING THE TOTEM.
THOSE DAYS ARE DONE.
WE'RE FIXING THE PILLAR--WE'RE ALL GOING HOME.
WHAT? HOW?!
THE LAB HERE... IT HAD THE TOOLS WE NEED.
SEE? NO MORE RANDOM JUMPS, NO MORE CHAOS.
HELL, SHAMAN, YOU CAN MAKE THE LAST JUMP AND DISASSEMBLE THE DAMN THING YOURSELF.
THE HELL HE WILL.

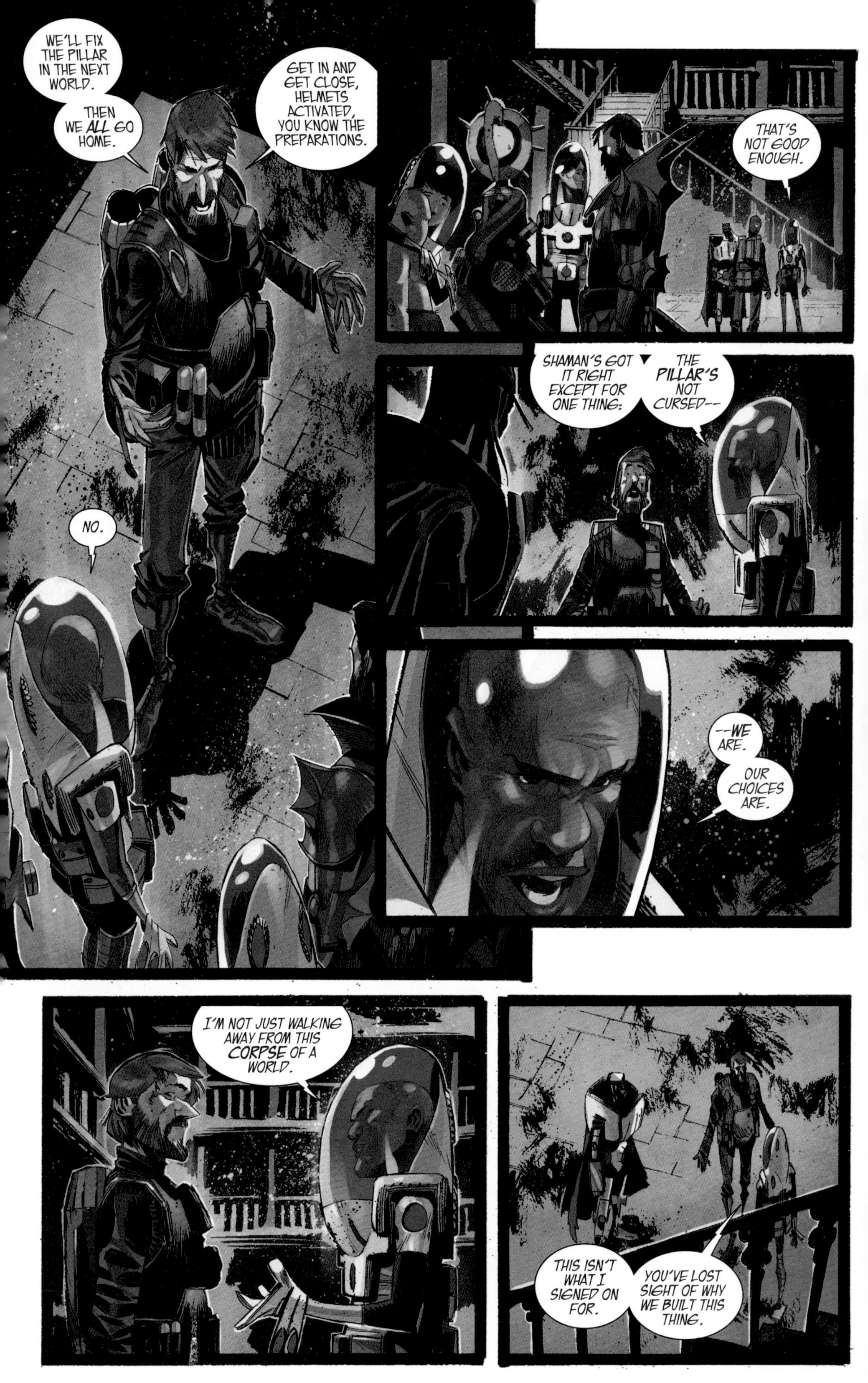
WE'LL FIX THE PILLAR IN THE NEXT WORLD.
THEN WE ALL GO HOME.
GET IN AND GET CLOSE, HELMETS ACTIVATED, YOU KNOW THE PREPARATIONS.
NO.
THAT'S NOT GOOD ENOUGH.
SHAMAN'S GOT IT RIGHT EXCEPT FOR ONE THING:
THE PILLAR'S NOT CURSED--
--WE ARE.
OUR CHOICES ARE.
I'M NOT JUST WALKING AWAY FROM THIS CORPSE OF A WORLD.
THIS ISN'T WHAT I SIGNED ON FOR.
YOU'VE LOST SIGHT OF WHY WE BUILT THIS THING.

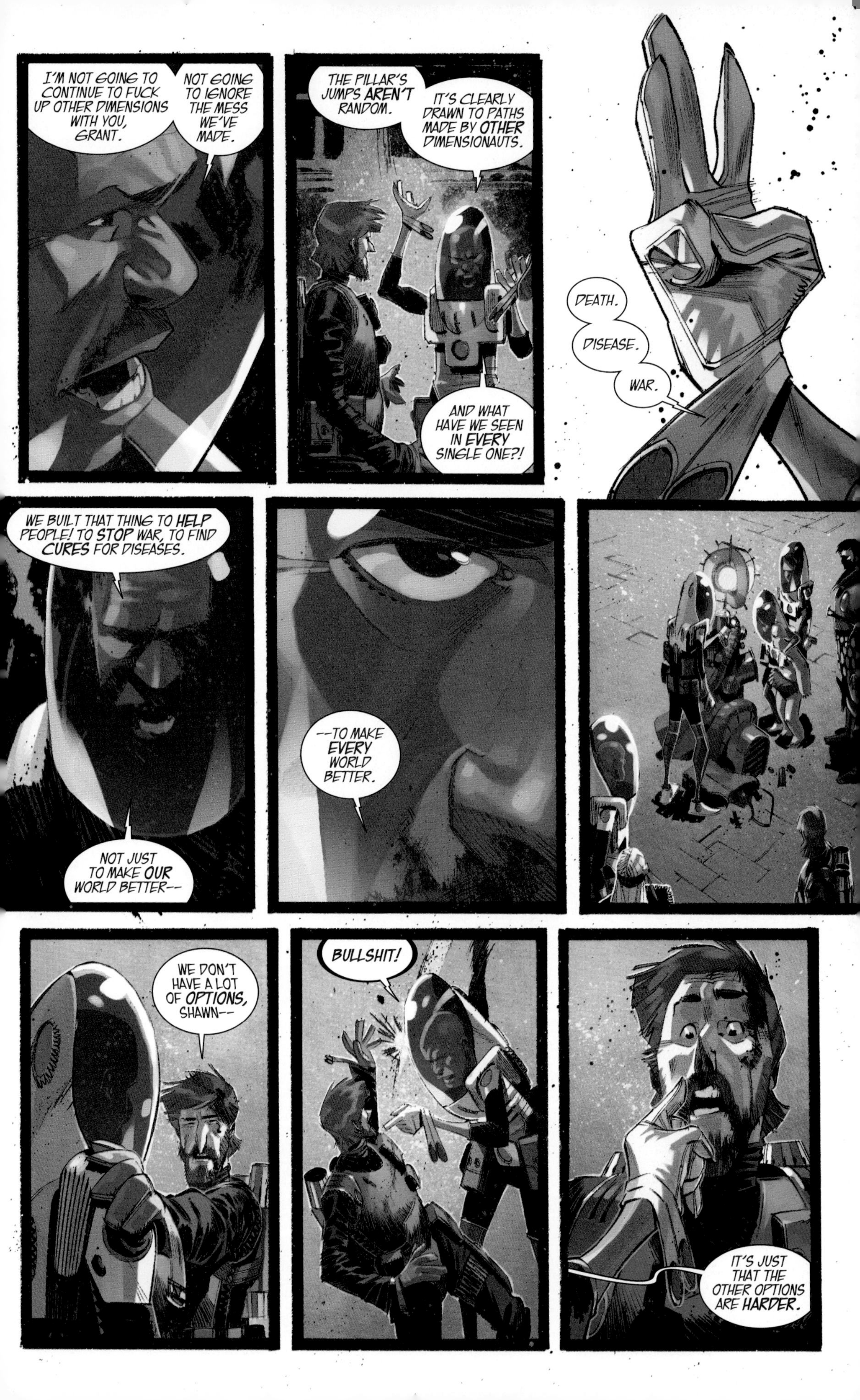
I'M NOT GOING TO CONTINUE TO FUCK UP OTHER DIMENSIONS WITH YOU, GRANT.
NOT GOING TO IGNORE THE MESS WE'VE MADE.
THE PILLAR'S JUMPS AREN'T RANDOM.
IT'S CLEARLY DRAWN TO PATHS MADE BY OTHER DIMENSIONAUTS.
AND WHAT HAVE WE SEEN IN EVERY SINGLE ONE?!
DEATH.
DISEASE.
WAR.
WE BUILT THAT THING TO HELP PEOPLE! TO STOP WAR, TO FIND CURES FOR DISEASES.
NOT JUST TO MAKE OUR WORLD BETTER--
--TO MAKE EVERY WORLD BETTER.
WE DON'T HAVE A LOT OF OPTIONS, SHAWN--
BULLSHIT!
IT'S JUST THAT THE OTHER OPTIONS ARE HARDER.

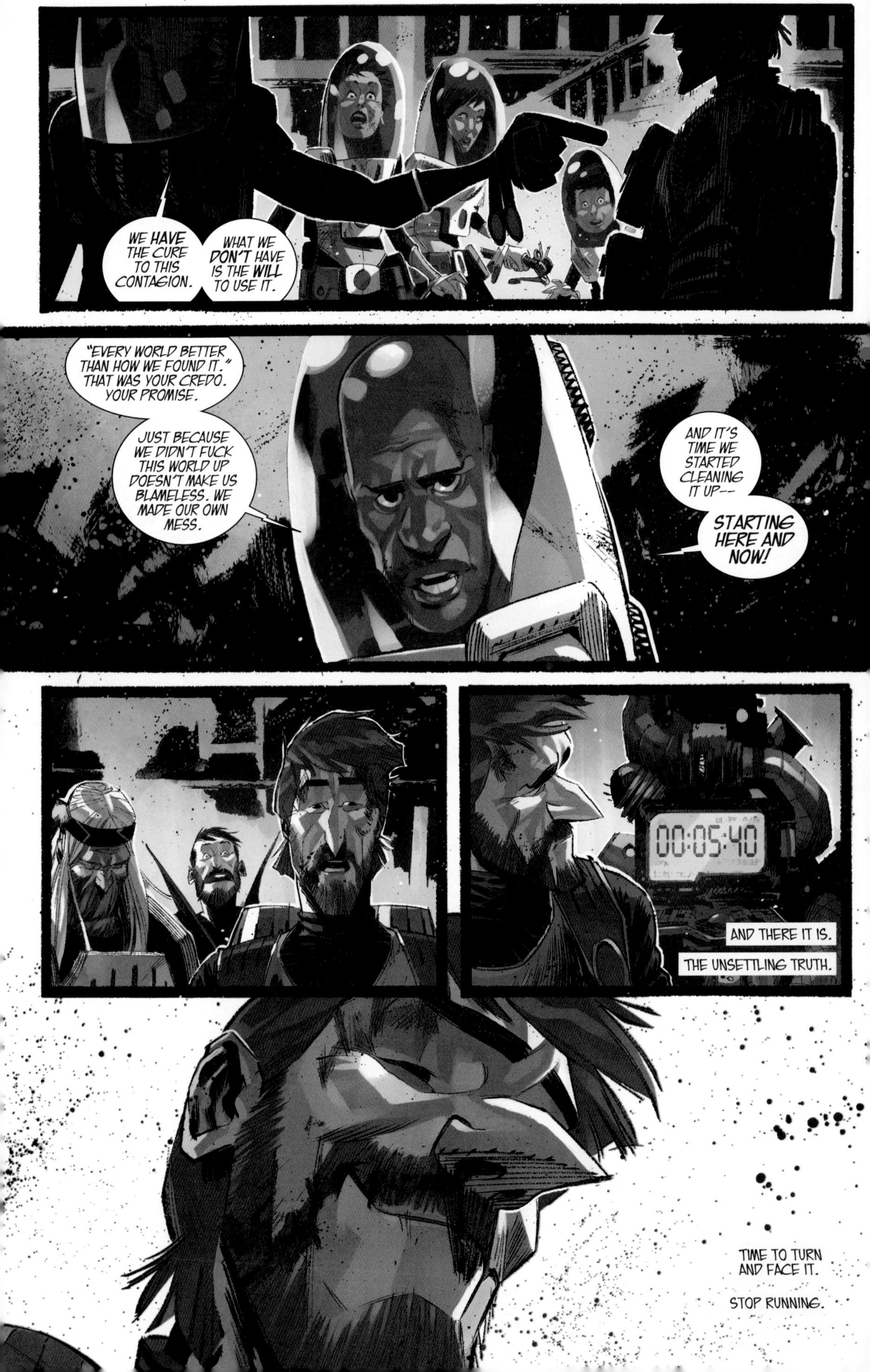
WE HAVE THE CURE TO THIS CONTAGION.
WHAT WE DON'T HAVE IS THE WILL TO USE IT.
"EVERY WORLD BETTER THAN HOW WE FOUND IT." THAT WAS YOUR CREDO. YOUR PROMISE.
JUST BECAUSE WE DIDN'T FUCK THIS WORLD UP DOESN'T MAKE US BLAMELESS. WE MADE OUR OWN MESS.
AND IT'S TIME WE STARTED CLEANING IT UP--
STARTING HERE AND NOW!
00:05:40
AND THERE IT IS.
THE UNSETTLING TRUTH.
TIME TO TURN AND FACE IT.
STOP RUNNING.

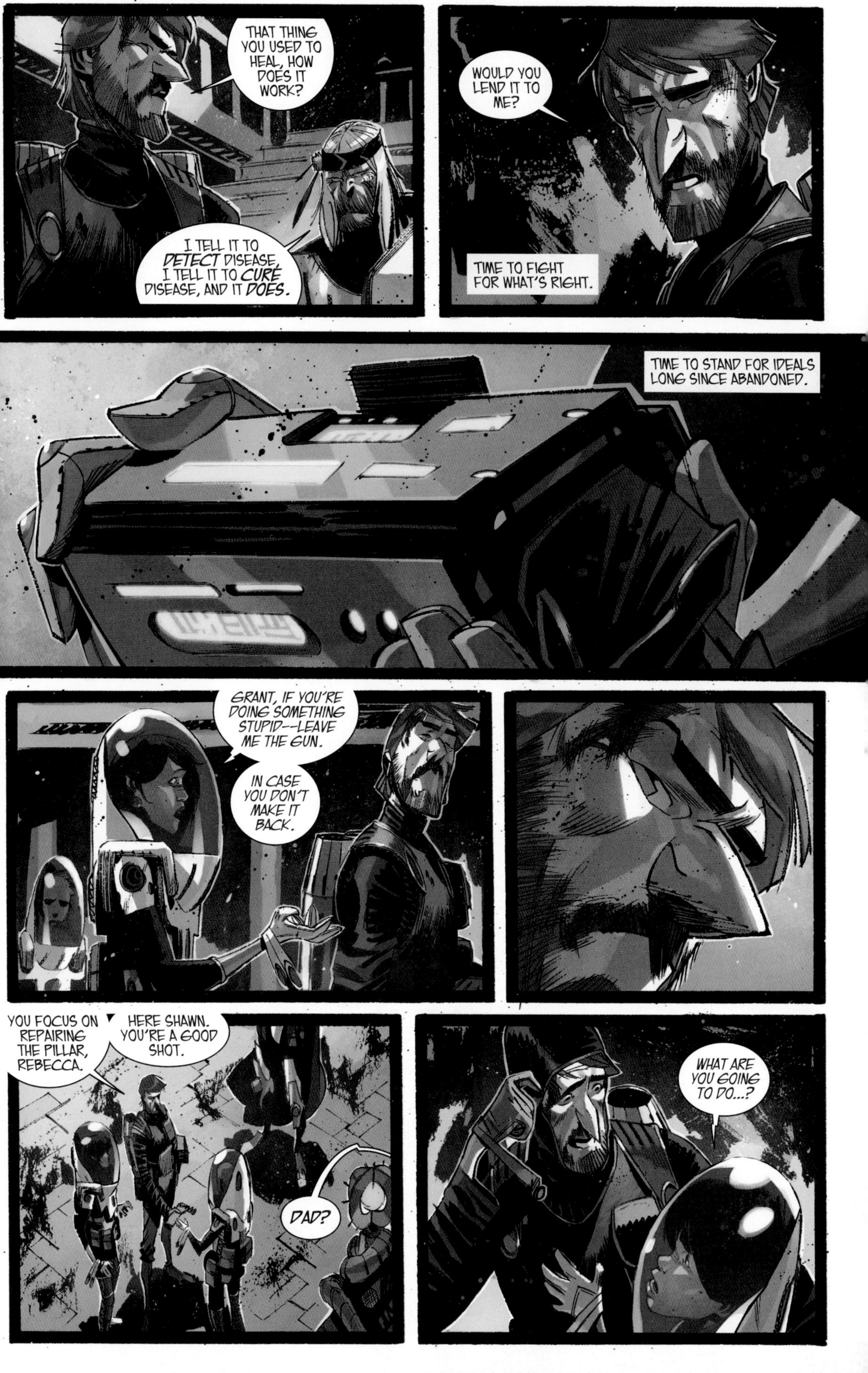
THAT THING YOU USED TO HEAL, HOW DOES IT WORK?
I TELL IT TO DETECT DISEASE, I TELL IT TO CURE DISEASE, AND IT DOES.
WOULD YOU LEND IT TO ME?
TIME TO FIGHT FOR WHAT'S RIGHT.
TIME TO STAND FOR IDEALS LONG SINCE ABANDONED.
GRANT, IF YOU'RE DOING SOMETHING STUPID--LEAVE ME THE GUN.
IN CASE YOU DON'T MAKE IT BACK.
YOU FOCUS ON REPAIRING THE PILLAR, REBECCA.
HERE SHAWN. YOU'RE A GOOD SHOT.
DAD?
WHAT ARE YOU GOING TO DO...?

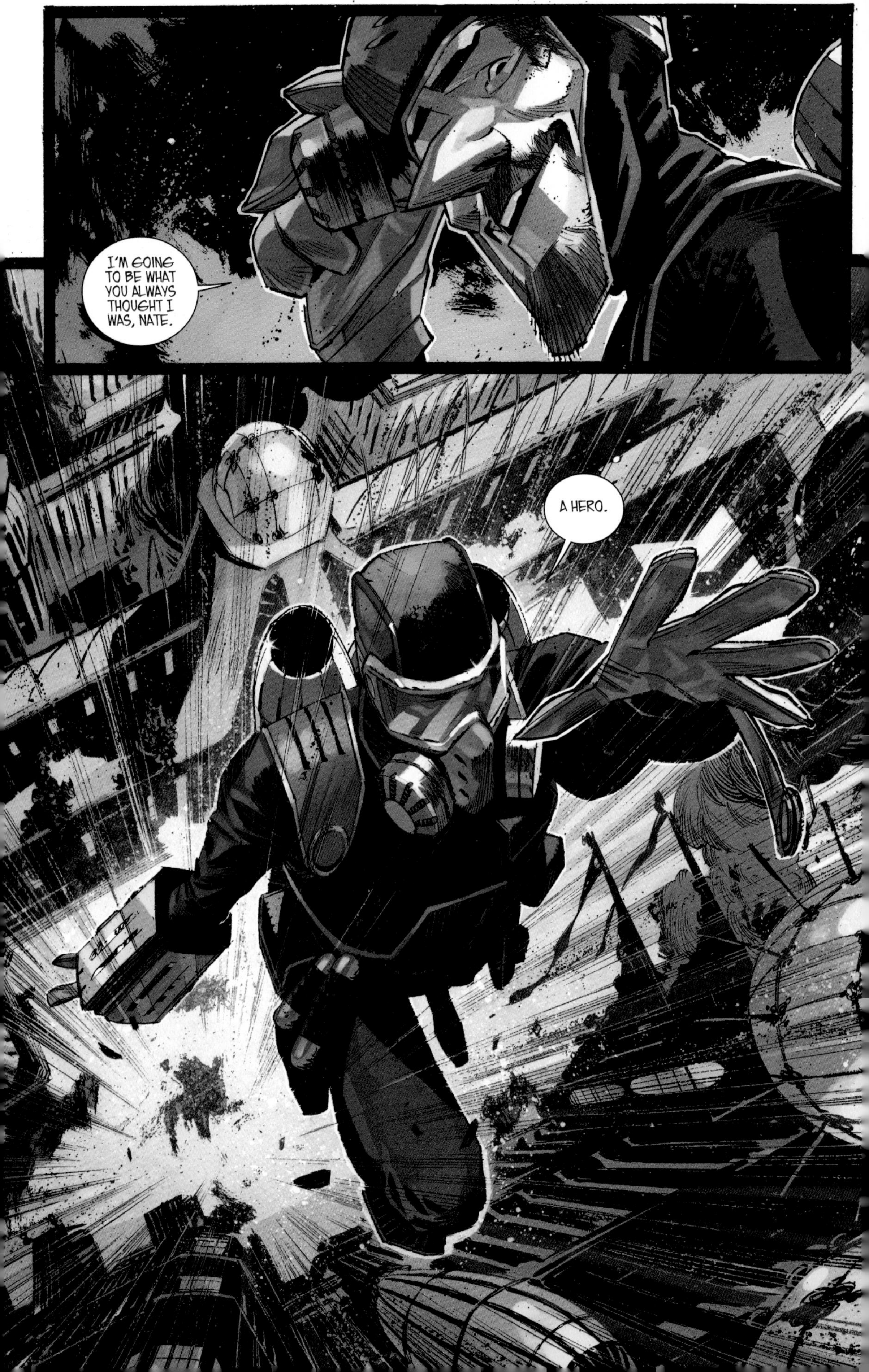
I'M GOING TO BE WHAT YOU ALWAYS THOUGHT I WAS, NATE.
A HERO.

# 15

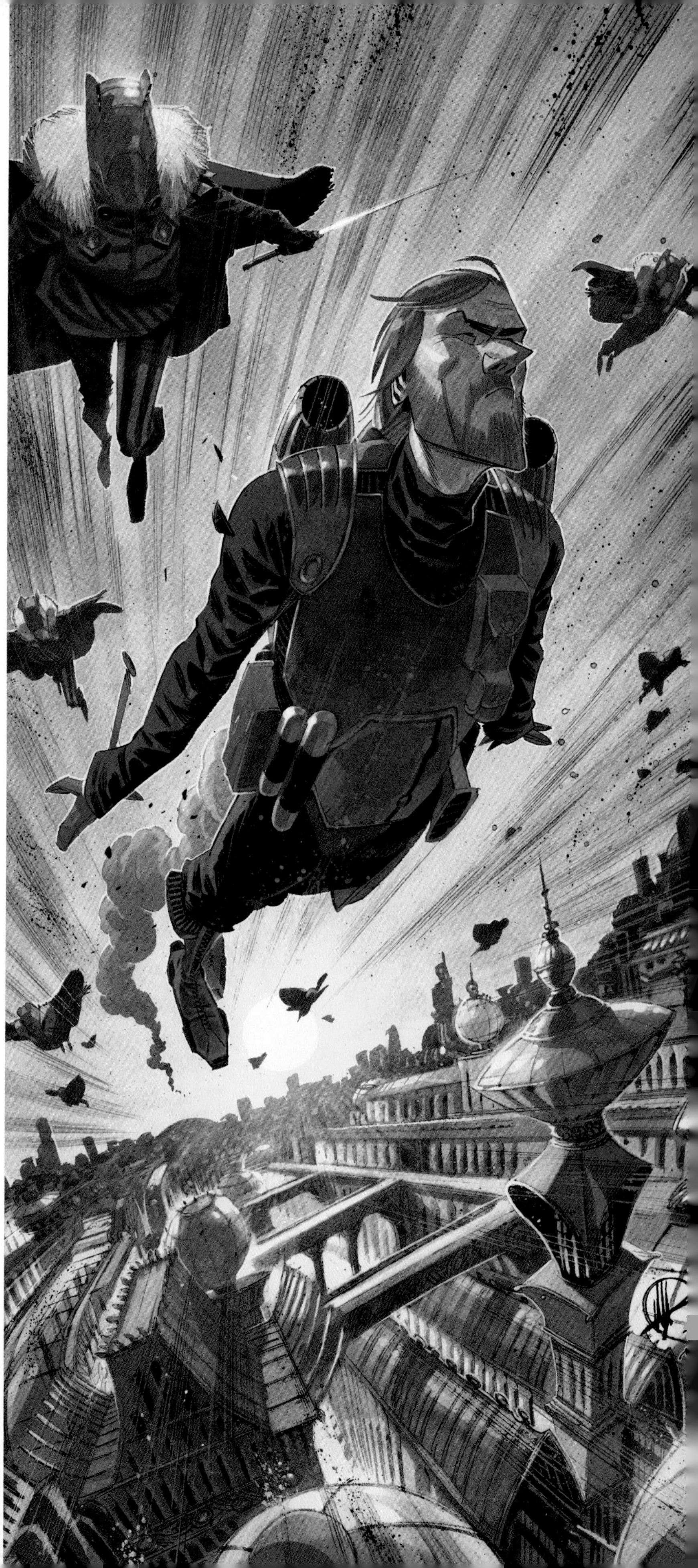

INSTITUTIONAL LEARNING FACILITIES ARE TRAPS INTENDED TO CONTROL THE MIND, SUBDUE THE SOUL, AND KEEP YOU IN DEBT UNTIL YOU'RE TOO OLD TO CAUSE TROUBLE.

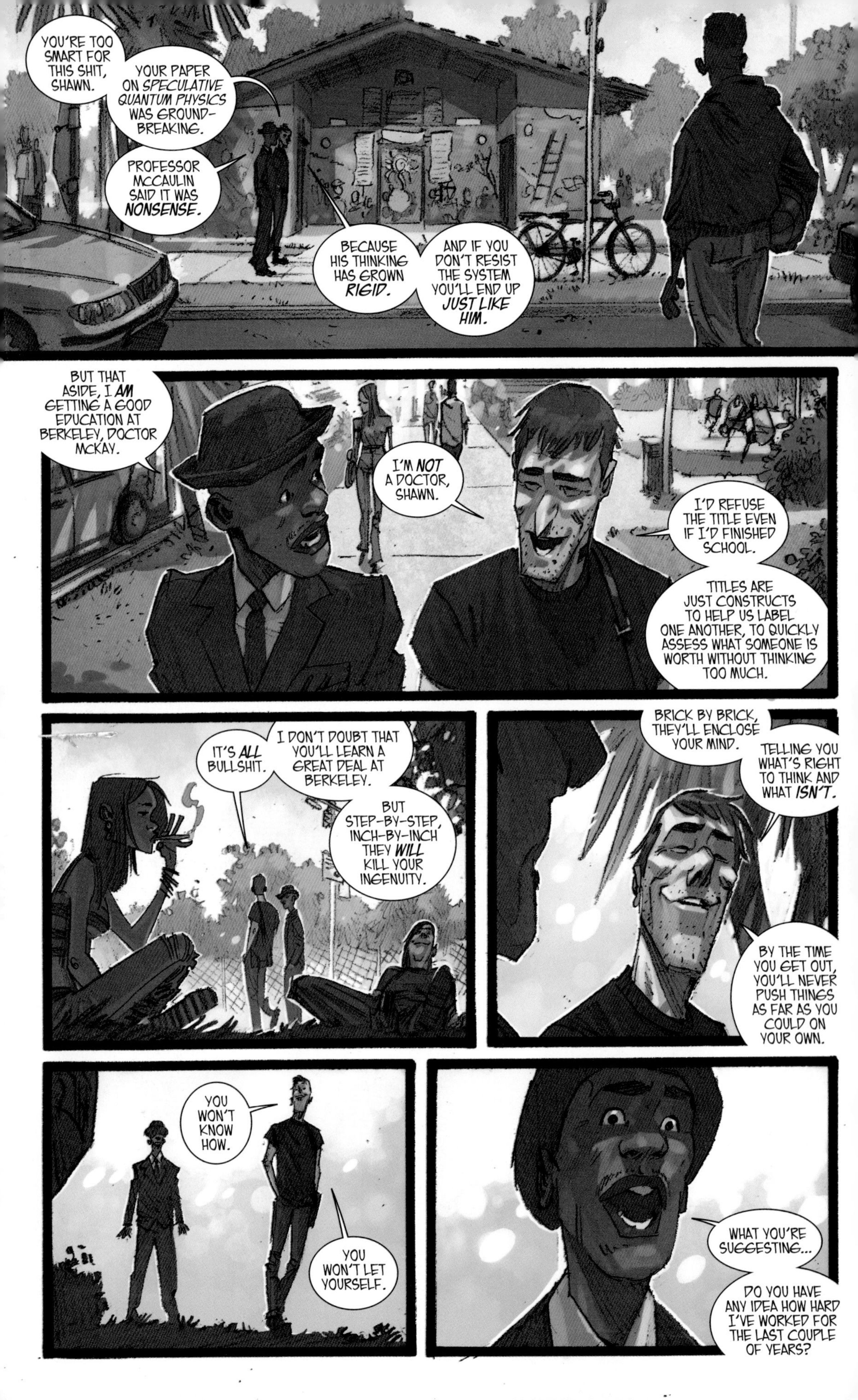
YOU'RE TOO SMART FOR THIS SHIT, SHAWN.
YOUR PAPER ON SPECULATIVE QUANTUM PHYSICS WAS GROUND-BREAKING.
PROFESSOR MCCAULIN SAID IT WAS NONSENSE.
BECAUSE HIS THINKING HAS GROWN RIGID.
AND IF YOU DON'T RESIST THE SYSTEM YOU'LL END UP JUST LIKE HIM.
BUT THAT ASIDE, I AM GETTING A GOOD EDUCATION AT BERKELEY, DOCTOR MCKAY.
I'M NOT A DOCTOR, SHAWN.
I'D REFUSE THE TITLE EVEN IF I'D FINISHED SCHOOL.
TITLES ARE JUST CONSTRUCTS TO HELP US LABEL ONE ANOTHER, TO QUICKLY ASSESS WHAT SOMEONE IS WORTH WITHOUT THINKING TOO MUCH.
IT'S ALL BULLSHIT.
I DON'T DOUBT THAT YOU'LL LEARN A GREAT DEAL AT BERKELEY.
BUT STEP-BY-STEP, INCH-BY-INCH THEY WILL KILL YOUR INGENUITY.
BRICK BY BRICK, THEY'LL ENCLOSE YOUR MIND.
TELLING YOU WHAT'S RIGHT TO THINK AND WHAT ISN'T.
BY THE TIME YOU GET OUT, YOU'LL NEVER PUSH THINGS AS FAR AS YOU COULD ON YOUR OWN.
YOU WON'T KNOW HOW.
YOU WON'T LET YOURSELF.
WHAT YOU'RE SUGGESTING...
DO YOU HAVE ANY IDEA HOW HARD I'VE WORKED FOR THE LAST COUPLE OF YEARS?

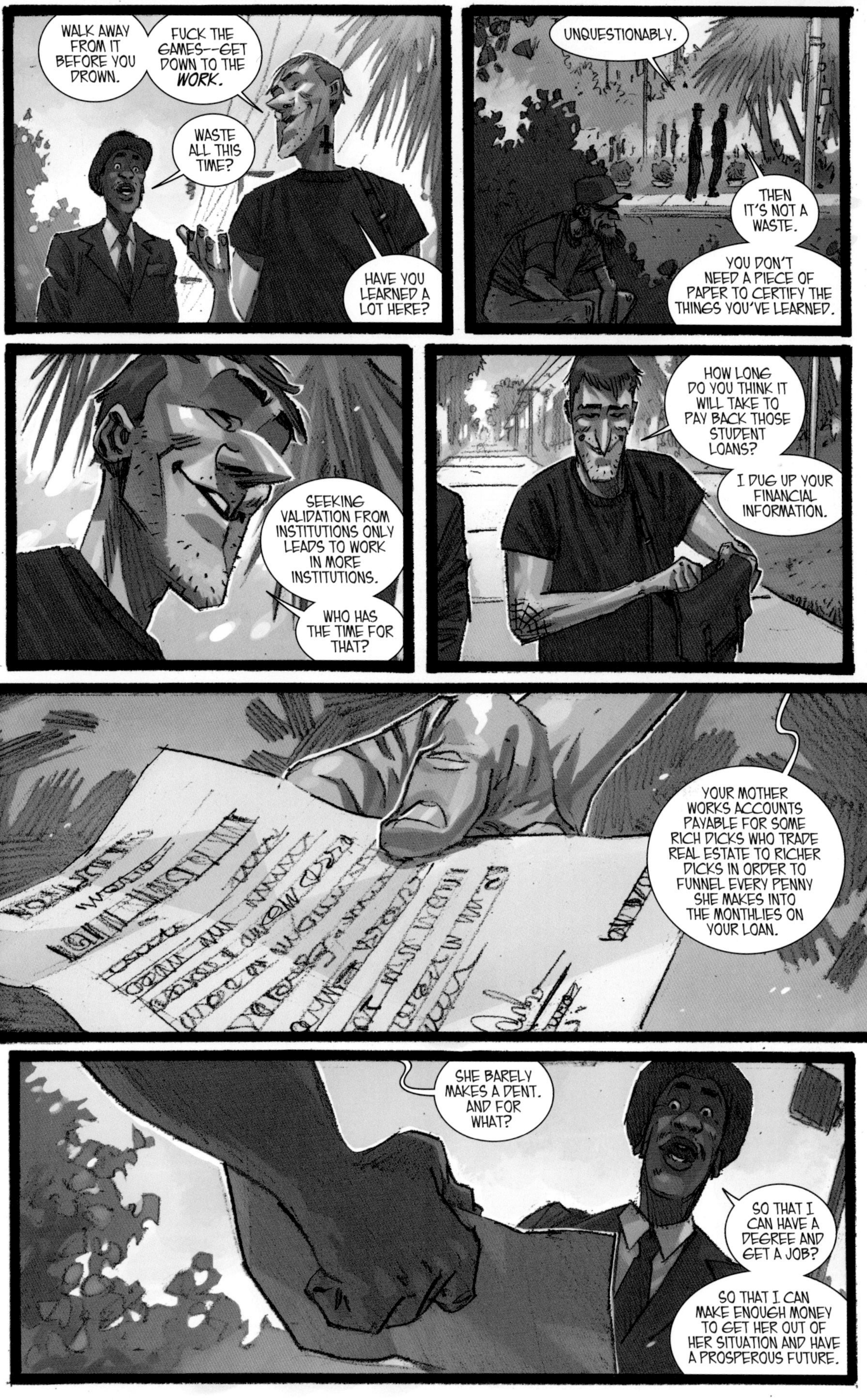
WALK AWAY FROM IT BEFORE YOU DROWN.
FUCK THE GAMES--GET DOWN TO THE WORK.
WASTE ALL THIS TIME?
HAVE YOU LEARNED A LOT HERE?
UNQUESTIONABLY.
THEN IT'S NOT A WASTE.
YOU DON'T NEED A PIECE OF PAPER TO CERTIFY THE THINGS YOU'VE LEARNED.
SEEKING VALIDATION FROM INSTITUTIONS ONLY LEADS TO WORK IN MORE INSTITUTIONS.
WHO HAS THE TIME FOR THAT?
HOW LONG DO YOU THINK IT WILL TAKE TO PAY BACK THOSE STUDENT LOANS?
I DUG UP YOUR FINANCIAL INFORMATION.
YOUR MOTHER WORKS ACCOUNTS PAYABLE FOR SOME RICH DICKS WHO TRADE REAL ESTATE TO RICHER DICKS IN ORDER TO FUNNEL EVERY PENNY SHE MAKES INTO THE MONTHLIES ON YOUR LOAN.
SHE BARELY MAKES A DENT. AND FOR WHAT?
SO THAT I CAN HAVE A DEGREE AND GET A JOB?
SO THAT I CAN MAKE ENOUGH MONEY TO GET HER OUT OF HER SITUATION AND HAVE A PROSPEROUS FUTURE.

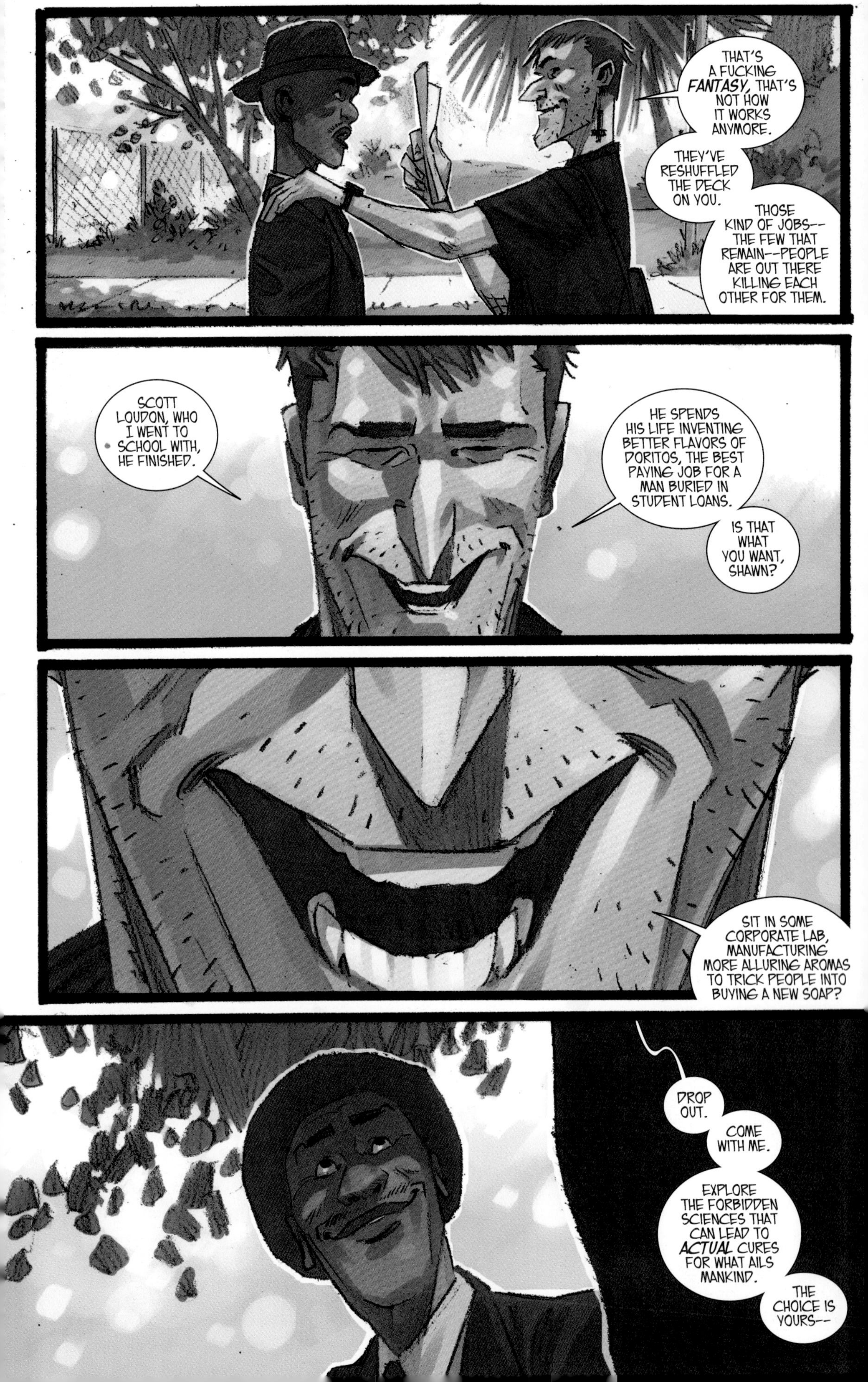
THAT'S A FUCKING *FANTASY*, THAT'S NOT HOW IT WORKS ANYMORE.
THEY'VE RESHUFFLED THE DECK ON YOU.
THOSE KIND OF JOBS-- THE FEW THAT REMAIN--PEOPLE ARE OUT THERE KILLING EACH OTHER FOR THEM.
SCOTT LOUDON, WHO I WENT TO SCHOOL WITH, HE FINISHED.
HE SPENDS HIS LIFE INVENTING BETTER FLAVORS OF DORITOS, THE BEST PAYING JOB FOR A MAN BURIED IN STUDENT LOANS.
IS THAT WHAT YOU WANT, SHAWN?
SIT IN SOME CORPORATE LAB, MANUFACTURING MORE ALLURING AROMAS TO TRICK PEOPLE INTO BUYING A NEW SOAP?
DROP OUT.
COME WITH ME.
EXPLORE THE FORBIDDEN SCIENCES THAT CAN LEAD TO *ACTUAL* CURES FOR WHAT AILS MANKIND.
THE CHOICE IS YOURS--

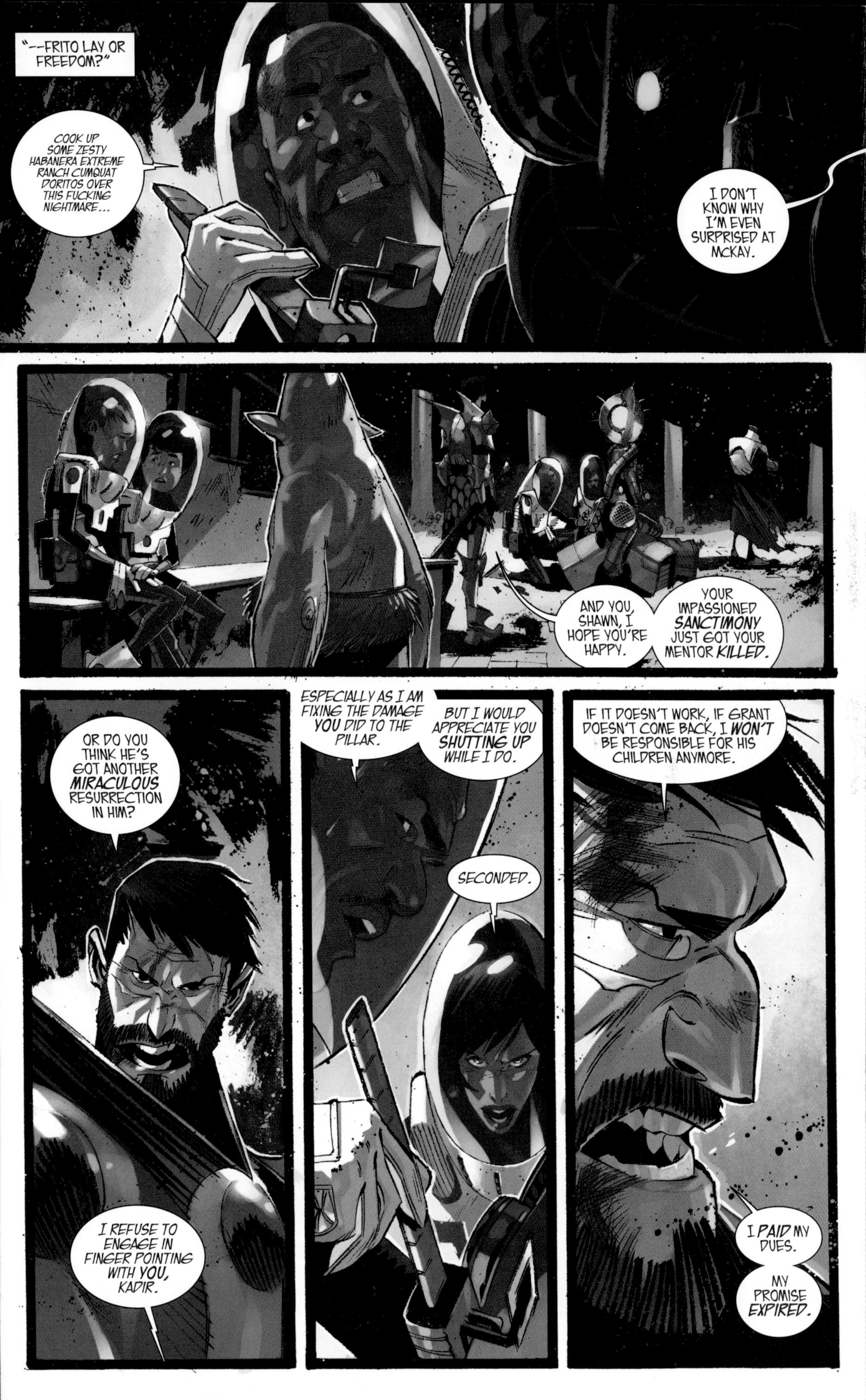
"--FRITO LAY OR FREEDOM?"
COOK UP SOME ZESTY HABANERA EXTREME RANCH CUMQUAT DORITOS OVER THIS FUCKING NIGHTMARE...
I DON'T KNOW WHY I'M EVEN SURPRISED AT MCKAY.
AND YOU, SHAWN, I HOPE YOU'RE HAPPY.
YOUR IMPASSIONED SANCTIMONY JUST GOT YOUR MENTOR KILLED.
OR DO YOU THINK HE'S GOT ANOTHER MIRACULOUS RESURRECTION IN HIM?
I REFUSE TO ENGAGE IN FINGER POINTING WITH YOU, KADIR.
ESPECIALLY AS I AM FIXING THE DAMAGE YOU DID TO THE PILLAR.
BUT I WOULD APPRECIATE YOU SHUTTING UP WHILE I DO.
SECONDED.
IF IT DOESN'T WORK, IF GRANT DOESN'T COME BACK, I WON'T BE RESPONSIBLE FOR HIS CHILDREN ANYMORE.
I PAID MY DUES.
MY PROMISE EXPIRED.

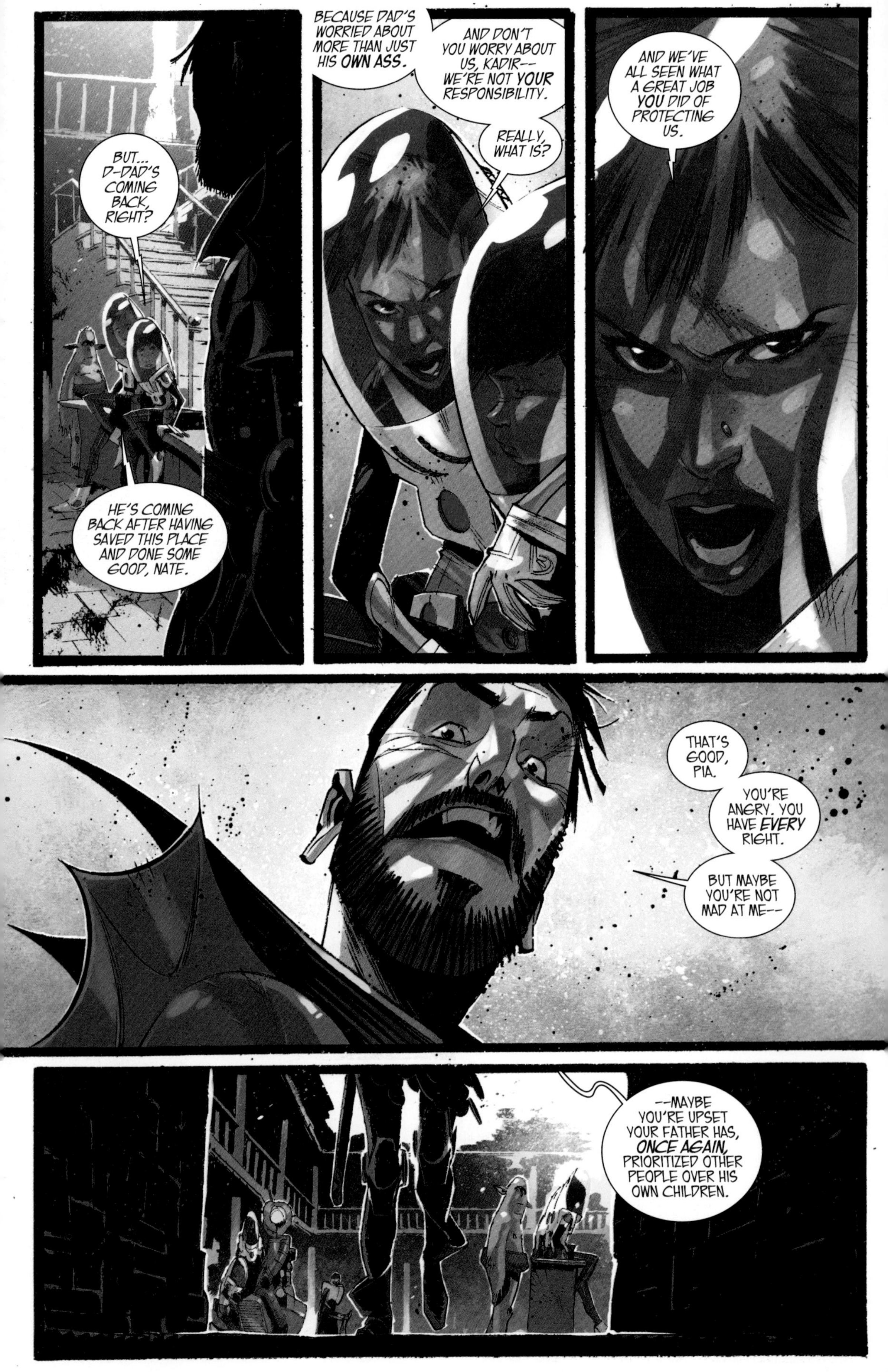
BUT... D-DAD'S COMING BACK, RIGHT?
HE'S COMING BACK AFTER HAVING SAVED THIS PLACE AND DONE SOME GOOD, NATE.
BECAUSE DAD'S WORRIED ABOUT MORE THAN JUST HIS OWN ASS.
AND DON'T YOU WORRY ABOUT US, KADIR-- WE'RE NOT YOUR RESPONSIBILITY.
REALLY, WHAT IS?
AND WE'VE ALL SEEN WHAT A GREAT JOB YOU DID OF PROTECTING US.
THAT'S GOOD, PIA.
YOU'RE ANGRY. YOU HAVE EVERY RIGHT.
BUT MAYBE YOU'RE NOT MAD AT ME--
--MAYBE YOU'RE UPSET YOUR FATHER HAS, ONCE AGAIN, PRIORITIZED OTHER PEOPLE OVER HIS OWN CHILDREN.

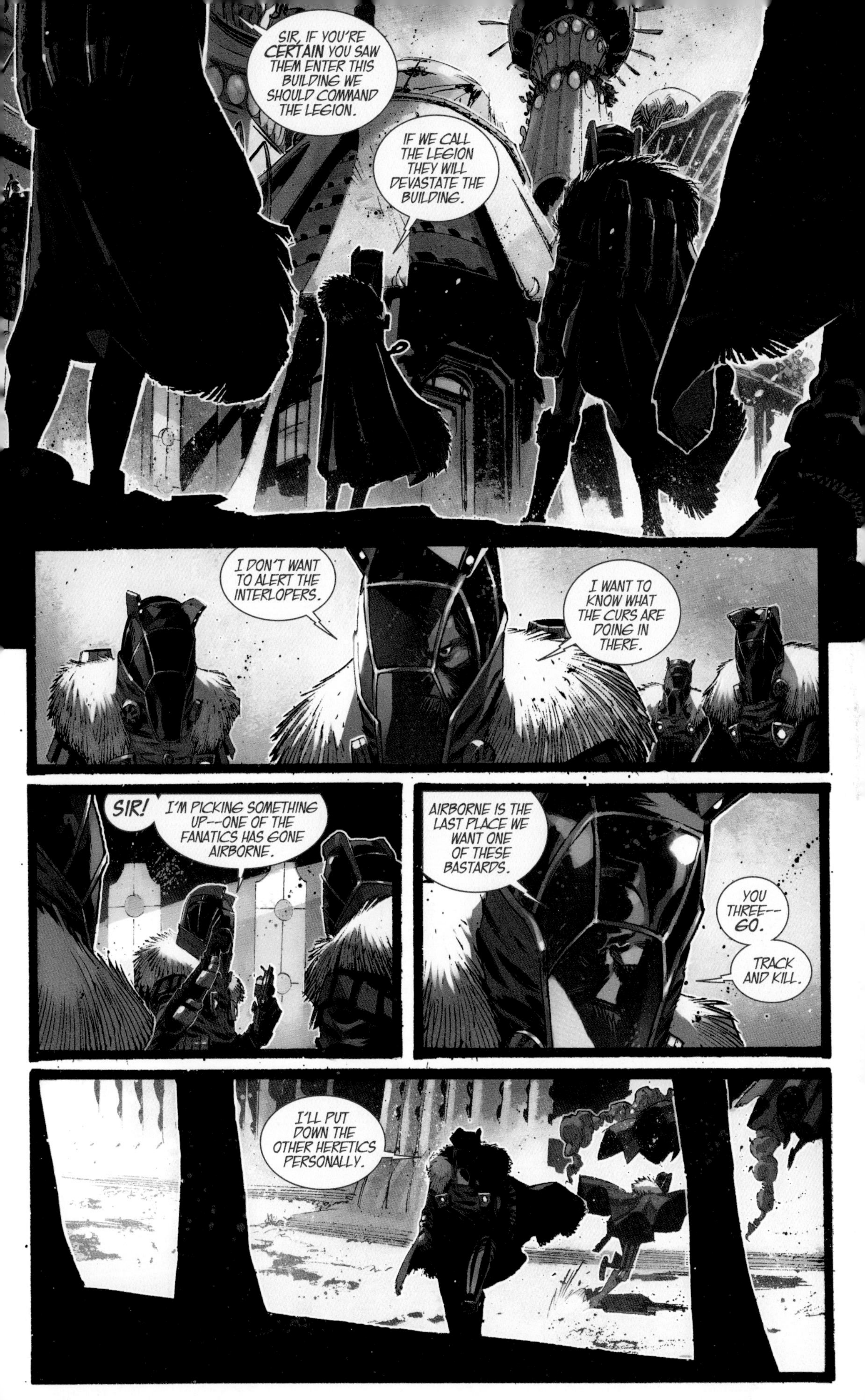
SIR, IF YOU'RE CERTAIN YOU SAW THEM ENTER THIS BUILDING WE SHOULD COMMAND THE LEGION.
IF WE CALL THE LEGION THEY WILL DEVASTATE THE BUILDING.
I DON'T WANT TO ALERT THE INTERLOPERS.
I WANT TO KNOW WHAT THE CURS ARE DOING IN THERE.
SIR!
I'M PICKING SOMETHING UP--ONE OF THE FANATICS HAS GONE AIRBORNE.
AIRBORNE IS THE LAST PLACE WE WANT ONE OF THESE BASTARDS.
YOU THREE--GO.
TRACK AND KILL.
I'LL PUT DOWN THE OTHER HERETICS PERSONALLY.

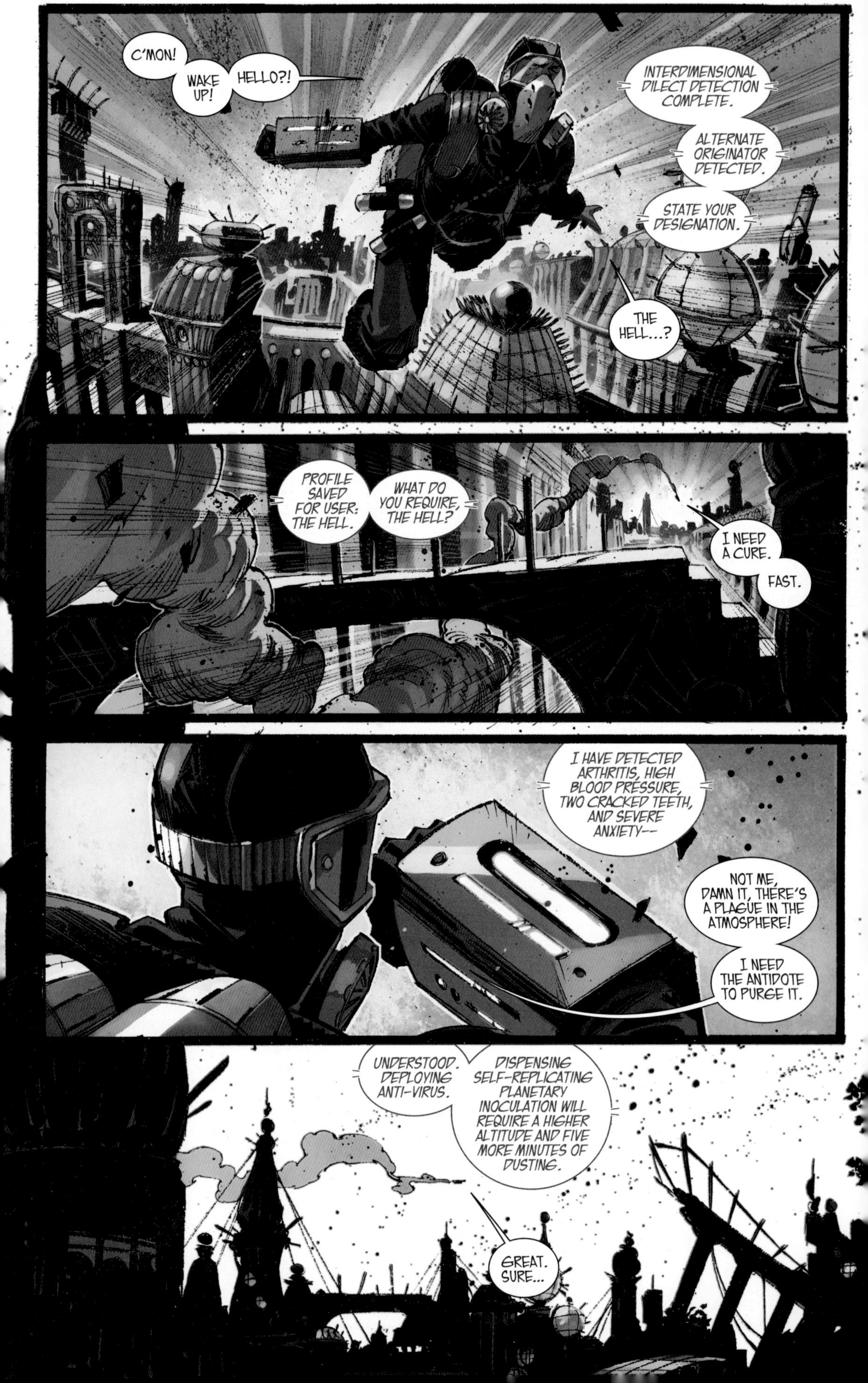
C'MON!
WAKE UP!
HELLO?!
INTERDIMENSIONAL DILECT DETECTION COMPLETE.
ALTERNATE ORIGINATOR DETECTED.
STATE YOUR DESIGNATION.
THE HELL...?
PROFILE SAVED FOR USER: THE HELL.
WHAT DO YOU REQUIRE, THE HELL?
I NEED A CURE.
FAST.
I HAVE DETECTED ARTHRITIS, HIGH BLOOD PRESSURE, TWO CRACKED TEETH, AND SEVERE ANXIETY--
NOT ME, DAMN IT, THERE'S A PLAGUE IN THE ATMOSPHERE!
I NEED THE ANTIDOTE TO PURGE IT.
UNDERSTOOD. DEPLOYING ANTI-VIRUS.
DISPENSING SELF-REPLICATING PLANETARY INOCULATION WILL REQUIRE A HIGHER ALTITUDE AND FIVE MORE MINUTES OF DUSTING.
GREAT. SURE...

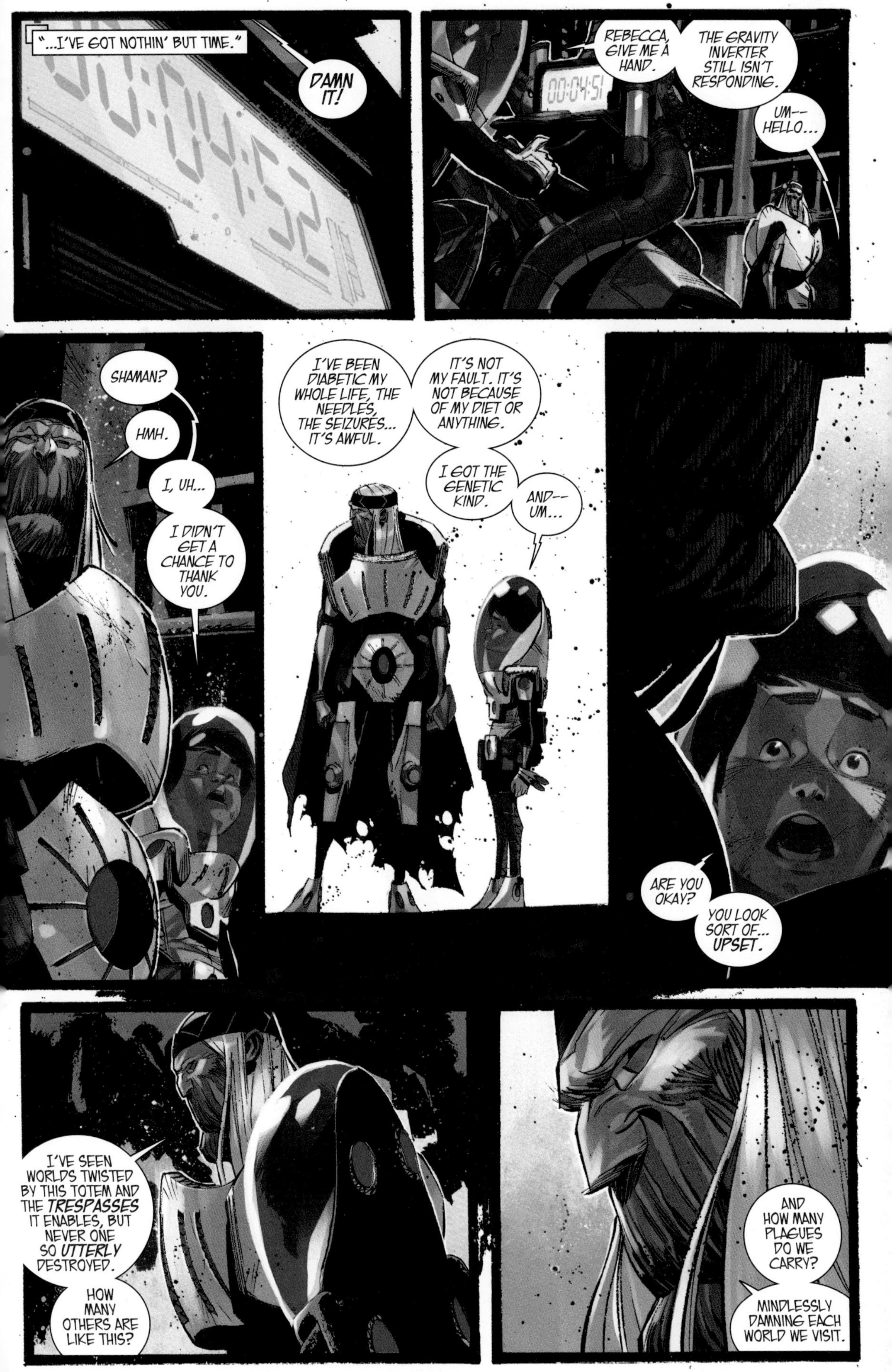
"...I'VE GOT NOTHIN' BUT TIME."
DAMN IT!
00:04:51
REBECCA, GIVE ME A HAND.
THE GRAVITY INVERTER STILL ISN'T RESPONDING.
UM-- HELLO...
SHAMAN?
HMH.
I, UH...
I DIDN'T GET A CHANCE TO THANK YOU.
I'VE BEEN DIABETIC MY WHOLE LIFE, THE NEEDLES, THE SEIZURES... IT'S AWFUL.
IT'S NOT MY FAULT. IT'S NOT BECAUSE OF MY DIET OR ANYTHING.
I GOT THE GENETIC KIND.
AND-- UM...
ARE YOU OKAY?
YOU LOOK SORT OF... UPSET.
I'VE SEEN WORLDS TWISTED BY THIS TOTEM AND THE TRESPASSES IT ENABLES, BUT NEVER ONE SO UTTERLY DESTROYED.
HOW MANY OTHERS ARE LIKE THIS?
AND HOW MANY PLAGUES DO WE CARRY?
MINDLESSLY DAMNING EACH WORLD WE VISIT.

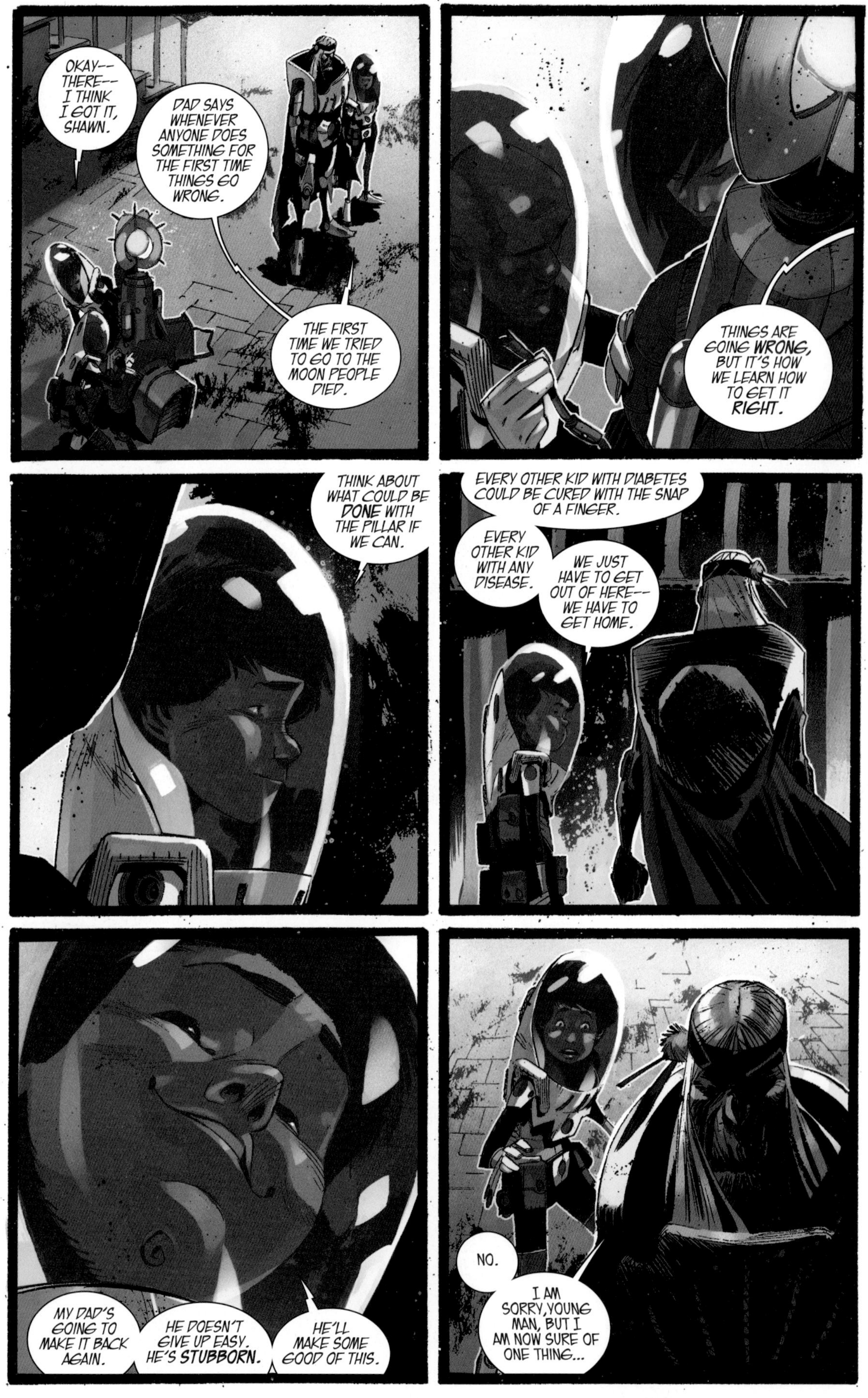
OKAY-- THERE-- I THINK I GOT IT, SHAWN.
DAD SAYS WHENEVER ANYONE DOES SOMETHING FOR THE FIRST TIME THINGS GO WRONG.
THE FIRST TIME WE TRIED TO GO TO THE MOON PEOPLE DIED.
THINGS ARE GOING WRONG, BUT IT'S HOW WE LEARN HOW TO GET IT RIGHT.
THINK ABOUT WHAT COULD BE DONE WITH THE PILLAR IF WE CAN.
EVERY OTHER KID WITH DIABETES COULD BE CURED WITH THE SNAP OF A FINGER.
EVERY OTHER KID WITH ANY DISEASE.
WE JUST HAVE TO GET OUT OF HERE-- WE HAVE TO GET HOME.
MY DAD'S GOING TO MAKE IT BACK AGAIN.
HE DOESN'T GIVE UP EASY. HE'S STUBBORN.
HE'LL MAKE SOME GOOD OF THIS.
NO.
I AM SORRY, YOUNG MAN, BUT I AM NOW SURE OF ONE THING...

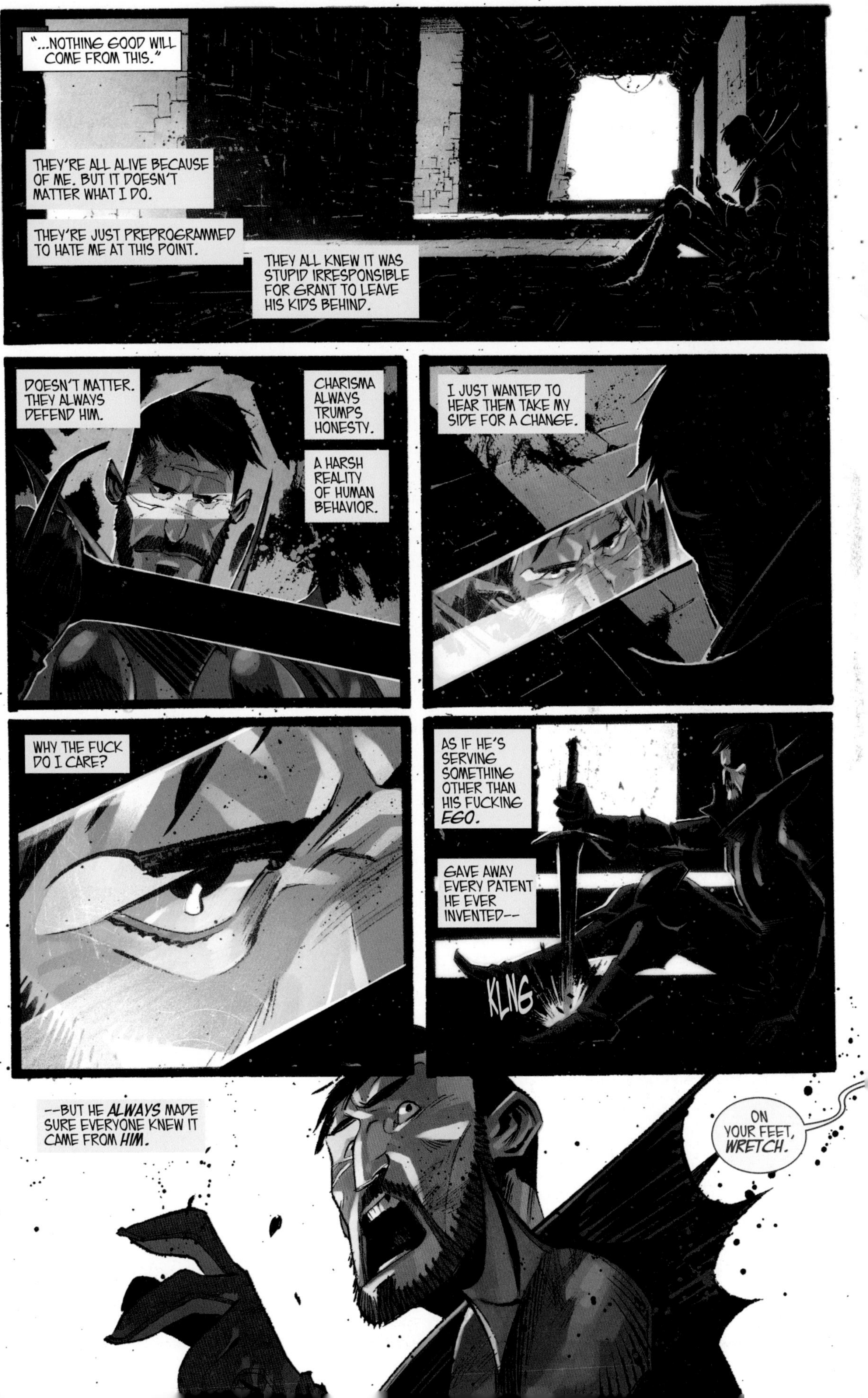
"...NOTHING GOOD WILL COME FROM THIS."
THEY'RE ALL ALIVE BECAUSE OF ME. BUT IT DOESN'T MATTER WHAT I DO.
THEY'RE JUST PREPROGRAMMED TO HATE ME AT THIS POINT.
THEY ALL KNEW IT WAS STUPID IRRESPONSIBLE FOR GRANT TO LEAVE HIS KIDS BEHIND.
DOESN'T MATTER. THEY ALWAYS DEFEND HIM.
CHARISMA ALWAYS TRUMPS HONESTY.
A HARSH REALITY OF HUMAN BEHAVIOR.
I JUST WANTED TO HEAR THEM TAKE MY SIDE FOR A CHANGE.
WHY THE FUCK DO I CARE?
AS IF HE'S SERVING SOMETHING OTHER THAN HIS FUCKING *EGO*.
GAVE AWAY EVERY PATENT HE EVER INVENTED--
KLNG
--BUT HE *ALWAYS* MADE SURE EVERYONE KNEW IT CAME FROM *HIM*.
ON YOUR FEET, *WRETCH*.

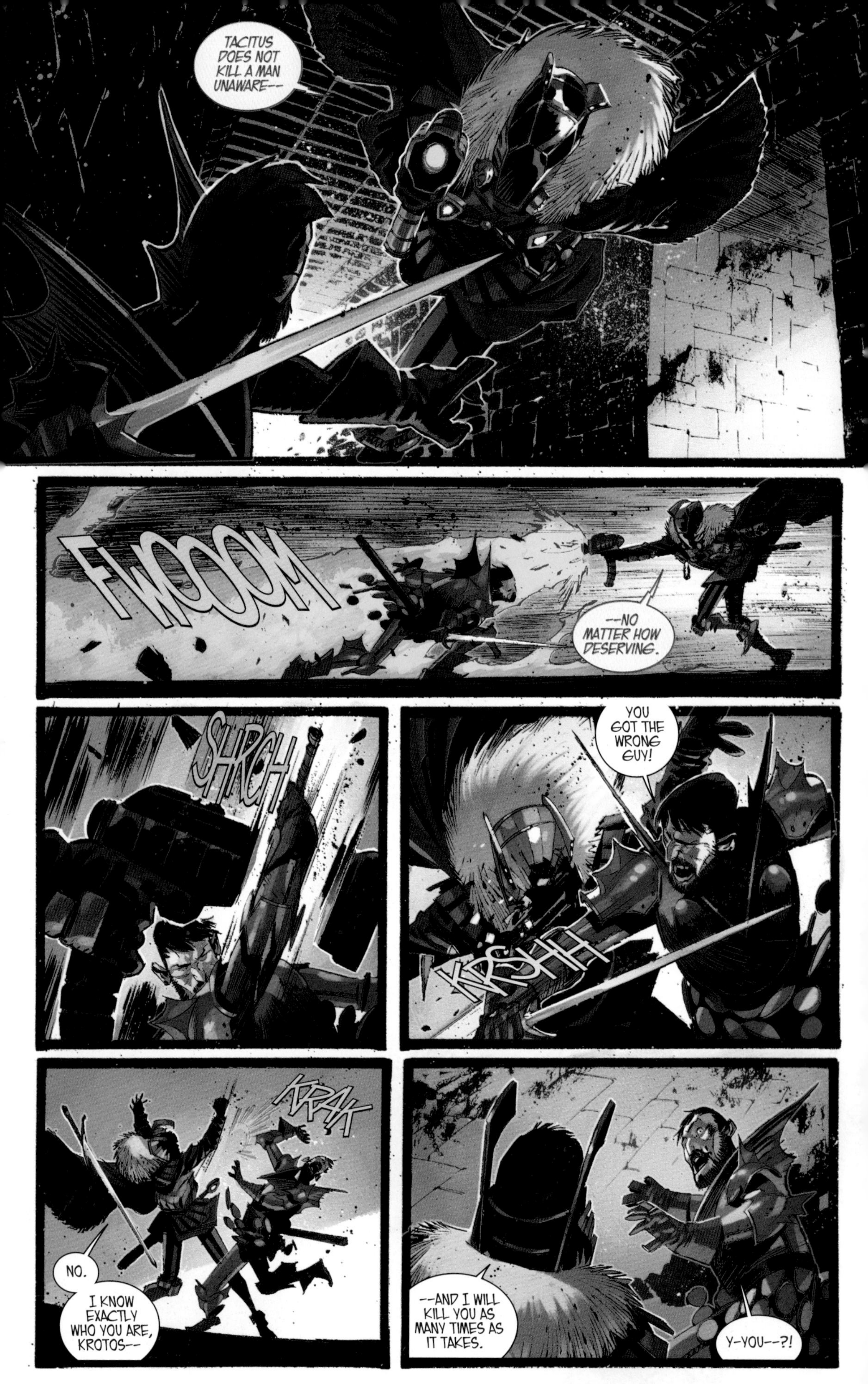
TACITUS DOES NOT KILL A MAN UNAWARE--
FWOOOM
--NO MATTER HOW DESERVING.
SHRCH
YOU GOT THE WRONG GUY!
KRSHH
KRAK
NO.
I KNOW EXACTLY WHO YOU ARE, KROTOS--
--AND I WILL KILL YOU AS MANY TIMES AS IT TAKES.
Y-YOU--?!

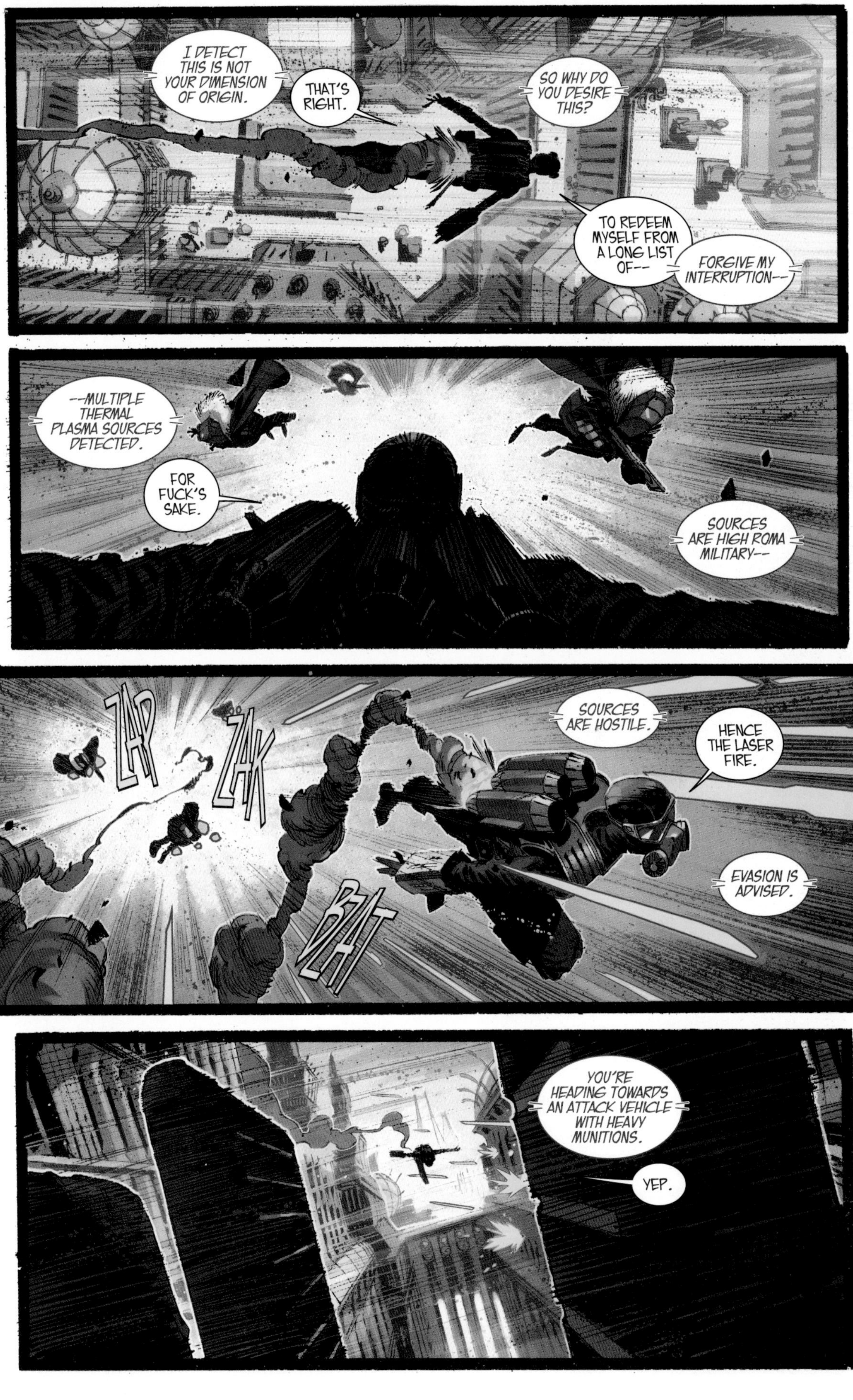
I DETECT THIS IS NOT YOUR DIMENSION OF ORIGIN.
THAT'S RIGHT.
SO WHY DO YOU DESIRE THIS?
TO REDEEM MYSELF FROM A LONG LIST OF--
FORGIVE MY INTERRUPTION--
--MULTIPLE THERMAL PLASMA SOURCES DETECTED.
FOR FUCK'S SAKE.
SOURCES ARE HIGH ROMA MILITARY--
ZAP
ZAK
SOURCES ARE HOSTILE.
HENCE THE LASER FIRE.
EVASION IS ADVISED.
BZAT
YOU'RE HEADING TOWARDS AN ATTACK VEHICLE WITH HEAVY MUNITIONS.
YEP.

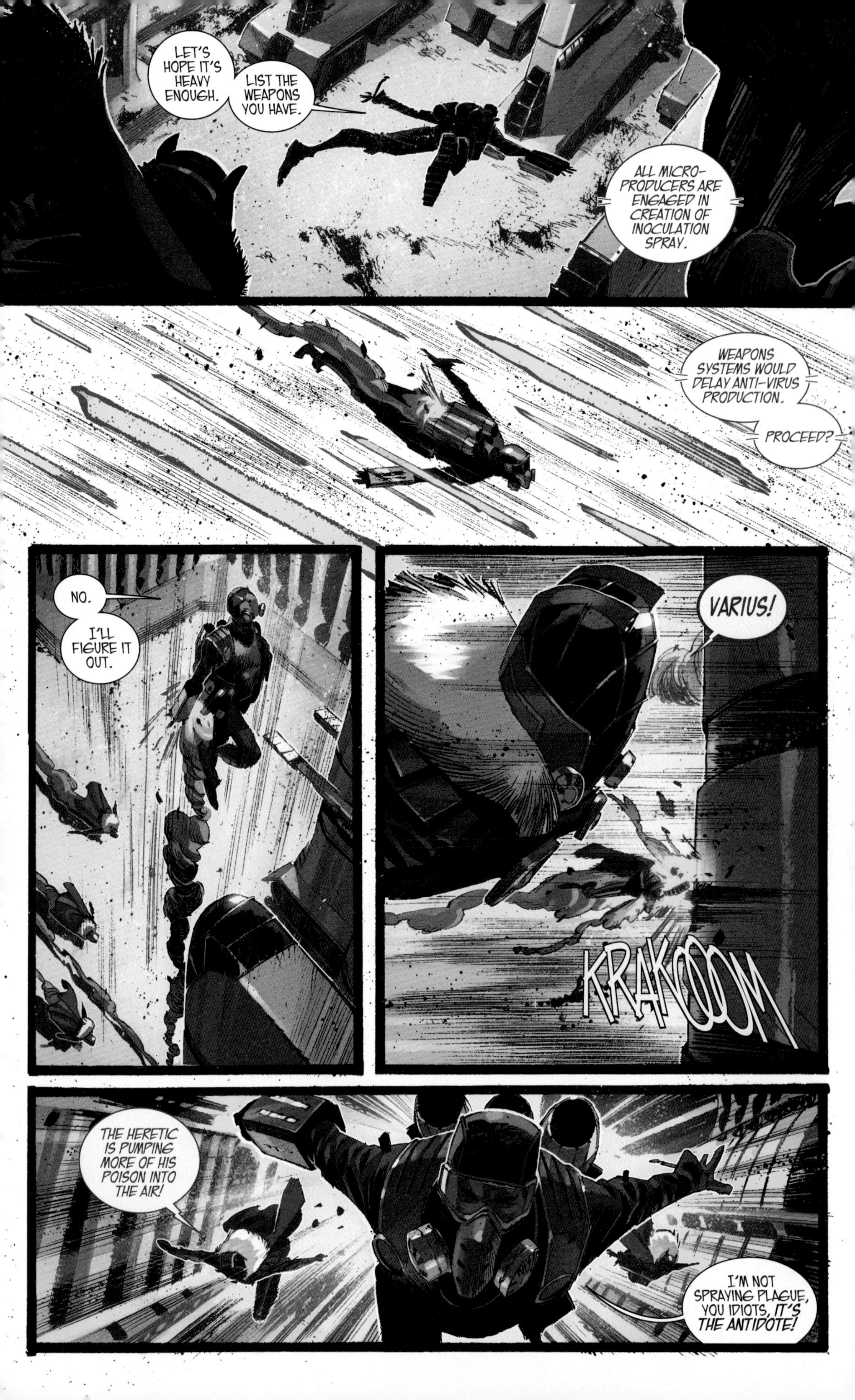
LET'S HOPE IT'S HEAVY ENOUGH.
LIST THE WEAPONS YOU HAVE.
ALL MICRO-PRODUCERS ARE ENGAGED IN CREATION OF INOCULATION SPRAY.
WEAPONS SYSTEMS WOULD DELAY ANTI-VIRUS PRODUCTION.
PROCEED?
NO.
I'LL FIGURE IT OUT.
VARIUS!
KRAKOOOM
THE HERETIC IS PUMPING MORE OF HIS POISON INTO THE AIR!
I'M NOT SPRAYING PLAGUE, YOU IDIOTS, IT'S THE ANTIDOTE!

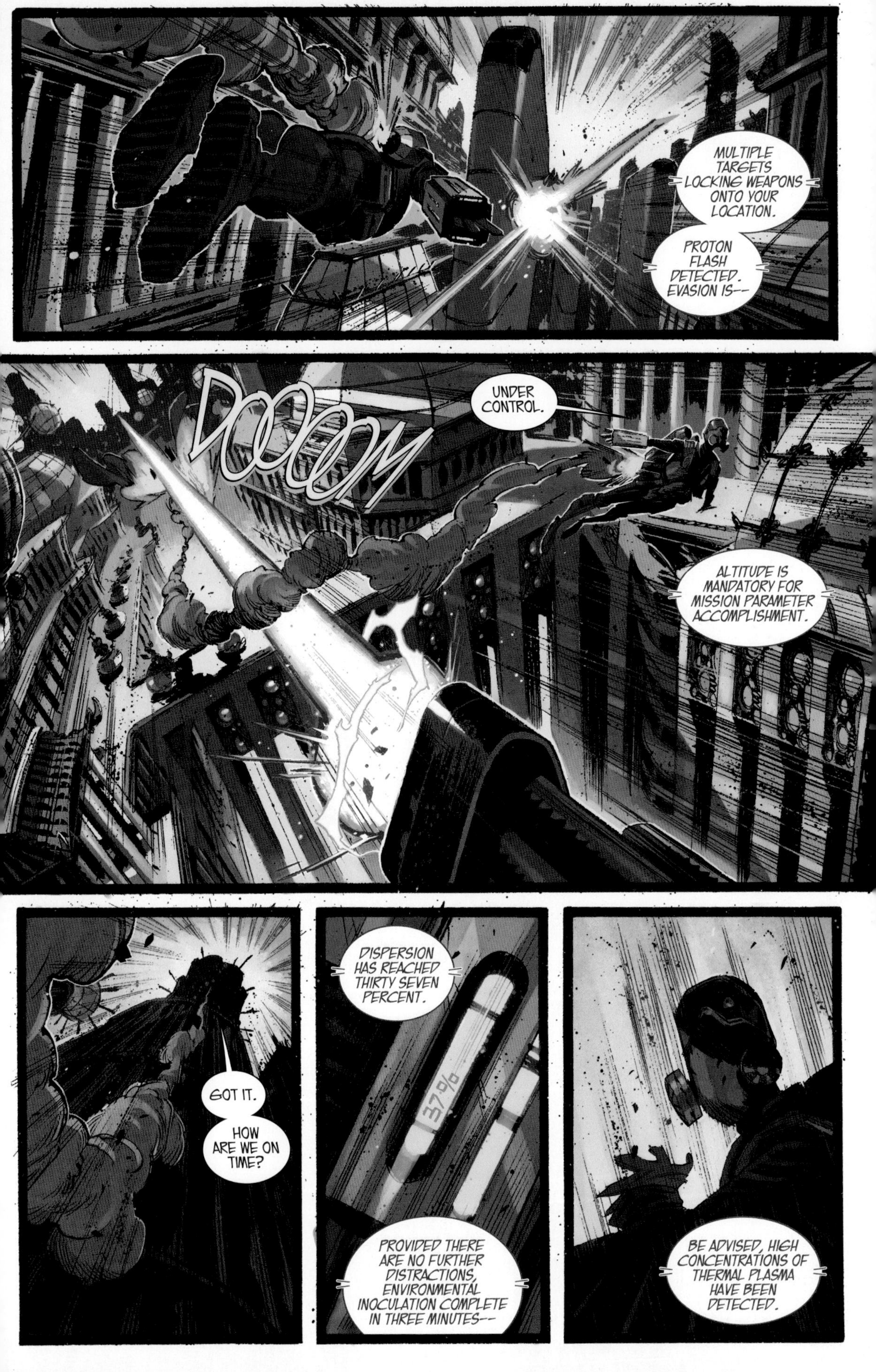
MULTIPLE TARGETS LOCKING WEAPONS ONTO YOUR LOCATION.
PROTON FLASH DETECTED. EVASION IS--
DOOOOOM
UNDER CONTROL.
ALTITUDE IS MANDATORY FOR MISSION PARAMETER ACCOMPLISHMENT.
GOT IT.
HOW ARE WE ON TIME?
DISPERSION HAS REACHED THIRTY SEVEN PERCENT.
37%
PROVIDED THERE ARE NO FURTHER DISTRACTIONS, ENVIRONMENTAL INOCULATION COMPLETE IN THREE MINUTES--
BE ADVISED, HIGH CONCENTRATIONS OF THERMAL PLASMA HAVE BEEN DETECTED.

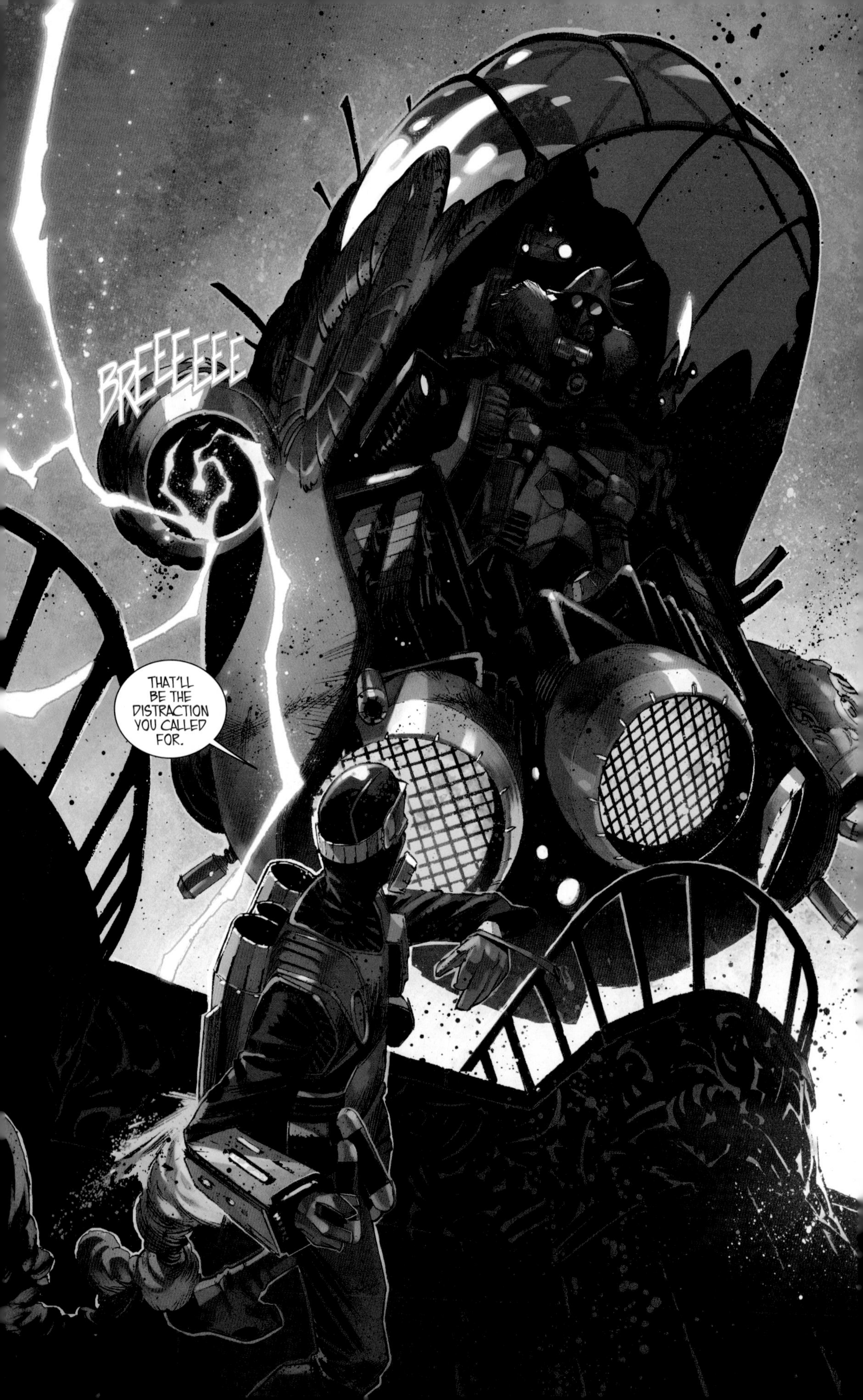
BREEEEEE
THAT'LL BE THE DISTRACTION YOU CALLED FOR.

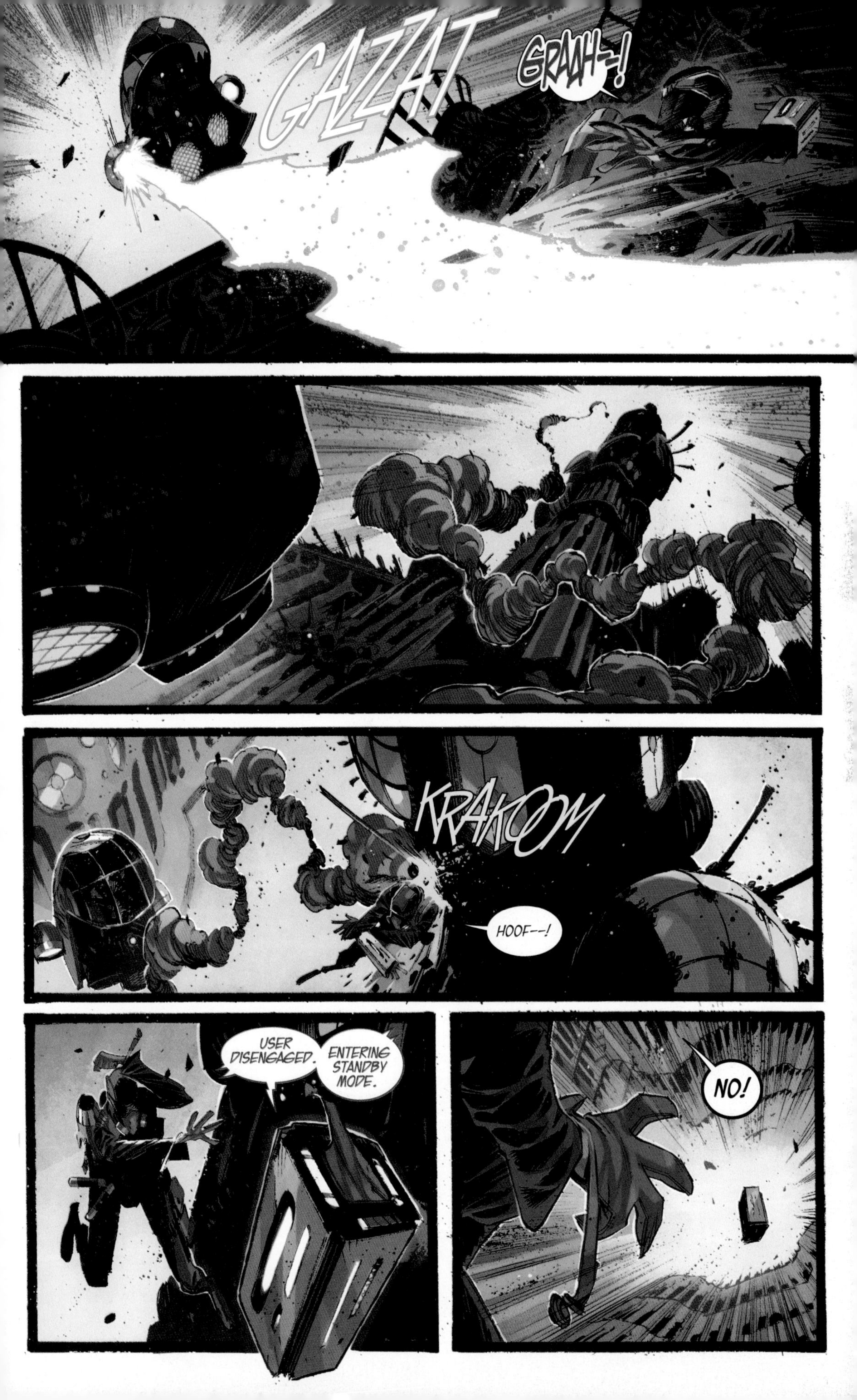
GAZZAT
GRAAH--!
KRAKOOM
HOOF--!
USER DISENGAGED.
ENTERING STANDBY MODE.
NO!

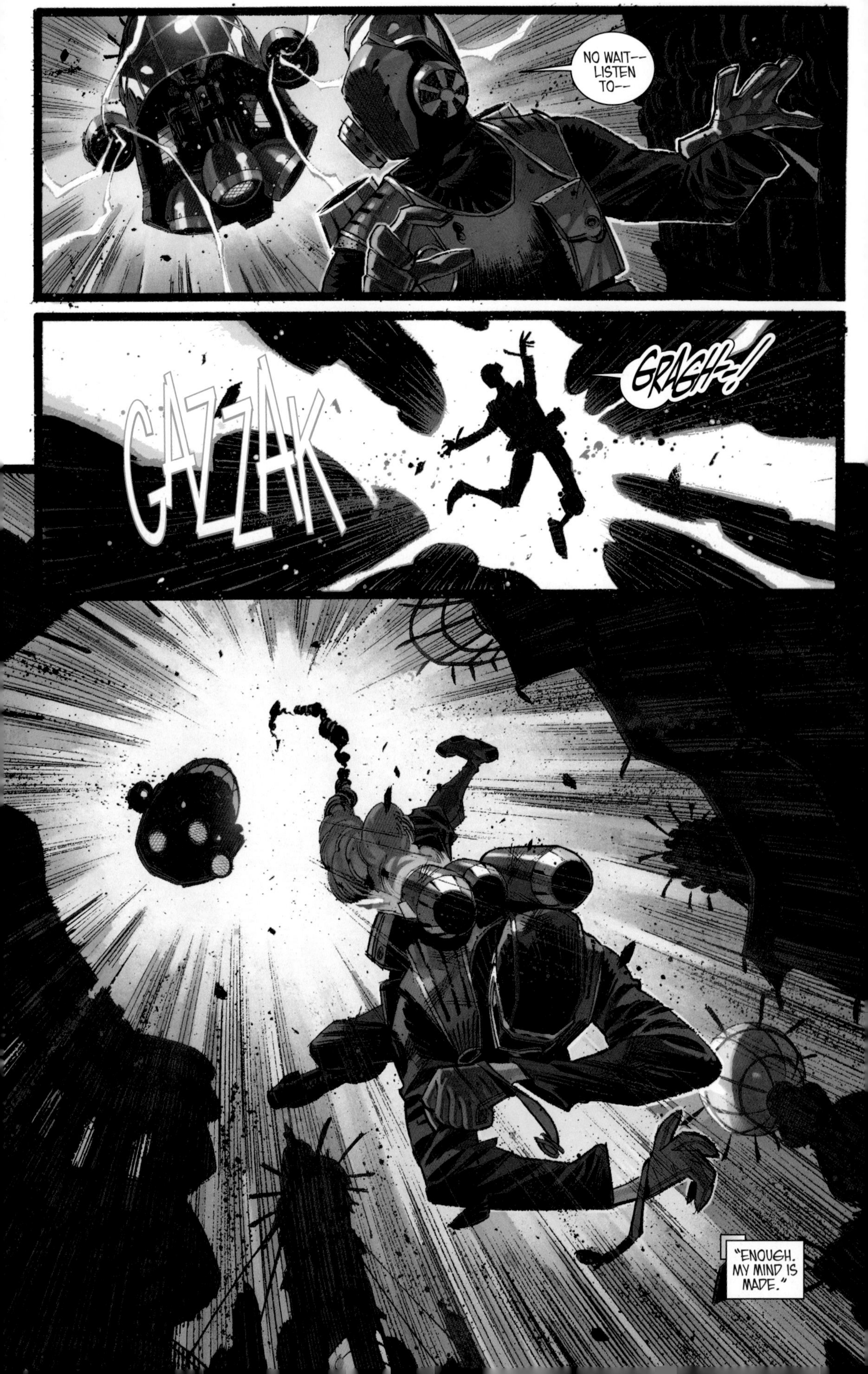
NO WAIT--
LISTEN
TO--
GAZZAK
GRASH--!
"ENOUGH.
MY MIND IS
MADE."

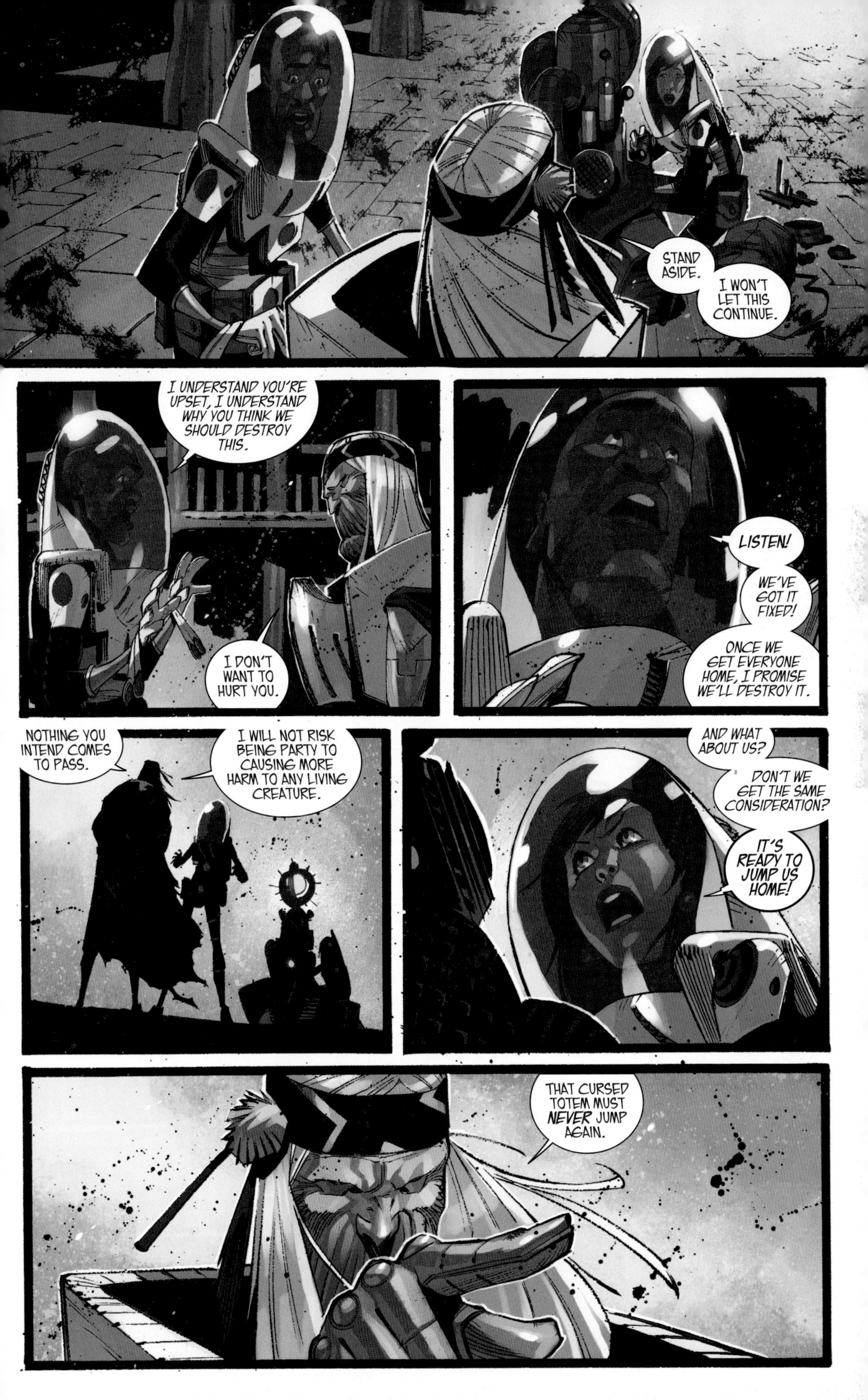
STAND ASIDE.
I WON'T LET THIS CONTINUE.
I UNDERSTAND YOU'RE UPSET, I UNDERSTAND WHY YOU THINK WE SHOULD DESTROY THIS.
I DON'T WANT TO HURT YOU.
LISTEN!
WE'VE GOT IT FIXED!
ONCE WE GET EVERYONE HOME, I PROMISE WE'LL DESTROY IT.
NOTHING YOU INTEND COMES TO PASS.
I WILL NOT RISK BEING PARTY TO CAUSING MORE HARM TO ANY LIVING CREATURE.
AND WHAT ABOUT US?
DON'T WE GET THE SAME CONSIDERATION?
IT'S READY TO JUMP US HOME!
THAT CURSED TOTEM MUST *NEVER* JUMP AGAIN.

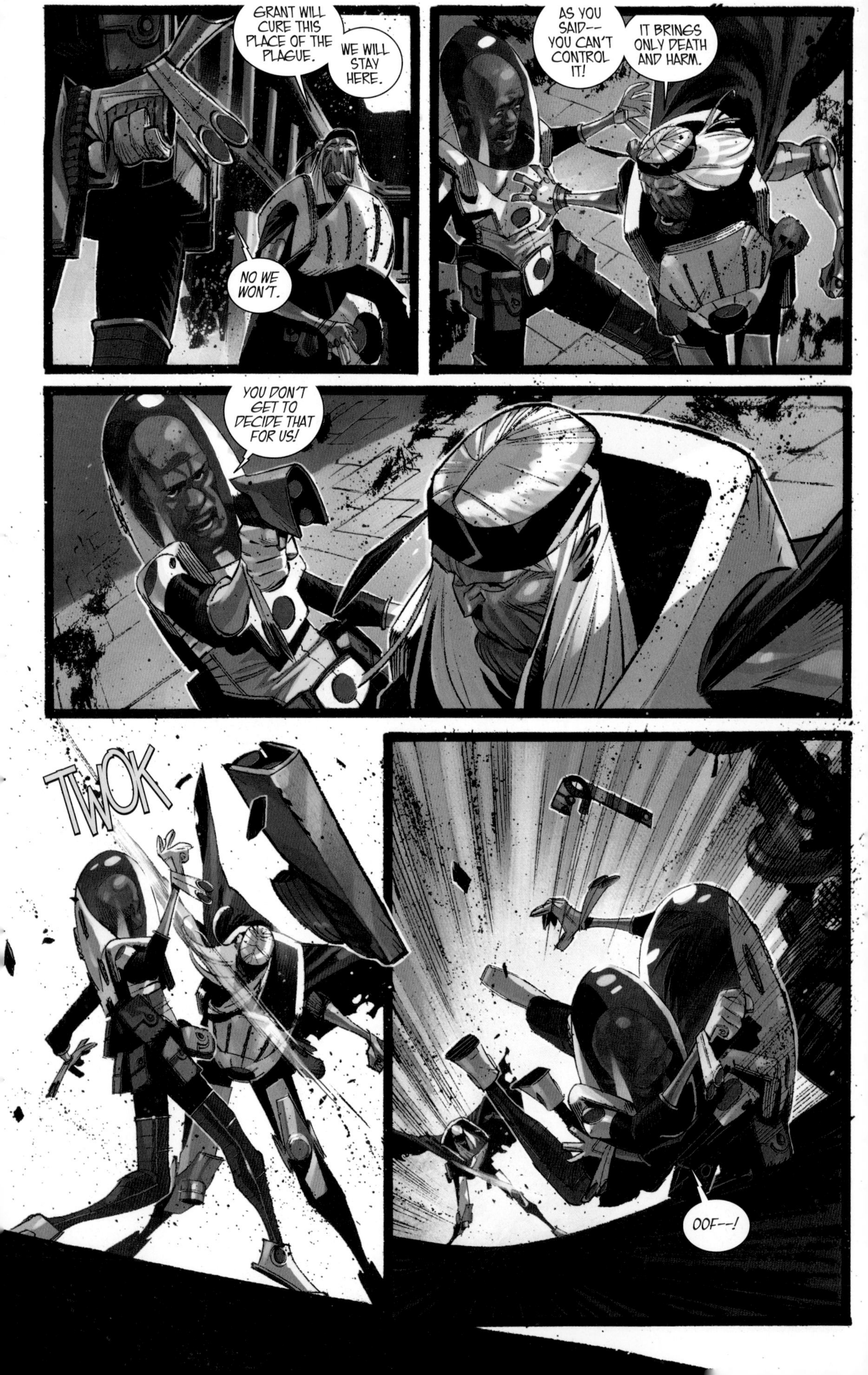
GRANT WILL CURE THIS PLACE OF THE PLAGUE.
WE WILL STAY HERE.
NO WE WON'T.
AS YOU SAID-- YOU CAN'T CONTROL IT!
IT BRINGS ONLY DEATH AND HARM.
YOU DON'T GET TO DECIDE THAT FOR US!
TWOK
OOF--!

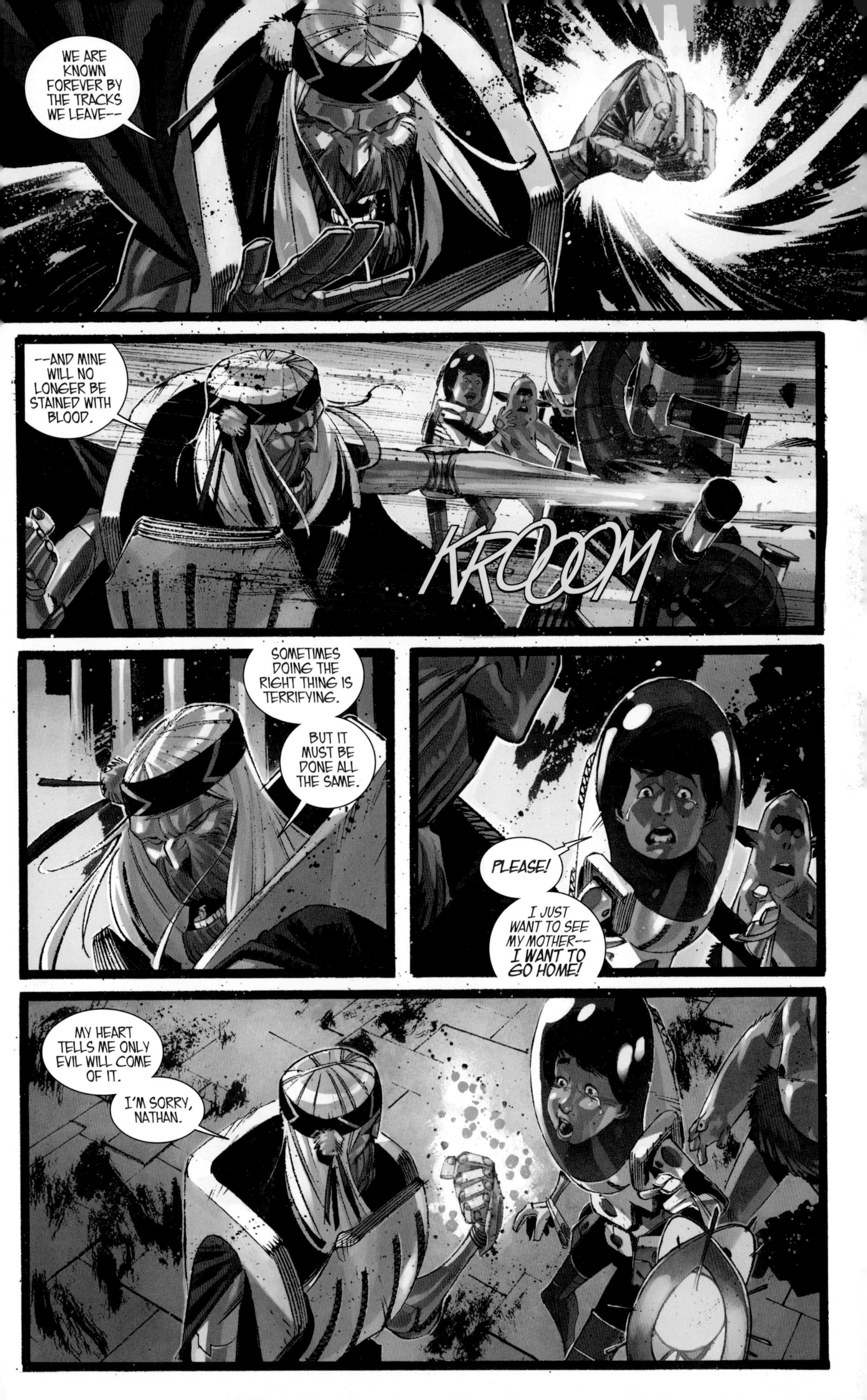
WE ARE KNOWN FOREVER BY THE TRACKS WE LEAVE--
--AND MINE WILL NO LONGER BE STAINED WITH BLOOD.
KROOOM
SOMETIMES DOING THE RIGHT THING IS TERRIFYING.
BUT IT MUST BE DONE ALL THE SAME.
PLEASE!
I JUST WANT TO SEE MY MOTHER-- I WANT TO GO HOME!
MY HEART TELLS ME ONLY EVIL WILL COME OF IT.
I'M SORRY, NATHAN.

KAZAAT

GURKK––

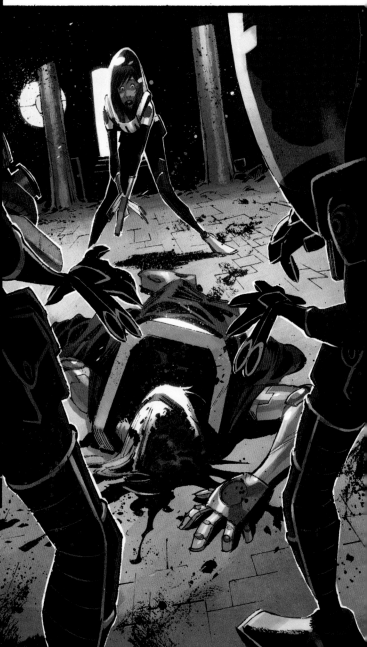

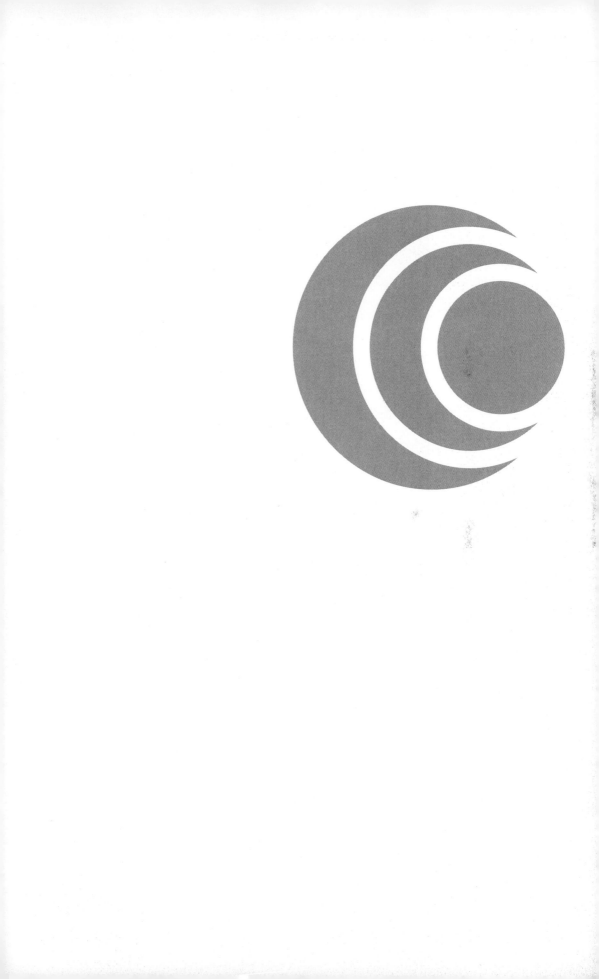

# 16

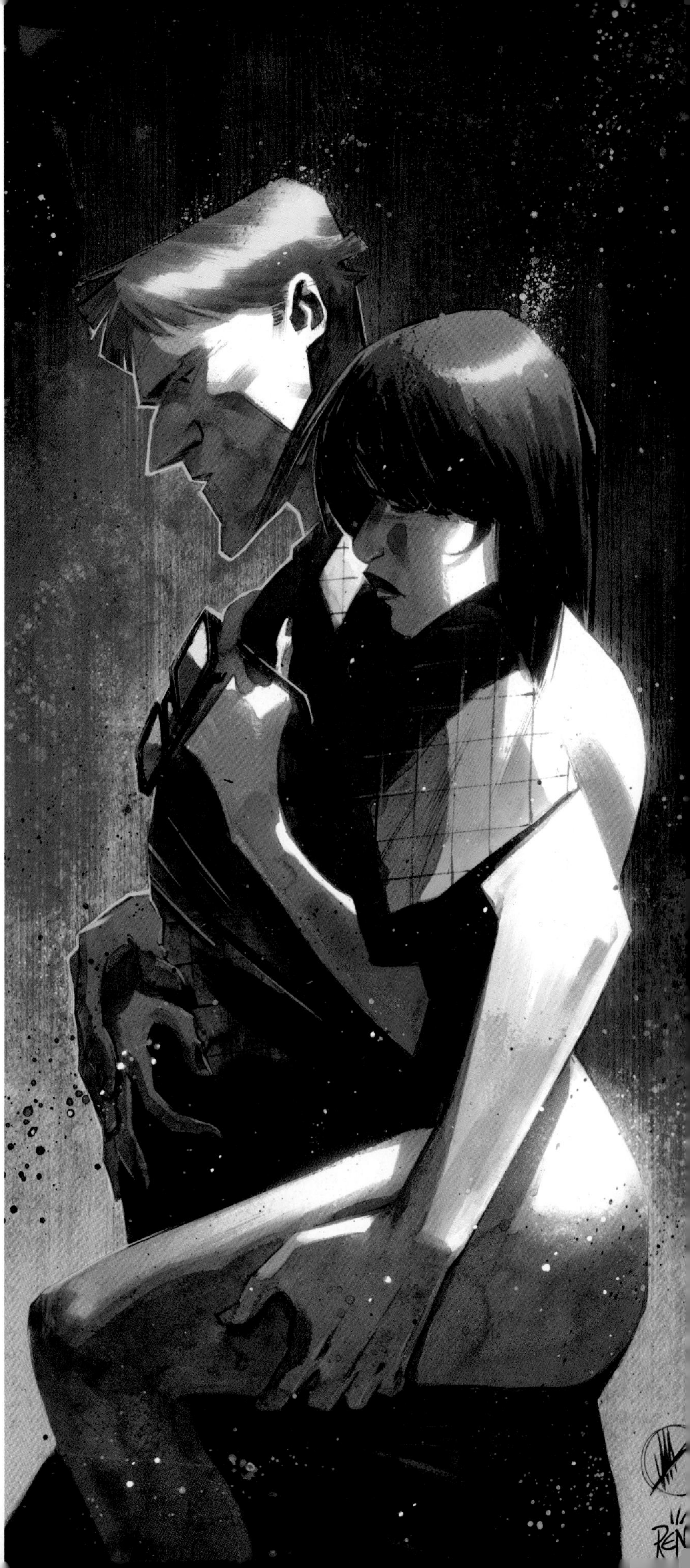

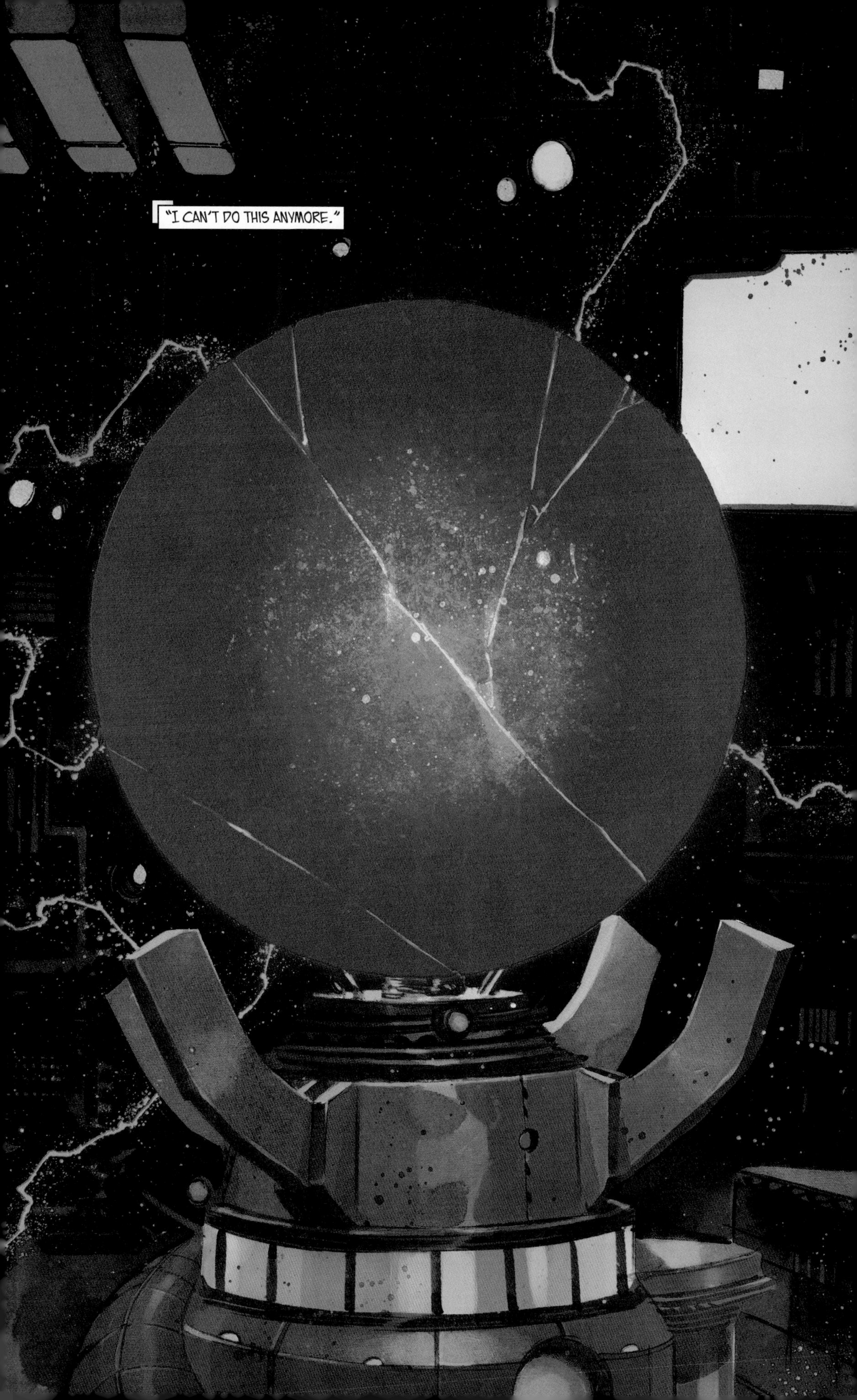
"I CAN'T DO THIS ANYMORE."

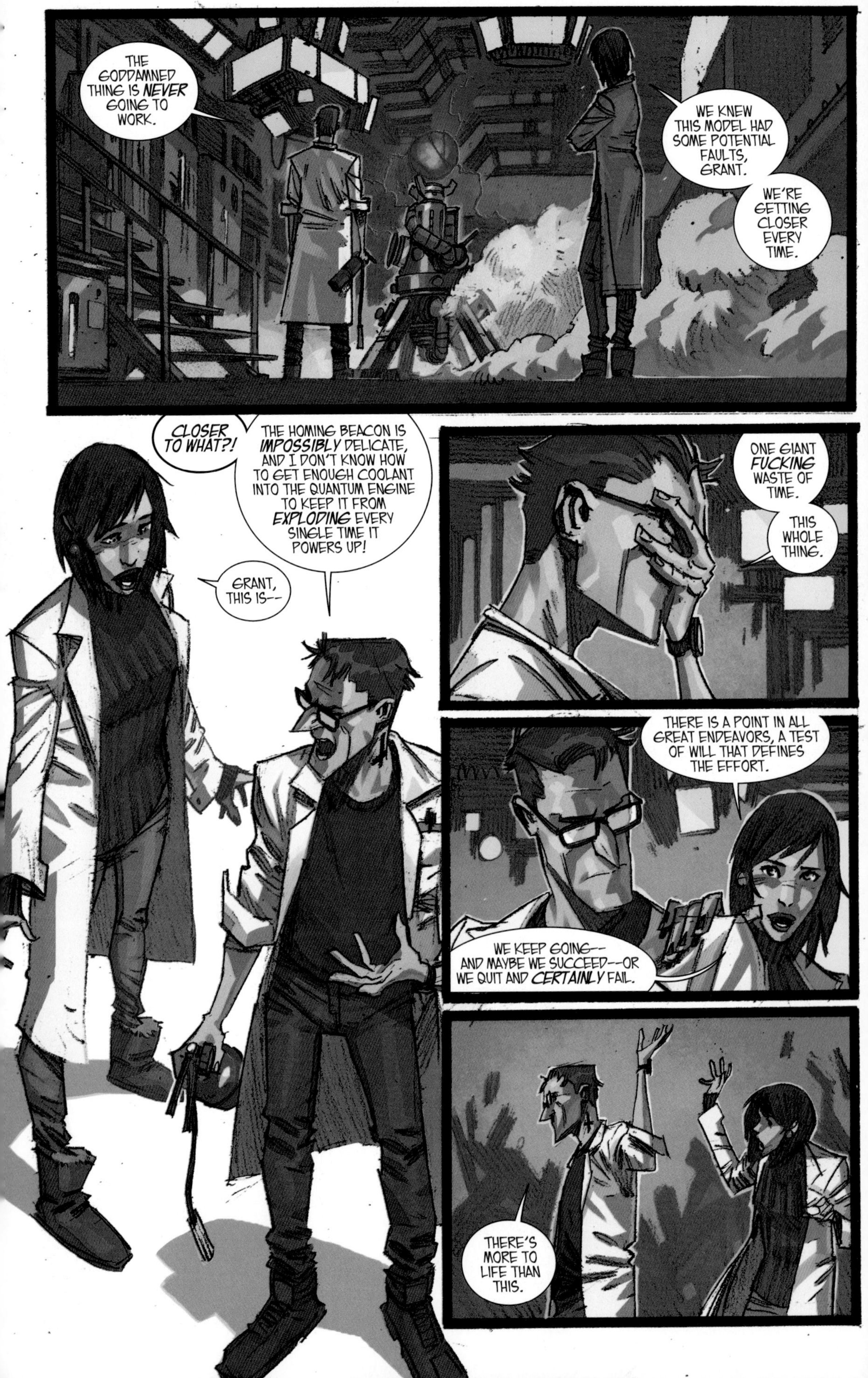
THE GODDAMNED THING IS NEVER GOING TO WORK.
WE KNEW THIS MODEL HAD SOME POTENTIAL FAULTS, GRANT.
WE'RE GETTING CLOSER EVERY TIME.
CLOSER TO WHAT?!
THE HOMING BEACON IS IMPOSSIBLY DELICATE, AND I DON'T KNOW HOW TO GET ENOUGH COOLANT INTO THE QUANTUM ENGINE TO KEEP IT FROM EXPLODING EVERY SINGLE TIME IT POWERS UP!
GRANT, THIS IS--
ONE GIANT FUCKING WASTE OF TIME.
THIS WHOLE THING.
THERE IS A POINT IN ALL GREAT ENDEAVORS, A TEST OF WILL THAT DEFINES THE EFFORT.
WE KEEP GOING-- AND MAYBE WE SUCCEED--OR WE QUIT AND CERTAINLY FAIL.
THERE'S MORE TO LIFE THAN THIS.

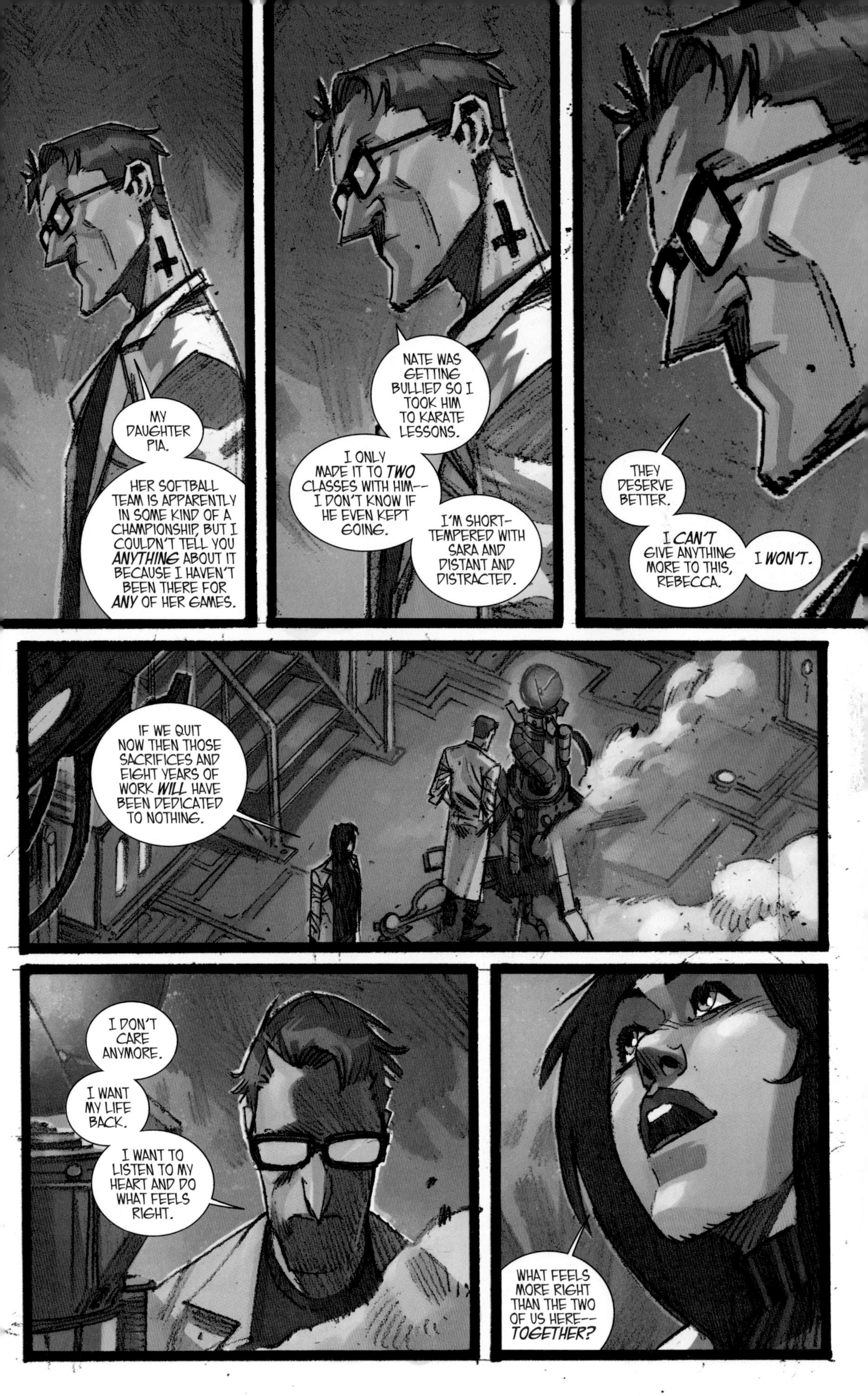
MY DAUGHTER PIA.
HER SOFTBALL TEAM IS APPARENTLY IN SOME KIND OF A CHAMPIONSHIP, BUT I COULDN'T TELL YOU ANYTHING ABOUT IT BECAUSE I HAVEN'T BEEN THERE FOR ANY OF HER GAMES.
NATE WAS GETTING BULLIED SO I TOOK HIM TO KARATE LESSONS.
I ONLY MADE IT TO TWO CLASSES WITH HIM-- I DON'T KNOW IF HE EVEN KEPT GOING.
I'M SHORT-TEMPERED WITH SARA AND DISTANT AND DISTRACTED.
THEY DESERVE BETTER.
I CAN'T GIVE ANYTHING MORE TO THIS, REBECCA.
I WON'T.
IF WE QUIT NOW THEN THOSE SACRIFICES AND EIGHT YEARS OF WORK WILL HAVE BEEN DEDICATED TO NOTHING.
I DON'T CARE ANYMORE.
I WANT MY LIFE BACK.
I WANT TO LISTEN TO MY HEART AND DO WHAT FEELS RIGHT.
WHAT FEELS MORE RIGHT THAN THE TWO OF US HERE-- TOGETHER?

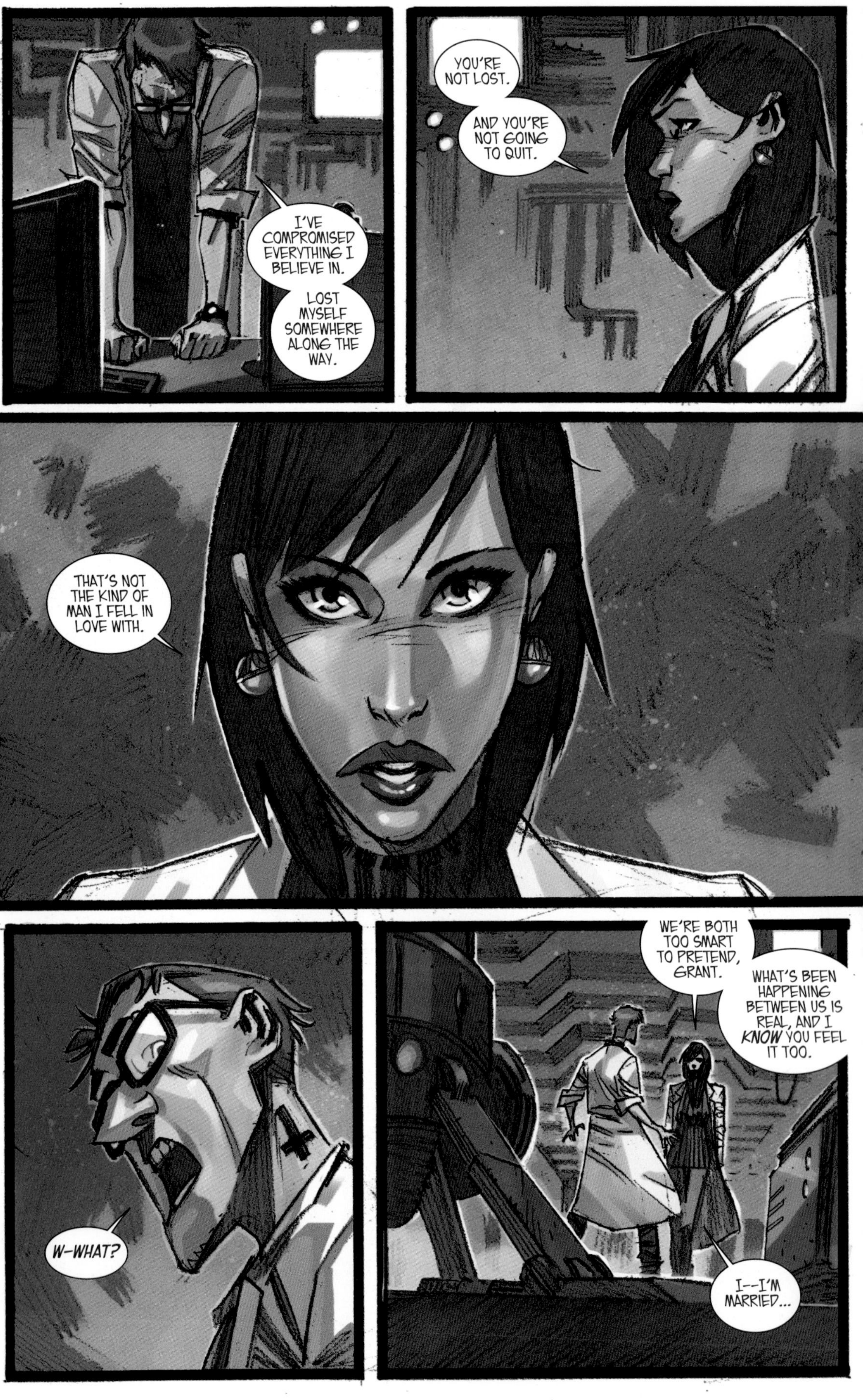
I'VE COMPROMISED EVERYTHING I BELIEVE IN.
LOST MYSELF SOMEWHERE ALONG THE WAY.
YOU'RE NOT LOST.
AND YOU'RE NOT GOING TO QUIT.
THAT'S NOT THE KIND OF MAN I FELL IN LOVE WITH.
W--WHAT?
WE'RE BOTH TOO SMART TO PRETEND, GRANT.
WHAT'S BEEN HAPPENING BETWEEN US IS REAL, AND I *KNOW* YOU FEEL IT TOO.
I--I'M MARRIED...

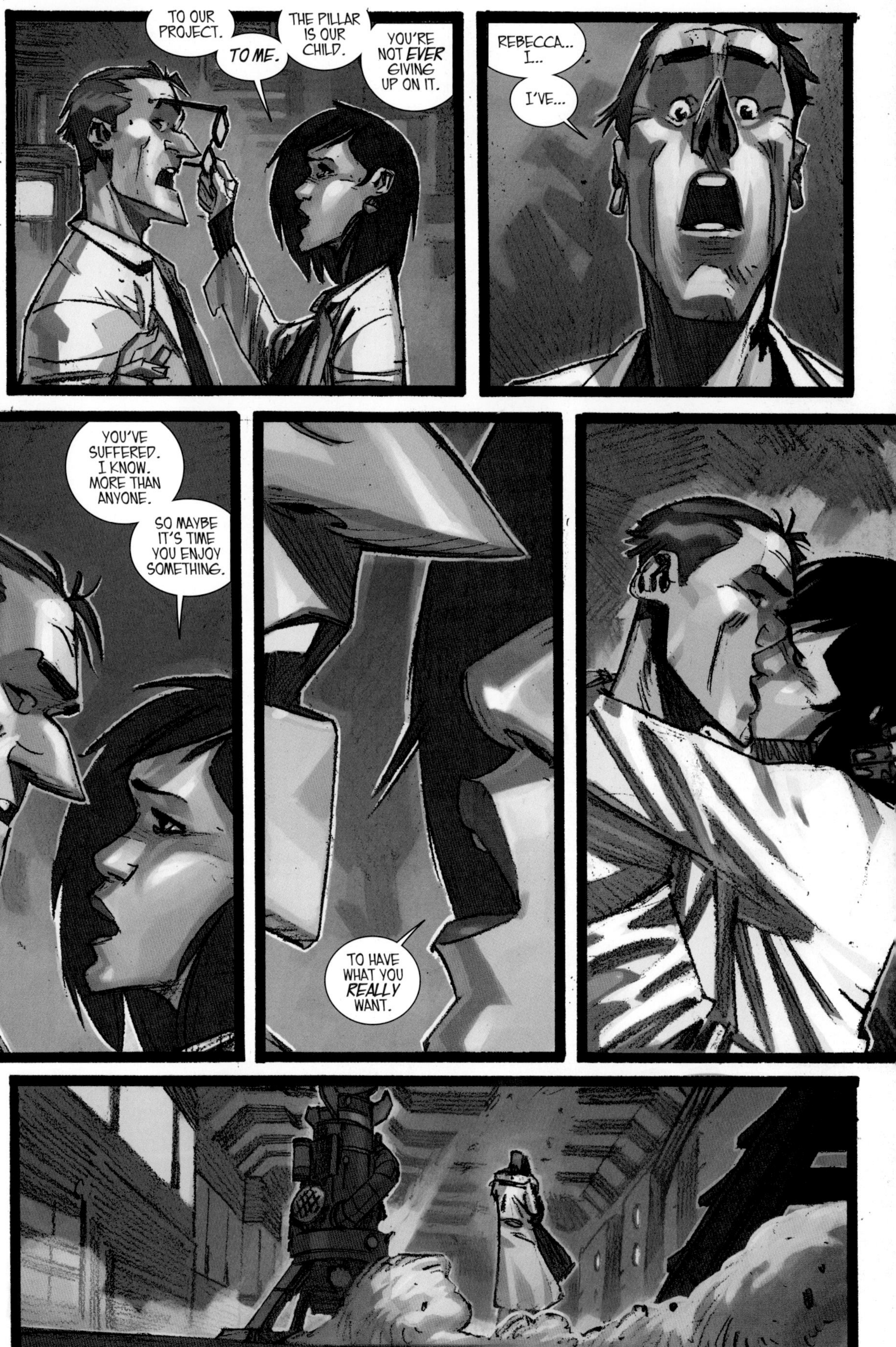

TO OUR PROJECT.
TO ME.
THE PILLAR IS OUR CHILD.
YOU'RE NOT EVER GIVING UP ON IT.
REBECCA... I...
I'VE...
YOU'VE SUFFERED. I KNOW. MORE THAN ANYONE.
SO MAYBE IT'S TIME YOU ENJOY SOMETHING.
TO HAVE WHAT YOU REALLY WANT.

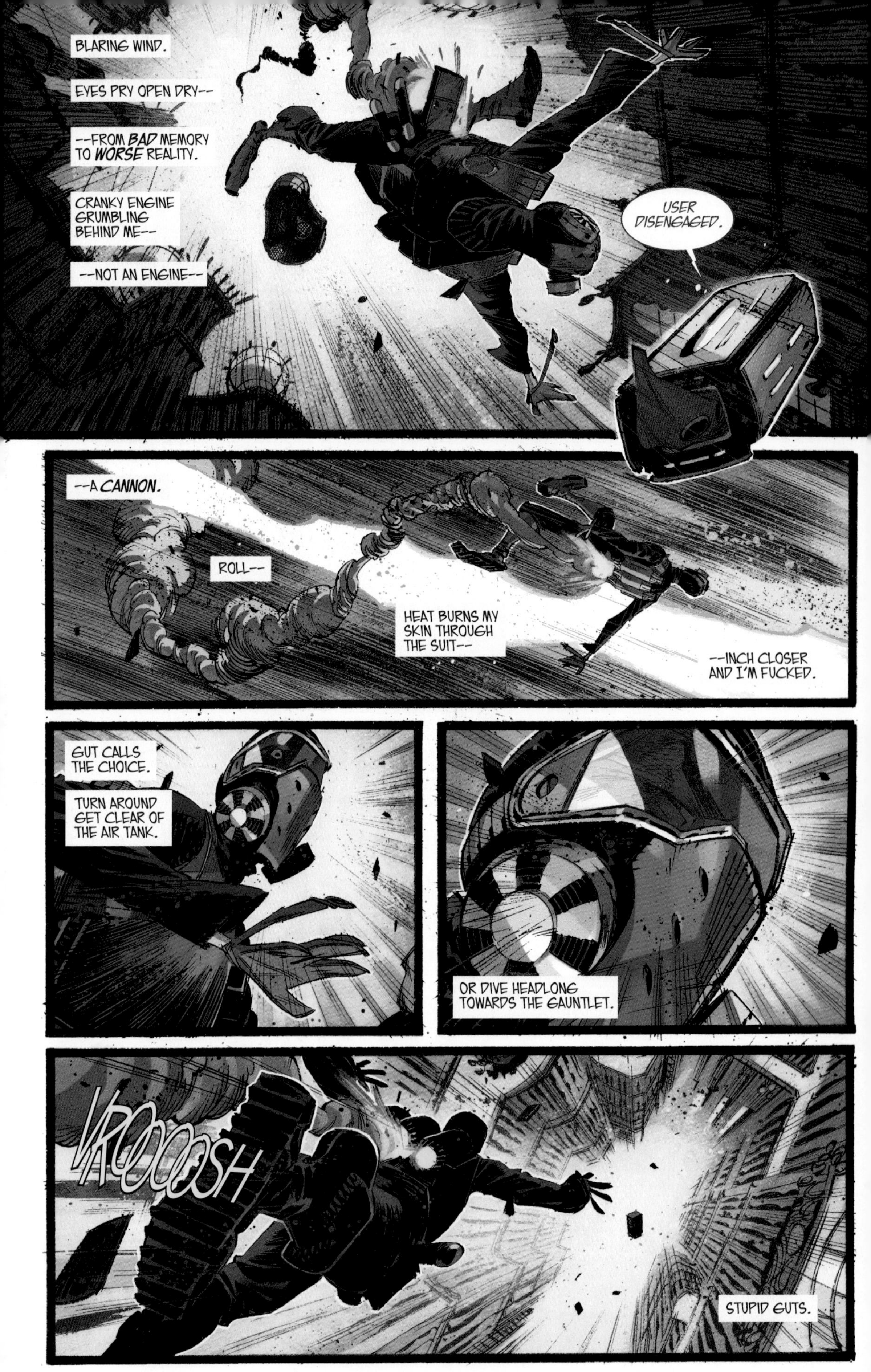
BLARING WIND.
EYES PRY OPEN DRY--
--FROM BAD MEMORY TO WORSE REALITY.
CRANKY ENGINE GRUMBLING BEHIND ME--
--NOT AN ENGINE--
USER DISENGAGED.
--A CANNON.
ROLL--
HEAT BURNS MY SKIN THROUGH THE SUIT--
--INCH CLOSER AND I'M FUCKED.
GUT CALLS THE CHOICE.
TURN AROUND GET CLEAR OF THE AIR TANK.
OR DIVE HEADLONG TOWARDS THE GAUNTLET.
VROOOOSH
STUPID GUTS.

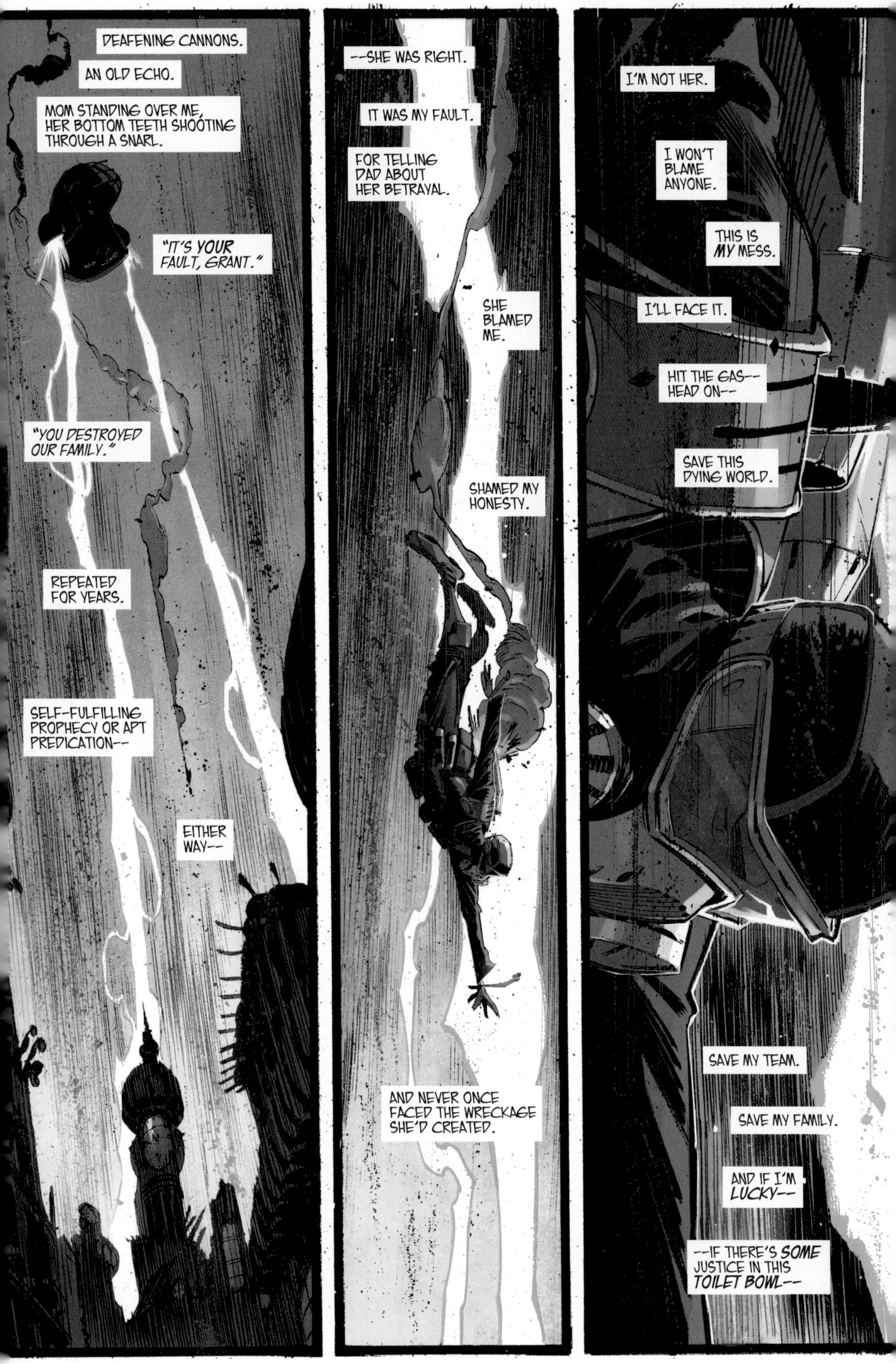
DEAFENING CANNONS.
AN OLD ECHO.
MOM STANDING OVER ME, HER BOTTOM TEETH SHOOTING THROUGH A SNARL.
"IT'S *YOUR* FAULT, GRANT."
"YOU DESTROYED OUR FAMILY."
REPEATED FOR YEARS.
SELF-FULFILLING PROPHECY OR APT PREDICATION--
EITHER WAY--
--SHE WAS RIGHT.
IT WAS MY FAULT.
FOR TELLING DAD ABOUT HER BETRAYAL.
SHE BLAMED ME.
SHAMED MY HONESTY.
AND NEVER ONCE FACED THE WRECKAGE SHE'D CREATED.
I'M NOT HER.
I WON'T BLAME ANYONE.
THIS IS *MY* MESS.
I'LL FACE IT.
HIT THE GAS-- HEAD ON--
SAVE THIS DYING WORLD.
SAVE MY TEAM.
SAVE MY FAMILY.
AND IF I'M *LUCKY*--
--IF THERE'S *SOME* JUSTICE IN THIS *TOILET BOWL*--

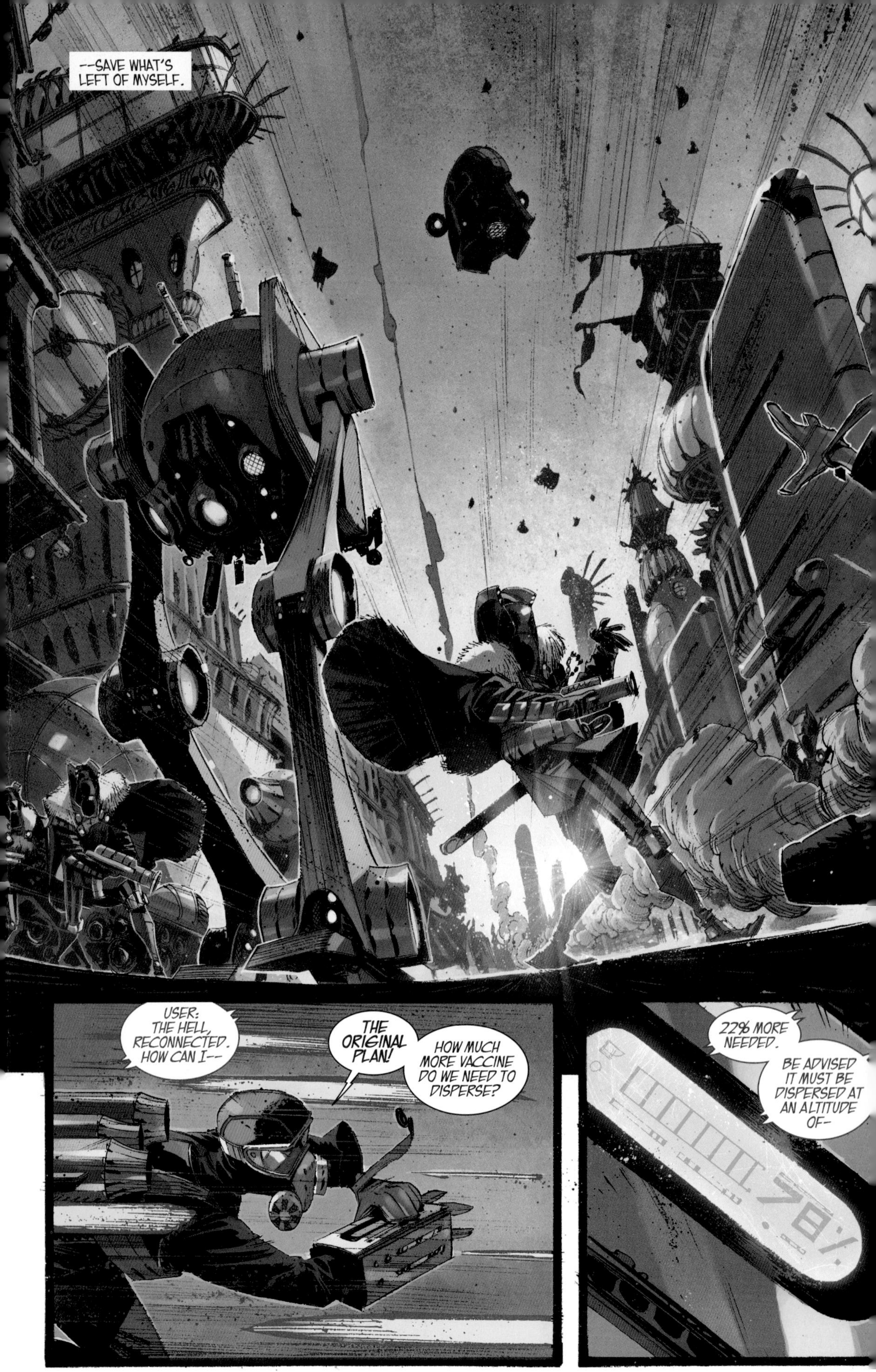
--SAVE WHAT'S LEFT OF MYSELF.
USER: THE HELL, RECONNECTED. HOW CAN I--
THE ORIGINAL PLAN!
HOW MUCH MORE VACCINE DO WE NEED TO DISPERSE?
22% MORE NEEDED.
BE ADVISED IT MUST BE DISPERSED AT AN ALTITUDE OF-
78%

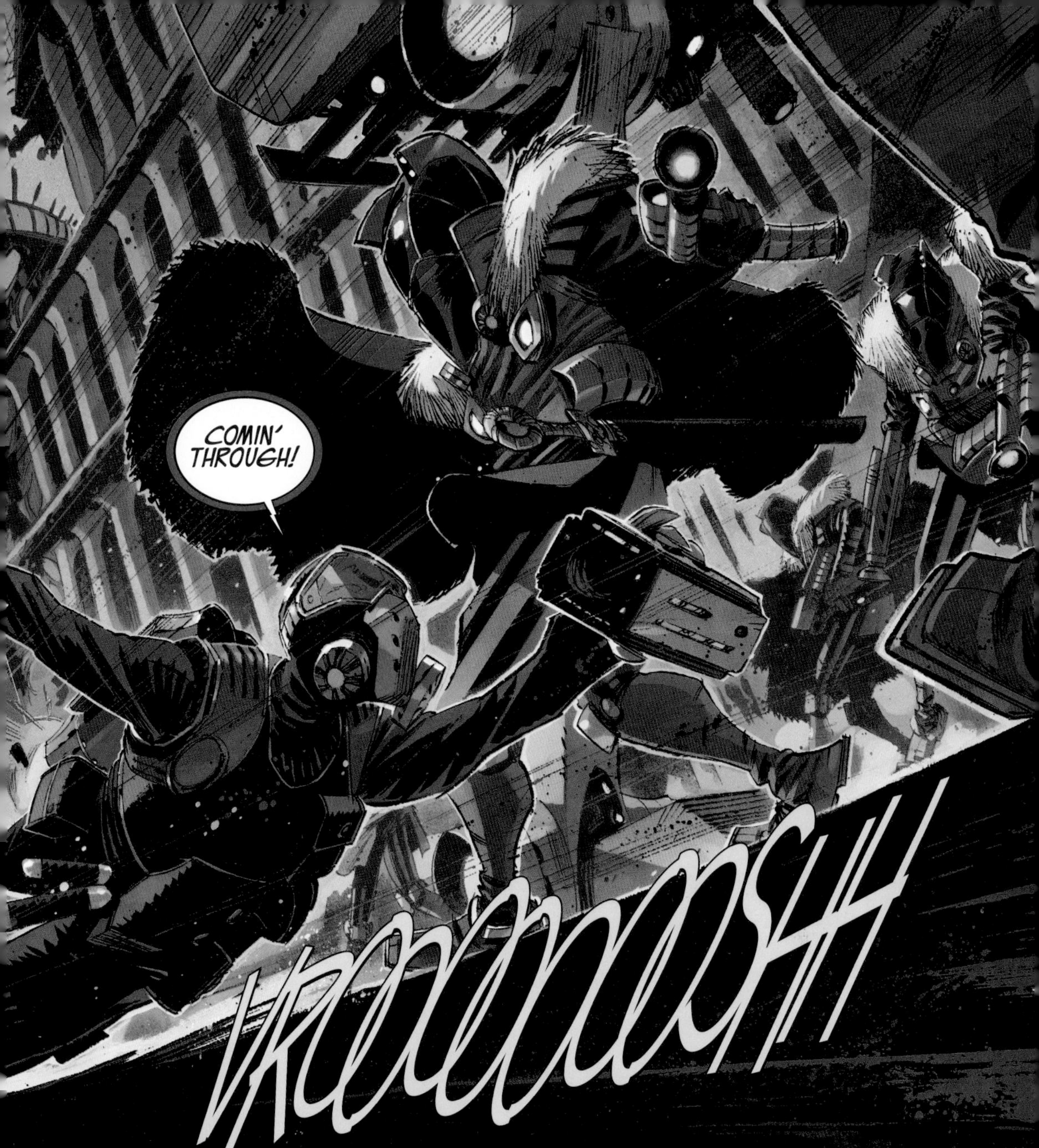
COMIN' THROUGH!
VROOOOOOSH

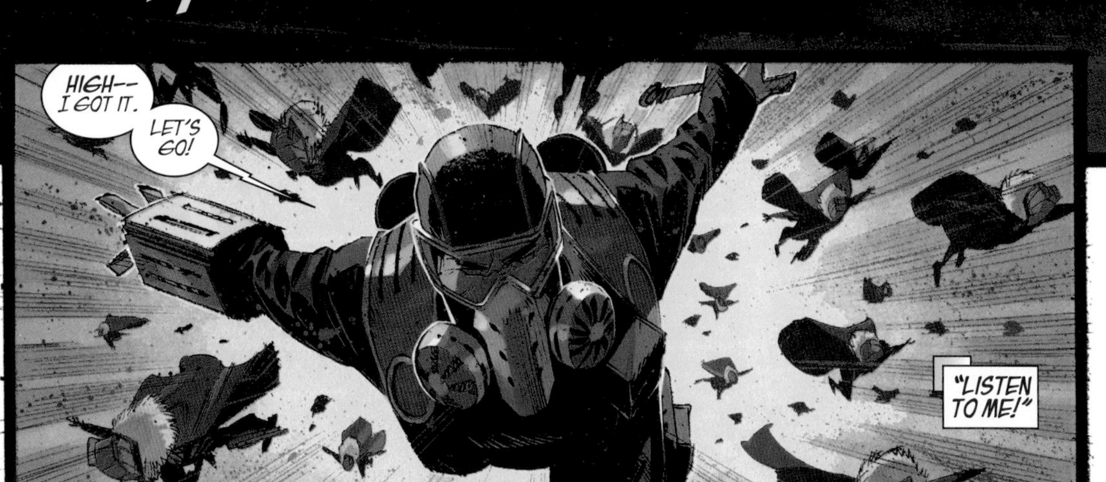
HIGH-- I GOT IT.
LET'S GO!
"LISTEN TO ME!"

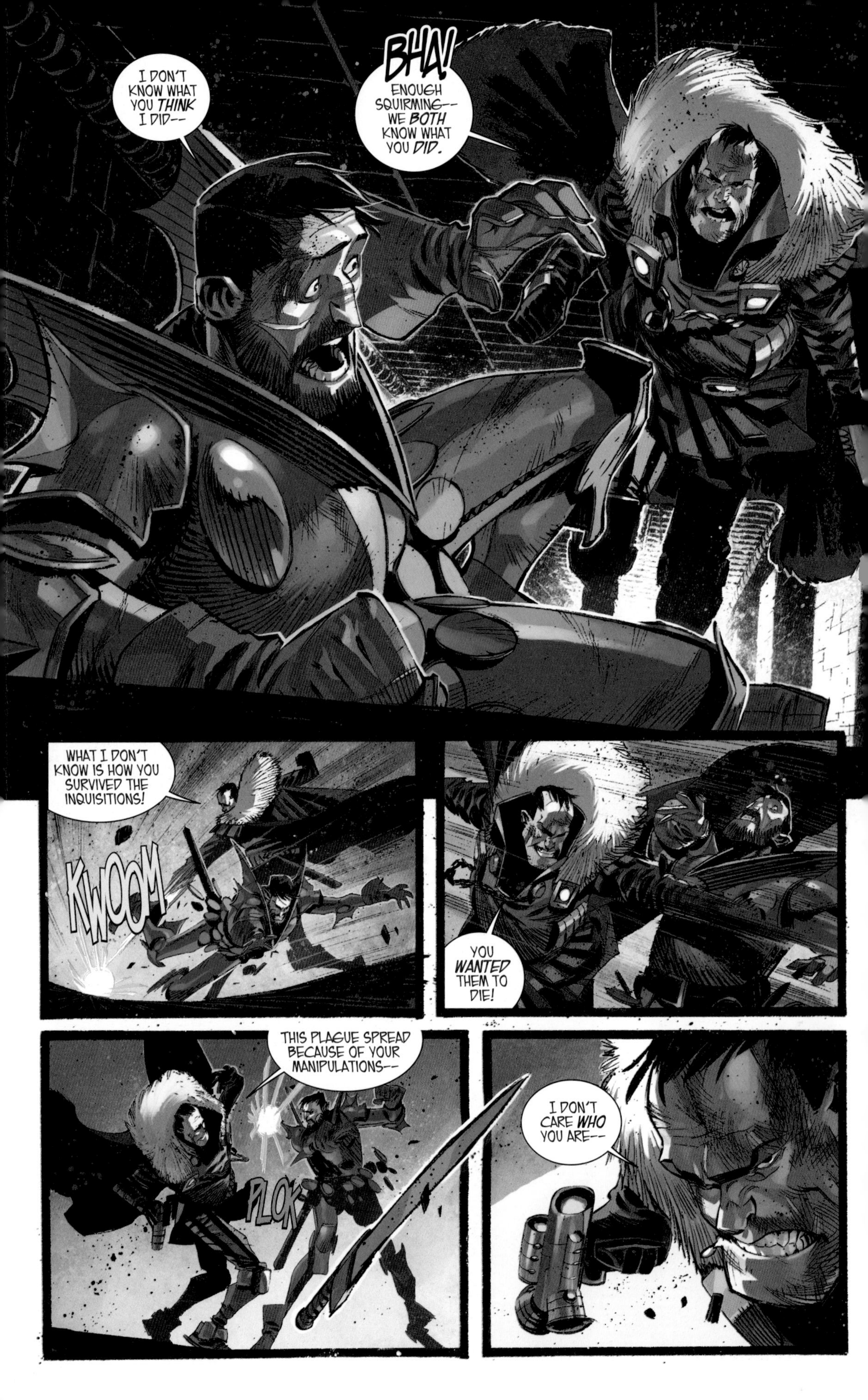
I DON'T KNOW WHAT YOU THINK I DID--
BHA!
ENOUGH SQUIRMING--WE BOTH KNOW WHAT YOU DID.
WHAT I DON'T KNOW IS HOW YOU SURVIVED THE INQUISITIONS!
KWOOM
YOU WANTED THEM TO DIE!
THIS PLAGUE SPREAD BECAUSE OF YOUR MANIPULATIONS--
PLOK
I DON'T CARE WHO YOU ARE--

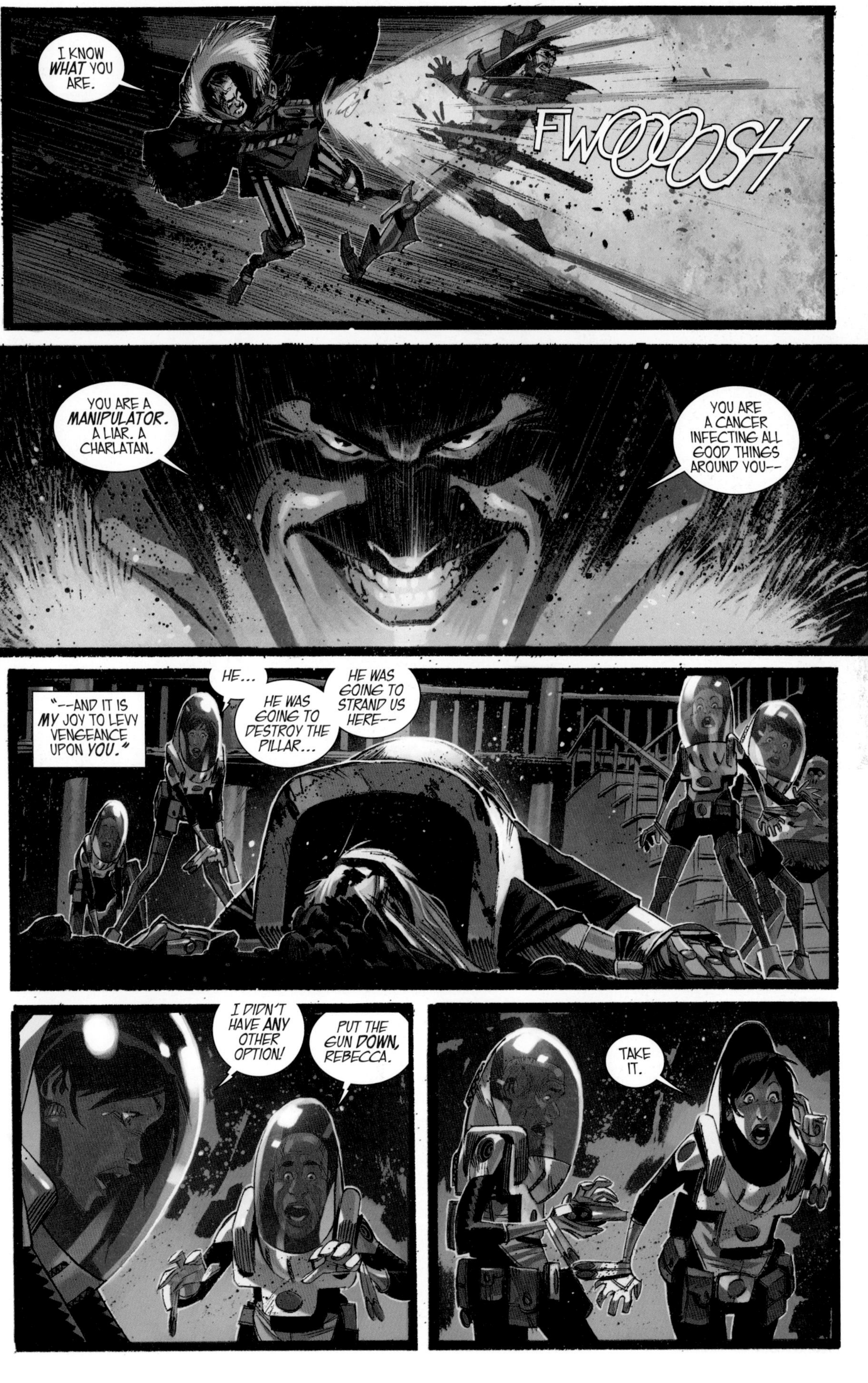
I KNOW **WHAT** YOU ARE.
FWOOOOSH
YOU ARE A **MANIPULATOR.** A LIAR. A CHARLATAN.
YOU ARE A CANCER INFECTING ALL GOOD THINGS AROUND YOU--
"--AND IT IS **MY** JOY TO LEVY VENGEANCE UPON **YOU.**"
HE...
HE WAS GOING TO DESTROY THE PILLAR...
HE WAS GOING TO STRAND US HERE--
I DIDN'T HAVE **ANY** OTHER OPTION!
PUT THE GUN **DOWN,** REBECCA.
TAKE IT.

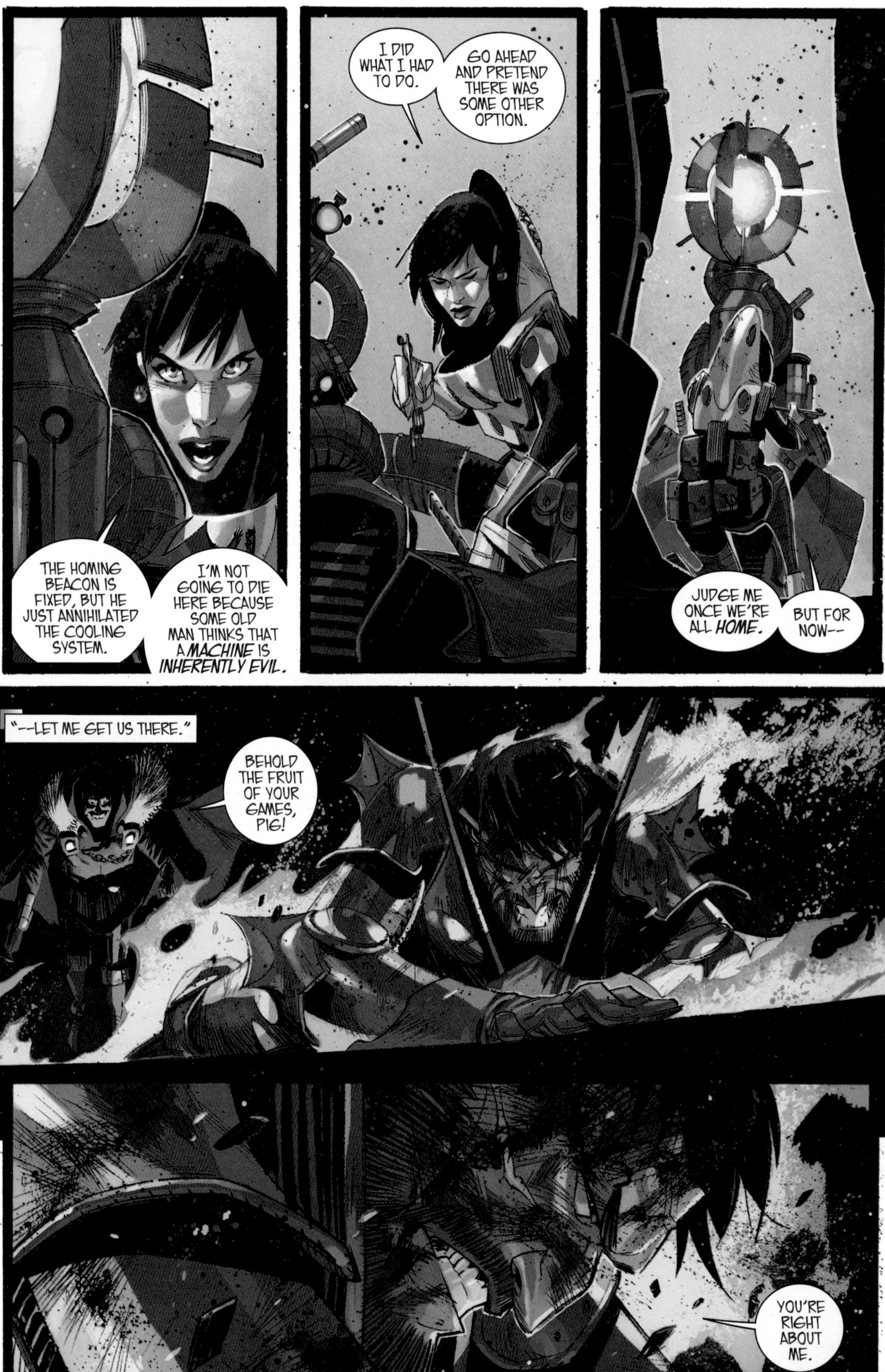
THE HOMING BEACON IS FIXED, BUT HE JUST ANNIHILATED THE COOLING SYSTEM.
I'M NOT GOING TO DIE HERE BECAUSE SOME OLD MAN THINKS THAT A *MACHINE* IS *INHERENTLY EVIL.*
I DID WHAT I HAD TO DO.
GO AHEAD AND PRETEND THERE WAS SOME OTHER OPTION.
JUDGE ME ONCE WE'RE ALL *HOME.*
BUT FOR NOW--
"--LET ME GET US THERE."
BEHOLD THE FRUIT OF YOUR GAMES, PIG!
YOU'RE RIGHT ABOUT ME.

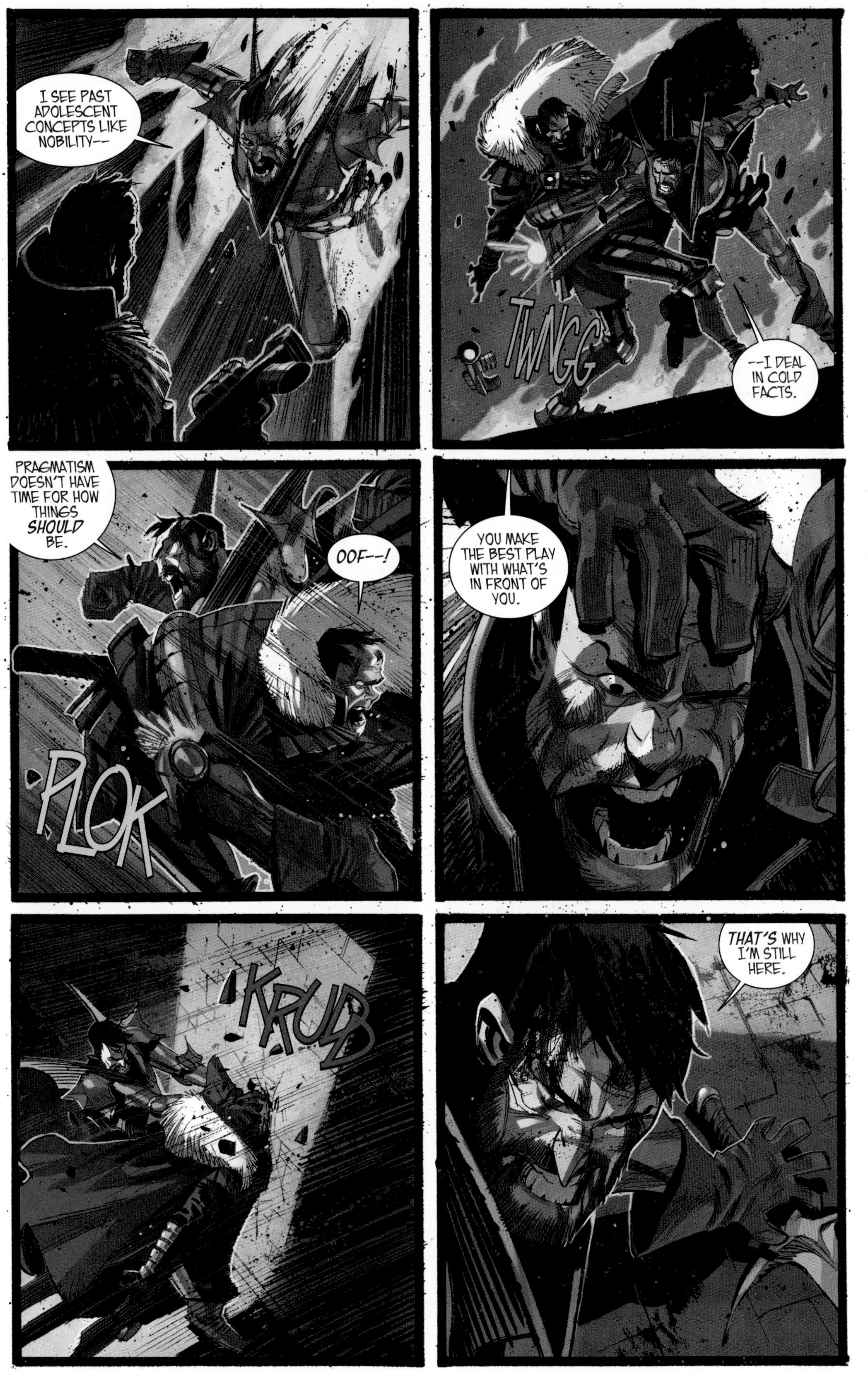
I SEE PAST ADOLESCENT CONCEPTS LIKE NOBILITY--
TWNGG
--I DEAL IN COLD FACTS.
PRAGMATISM DOESN'T HAVE TIME FOR HOW THINGS *SHOULD* BE.
OOF--!
PLOK
YOU MAKE THE BEST PLAY WITH WHAT'S IN FRONT OF YOU.
KRUD
*THAT'S* WHY I'M STILL HERE.

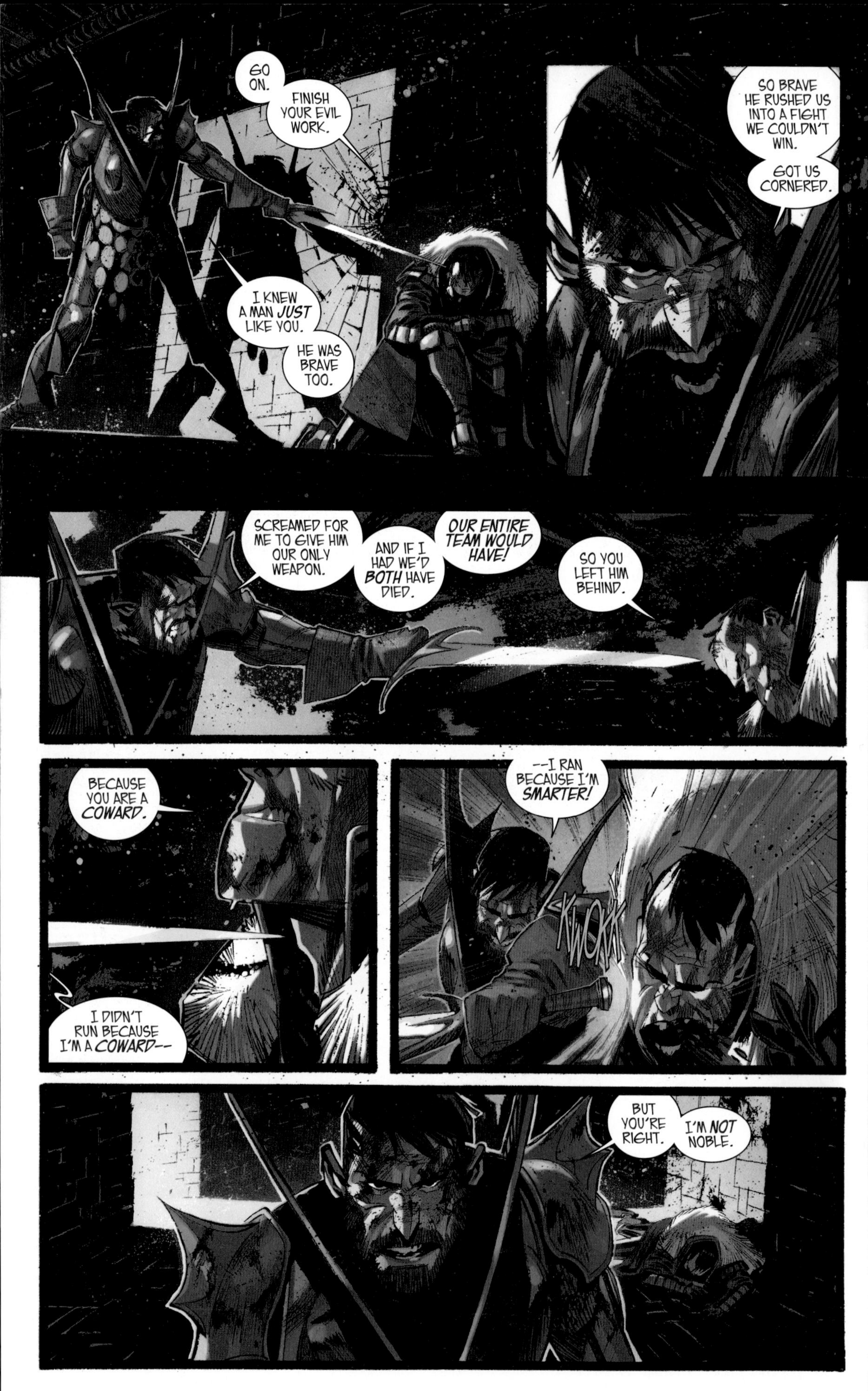
GO ON.
FINISH YOUR EVIL WORK.
I KNEW A MAN JUST LIKE YOU.
HE WAS BRAVE TOO.
SO BRAVE HE RUSHED US INTO A FIGHT WE COULDN'T WIN.
GOT US CORNERED.
SCREAMED FOR ME TO GIVE HIM OUR ONLY WEAPON.
AND IF I HAD WE'D BOTH HAVE DIED.
OUR ENTIRE TEAM WOULD HAVE!
SO YOU LEFT HIM BEHIND.
BECAUSE YOU ARE A COWARD.
I DIDN'T RUN BECAUSE I'M A COWARD--
--I RAN BECAUSE I'M SMARTER!
KWOKK
BUT YOU'RE RIGHT.
I'M NOT NOBLE.

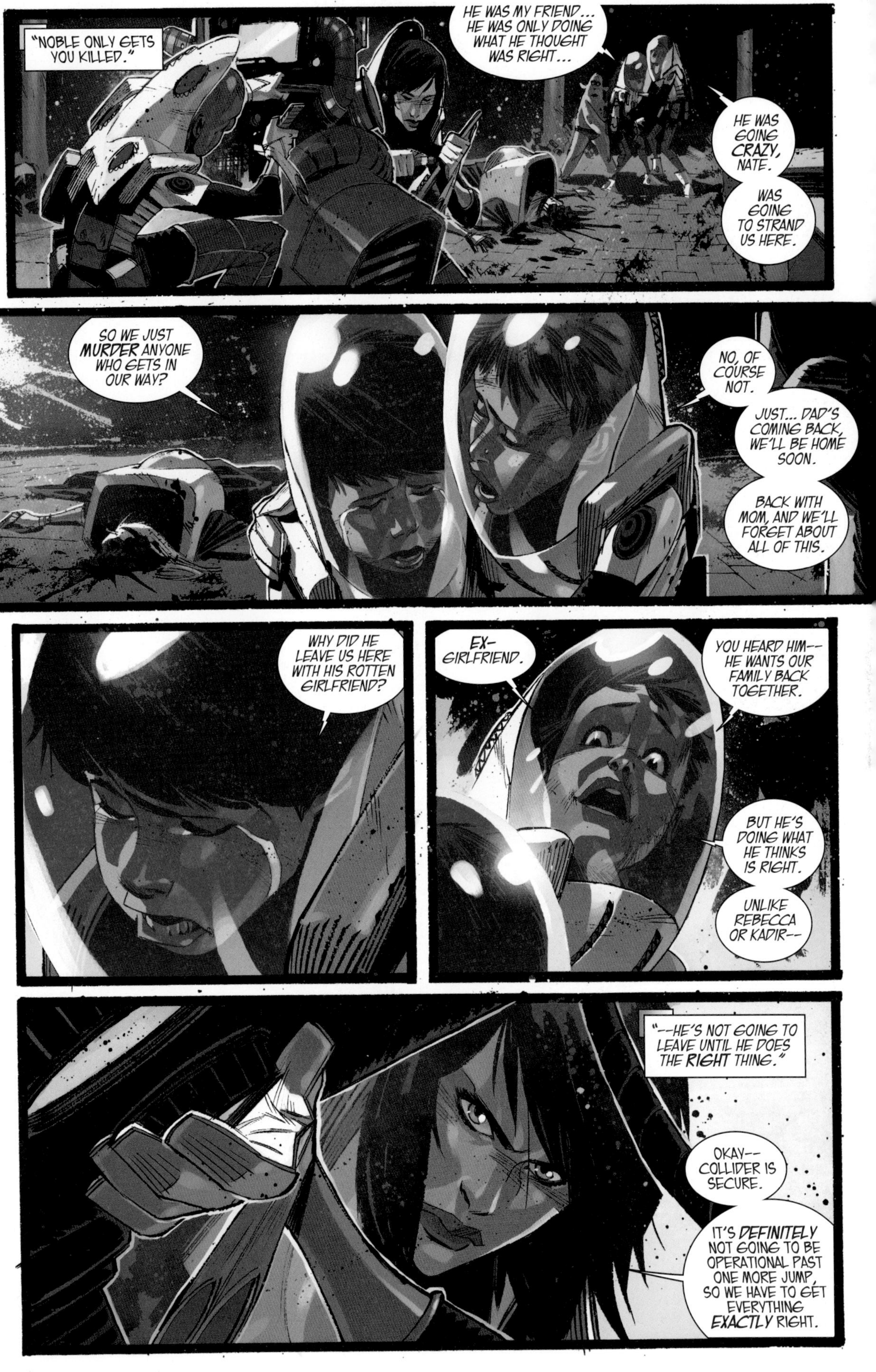
"NOBLE ONLY GETS YOU KILLED."
HE WAS MY FRIEND... HE WAS ONLY DOING WHAT HE THOUGHT WAS RIGHT...
HE WAS GOING CRAZY, NATE.
WAS GOING TO STRAND US HERE.
SO WE JUST MURDER ANYONE WHO GETS IN OUR WAY?
NO, OF COURSE NOT.
JUST... DAD'S COMING BACK, WE'LL BE HOME SOON.
BACK WITH MOM, AND WE'LL FORGET ABOUT ALL OF THIS.
WHY DID HE LEAVE US HERE WITH HIS ROTTEN GIRLFRIEND?
EX-GIRLFRIEND.
YOU HEARD HIM--HE WANTS OUR FAMILY BACK TOGETHER.
BUT HE'S DOING WHAT HE THINKS IS RIGHT.
UNLIKE REBECCA OR KADIR--
"--HE'S NOT GOING TO LEAVE UNTIL HE DOES THE RIGHT THING."
OKAY--COLLIDER IS SECURE.
IT'S DEFINITELY NOT GOING TO BE OPERATIONAL PAST ONE MORE JUMP, SO WE HAVE TO GET EVERYTHING EXACTLY RIGHT.

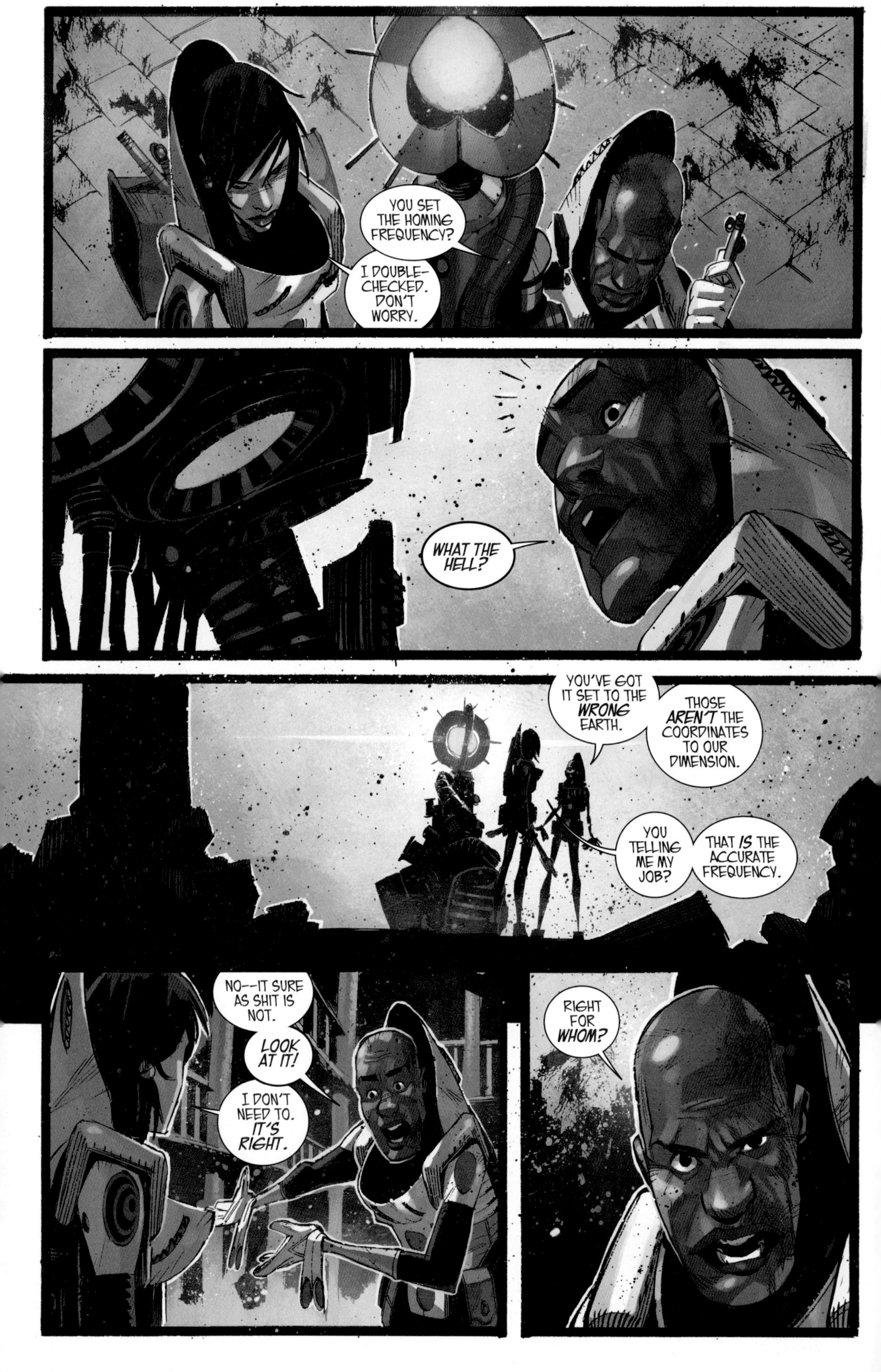
YOU SET THE HOMING FREQUENCY?
I DOUBLE-CHECKED. DON'T WORRY.
WHAT THE HELL?
YOU'VE GOT IT SET TO THE WRONG EARTH.
THOSE AREN'T THE COORDINATES TO OUR DIMENSION.
YOU TELLING ME MY JOB?
THAT IS THE ACCURATE FREQUENCY.
NO--IT SURE AS SHIT IS NOT.
LOOK AT IT!
I DON'T NEED TO. IT'S RIGHT.
RIGHT FOR WHOM?

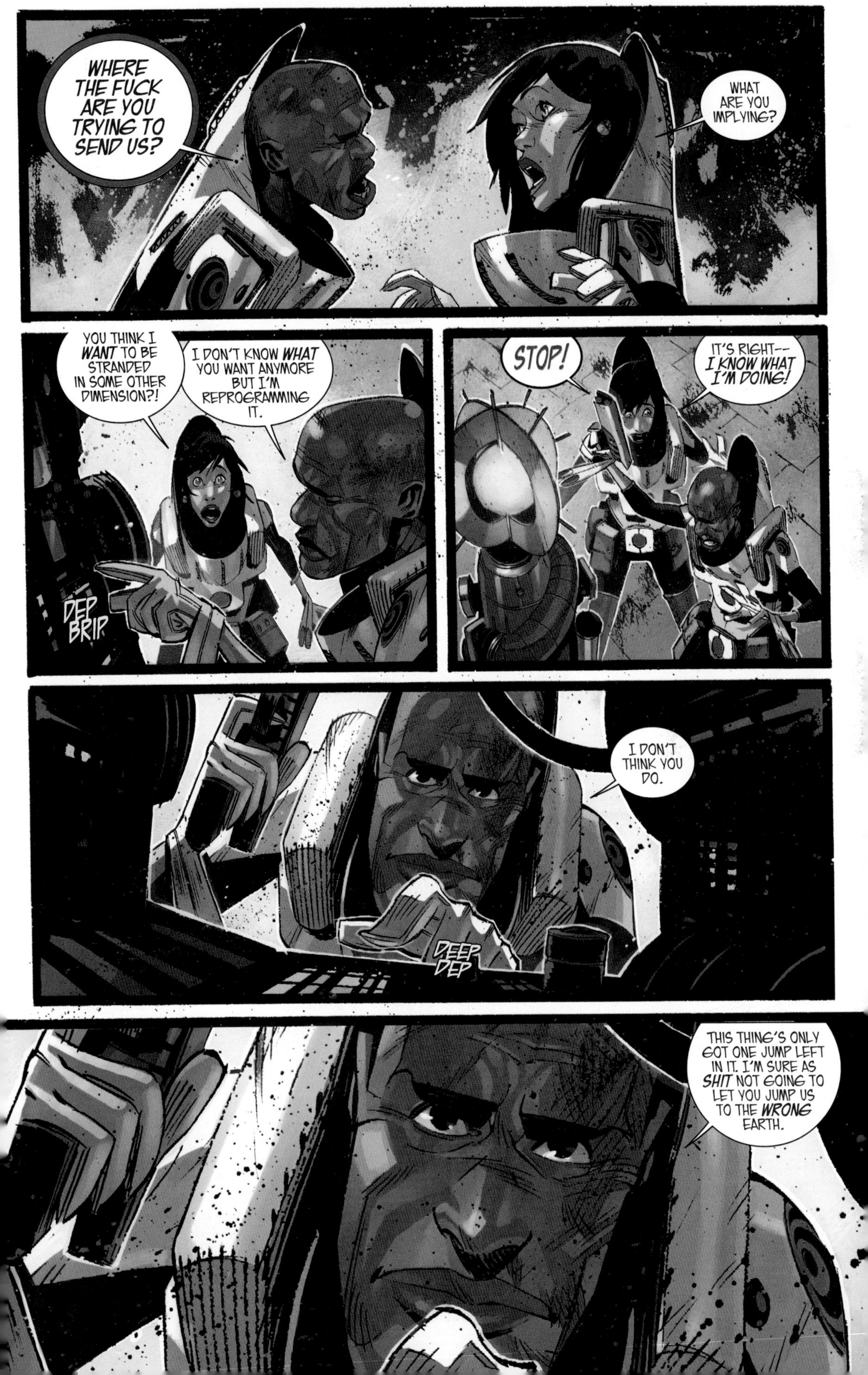
WHERE THE FUCK ARE YOU TRYING TO SEND US?
WHAT ARE YOU IMPLYING?
YOU THINK I *WANT* TO BE STRANDED IN SOME OTHER DIMENSION?!
I DON'T KNOW *WHAT* YOU WANT ANYMORE BUT I'M REPROGRAMMING IT.
DEP BRIP
STOP!
IT'S RIGHT-- *I KNOW WHAT I'M DOING!*
I DON'T THINK YOU DO.
DEEP DEP
THIS THING'S ONLY GOT ONE JUMP LEFT IN IT. I'M SURE AS *SHIT* NOT GOING TO LET YOU JUMP US TO THE *WRONG* EARTH.

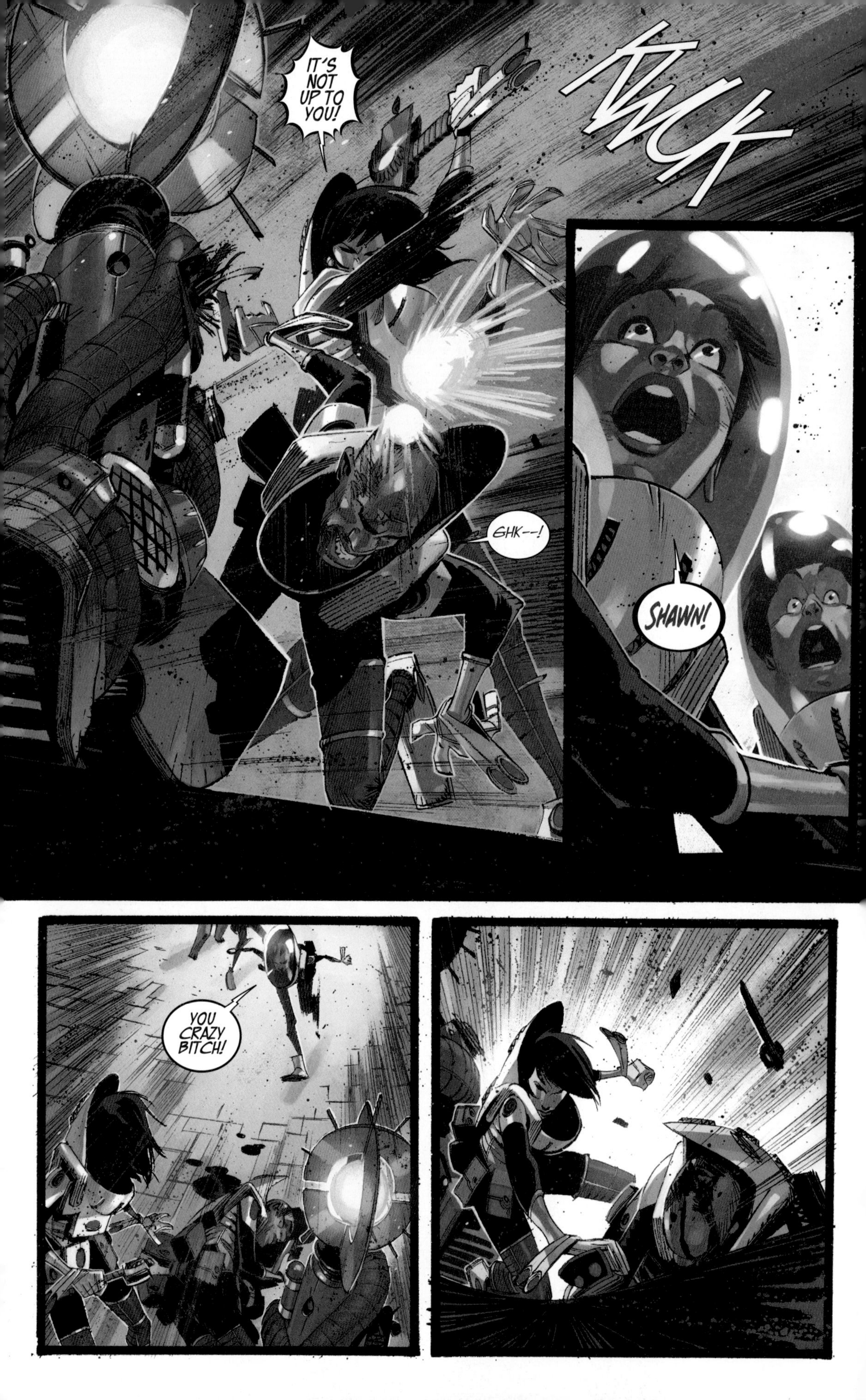
IT'S NOT UP TO YOU!
KLICK
GHK--!
SHAWN!
YOU CRAZY BITCH!

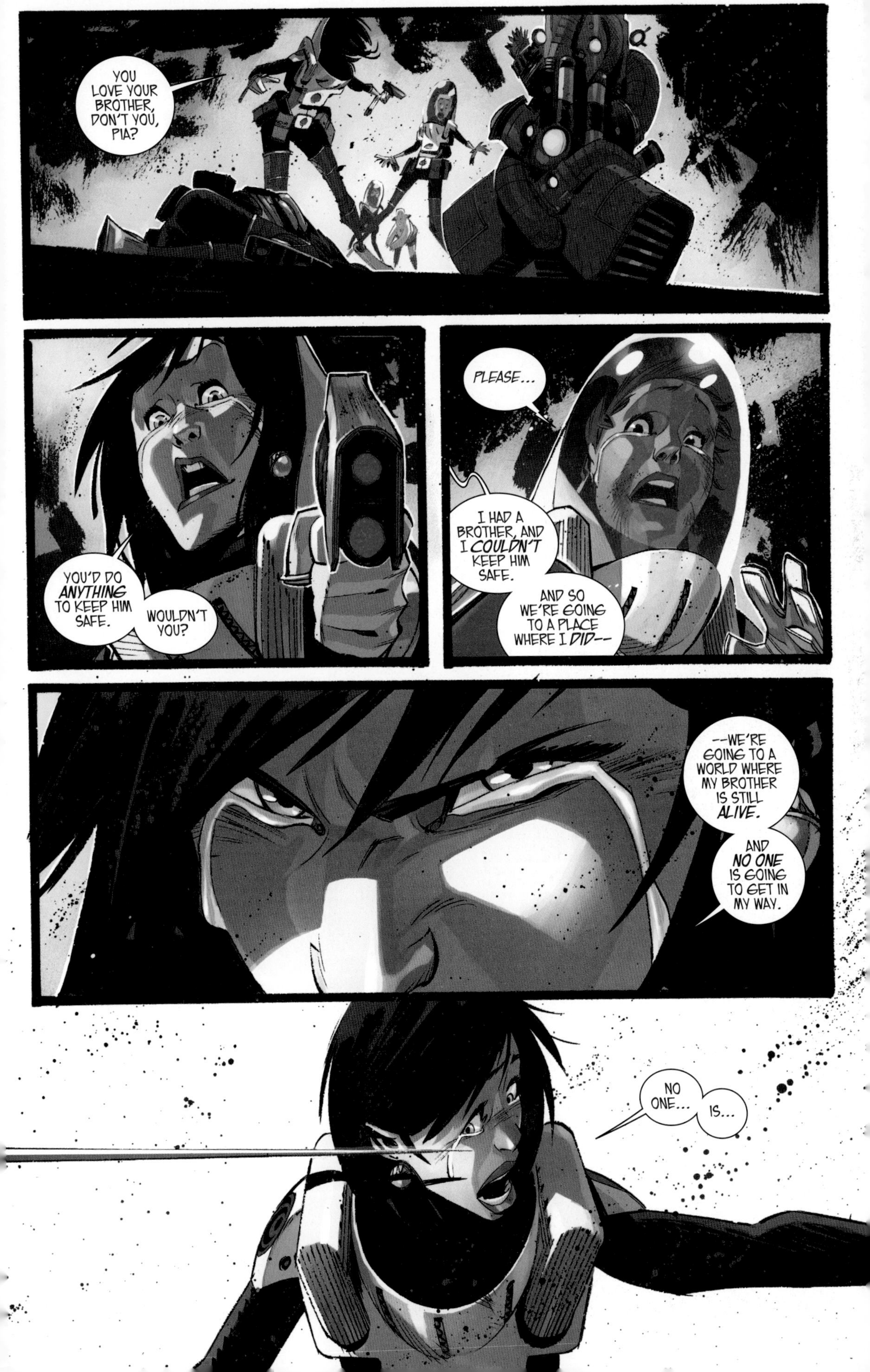
YOU LOVE YOUR BROTHER, DON'T YOU, PIA?
YOU'D DO ANYTHING TO KEEP HIM SAFE.
WOULDN'T YOU?
PLEASE...
I HAD A BROTHER, AND I COULDN'T KEEP HIM SAFE.
AND SO WE'RE GOING TO A PLACE WHERE I DID--
--WE'RE GOING TO A WORLD WHERE MY BROTHER IS STILL ALIVE.
AND NO ONE IS GOING TO GET IN MY WAY.
NO ONE...
IS...

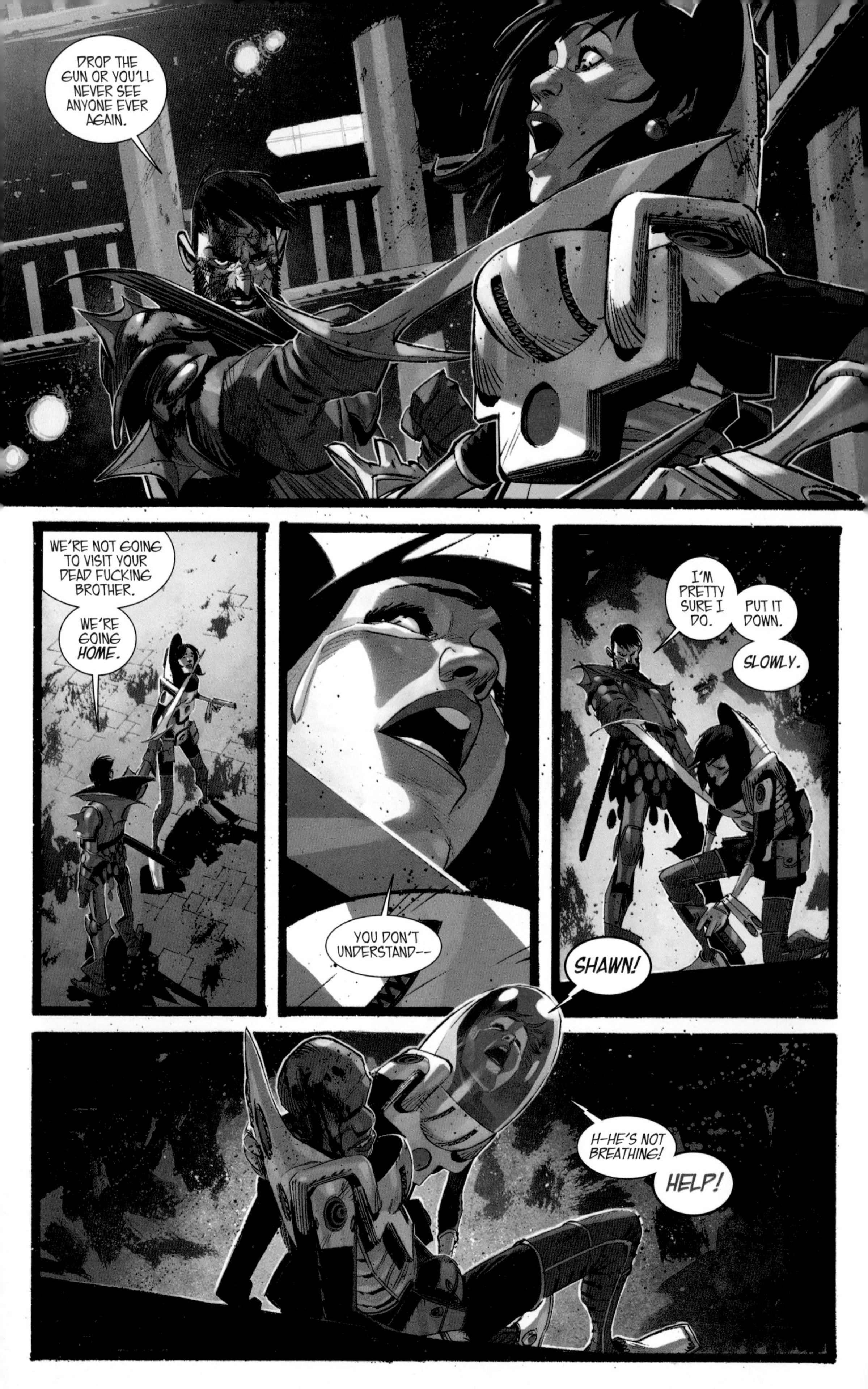
DROP THE GUN OR YOU'LL NEVER SEE ANYONE EVER AGAIN.
WE'RE NOT GOING TO VISIT YOUR DEAD FUCKING BROTHER.
WE'RE GOING HOME.
YOU DON'T UNDERSTAND--
I'M PRETTY SURE I DO.
PUT IT DOWN.
SLOWLY.
SHAWN!
H-HE'S NOT BREATHING!
HELP!

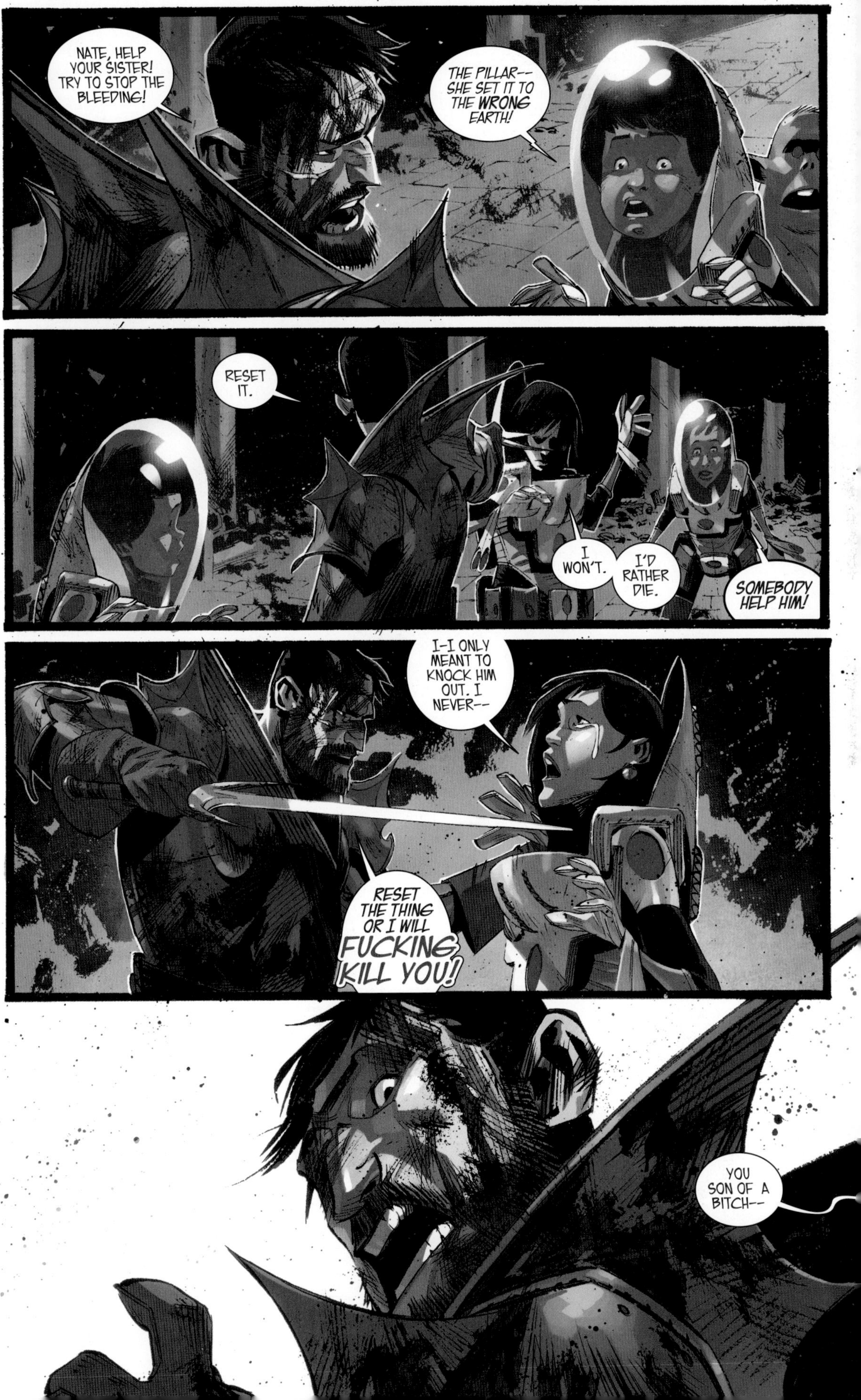
NATE, HELP YOUR SISTER! TRY TO STOP THE BLEEDING!
THE PILLAR-- SHE SET IT TO THE WRONG EARTH!
RESET IT.
I WON'T.
I'D RATHER DIE.
SOMEBODY HELP HIM!
I-I ONLY MEANT TO KNOCK HIM OUT. I NEVER--
RESET THE THING OR I WILL FUCKING KILL YOU!
YOU SON OF A BITCH--

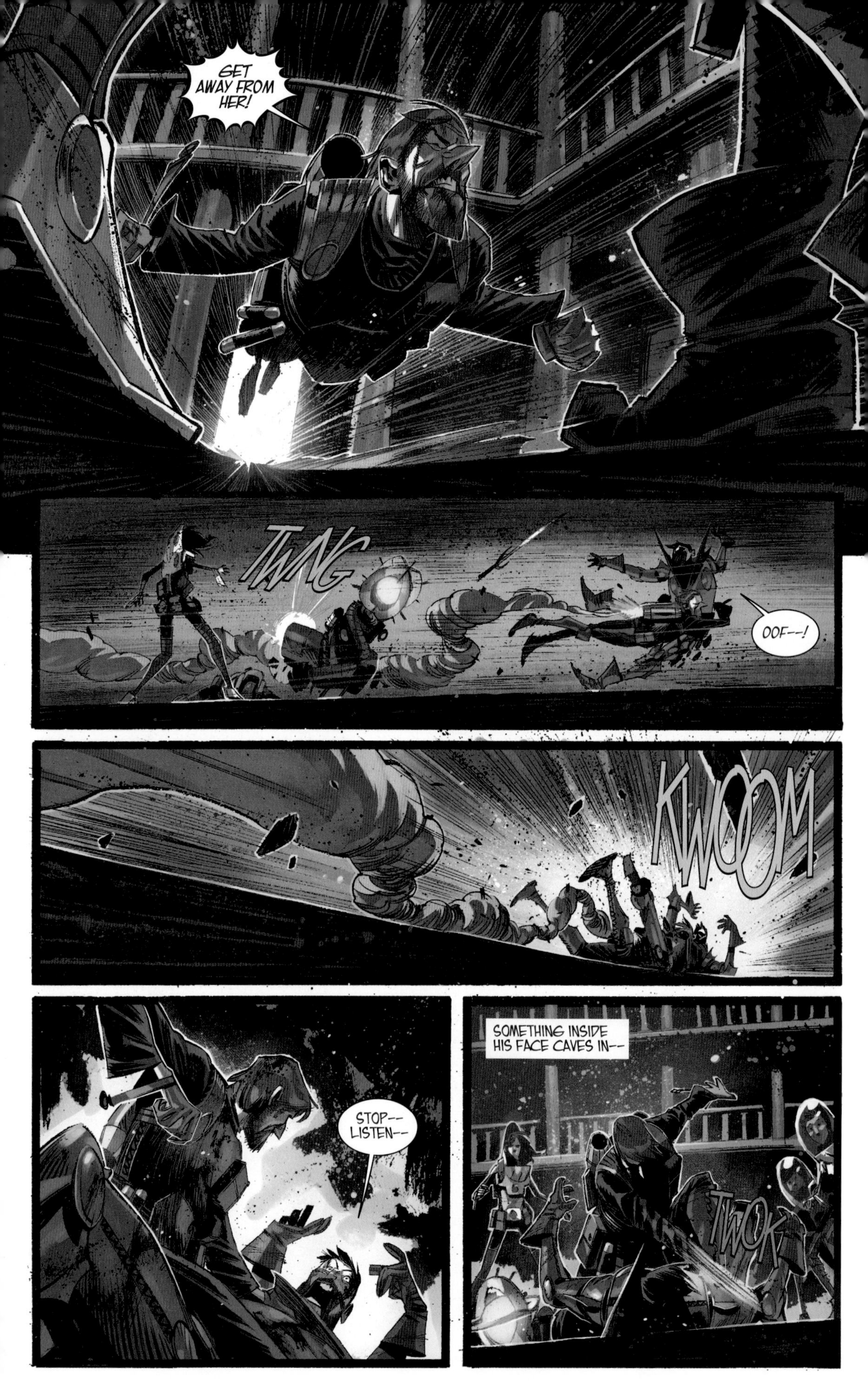
GET AWAY FROM HER!
TWANG
OOF--!
KWOOM
STOP-- LISTEN--
SOMETHING INSIDE HIS FACE CAVES IN--
TWOK

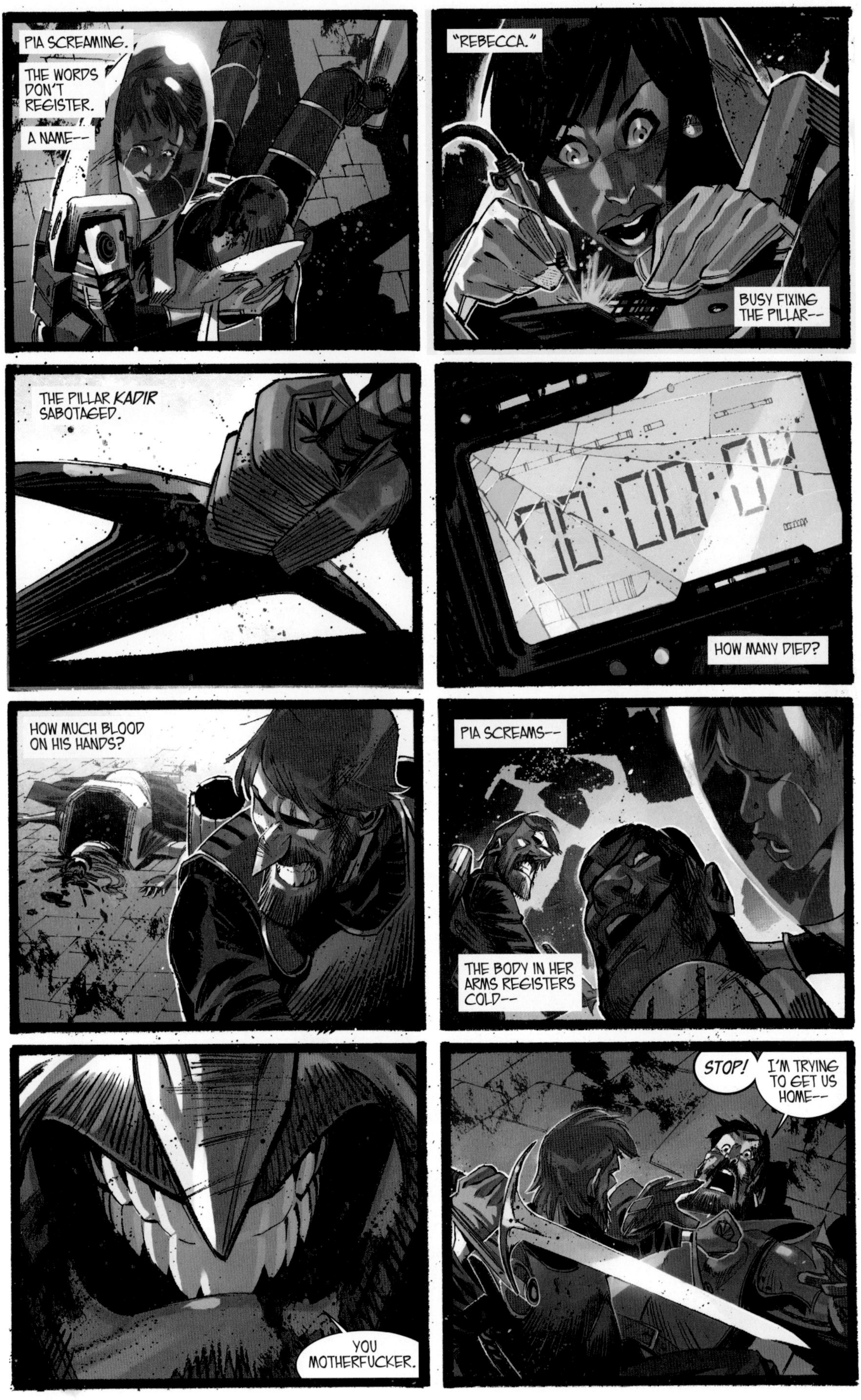
PIA SCREAMING.
THE WORDS DON'T REGISTER.
A NAME--
"REBECCA."
BUSY FIXING THE PILLAR--
THE PILLAR *KADIR* SABOTAGED.
00:00:04
HOW MANY DIED?
HOW MUCH BLOOD ON HIS HANDS?
PIA SCREAMS--
THE BODY IN HER ARMS REGISTERS COLD--
YOU MOTHERFUCKER.
STOP!
I'M TRYING TO GET US HOME--

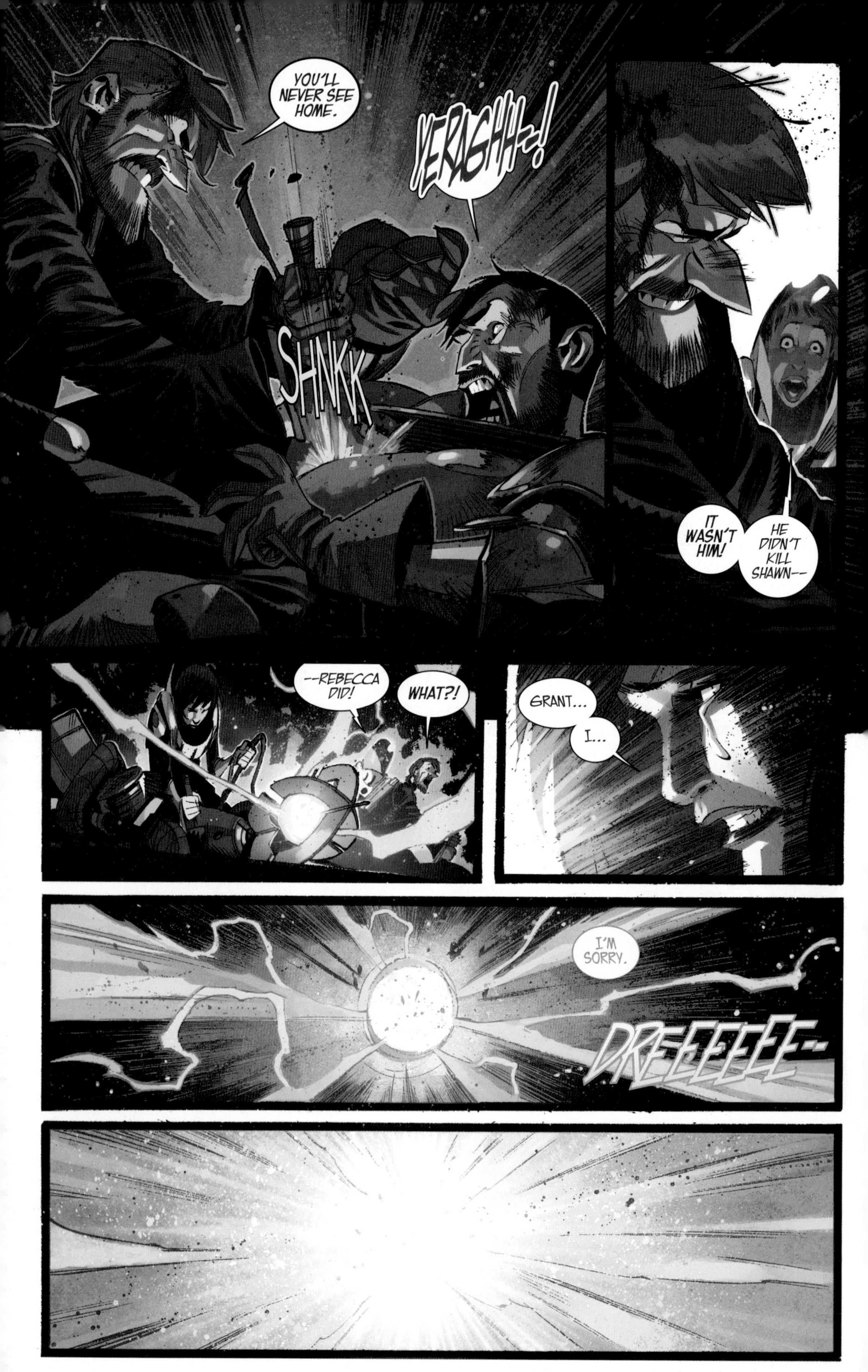
YOU'LL NEVER SEE HOME.
YERAGHH--!
SHNKK
IT WASN'T HIM!
HE DIDN'T KILL SHAWN--
--REBECCA DID!
WHAT?!
GRANT...
I...
I'M SORRY.
DREEEEEE--

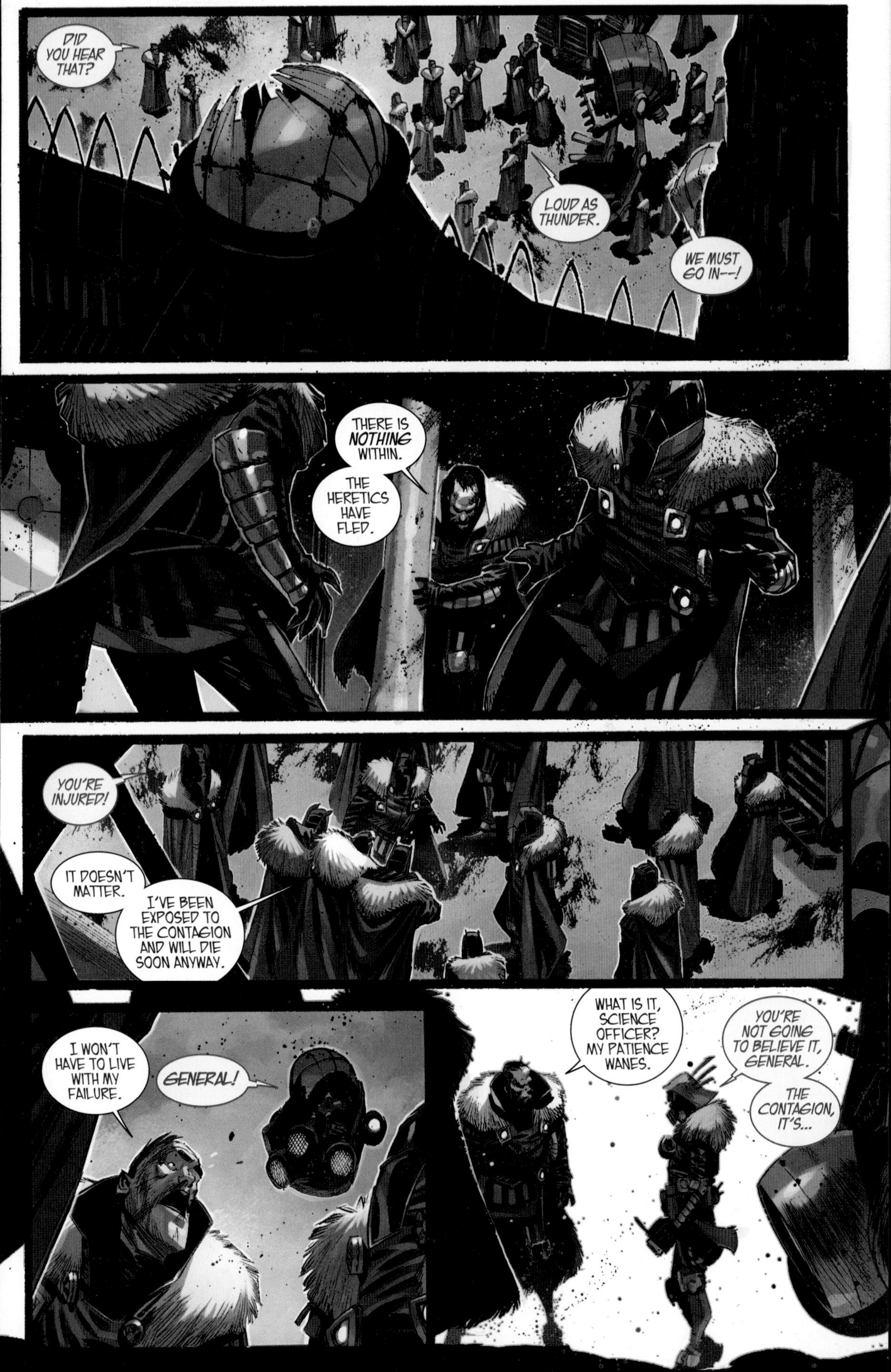
DID YOU HEAR THAT?
LOUD AS THUNDER.
WE MUST GO IN--!
THERE IS NOTHING WITHIN.
THE HERETICS HAVE FLED.
YOU'RE INJURED!
IT DOESN'T MATTER.
I'VE BEEN EXPOSED TO THE CONTAGION AND WILL DIE SOON ANYWAY.
I WON'T HAVE TO LIVE WITH MY FAILURE.
GENERAL!
WHAT IS IT, SCIENCE OFFICER? MY PATIENCE WANES.
YOU'RE NOT GOING TO BELIEVE IT, GENERAL.
THE CONTAGION, IT'S...

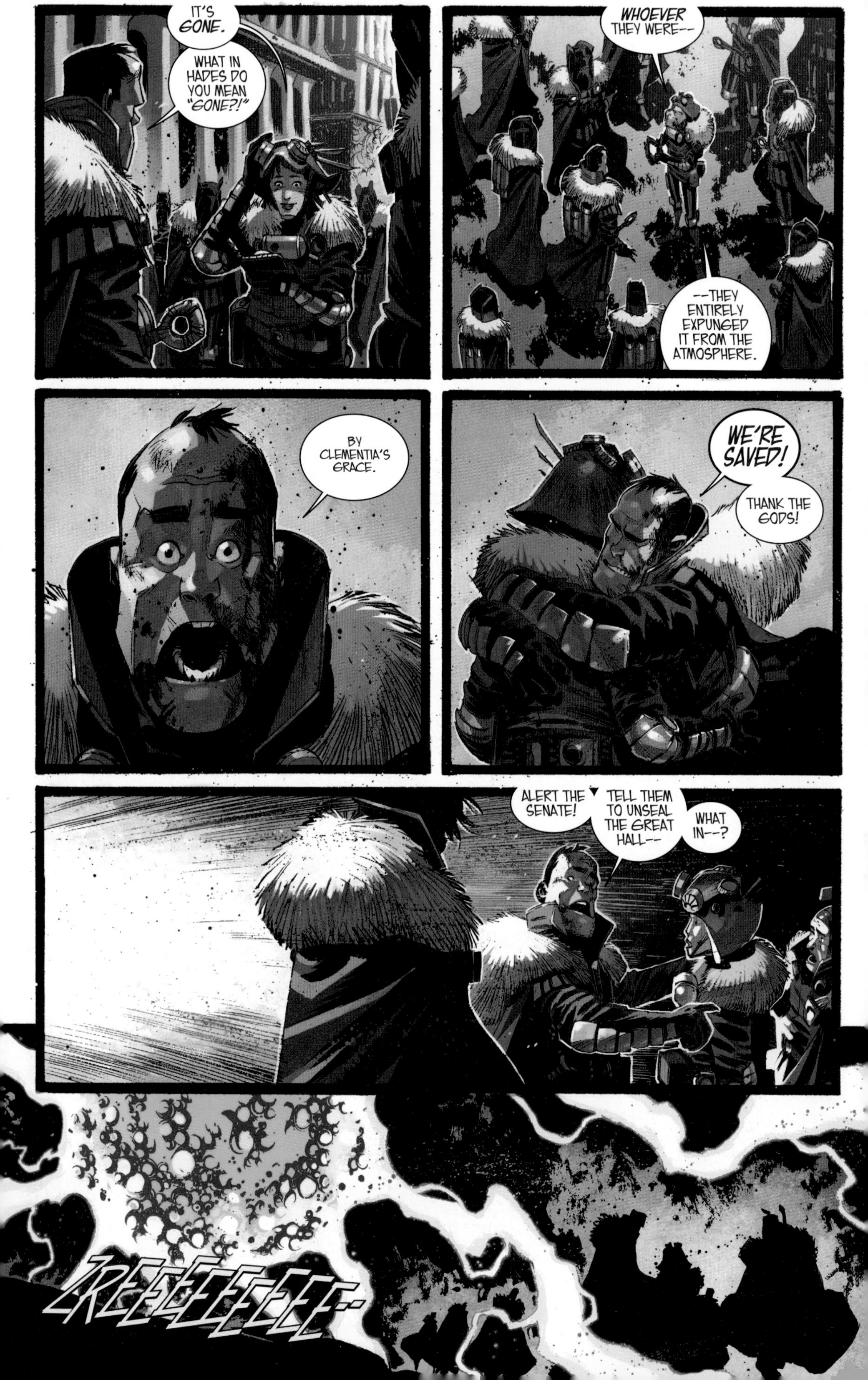
IT'S GONE.
WHAT IN HADES DO YOU MEAN "GONE?!"
WHOEVER THEY WERE--
--THEY ENTIRELY EXPUNGED IT FROM THE ATMOSPHERE.
BY CLEMENTIA'S GRACE.
WE'RE SAVED!
THANK THE GODS!
ALERT THE SENATE!
TELL THEM TO UNSEAL THE GREAT HALL--
WHAT IN--?
ZREEEEEEEEEE--

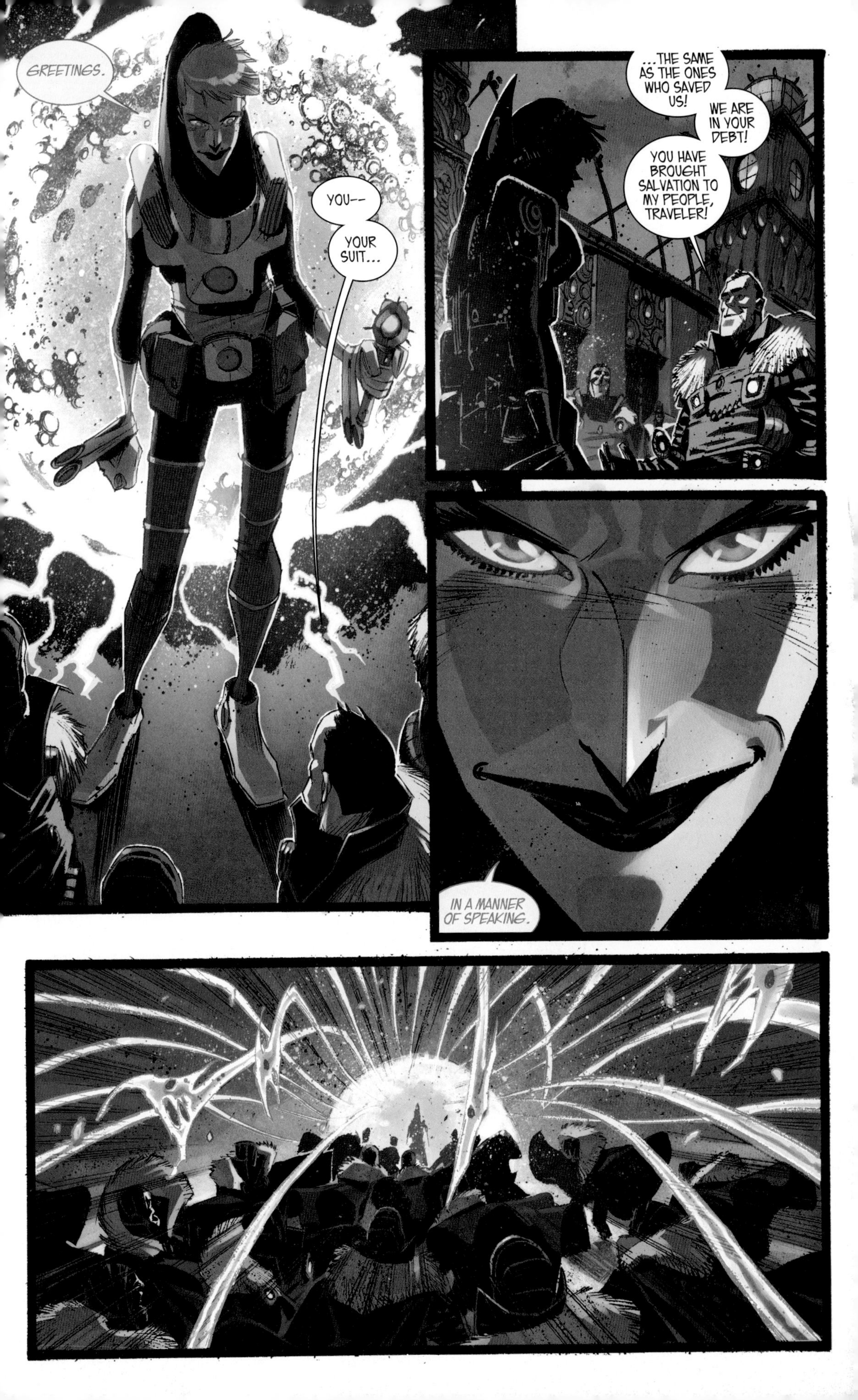
GREETINGS.
YOU--
YOUR SUIT...
...THE SAME AS THE ONES WHO SAVED US!
WE ARE IN YOUR DEBT!
YOU HAVE BROUGHT SALVATION TO MY PEOPLE, TRAVELER!
IN A MANNER OF SPEAKING.

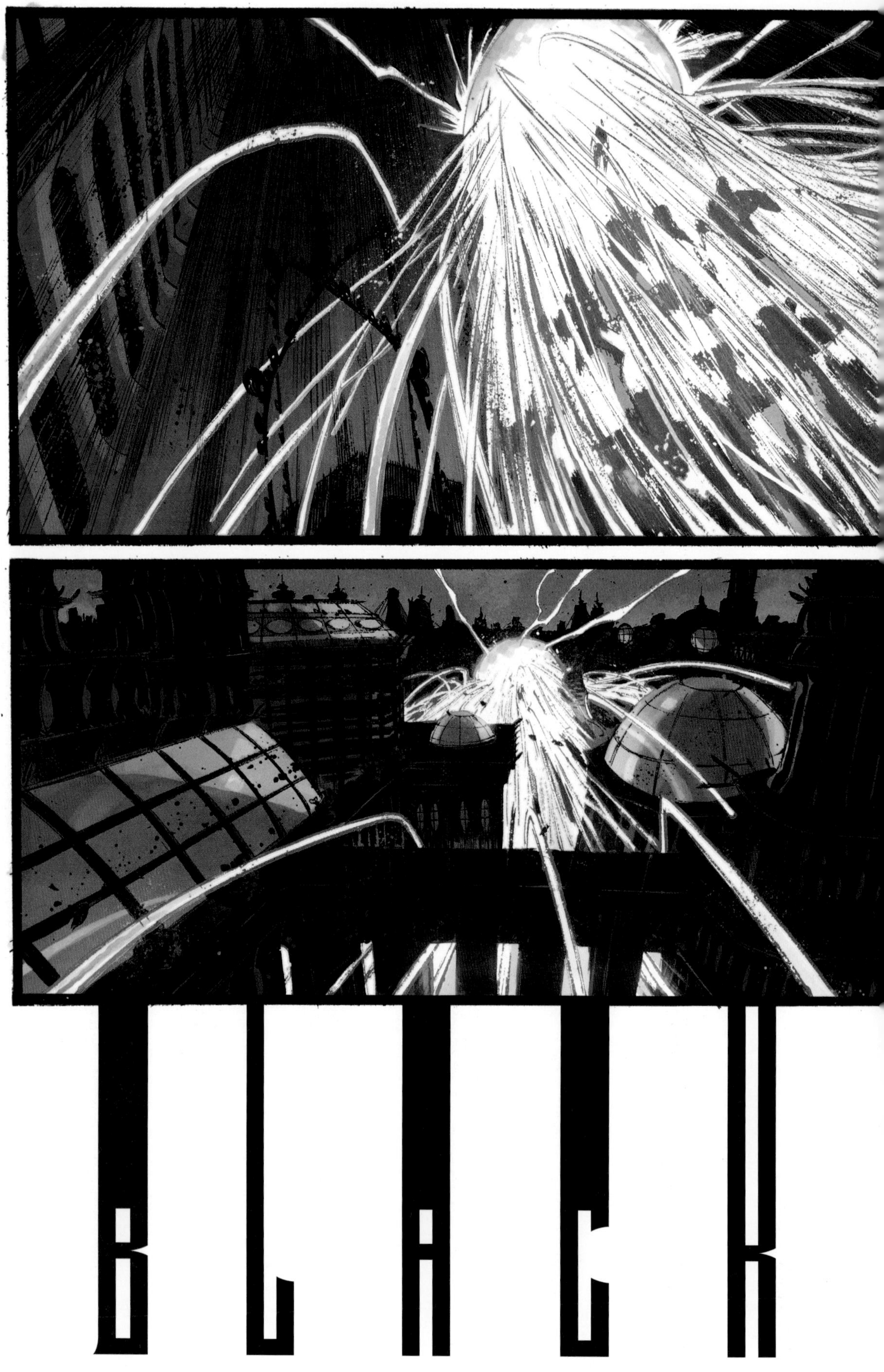

# BLACK

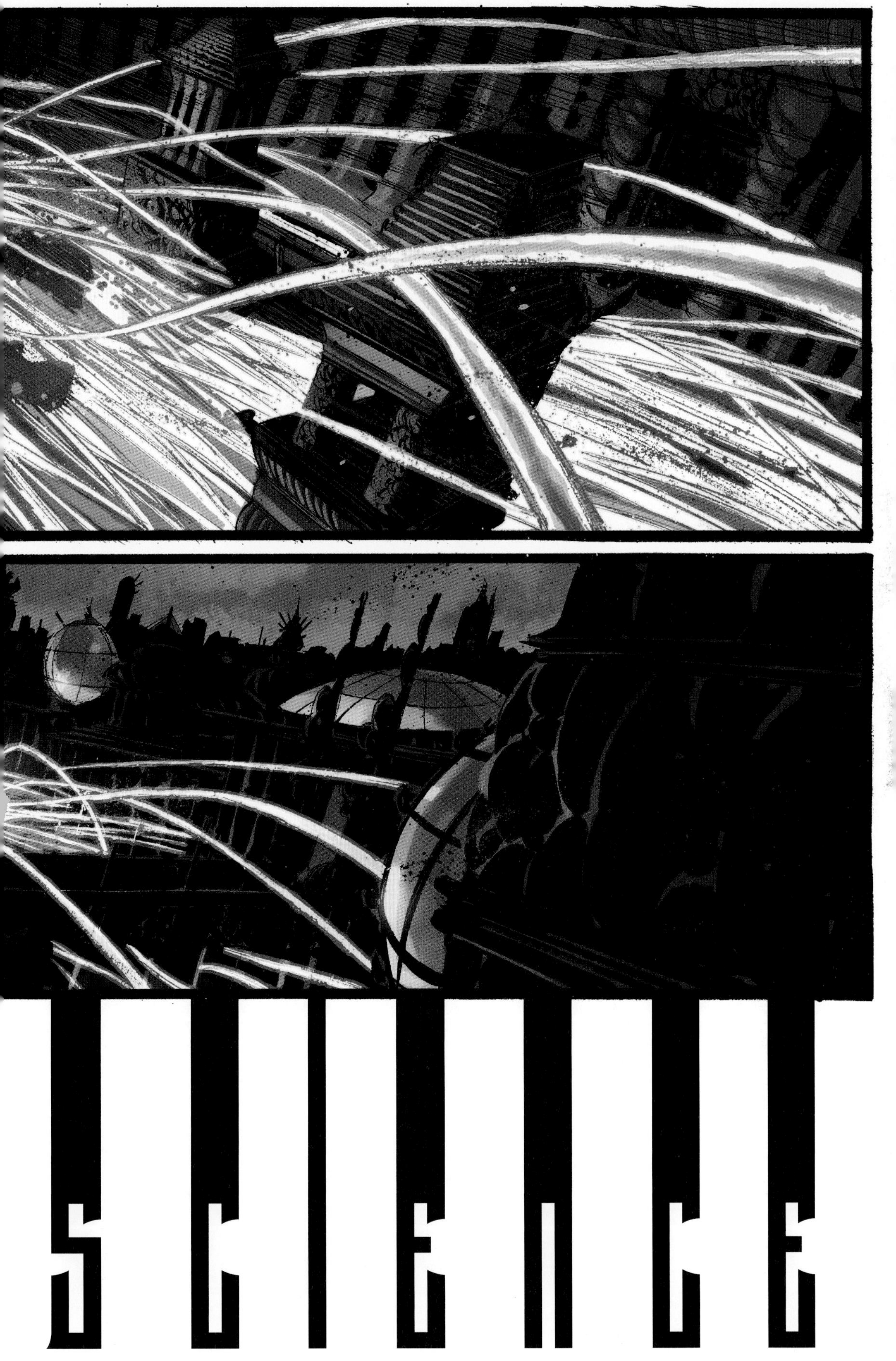

# SCIENCE

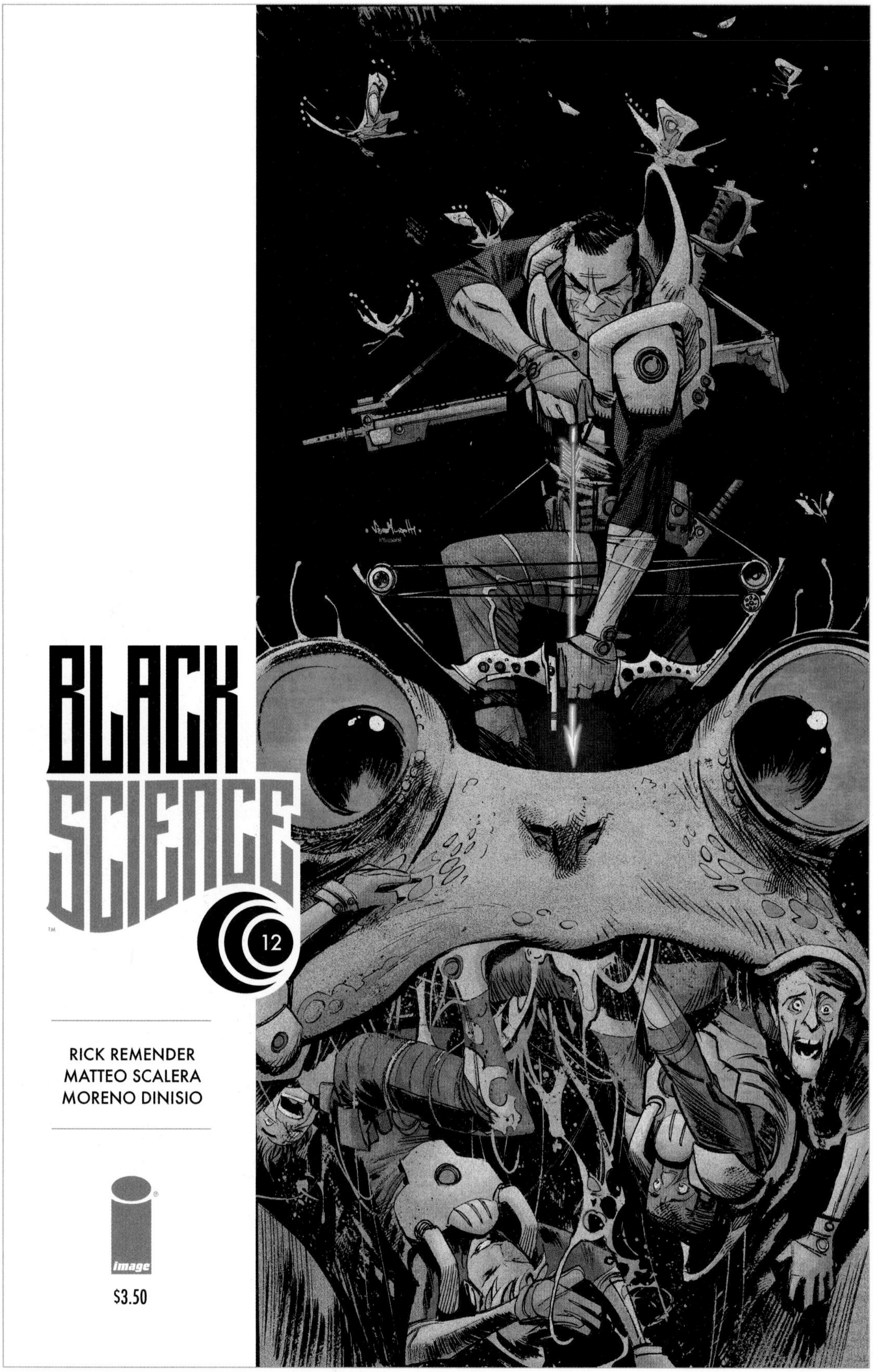
BLACK
SCIENCE
12
RICK REMENDER
MATTEO SCALERA
MORENO DINISIO
image
$3.50

#12 VARIANT BY SEAN MURPHY AND MATT HOLLINGSWORTH

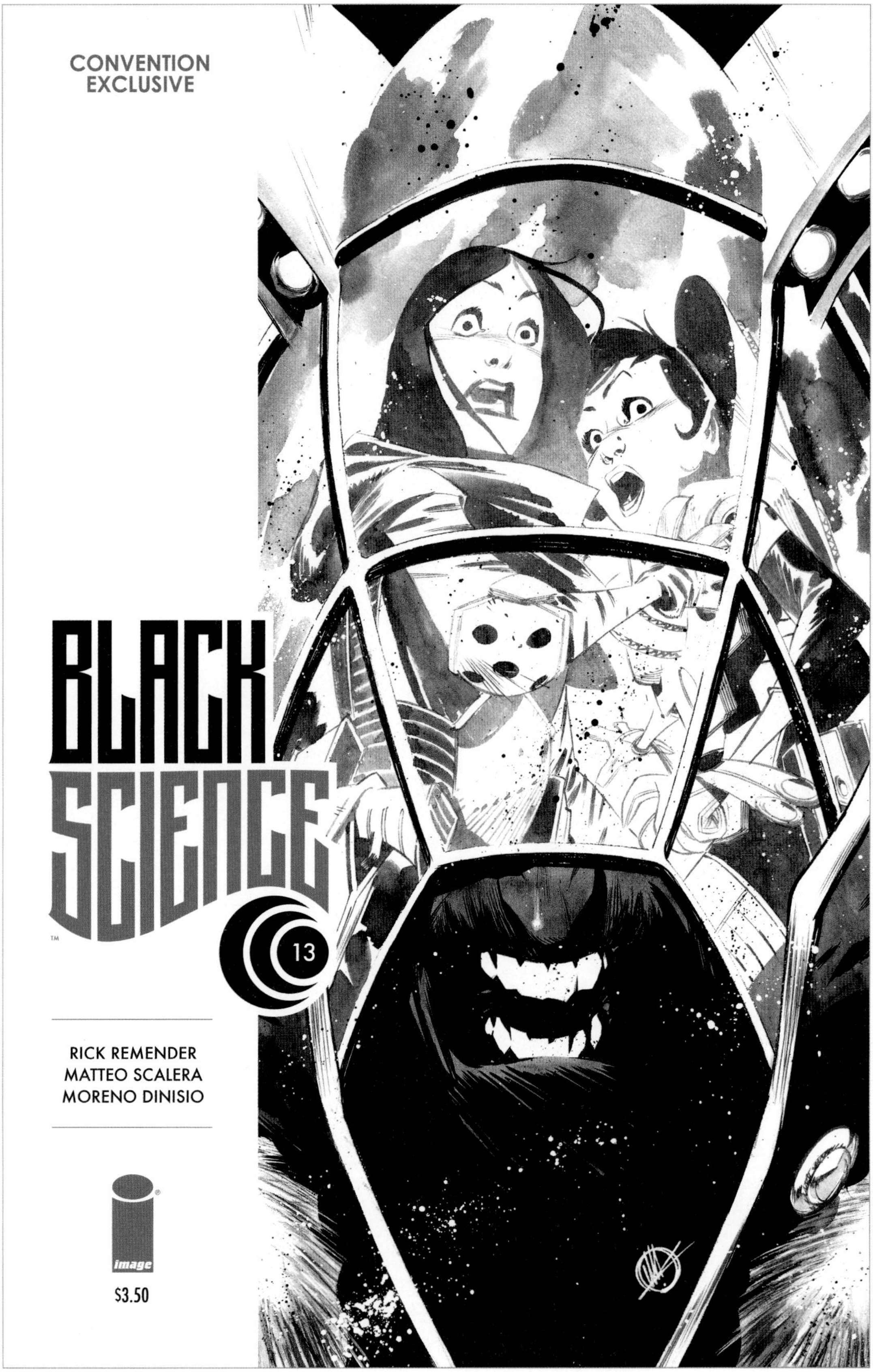
CONVENTION EXCLUSIVE
BLACK SCIENCE
13
RICK REMENDER
MATTEO SCALERA
MORENO DINISIO
image
$3.50

#13 WONDERCON EXCLUSIVE VARIANT BY MATTEO SCALERA

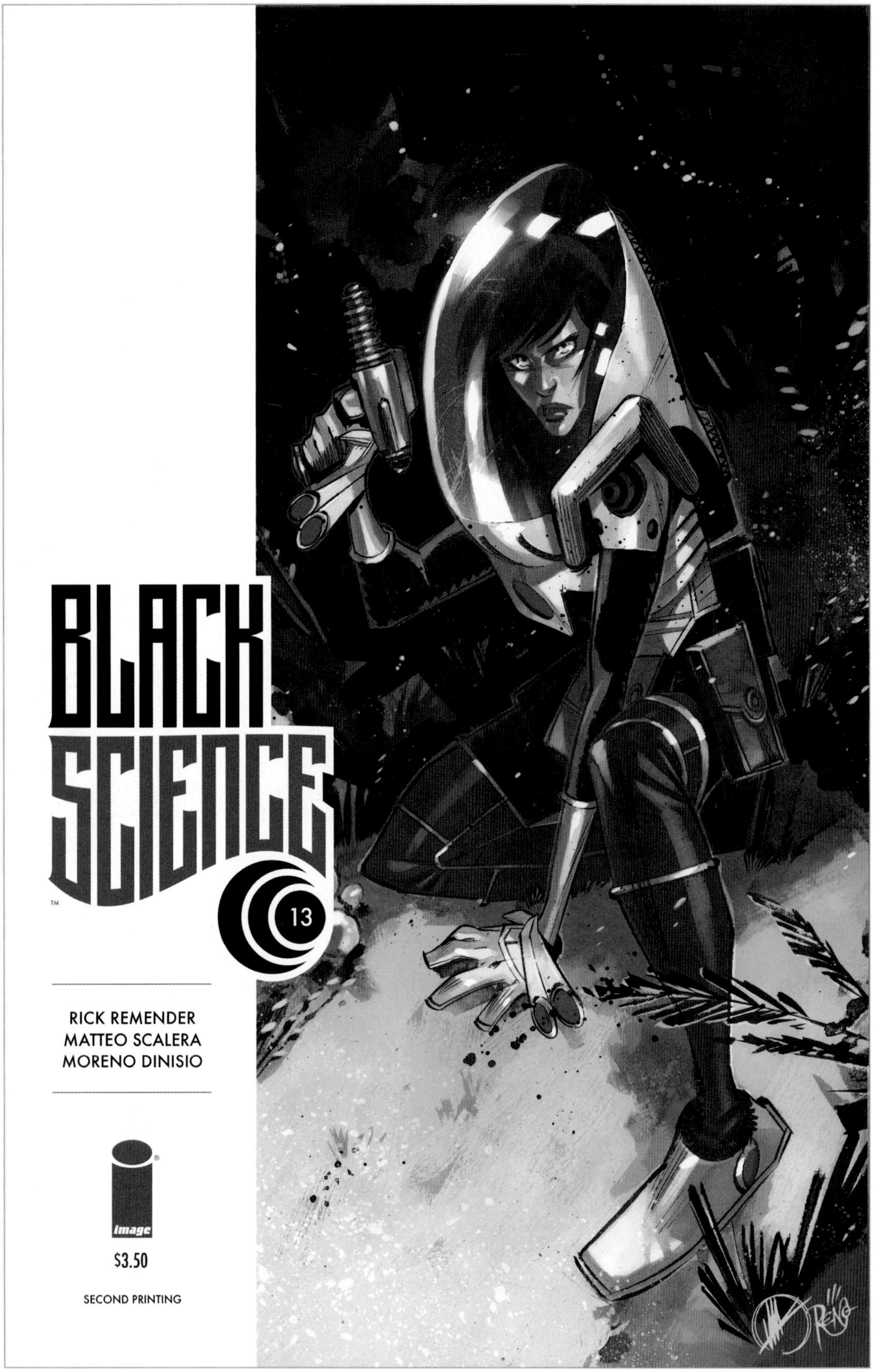
BLACK SCIENCE
TM
13
RICK REMENDER
MATTEO SCALERA
MORENO DINISIO
image
$3.50
SECOND PRINTING

#13 SECOND PRINTING VARIANT BY MATTEO SCALERA AND MORENO DINISIO

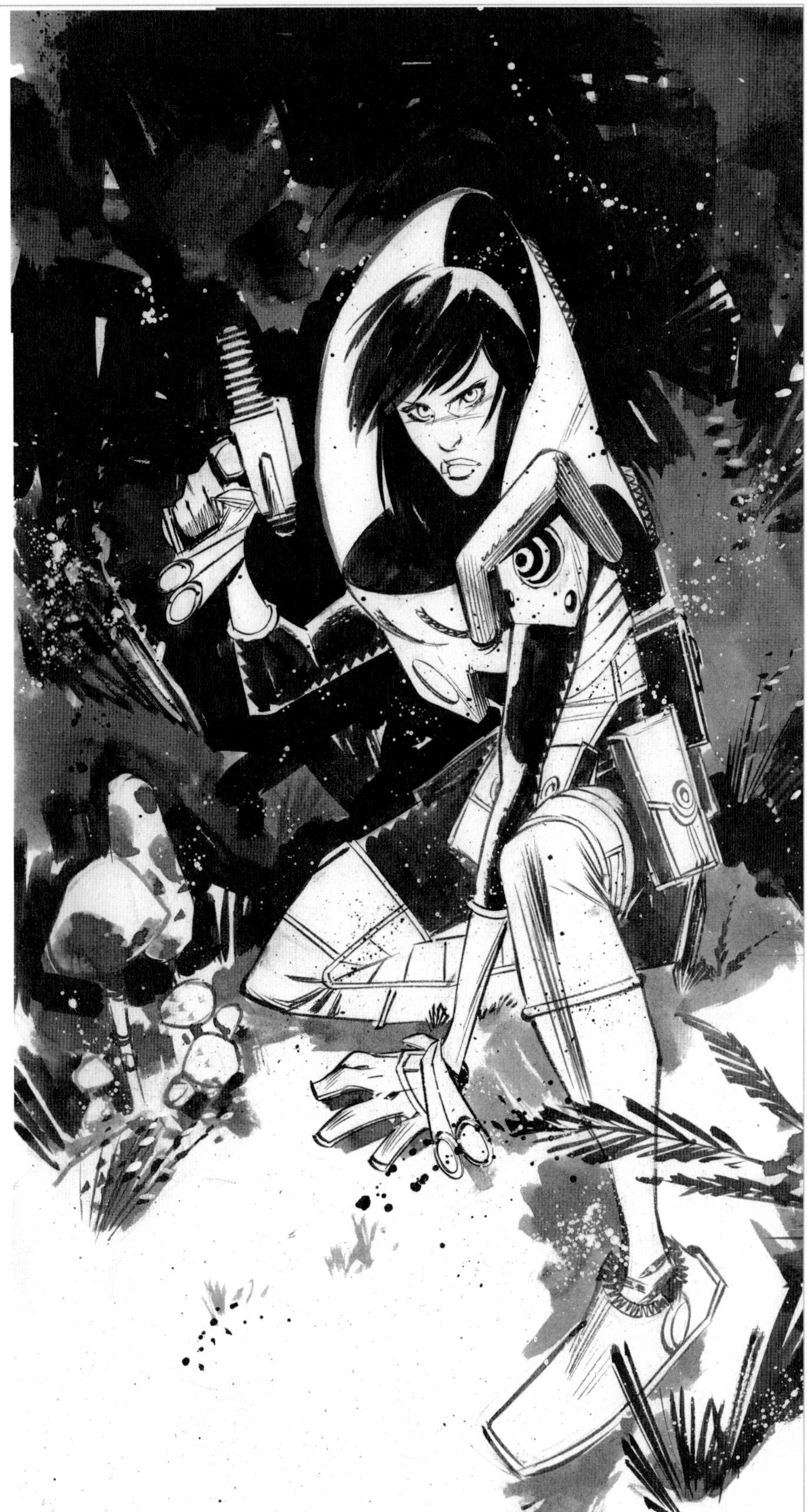

#13 SECOND PRINTING VARIANT PENCILS BY MATTEO SCALERA

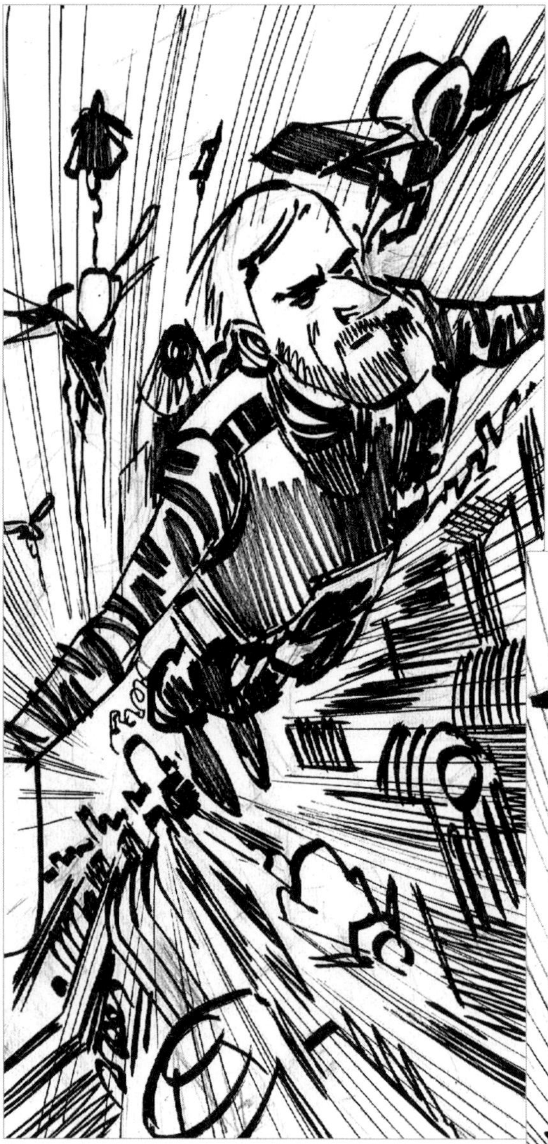

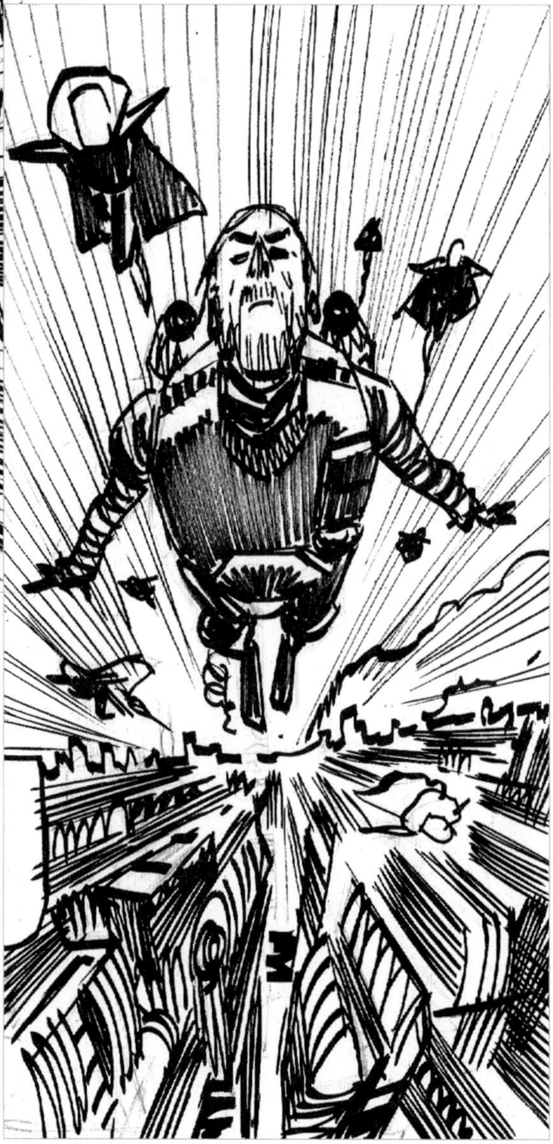

#15 COVER LAYOUTS

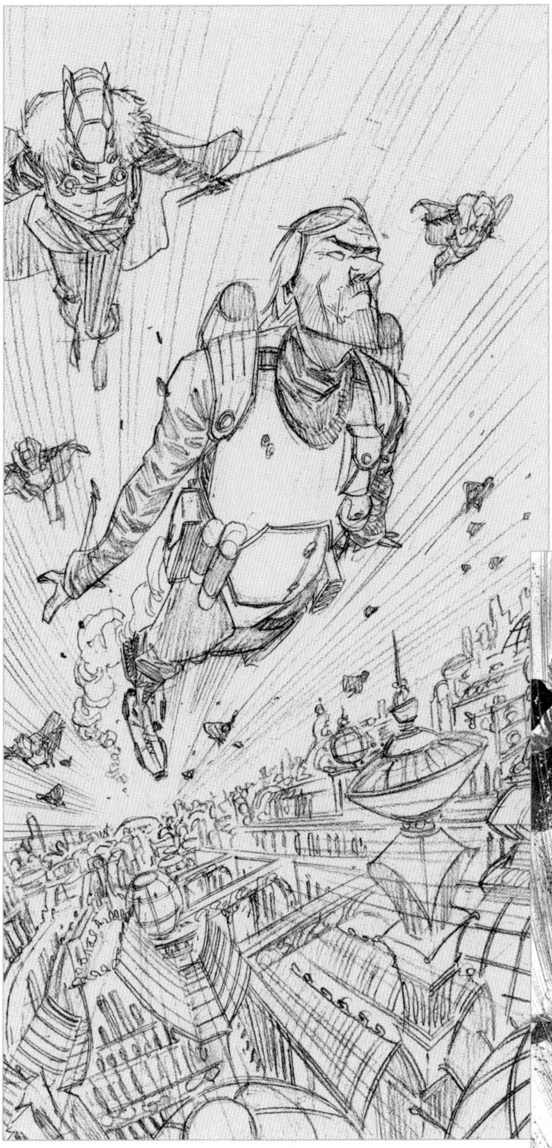

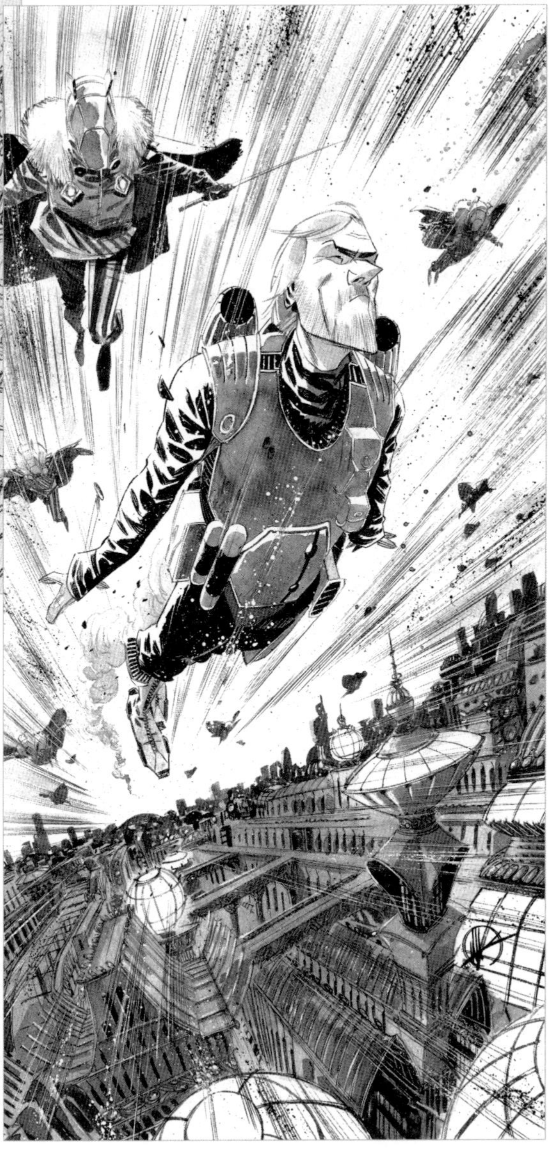

#15 COVER PENCILS & INKS

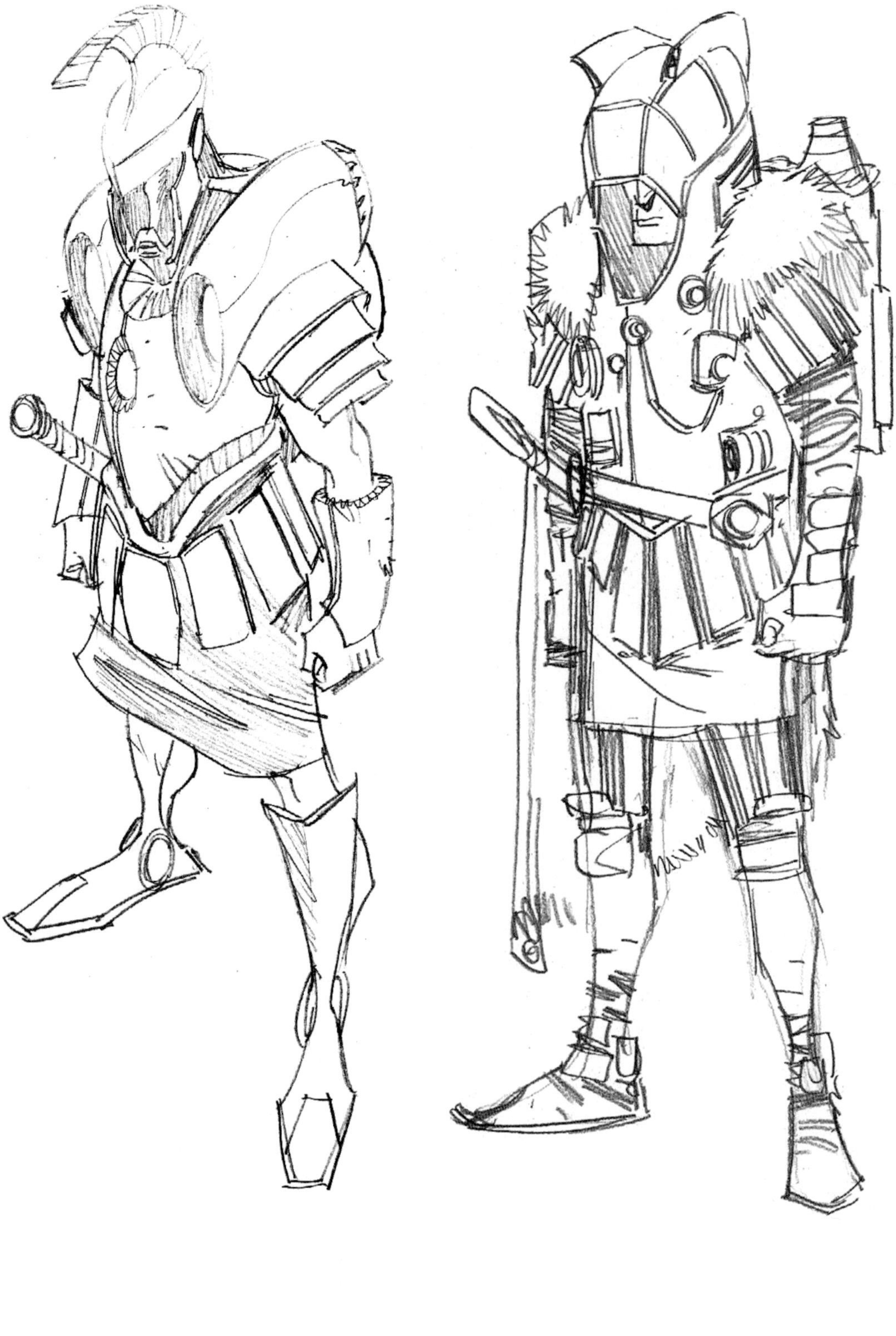

CENTURION DESIGNS BY MATTEO SCALERA

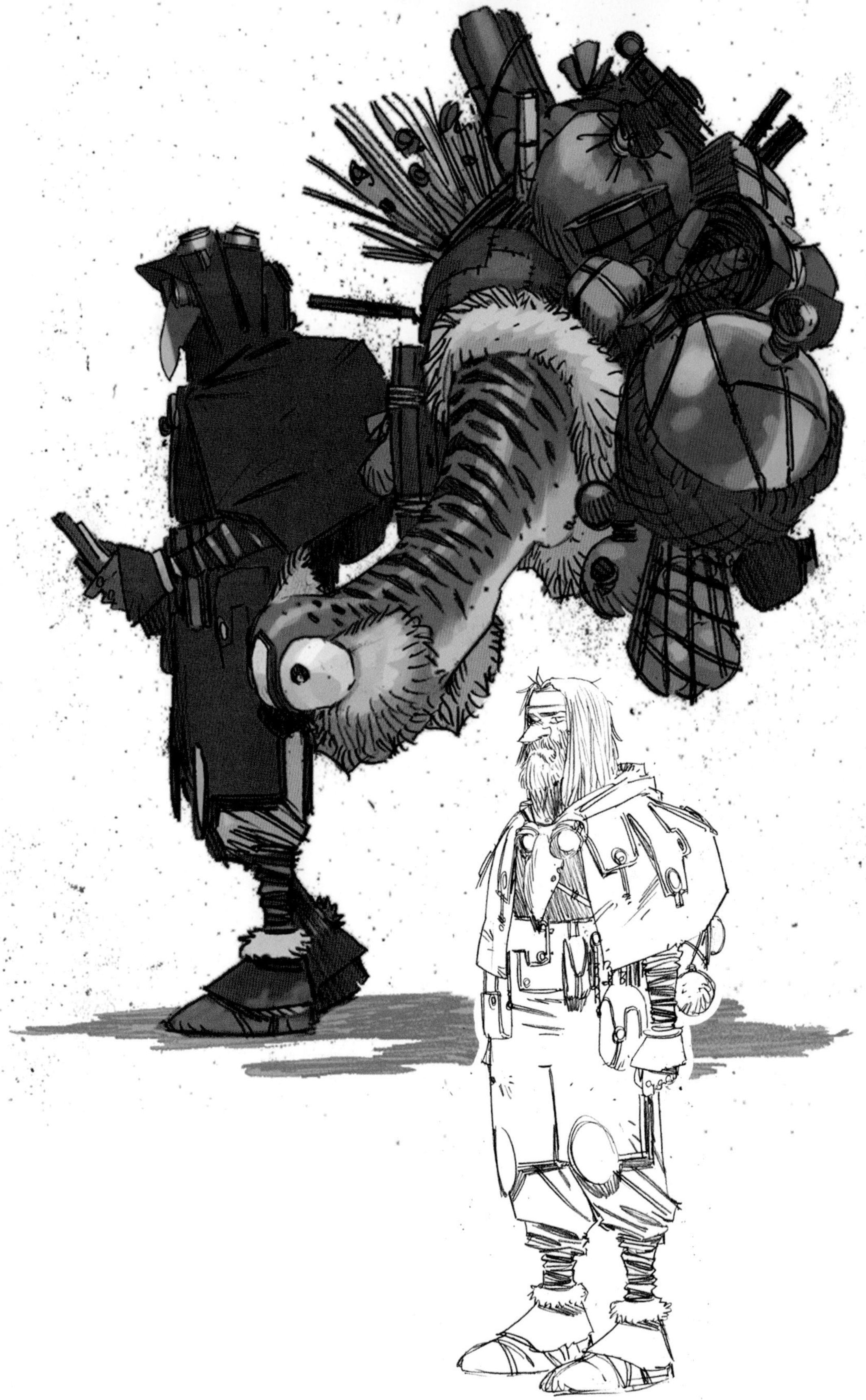

CONCEPT ART FOR THE NEXT STORY ARC BY MATTEO SCALERA WITH COLORS BY MORENO DINISIO

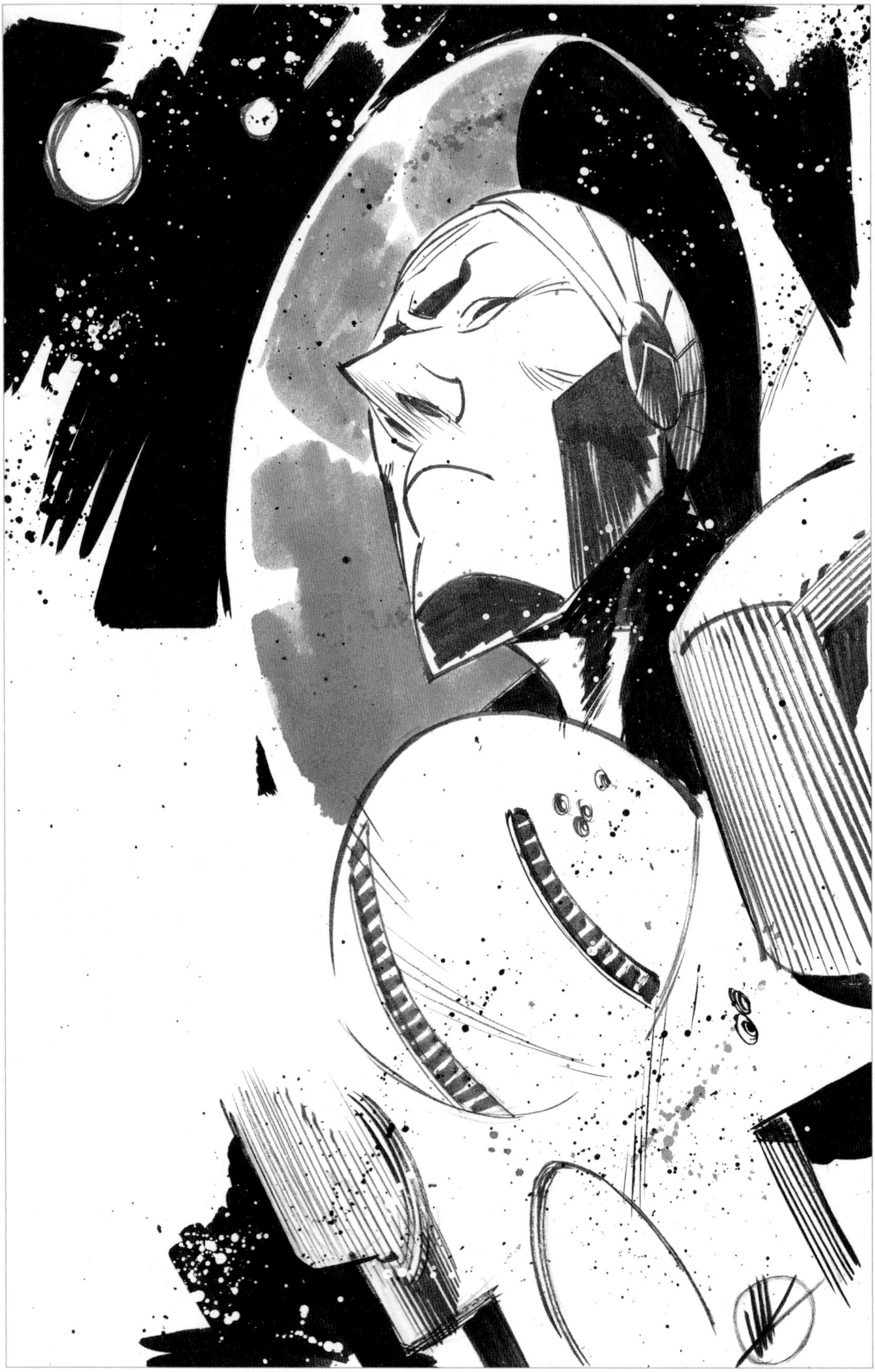

COMMISSION ART BY MATTEO SCALERA